Seeds of Gaia

By Rick Partlow

Chapter One

The fabric of spacetime writhed in birth agony and delivered the sharpened wedge of a starship. Fusion flares lit at the spacecraft's drive plates, sending it desperately lurching away from the already-closing rift in space and the looming mass of Proxima Centauri at a punishing five gravities of acceleration. The reason for its haste emerged from the awful nothingness of Transition Space a hundred thousand kilometers closer to the star: a naturalistic, predatory shape bristling with weapons pods and fitted with massively outsized fusion drives.

Deep within the pursuit ship *Raven*, encased in the gelatinous fluid of an acceleration tank, Captain Samuel Avalon watched his prey through a neural feed from the exterior sensors. With a thought, he called up the intercept course his navigator had already plotted, watching the animated line overlay itself on the sensor image of the fleeing bandit.

Estimated intercept time? he asked, his implanted neurolink relaying the question to the navigator's g-tank.

One hour at maximum g's, came the immediate reply.

Execute.

Sam felt his chest squeezed by a giant fist and remembered to whisper a prayer of thanks to Gaia for the blessings of oxygenated biotic fluid. Without the g-tanks, twenty gravities' acceleration would have ruptured his organs and left him choking in his own blood.

Bandits increasing acceleration to eight g's, his weapons' officer announced. *They* really *don't want to talk to us Sam.*

Devon, Sam called to the navigator, *can we still get them before they reach the antipodal Transition point?*

Not at this rate Sam, the woman replied. He could almost see her shaking her head. *Our only chance is if they don't have g-tanks. They won't be able to keep up this sort of acceleration long without 'em.*

We can't chance that, he decided. *They've already killed three freighter crews...we can't let them do it again. Arvid,* he addressed the weapon's officer, *take out his drives. Make it as clean as you can.*

Launching.

The Patrol cutter shuddered as the flattened dart of a missile detached itself from the outer hull, maneuvering jets kicking it away from the vessel before its drives lit in a flash of annihilated antihydrogen. The missile streaked away from the cutter as if the ship were standing still, accelerating towards the fleeing bandit at over a hundred gravities.

Throttle us down to one g and let's get out of these tanks, Sam declared. The missile would stop the bandits or it wouldn't---there was no point in wasting fuel to be there a few hours sooner.

The pressure eased from his chest and almost immediately the fluid began draining from the g-tank. Taking a breath of air for the first time in over an hour, he gagged, choking out the remains of the oxygenated fluid from his lungs before it had a chance to evaporate. The last of it drained from the tank and then the seal hissed open, letting in a rush of cold air and sending him into involuntary shivers.

The others were stumbling from their cabinets as he made his way out of the g-chamber and into the communal shower. Sprays of warm water erupted from the walls, scrubbing the dried biotic gel from his skin and hair as the rest of the ship's crew filed in behind him.

"The hunter-killer should arrive on target in less than half an hour, Sam," Devon told him, leaning back to let the streams of water at her close-cropped hair. She had an athlete's physique, but after two years of serving with the same crew, Sam hardly glanced at it anymore.

"Do you think we can get a clean hit?" Carlos, the ship's medical officer asked her as he moved into the shower.

"No way of knowing," she shook her head. "The bandit ship is a freighter hull, but you know how they chop those things up. They could have a shitload of armor or they could have stripped off most of their shielding to mount weapons and fuel pods."

"Why worry about those SOB's?" Arvid muttered. "They knew what the risks were when they decided to work for the Consensus. Damn Earthers are getting what they deserve."

"We worry about those SOB's," Sam fixed the smaller man with a glare, "because they are human beings, just like us." The others fell into embarrassed silence, not meeting his gaze. "Get dressed and get to the control room."

Sam turned and walked through the warm air of the dryers, trying not to look back at them. He knew he was hard on Arvid, but they couldn't let themselves become like the Earthers, couldn't allow themselves to have such disrespect for life. If that happened, there would be nothing left worth fighting for.

*   *   *

Less than ten minutes later, the entire crew was strapped into acceleration couches in the ship's main control room and Sam Avalon was staring at the tactical holodisplay, watching the blue arrow representing his missile closing on the red dot of the bandit ship.

"He isn't increasing his boost," Devon commented.

"They must not be equipped with g-tanks," Carlos said. "I'd be surprised if any of them were still conscious."

"The missile has hit burnout," Arvid announced. "Still gonna take them before they hit the Transition point."

Sam thought, not for the first time, how pressing and instinctive the human need for conversation was. Each of them had a computer link and transmitter implanted at the base of their skull and could wordlessly access tactical displays, technical readouts and situational updates from the computer or from each other, yet each of them still felt the need to make such periodic announcements. He didn't bother trying to prevent it---he might as well have asked them not to breathe.

"We all clear of civvie traffic?" Carlos asked.

"I ran a general area scan when we jumped in," Devon replied. "Nothing then, let me…"

There was a discontinuity.

For a moment, none of them were aware anything had happened---it was as if they had blinked in unison. Then Sam noticed that the red dot representing the bandit had disappeared from the tactical holotank.

"What the hell?" he blurted, leaning forward against his acceleration restraints. "Where are they Devon? Did they jump?"

"No, they're just gone." Devon shook her head. "Our missile, too…not a shred of wreckage. What in Gaia's name?" She looked over at him, frowning in perplexity. "We were just hit with a massive EMP, Sam--- all of our sensors were out for almost a second."

"An Electromagnetic Pulse?" he repeated. "From what?"

"I don't know, even the cameras blanked out."

"I can try to get a feed from the Resolution habitats in the Centauri Belt," Arvid suggested, making the connection without waiting for permission.

The *Raven*'s AI negotiated with those of the collection of asteroid habitats and within seconds, each of the crew was watching a video feed from an optical telescope located near the inner edge of the belt. Frame by frame, the images downloaded into their individual neurolinks, beginning with the view of the fleeing bandit craft, its fusion drive glowing like a miniature star. With the next frame, the dart of the intercept missile came into the picture, a computer-generated outline allowing them to see it against the black background.

The missile drew closer to the bandit ship, and when it was only a thousand kilometers away, *something* superimposed itself on the blackness, something huge and gray and formless that wiped out everything else in the frame. And then there was nothing.

Raven, Sam ordered the ship's computer, *enhance that image...get me an ID.*

Working on it, Sam, the AI promised. There was a long pause, and when the computer spoke to him again, it was with a hesitancy that Sam had never heard before. *Sam, I recommend we make for Aphrodite at maximum emergency speed.*

"Hey Sam, what gives?" Arvid asked plaintively. "*Raven* just shut me out of the net."

"Me too," Devon confirmed, frowning.

Tell me Raven, Sam ordered.

Let me show you, Sam.

He found himself floating in the darkness, watching the frozen image of the bandit starship, the replay slowed down an order of magnitude below normal speed. It still only occupied the image for a moment, less than a heartbeat, but there was no doubt as to what it was. Basically cylindrical in shape, its fore-end was a gigantic funnel a dozen times the size of the main body, while the aft was a cauldron of fusion fire, an engine so powerful it was contained only with magnetic fields.

Its course passed hundreds of thousands of kilometers beyond the bandit ship, but the unsuspecting starship disintegrated in its wake, torn apart at the molecular level by an electromagnetic field so powerful it could collect interstellar hydrogen for use as fuel. The intercept missile, another two hundred thousand klicks distant, spontaneously detonated, its explosion lost in the passage of the…the alien. Sam had to force himself to use the word.

But there was no other word to use. No human had built that ship, he was sure. And so, after nearly three thousand years in space, after a century of routine star travel via the Transition Lines, he, Captain Samuel Abanks-Avalon, was the first human to encounter an alien intelligence.

No, not the first…the bandits were the first. Unfortunately for them.

Where is it going? He asked the *Raven*'s computer.

At its present trajectory, it will skim the outer atmosphere of Proxima Centauri, Raven told him, *presumably to pick up extra fuel. After that…it is on a direct collision course with the Earth, at nearly ninety percent of lightspeed.*

Sam's chest tightened as the AI's words sunk in.

That thing has to be the size of a small planet, he said slowly. *If it hits at that velocity…*

If it is not stopped, the computer told him, *in five years there will be nothing left of Earth but a cloud of rubble.*

"Devon," Sam fairly snarled the words, noticing the shocked expressions on the faces of the others but not caring, "get us to the Transition Point. Fastest circuit back to Aphrodite. Get us home *now*."

Chapter Two

Priscilla opened her eyes for the first time and realized she was no longer herself. She sat up, shivering with the chill in the air, feeling the cloying stickiness of biotic fluid on her skin.

"Good morning," said a voice from somewhere above her.

She tried to focus on the source of the words, but her eyes didn't want to work yet. It didn't matter. Among the vast knowledge with which she had been "born" was the knowledge of who was speaking.

"Is it morning?" she asked, surprised she could manage sarcasm so early.

"Somewhere. Your shuttle leaves in twenty hours. You'll be travelling on a Patrol cutter, the *Raven*. Commanded by Captain Samuel Abanks-Avalon, the man who discovered the artifact."

"I have his personnel file," Priscilla realized, frowning. "He could be a problem."

"We do what we can with what we have," the voice replied. "It would be wrong to exclude the man who discovered this threat. But I leave the details up to you." There was a humorous edge to the voice. "You have my complete trust."

"Of course," Priscilla said, smiling thinly. She rubbed her eyes until her vision finally cleared. What she saw did not surprise her. "Let's get to work."

*   *   *

As he crossed the suspended walkway between the Aphrodite shuttleport and the Resolution Government Megaplex, Sam Avalon paused to regard the new Jerusalem that was Dauphin City. It stretched out before him for a hundred kilometers on any side, a crystalline jewel inlaid in a living planet, glowing in the midday light of Epsilon Eridani. Mother had built the City first, before her nanomachines had gone to work terraforming the planet or cloning its future inhabitants. She had built it as a symbol of her love for her children. The sight of it still took his breath away after all these years.

Smiling softly, he passed through into the twentieth-floor entrance of the kilometer-wide headquarters of the Diaspora Resolution. After months cooped up in a ship with the same half dozen people, it felt extraordinary to be among the throng of humanity passing through the halls of the gigantic Government Complex. Some experienced agoraphobia upon their return from space, but not Sam; he drank it in like a fine wine.

These past few weeks aboard ship had been the worst in his memory. After reporting the alien starship, they had been sent on a month-long patrol of outlying systems, carefully planned to keep them away from any human contact. Sam had thought they were going to be shut out of it until the Resolution was ready to make a public announcement, but here he was, recalled to Aphrodite for a mission briefing, and no announcement had been made. He hoped the rest of the crew could keep their mouths shut until they lifted again.

Sam made his way through the labyrinthine halls of the complex, catching a ride on a lift that took him deep into the underground levels and nearly a half a kilometer closer to the center of the building. As he approached the center, Sam noticed that the human traffic began to thin out, and the uniforms began to change: the bright blue of the Patrol and the forest-green of the Scouts gradually gave way to the gray of the Intelligence Corps and the stark whites of the Political Service. The Grays and the Whites made him feel uncomfortable, like an unruly child sent to the counselor's office for correction.

But no one questioned his presence, even when he entered the Holiest of Holies, the Central Planning Office. It was here that Mother interfaced with her children through a sophisticated network of Artificial Intelligence nodes linked to her orbital home. Outside the entrance was a life-sized model of the original Gaia Probe, a spherical Mylar bubble three meters across. Launched from Earth during the legendary Golden Age late in the Twenty-First Century, the Gaia Probe had been the life's work of Dr. Charles Dauphin. Forty years of effort to unite such diverse fields as AI computer systems, nanotechnology, cloning, interstellar transport and planetary engineering had all culminated in that one bubble of hope, containing genetic samples of thousands of different life forms, a small nanotech self-replication factory and the most sophisticated Artificial Intelligence the Twenty-First Century had produced, Mother.

Sam hesitated before the display, watching the hologram recreation of the launch of the Gaia probe from lunar orbit late in the Twenty-First Century. An electromagnetic cannon had given the probe its initial impetus, then a solar-powered microwave laser had carried it to Epsilon Eridani. The plan had been for a dozen of the probes to be launched in a twenty-year period; but before Mother had made it halfway to her destination, the Consensus Government had collapsed like the beautiful but fragile thing it was. Charles Dauphin had died in the brutal civil war that had followed, swallowed in a wave of military nanotech that had killed billions and swept the Earth clean of high technology. He had never known that his heritage had indeed made it to the stars.

And Mother had given birth to far more than he ever could have dreamed. Not only had she transformed Aphrodite and Hephaestus from desolate lifelessness into life-bearing jewels, she had also constructed copies of herself and launched them to other star systems, finishing the work Dauphin had started. A millennium later, the discovery of Transition Space had united all her children into the Diaspora Resolution, a union of more than two dozen systems and twenty habitable worlds.

There, the narration ended, looping back to the beginning of the recording, and Sam proceeded into the Planning Center. He was struck almost immediately by the relative lack of people. On a purely intellectual level, he knew that the lavishly decorated walls disguised an incredible amount of raw computing power, but a small part of him couldn't shake the impression that the endless hallways had been constructed merely to make the trek to the Central Conference Room seem more intimidating.

They were waiting for him there, and he thought for one, blood-curdling moment that he was late, but a quick check of his headcomp reassured him that he was ten minutes early. Damn, this *must* be a critical situation if even the Whitesuits were showing up early for meetings. There were four of them seated at the table, deep in a conversation that ended abruptly as he entered the open doorway and came to attention.

"Captain Samuel Abanks-Avalon, Resolution Patrol Service, reporting as ordered," he clipped off in his best Academy voice.

"At ease, Captain," the senior political officer present told him. "Pull up a chair and let's get down to business. We don't have much time."

"Yes ma'am," he nodded to her. He accessed her ID file with his headcomp: her name was Ursa Tellesian and she had a stern bearing that reminded him of one of his Primary-Ed teachers…but then, almost all of the politicos he'd met reminded him of his Primary-Ed teachers.

"Captain Avalon, I'm sorry if it seemed to you that you and your crew had been shut out of the loop after your historic discovery, but it was necessary. Upon receipt of your report, we immediately sent an investigative team to the alien ship's projected system of origin." A large hologram sprang to life at the center of the room, showing a G-class star and then panning out quickly to a planet at around one and a half Astronomical Units. It was a living world, that much was obvious from an orbital view---small, scattered green continents dotted a vast blue of water oceans.

"Did they make contact with the aliens?" Sam asked with palpable excitement.

"There were no aliens to contact," another of the Whitesuits at the table answered. He was a broad-bodied man whose ID registered him as Dr. Kama T'Leva, one of the chief researchers of the Resolution Science Council. "In fact, there was no higher animal life on the planet whatsoever. Nothing but bacteria and primitive lichens. It looked very much like a half-completed terraforming job."

"You're not saying…" Sam shut his mouth, unwilling to put it into words.

"We're not saying anything." A woman at the opposite end of the table stood and erased the hologram with a wave of her hand. "We don't have time for theatrics and we don't have time for speculation."

Sam stared at her, not because of her pronouncement, and not just because she had *no* ID file registered with the housekeeping computer, but because of *her*. Sam was not a man easily distracted by a pretty face, but this woman went far beyond pretty. She was *perfect*, and not just in appearance. There was an unmistakable grace in the way she moved, a grace he had seen in null-grav ballet dancers and martial arts masters and damn few others. Matched with the almost haughty self-assurance with which she held herself, Sam had the feeling he was looking at a fairy queen out of a medieval fantasy.

"Captain Avalon," she continued, "this is the situation. A cursory look at the features of the world in the ship's system of origin told our investigators that it had been terraformed. But there is no Mother computer, no Terran species introduced larger than bacteria, and no trace of any Gaia probe. Mother has no record of ever dispatching a probe to the system. If there was a Gaia probe sent to this world, we have no knowledge of who sent it or where it came from. But the aliens who once lived on that world did…or thought they did."

"Gaia's blood…" Sam murmured. "You mean that world…"

"Not only had life," she confirmed his worst fears, "but intelligent life. A technological civilization." She let out a long breath and for the first time he could see emotion play across her perfect face. She pushed a stand of light-brown hair out of her eyes. "We discovered remains, records on one of their moons. They were remarkably advanced in some areas. Unfortunately for them, nanotechnology was not one of those areas. They watched helplessly as their world was transformed from one perfect for them to one where the air and water were poisonous.

"From the little we were able to glean from the remains of the moonbase, they held their world in a sort of religious awe. It was part of them, part of what they considered their collective spirit. They could have fusion bombed the terraformed ecology from orbit and re-engineered the world as it was, but to them that would not be the same. They thought of themselves as empty shells with no spirit, living ghosts of a race. So most of them stayed there and died with their world."

Sam closed his eyes and swallowed hard, trying to keep his emotions under control. Billions of intelligent beings wiped out as if they were a bacterial culture…

"Most," she went on, "but not all. Around a million of their best scientists, researchers and engineers went into orbital colonies and began a crash construction program that took over three centuries." She shook her head. "It's amazing really. They developed an incredibly sophisticated electromagnetic field technology basically from scratch...and 347 years later, they had built a starship."

"What the hell kind of ship is it though?" Sam had to ask. "I've never seen anything like it---how can it maintain that sort of acceleration over interstellar distances?"

"It's something that used to be called a Bussard ramjet," Dr. T'Leva interjected. "It uses electromagnetic ramscoops to collect interstellar hydrogen and fuses it. The old Consensus, as advanced as they were, never came close to having the kind of technology to build one---and we didn't need one after we discovered the Transition drive."

"At any rate," the woman took back over, shooting the scientists a harsh glance, "they built it, and they launched it and then they blew up their space habitat and killed themselves. And right now, an object twenty kilometers long and travelling at a very good percentage of the speed of light is heading toward Earth."

"How did they find out where the probe came from?" Sam asked. "Assuming it did come from Earth, I mean."

"We don't know. There's a hell of a lot we don't know, but we can't wait for more information; we have to act now."

"So it's headed for Earth," Sam prompted. "How are we going to stop it?"

"That's the meat of our problem," she acknowledged. "There are no star systems between the Centauri system and Earth, so there is no Transition line terminus where we can position an intercept, and no way to bring enough raw materials there even if we could reach it. Which means we *have* to base our activities in the Solar System...with all the political obstacles that involves."

"*Can* we stop it?" Sam asked. "I mean, how do you stop something that big and going that fast? Put an asteroid in front of it?"

"We doubt that would accomplish anything," Dr. T'Leva shook his head. "The device must have automatic defenses to take care of such dangers. To stop this weapon, we will have to use something more sophisticated." He half-smiled, stepping naturally into a pedantic mode. "The best way is to construct a very large Teller-Fox warp device, like the one used in the Transition drive but in a fixed position, and send the whole ship into T-space."

"And you think the Consensus is just going to sit around and watch that?" Sam cocked an eyebrow.

"That will be our job, Captain Avalon," the woman told him. "My name is Priscilla, and I will be leading a delegation to Earth to attempt to convince them to let us try to stop the weapon. You and your crew will provide transportation and support for the duration of the mission. Your ship is being refitted as we speak and we will be leaving orbit in six hours."

"I'm honored to be chosen for such an important mission, Priscilla," he told her. "I hope my crew and I perform to your satisfaction."

"I'm certain you'll do what I expect of you," she replied, with what he could have sworn was a barely concealed smirk.

"Captain Avalon," political officer Tellesian spoke up once more, "we shouldn't keep you any longer. You will need to go supervise the refitting of your ship and brief your crew. Priscilla and the rest of the diplomatic crew will be joining you in a few hours."

"Ma'am." He nodded, rising from his seat, and exiting the room, pausing for one final glance at Priscilla. Of all the mysteries he had just been presented, she was perhaps the least understandable. Why were high-ranking scientific and political officers kowtowing to someone without even an official ID? Just who was she?

He let the questions fade as he left the room. One last thought stuck with him: it was fortunate that no colonists had been produced by the probe that had terraformed the alien's world. He couldn't imagine a colony of humans bearing the guilt of living each day on the bones of an entire race, knowing they existed only because of a horrible genocide.

*   *   *

Sam Avalon watched with skepticism and growing impatience as the technicians refitted his ship with the necessary equipment for the coming mission. As honored and excited as he was to be included on something so momentous, had it been practical to pace in zero gravity he would have been wearing a groove into the floor of the drydock.

You seem agitated, Sam, Raven's voice echoed in his head. *Is there a problem?*

You ever get antsy, Raven? he asked the AI. *Kind of worried for no good reason?*

Never, Sam and neither do you. When humans do something without knowing the reason, it is a response to internal or external feedback of which they are not aware consciously. The difference between us is that I have no "instincts." All my sensory input is deliberate. All my decisions are conscious and unaffected by body chemicals. I may be an Artificial Intelligence, but I am not an artificial human *intelligence.*

Do you consider that a weakness or a strength? Sam wondered.

Neither. It is just what I am.

"Avalon?" A voice behind Sam turned him around, his hand automatically slapping against the wall to stop the spin.

What he saw, floating awkwardly with a look that was a mixture of disgust and panic, was a short, pudgy male dressed in the whites of the Political Service. But this man was no ambassador or negotiator---the triangle patch on the left breast of his uniform marked him as far more than that.

"I'm Captain Avalon," Sam replied, trying to hide his distaste, yet knowing that with this man, hiding anything would be next to impossible. "What can I do for you?"

"Well, if you're the naïve do-gooder running this fiasco, I'm the unlucky son of a bitch who was shanghaied into doing your dirty work."

Sam's jaw dropped and he had to force himself not to simply stare at the man in astonishment.

"Aren't you…" he stammered. "I mean, you're a Sensitive, right?"

"Didn't I just say that?" He snapped.

Thoroughly nonplussed, Sam accessed the man's ID file through the station's computer and saw that his name was Mawae Fallayah Danabri and he was indeed a Sensitive, as impossible as that seemed given his behavior. He also saw, much to his surprise, a list of commendations and awards for diplomatic service a meter long.

"Your luggage is already aboard, Mr. Danabri," he said, not sure how to respond to the rude little man. "*Raven*'s AI will show you to your cabin."

"Of course," Danabri sneered, brushing past Sam--- not an easy thing to do in zero gravity, but he had obviously practiced---and heading for the open hatch of the ship. "Why provide the courtesy of a human when a piece of machinery can do the job more efficiently?"

Sam was still staring after him in profound bemusement when a hand touched his arm, sending an almost electric shock through him.

"Captain Avalon," Priscilla said, "is your crew aboard?"

"Yes…" He stumbled over his words, used to addressing superiors by their title but realizing that she hadn't given him one. "…Priscilla. And one of your people, Sensitive Danabri, just boarded. Will you be bringing any other specialists along?"

"No, this is strictly a diplomatic mission," she told him. "It was thought that bringing along technical personnel would seem presumptuous."

"And you…you've worked with Sensitive Danabri before?"

"Not personally," she said. "But I have been assured he is the best available. Why do you ask?"

"No reason." He shook his head. "Allow me to show you to your cabin."

"No need for that." She floated past him perfunctorily. "I can access your ship's AI."

Raven, he whispered silently, *I don't suppose there's any scientific basis for premonitions, is there?*

Of course not, Sam, the computer admonished him. *If psychic abilities existed, the Resolution would hardly have to put so many resources towards raising and training Sensitives to read human body language and voice inflection.*

Damn good thing, he nodded to himself, heading into the ship.

Chapter Three

Reality solidified around Sam Avalon and darkness filled the void left by the absence of existence that was Transition Space.

"There's Mars," Devon breathed in obvious relief, nodding toward a small, red star in the holotank, nearly half an AU away.

Sam knew how she felt. He didn't think he had *ever* been so grateful to see a journey's end in his whole life.

"Contact the Collective," Sam ordered. "Let them know we're coming."

As D'jonni, the communications officer, carried out his directive, Sam sneaked a glance back at Mawae Danabri, knowing the Sensitive would notice but not caring. Things had begun badly with the man, and had only gotten worse as the voyage wore on. It had all come to a head just a few days ago during lunch…

*   *   *

"Is this what you people call food?" Mawae Danabri whined, tossing away a half-empty ration packet. Sam watched the plastic pouch cartwheel across the room, trailing little globules of meat broth, and made himself do a breathing exercise to avoid leaping across the room and throttling the Sensitive.

Arvid caught the packet and waved the loose bubbles of soup back into it, throwing Sam a pained look. Six days in Transition Space with the abrasive little man had worn down the patience of everyone on board.

"Is there something else you would prefer, Sensitive Danabri?" Devon asked, always the peacemaker.

"There are many things I would prefer," Danabri sighed, letting himself float up against the safety webbing across his lap. "I would prefer to be dining at the Café du Lac on Amethyst. I would prefer to be part of a society where I wasn't addressed by my function, as if I were some sort of goddamned cleaning robot. I would prefer it if I hadn't been programmed on a genetic level and enslaved from birth as a human tool for the Diplomatic Corps. I would *quite* prefer it if I were in my own universe instead of somewhere so strange that if I looked at it I wouldn't even see it. But most of all," he growled, his voice raising, "I would prefer it if I had some fucking *gravity* so I didn't feel as if I were going to puke every single minute!"

"*Citizen* Danabri," Priscilla spoke up, and everyone's head swung around, watching her propel herself into the chamber, "if you would take your anti-nausea medication, you would find your equilibrium to be adequate to the task." She moved to the table and strapped herself into a restraint web. "As for your political complaints, I don't recall there being any restrictions on emigration for citizens of the Resolution. If you don't care for your function in our society, you could simply request asylum on Mars. Or I am sure the Consensus government would be simply delighted to offer you a place in *their* society..."

Arvid went into an impromptu coughing fit to cover his uncontrollable laughter, and it took all of Sam's willpower not to do the same.

Danabri didn't laugh, but he also didn't seem angry. He simply stared at her with a look that Sam thought was more wistful than anything else.

"It's easy for you to be dismissive," he said quietly, staring her in the eye. "How can a goddess understand mere mortals?"

Sam thought that was a particularly hyperbolic analogy but for some reason it seemed to visibly affect

Priscilla. She looked away from the Sensitive's accusatory glance, and for a moment Sam thought she would retreat from the room. But finally, she gathered herself and replied.

"Perhaps being a goddess only seems easy when seen from below, Sens…Mawae Danabri. You decry your lack of choice, but how much choice do you suppose *I* have?"

"None of us have much choice, Priscilla," he responded with a humorless chuckle. "That is the trouble with our society."

"Yet is there another society available to us which you would prefer?"

He considered that for a moment before shaking his head and looking away.

"Then I trust I can depend on you to do your job to the best of your ability."

"As always," Danabri sighed, releasing himself from his restraints and giving a listless push out of the room.

Devon shot Sam a "what the hell was that" look, but all he could do was shrug helplessly.

"Could I speak to you for a moment, Priscilla?" Sam asked, wincing. He didn't really *want* to talk about this, but his crew would expect it and perhaps Priscilla would as well.

"Of course, Captain Avalon," she said, kicking off and leading him down the corridor into a computer maintenance bay.

She waited patiently as he shut the door behind them, and then turned to face her.

"It's about this Danabri," he said bluntly. "Are you sure he can do this? I don't mean to presume here, but we are talking about a critically important task, and a very delicate one at that. With his attitude, he's as likely to start a war with the Consensus as you are to convince them to allow us to help them."

"You forget a few things, Captain," Priscilla replied without a hint of anger at his questioning. "I will be doing the negotiating, not Sensitive Danabri, and I can assure you I am up to that task."

"Of that I have no doubt…" he began, but she cut him off with a raised hand.

"Let me assure you that Mother did not make this decision lightly. Sensitive Danabri has an outstanding record. He will not compromise our mission."

"What about his effect on my crew?"

"Captain Avalon, you are a professional, as am I, as is Sensitive Danabri. Just as you expect me to do my job and I expect him to do his, I trust that you will do yours, and take care of your crew's morale."

*   *   *

And that, of course, had been that. No help had been forthcoming from Priscilla and it had been up to him to head off any possible confrontations between Danabri and the crew. But thank the Mother, they were finally at Mars and at least facing the opportunity to get out of the cramped quarters of the ship and into a place with a bit more elbow room.

The Martian Collective central computer guided them in with an impersonal anonymity Sam wasn't used to: Resolution AI's were more talkative. Of course, Mars was *different*. Everyone knew that…even if damn few had actually been there. Sam was nearly as excited at the prospect of visiting Mars as he was nervous about their mission.

There were all kinds of stories about the Collective. Depending on whom you listened to, the Martians were either in bed with the Consensus, secretly passing them information on Resolution trade routes, or they were the purest ideological heirs to Charles Dauphin, living in peace and harmony with all other humans. Sam assumed the truth was somewhere in-between.

There was one mystery that was true and unsolved, however, and its evidence was right before Sam's eyes. When Mother had left Earth three thousand years ago, Mars was a red planet, its few thousand colonists confined to domed craters. Today, Mars was a living world, blue with the oceans and green with forests, rich with brown soil and a breathable atmosphere.

Terraforming was nothing new to the Resolution, of course…but to the Resolution, terraforming was a process governed by nanotechnology. Microscopic disassemblers reorganized atmospheres, freed oxygen from water ice and rock and prepared the way for the introduction of genetically engineered life forms. Here on Mars, however, there was not a trace of nanotechnology---and Mother knew, they had looked. Early Resolution diplomatic missions had taken surreptitious soil, water and atmosphere samples, searching for the discarded husks of ancient nanites, but not a single one had been found. As far as Resolution researchers could tell, Mars had been terraformed through a combination of brute force and biotechnology.

And that was where the mystery came in, of course, because there was not a single indication in the current Martian culture of such capabilities. If anything, they seemed inferior to even the Consensus, technologically. Yet there they were somehow, sitting on what was likely the first terraformed world in human history.

Sam felt the winds of the upper atmosphere buffet his ship as it descended along the guidance signal provided by the Collective computer and fought to keep his hands from clutching at the armrests of his acceleration couch. The *Raven* was perfectly capable of atmospheric insertion, particularly with the AI in control, but the thought of taking the big ship down to a planet always scared the living hell out of him. Not exactly something a starship captain should let on to the crew, he thought ruefully.

The *Raven* described a long, gentle spiral through the Martian atmosphere, coming lower over weathered sandstone mountains, speckled here and there with brown and green. Sam let himself be distracted by the surreal beauty of the world, watching carefully to catch glimpses of the broad-winged Shrieks that were the dominant aerial predator introduced by the Terraformers. Ten meters from wingtip to wingtip, they could kill a man as easily as they could the spindly-legged herbivores roaming the Martian plains.

As the mountains gave way to those plains, Sam could finally see their destination: the port city of Tarshish. Tarshish was unique on Mars. Though there were various small industrial centers and collections of homes around them, Tarshish was the only thing that could truly be called a modern city on the whole planet. On Resolution worlds, the humans were concentrated in the megaplexes in order to put less pressure on the planetary ecology, but the Martians seemed to rely on population control to accomplish that task. Or at least everyone assumed so; population control was another one of those things about which the Collective didn't talk to outsiders.

The spaceport at Tarshish was basic by Resolution standards---little more than a large, flat plain of fusion-formed concrete about a kilometer on a side---and it was nearly unoccupied at their arrival. From the air, Sam saw only a pair of orbital shuttles parked near the far end, surrounded by maintenance vehicles. The computer guided the *Raven* in a narrowing spiral to an area near the center of the field, slowing them in the process until it was safe to cut thrust to the main engines and shift power to the landing jets. Superheated air, drawn in through turbo intakes and run through ducts close to the ship's reactor, blasted a scorched pattern on the gray surface below them, depositing them on hydraulic landing treads with a gentle bump.

He let out a long-held breath and began unfastening his safety restraints.

"Collective Control says they have a car headed out to pick us up," D'jonni announced, speaking over the hiss of the pumps spraying coolant on the belly of the ship and the ground beneath her.

"Lock her down, people," Sam ordered, levering himself out of the command couch. "Arvid, you're in charge till the maintenance crews are done, then call me to find out where to link up with us."

"Aye, sir," Arvid sighed in resignation. No one looked forward to being stuck on the ship for refit duties.

"Don't worry." Sam clapped him on the shoulder. "I'll make sure you don't miss any of the fun. Everyone else," Sam looked around, "you remember the briefings. Don't ask too many questions, it's considered impolite here. In fact, given the sensitivity of the situation, you're better off not speaking to the locals unless spoken to, unless it involves something urgent. Let Priscilla, Sensitive Danabri or me do most of the talking."

Hell, we've been letting the little runt do all the talking this whole damn trip, Devon broadcast to him via his neurolink on a private channel. *Thank God it's the Martians' turn.*

Let's keep the neurolinks open for official matters, shall we? Sam responded silently, casting a baleful eye her way.

At least, Sam thought, the little shit wasn't paying attention to them or he would probably know they were talking about him. He was too busy enthusing over the return of gravity. Sam wasn't sure which was more annoying: Danabri's incessant whining over the lack of gravity or his inflated ebullience at its return. He pushed the thought aside as unworthy and led the impatient line of crewmembers to the ship's utility bay, where the main egress ramp was already lowering to the steaming concrete of the landing pad.

Raven, keep alert while we're gone, Sam ordered the ship's computer. *I don't distrust the Collective, but we're awfully close to the Consensus here…*

I understand, Captain Avalon, Raven replied. *I will keep in touch with you.*

Sam could already see the Collective vehicles approaching as he stepped out onto the concrete: three service trucks loaded with technicians and equipment and a single, boxy passenger van to take them to their meeting.

"The least they could have done was provide a decent luxury coach," Danabri grumbled when he saw it.

"Damned egalitarian of them, wasn't it?" Sam commented dryly.

"Is there any meaning behind it?" Priscilla asked. She had been strangely silent during the landing, but it was as if she suddenly switched on as she hit the landing pad, her eyes narrowing in thought.

"Most likely nothing significant." Danabri sniffed. "Other than possibly a desire to placate the Consensus by treating us as nothing special. The Collective isn't very ostentatious, as I am sure you're aware."

Before she could reply, the vehicles were upon them. As the service trucks pulled around to the rear of the ship, the van came to a halt directly in front of them and two Martians exited it. Characteristically tall and slender, the taller of the two men towered over Sam by a good half meter yet was only three quarters of his mass, looking down his long, aquiline nose at the heavy-worlder.

"We greet you in the name of the Collective Will of the Martian People," the taller man bowed cordially. Sam noticed the diplomat didn't offer a name: they'd been advised that this was a common Martian practice.

"And we thank you for agreeing to meet with us," Priscilla nodded. "I am Priscilla of the Resolution Diplomatic Corps."

"Please allow us to convey you to your temporary quarters, where you can prepare yourselves while we wait for the Consensus representatives to arrive."

Accustomed as Sam was to the uniformity of the Resolution Diplomatic Corps, the spare garb of the Martian diplomat still gave him pause. The tall man wore a simple, long-sleeved khaki tunic fastened in front, with pants of the same color and open-toed sandals. There was no mark of rank or station, nor were the clothes adorned with any personal touch. They were as simple as a military uniform, yet lacking even a military degree of individuality. The van's driver wore an identical set of clothes, which made Sam wonder how the Martians managed to identify functionaries without asking. It seemed somehow inefficient to his military sensibilities.

The van carried them across the concrete pad and onto a wide, paved access road into Tarshish. Sam settled into his comfortable if utilitarian seat and listened to Priscilla and the Martian diplomat trade careful inanities, awed by Priscilla's ability to keep the man talking without asking so much as his name. As he listened, he watched the city unfold around them, fascinated at how it managed to be simultaneously cosmopolitan and anachronistic. Tarshish was immense by Martian standards, and breathtakingly beautiful, its surreal spires and pyramids climbing into the purple-tinted sky with fragile elegance.

But the fantasy towers were girded with old-fashioned surface streets, built for individual groundcars, a system unheard of in the Resolution and not even seen on Earth for the last several centuries. Again, it was a system unworkable for the sorts of populations common on Resolution worlds, but perfectly suited for Mars.

The whole planet was a giant question that they were bound by form to avoid asking. Sam reminded himself that he was trying to not think about it, but his reverie was broken by their abrupt arrival at their destination. As buildings went in the lavish city, this one was nothing special, just a vaguely phallic obelisk a mere twelve stories tall and a hundred meters in diameter at its base.

"We trust your accommodations will be to your satisfaction," the Martian diplomat bowed to them as they disembarked the van. "Please make yourselves at home. We have a complete housekeeping system in place, but if there is anything it does not provide you, feel free to contact us. You may consider the city yours to discover, though we recommend that if you wish to explore outside of it, you should call for a guide, as there are dangerous animals in the wilds."

"When can we expect the Consensus ambassadors?" Priscilla asked him.

"Their ship is expected in fourteen hours, twenty-four minutes," the diplomat informed her. "Naturally, it is at their discretion at what point after that they wish to meet with you."

"We thank you for your gracious welcome." Priscilla nodded to him formally. He bowed in return, and then boarded the van.

"That's about the weirdest damn thing I ever saw," Carlos blurted as the vehicle drove away. "How can you have any kind of human society without telling people your name or asking them any questions?"

"How often do we get honest answers to our questions anyway?" Danabri muttered, staring after the departing vehicle.

"We were briefed what to expect," Sam answered with a shrug. "Let's leave the diplomacy to the diplomats and concentrate on settling in and doing our jobs. Devon."

He turned to the navigator. "Make sure everyone finds a room, then get on the horn to Arvid and see that he's relieved at the ship."

"Aye, sir," she nodded, then led the rest of the crew into the building. Danabri trailed them inside, frowning thoughtfully. Sam wondered what was bothering the man: he was too quiet.

Priscilla turned to him as they stood alone outside the doorway to the building. She seemed agitated and uncomfortable, uncharacteristically searching for something to do with her hands.

"Captain Avalon," she began, "I just wanted you to know that I do appreciate the manner in which you've carried out your duties. I know I've been a bit...brusque with you and your crew, but it is nothing personal, I assure you."

"Rest assured, Citizen Priscilla," he replied with more than a little irony, "I never once thought there was anything personal."

"It's simply that I am unused to working under these conditions," she went on, either oblivious to his tone or ignoring it. "I usually deal with matters in a more...controlled environment."

"One thing you learn quickly in the Patrol, Citizen Priscilla, is that life is frequently an uncontrolled environment. It's one of the things I like about the job."

She pierced him with a curious glance. "You say that, yet I know you also love the stability and organization of the service."

"The service, the Resolution, they are all my home," Sam shrugged. "They gave me life, gave me a purpose...but home is a place you start, not a place you stay forever."

"That's an interesting outlook, Captain," Priscilla admitted. "You've given me something to think about."

"Then I apologize." He grinned, heading for the door to the guesthouse. "Because Mother knows, you have quite enough to think about as it is."

Chapter Four

"This is the best goddamned meal I ever had," Mawae Danabri muttered around a mouthful of beef and gravy.

"It's always nice to eat under gravity after a long journey." Devon nodded diplomatically, studiously avoiding looking at the man as she ate so as not to ruin her appetite.

Everyone had gathered in the guesthouse's spacious, well-stocked dining room after settling into their quarters: it had become something of a tradition for Sam's crew through the years to share their first meal after landing, and Danabri and Priscilla had tagged along.

Sam wasn't sure how he felt about that. The post-mission meal was a time to blow off steam after adhering to strict professionalism for many weeks on ship. With the two outsiders present, they had to rein in their comments; Sam could see the resentment in his people's faces.

But…for some reason, he was glad that Priscilla had come down to eat with them. He wasn't sure why he was glad, but somehow the action made her seem more human. She wasn't near as talkative as Danabri, however; the man hadn't ceased to effuse about how happy he was to have gravity back.

"So what do we do now, boss?" Arvid wanted to know. Carlos had taken his place at the ship after grabbing a quick bite.

"I guess it's safe to assume no one feels like sleeping," Sam mused. "And it seems the Earthers won't be here till tomorrow at the earliest. How about we take a tour of the city?"

"I'm up for that," Devon smiled. "Not every day you get to go to Mars and do some sightseeing."

Arvid and D'jonni nodded eagerly, pushing away from the table; to Sam's surprise, so did Mawae Danabri.

"I think I'll tag along," the Sensitive decided. "These Martians are pleasantly unreadable...it will be nice to be able to walk through a crowd without knowing what everyone is thinking."

"What about you, Citizen Priscilla?" Sam asked hopefully. "Care to join us?"

"I should stay." Priscilla shook her head. "I should prepare for the meetings..."

"I would think after nearly two weeks shipboard, you're as prepared as you can be," Sam retorted, smiling to take the edge off the comment.

She looked at him sharply, as if she were about to disagree, but again he saw a flicker of indecision in her eyes, and a look of discomfort as if she were not used to the event. Finally, she shrugged.

"You may be right, Captain Avalon," she said. "Perhaps what I really need is to get my mind off all this for a while."

"After all, how often do you get to visit Mars?"

Sam offered her his arm. He felt an electric tingle through his whole body when she took it.

*   *   *

Tarshish was even more impressive on foot, Sam thought. Once they got past the neighborhood of government buildings, the inner city became a hodgepodge of bazaars and shops, selling almost anything imaginable. There was artwork, clothing and food from a dozen different worlds and a hundred different asteroid settlements and space colonies, peddled from outdoor stalls and decorative shops and everything in-between.

Everywhere there were milling crowds of offworlders, both shopping and hocking their wares; even

31

the custodial workers were recognizably non-Martians. Sam's head spun trying to catalog them all: here a Belter freighter crew, sporting the close-cut Mohawks and facial tattoos characteristic of spacers in the loosely aligned collection of settlements in the Solar asteroid belt. There, a diplomatic team from the Jovian mining colonies, their skin dark and rubbery, their bodies engineered centuries ago to withstand the electromagnetic belts surrounding Jupiter and bathing the colonies on its moons with lethal radiation. Resolution technology had allowed the construction of permanent energy shields that made the colonies livable for unmodified humans, but the Jovians carried their heritage in their genes and there was no going back.

There were Earthers of various stripe scattered through the crowd as well, though Sam understood from his intelligence briefings that they were usually transplants born on one of the handful of star colonies that the Consensus had managed to establish in the brief years since stealing the Transition drive from the Resolution.

What there was a decided lack of was Resolutionists. Sam knew that most Resolution traders felt uncomfortable operating so close to the Consensus, but he felt as if he stood out like an advertising hologram.

"I don't think I've ever seen so many different people from so many different worlds in one place," Sam confessed to Priscilla as they walked together behind the rest of the group. "Not even in the Patrol Academy."

"This place is a regular Casablanca." She nodded, taking it all in with wide eyes.

"A which?" Sam frowned.

"Sorry," she said with a chuckle. "Old Earth reference. Casablanca was a city in Africa, used as a meeting place by diplomats, traders, spies and criminals for several decades before the Collapse."

"Are you a student of old Earth history?" Sam asked.

"I am a student of just about everything, Captain Avalon," she replied distractedly, still absorbed by the bustle of the city. "I wonder what the significance is of the lack of native Martians in this district."

"Maybe they find that offworlders ask too many questions," Sam suggested.

"Perhaps," she allowed, "but not even a subclass of traders to do business down here?" She shook her head. "There have been plenty of separatist communities in human history, but no matter how apart they considered themselves, some few individuals always managed to hide their distaste and trade with outsiders. And the Martians don't even seem to have that sort of distaste. It's strange."

"I wish we knew more about Old Earth," Sam said wistfully. "So much was lost in the Collapse, and even much of what's left is tightly controlled by the Consensus government. Sometimes I feel like we've all lost a part of ourselves."

"That's a rare attitude among Patrol officers," Priscilla observed, picking through a pile of hand-woven rugs at an outdoor shop. The owner, a short, grizzled Earther, frowned at their Resolution uniforms but said nothing. "Most seem to resent the Consensus, and everything that goes with it."

"Earth isn't the Consensus, and the Consensus isn't Earth," Sam replied, trying not to notice the glare from the rug merchant. "We are all humans, and we all come from the same place, and long after the Consensus and the Resolution are gone, that will still be true."

She glanced at him sharply. "You speak so casually of the Resolution ending."

"I may not know all I wish to of history, Priscilla," Sam told her quietly, deliberately moving away from the Earther merchant, "but I do know of a parable that predates the Collapse as long as the Collapse predates us. A powerful ruler once commissioned a sage to come up with a phrase that would fit all occasions, whether sad or joyous, momentous or trivial. The man thought about it for many months before returning to the King with his choice. The phrase he chose was 'This too shall pass.' I try to remind myself of that whenever I get too proud of human accomplishment."

"I see when I return to Aphrodite," Priscilla said in obvious amusement, "that I must make plans to institute a new branch of the Patrol to be populated entirely by philosophers."

"All humans are philosophers. We live our lives by personal philosophies, spoken or unspoken." Sam smiled, idly running a finger over a statue of pure nickel iron imported from the solar Belt. "Patrol officers just have more time to think about it. Though the more I study it, the more it seems that the longer humans live, the less they think about how they live. Back when death was an imminent reality for all adults, people were more concerned with living ethically."

"Sam," Devon called to him from further down the street, waving him toward a small shop. "Come look at this."

Sam and Priscilla followed her into the darkened recesses of the corner shop, through a maze of hanging tapestries inlaid with holographic displays, their light sending out arcane shadows in the confines of the little building. In the back of the shop, they found Danabri, Arvid and D'jonni huddled with a plainly dressed woman with a particular ageless look that Sam associated immediately with a Resolutionist.

"Sam," Devon introduced, "this is Jeddah Valley. She's originally from Demeter."

"I saw your crew, Captain, and had to say hello." The woman took his hand. "It's so rare to find anyone from home here in Tarshish."

"How did someone from Demeter wind up running a shop in Tarshish?" Priscilla asked the woman.

"I worked as crew on a freighter to the Belt, fifteen years ago," Jeddah told him. "They had a containment problem out near Ceres and had to dump their reactor. The rest of the crew hired passenger space on a ship home, but I had something of the wanderlust, so I decided to take the hop to Mars. I hooked up with a merchant, worked for him till he decided to move on, and then I bought out his shop." She shrugged, smiling. "I imagine someday I'll move on myself, but I'm not quite tired of this place just yet."

"Sam," Devon said, her voice emphatic, "you need to look at this."

Sam followed her gesture, stepping through as the others parted. Hanging from the back wall was a tapestry inlaid with the holographic display of...

Sam blinked.

Inlaid on the tapestry was the image of the starship, the Bussard ramjet they had seen in the Centauri system. Not one like it, not merely the same design, but the same ship.

"How the hell..." Sam began, but words ran out.

"Citizen Valley," Priscilla demanded, "where did you acquire this image?"

"Yes, Devon was telling me you would be interested in this." Jeddah nodded. "My old boss, the previous owner here, bought this off a crewman on a Belt freighter, one of the new ones with the Transition drive they bought off the Resolution a few years back. The navigator said they saw this out in some unnamed system where they were making a connection, but no one ever believed him. He used to make these tapestries for a little extra money, so he made one of what he saw."

"Why wouldn't anyone believe him?" Sam asked. "Surely the ship's captain could back it up with the sensor log."

"Apparently," Jeddah said with a sly grin, "they were running Resolution technology to the Earthers and the captain wasn't too keen on keeping an accurate log."

"Gaia's Teeth," Sam muttered. "How long ago did he say he saw the thing?"

"Not sure, really," she admitted, shaking her head. "Danaan, the old owner here, talked to him more than I did. But it was ten years ago when he came in here, and he must have seen it a few years before that…his story was already a joke in the city by then."

"Devon," Sam said tightly, "do me a favor and use our discretionary fund to buy this tapestry. Then take it back to the ship and have *Raven* run a comparison scan with the images in her memory."

"Yes, sir," Devon said with a nod. "Where should I meet you?"

"We'll be back at the guest house. I would imagine Citizen Priscilla just got something new to think about."

* * *

"You know what this means," Priscilla said quietly to him as they paced quickly back through the merchant district.

"We weren't the first people to see this thing," Sam said with a nod. "Which means, there's the possibility that at least the Martians already knew about it."

"I wonder if they're the only ones," Priscilla murmured. "Come on." She suddenly tugged at his arm, leading him off down a side street.

"Where are we going?" Sam wondered with a confused frown, quickening his pace to follow her.

We're being followed, she told him over his neurolink. *For the last half a kilometer. At least three men, fifty meters back…don't look yet.*

Raven, do you read? Sam tried to call the ship's computer using his implant transmitter. Raven? *Devon, can you hear me?*

We're being jammed, Priscilla guessed. *Take this next left turn and you can get a glimpse of them...don't be too obvious though.*

Sam followed her through a sharp left at the next surface street and allowed himself a brief glimpse of their pursuers: there were three men, dressed in the manner of an independent insystem freighter crew. Sam knew that was a deception because they all had the build of men who lived at or near standard gravity. They couldn't be Resolutionists, so that left either Earthers or Earther colonists.

Priscilla, we should try to lead them back to the Collective administration district.

If we do that, she protested, *we'll lose them and we'll never find out why they're following us.*

Yes, but if they intend us harm, we're helping them out by heading this way; we're nearly to the edge of the city.

Priscilla looked around for the first time at where they were: in a nearly deserted section of Tarshish surrounded by automated utility centers. The hum of generators and water pumps and the scuffle of their own feet on the pavement were the only noises. And then Sam heard the footsteps behind them starting to increase in pace.

"Too late," Sam said out loud as he turned to face them.

The three men halted abruptly in their charge at Sam's motion, pausing to glance questioningly at each other, and then back at Sam and Priscilla.

"Who are you and what do you want?" Priscilla demanded.

Sam didn't wait for an answer; instead he used the distraction of her question as an opportunity to launch himself into the nearest of them, a broad-bodied man with a single stripe of hair running from his forehead down past his collar. Taking advantage of the low Martian gravity, Sam leaped from a standing start into a jump side kick that took the Earther directly in the sternum and sent him flying backwards, had over heels.

Touching down from the kick, Sam spun into an elbow strike at the second of the group, a tall, rangy fellow with a tattoo of a wolf running down his right cheek. But the element of surprise was gone and the man had enough time to dodge to the side, turning a devastating temple strike into a blow to the side of the neck that still sent him stumbling away off-balance and in pain.

The third Earther grabbed for something at his belt as he turned toward the Patrol Captain, but both he and Sam were surprised when Priscilla lashed out at him with a vicious round kick that broke his forearm with a sickening crack. The device he'd been attempting to retrieve clattered to the pavement, but before Sam could either get a look at it or go to Priscilla's aid, the tattooed man was back on his feet. In his hand was a black, cylindrical device like the one the third attacker had dropped. Tattoo angled the thing toward the ground and touched a button on its side and Sam heard a faint hum issuing from it, could just barely see an interruption in the air below it.

Sam had a sickening feeling he knew what it was, and he threw himself backward as the Earther swung at him with the device. He rolled onto his shoulder and flipped back onto his feet in time to dodge Tattoo's next charge. Leaping to the side, he caught a glimpse of Priscilla finishing the assailant she'd already disarmed, executing a series of elbow and knee strikes so quickly he couldn't follow them.

He had little time to ponder her unexpected abilities, because Tattoo was circling around, trying to get an angle on him, swiping his weapon back and forth in a threatening figure eight. Sam quickly retreated, not sure of the thing's reach but knowing what it would do to him if he guessed wrong. As Tattoo advanced on him and he continued to backpedal, Sam suddenly felt a tingle along his spine just as he heard Priscilla's mental call, *Behind you!*

Acting on a combination of instinct and training, Sam ducked to the side as Tattoo swung his weapon and saw out of the corner of his eye the Mohawked Earther he'd kicked rushing him from behind. Tattoo, unable to control his swing, slashed his weapon right across Mohawk's upper torso, which separated from the rest of his body in a spray of arterial blood. Before the two halves of the dead Earther hit the ground, Sam and Priscilla were both in motion, coordinating their attack through their neurolinks.

Sam feinted a high kick, and before Tattoo could bring his weapon around to guard, Priscilla slammed her heel into the side of the man's knee. Sam heard the Earther's kneecap shatter, saw the man's mouth open in a scream, saw his hand open involuntarily around the grip of his weapon, held over his head in a defensive gesture...

As the device fell, it sliced through the top of Tattoo's skull, cleaving it neatly in two before sliding out and falling to the ground. Sam stepped back as the body collapsed in front of him, spraying blood across the pavement.

"Come on, let's go!"

Sam grabbed Priscilla's hand and set off at a sprint back towards the Collective government sector. He didn't know if there were any more of the Earthers around and he wasn't about to wait to find out.

"Shouldn't we call the authorities?" Priscilla asked, pacing him without difficulty.

"Once we're somewhere safe," Sam replied.

Devon, Sam called over his neurolink, hoping they were out of range of the jamming. *Devon, are you there?*

Nothing. Raven, he called, *do you read?*

Captain Avalon, I am gratified to hear from you. There has been trouble.

An attempt was made on our lives, but we're both okay, Sam told the ship's computer. *Is everyone else all right?*

Lieutenant Commander Conrad was also attacked, sir...

Devon? Sam interrupted, so surprised he almost stopped running. *Is she all right?*

She sustained a serious injury, but she will recover; she's in the medical unit here on board. No one else was hurt, but they are all here as well.

Contact the Collective authorities, Raven, Sam ordered the AI. *Inform them of both attacks and tell them they need to pick up the bodies of the men who tried to kill us.* Sam gave him a feed of the coordinates at which the attack had occurred. *Let them know we'll be waiting for them at our ship.*

Yes, Captain Avalon. If I may say so, I am glad you're unhurt.

Thanks. Tell the crew we'll be there in a few minutes.

"We need to get back to the ship," Sam gasped out to Priscilla, still running. "There's been..."

"Yes, I heard," she interrupted. "We'd better find a transport."

Sam was almost too distracted by the turn of events with his crew to be shocked that Priscilla could listen in on private neurolink conversations. He shook off the thought as he saw a private Offworlder-run cab sitting at a corner and began waving at it...

*   *   *

40

With the way things had been going, Sam half-expected *Raven* to be under missile attack when he arrived, but the spaceport was the very model of serenity. Sam absent-mindedly shoved a handful of Tradenotes at the cab driver, not caring if he was overpaying, then followed Priscilla out of the open-top vehicle and trotted toward the ship.

The boarding ramp lowered to meet them and they clambered up it, finding Lieutenant Arvid waiting for them in the utility bay, a frown describing his brown face.

"Thank Mother you're both all right," the weapons officer sighed. "When we couldn't reach you by neurolink, we thought the worst."

"How's Devon?" Sam asked. "Is she going to be okay?"

"She got a nasty slice right through the left shoulder blade," Arvid shook his head, "but we got her to the ship in time and the med unit is working on her now. *Raven* says she should be good as new by tomorrow morning.

"After you two left, Devon paid Jeddah, the Resolutionist shopkeeper," Arvid explained, "and then she started back for the guest quarters. Carlos and D'jonni talked with Jeddah for another minute while Danabri and I looked around the stands in front of the store. That's when we heard someone scream. We all ran out and found Devon being attacked by two Earthers…at least they looked like Earthers to me. They took off when they saw us coming, and we didn't chase them because we weren't sure if there were more of them and we wanted to get Devon to the ship."

"Why didn't you have her taken to a Collective medical center?" Priscilla wondered.

"We weren't sure about their technology," Arvid told her. "They can't have nanotech, not with the

Consensus breathing down their necks, and I knew what we had on board ship."

"Good decision," Sam told him, clapping a hand on his shoulder. "Did you call the Collective authorities and let them know what happened?"

"Yes, sir, they have people on the way to interview us and we called in descriptions of the attackers." He frowned more deeply. "I don't expect anything to come of it though. No one would plan something like this without some way of escaping capture."

"The ones we encountered won't be escaping anywhere," Sam muttered, leaning back against a workbench. The adrenaline rush was beginning to fade, and Sam could feel himself slipping into post-traumatic shock. He clenched his fists to keep his hands from shaking, not willing to use his pharmacy organ to dose himself with a sedative. "Maybe the Collective can find something on the bodies."

"I just wish we could have caught the guys that hurt Devon." Arvid shook his head. "At least we could have gotten the picture back from them."

"What?" Priscilla snapped. "What picture?"

"I'm sorry," Arvid stuttered hesitantly. "I thought someone told you. It was the tapestry we bought, the one with the alien ship on it. The Earthers…they took it."

Chapter Five

"What the hell do you mean there were no bodies?" Sam exploded, earning a sharp glance from Priscilla.

"As we have indicated," the Martian investigator repeated unflappably, "we did a thorough search of the area and found no signs of the men you claimed were injured in the altercation."

"What about security scanners?" Priscilla asked the man, holding up a hand to still protests from the other members of the ship's crew gathered in the meeting room with the two Martian officials. "Surely you run security scanners in the Offworlder districts."

"The scanners were scrambled," the Martian told them, "undoubtedly by the same interference that disabled your neurolink communicators. The same thing happened to the scanners near where your Navigator, Devon Bishop, was attacked."

"Have you interviewed witnesses of that attack, at least?" Sam wanted to know.

"They corroborate what your people said," the second Martian official replied, nodding---it was as if the two were interchangeable. "However, we have been unable to find any record of anyone that matches a description of the attackers. We did collect DNA samples from blood on the street near where you were attacked, and we will process them against those visitors who are registered, but if they managed to get onplanet without being recorded..."

"So that's it then," Sam muttered bitterly. He wasn't so upset with the inability of the Martians to find the attackers as he was at their cheerful and blasé attitude. "At least two people dead, one of my crew badly injured, and that's it."

"We shall, of course, do our best to find those responsible," one of the two assured him. "In the meantime, we urge you to be cautious. If these people are able to evade our security procedures, there is no telling what resources they have."

"How about letting us carry weapons then?" Arvid suggested.

"Personal weapons are strictly forbidden in the Collective," the Martian said sharply. "There are no exceptions."

"That didn't seem to bother those bastards that attacked us," Carlos snapped. "I guess it'll be some comfort if one of us is killed that at least the murderer will get arrested for illegal weapons possession…*if* you can catch him, that is."

"Medical Officer Raines," Sam hissed, eyes turning cold as he came to his feet, "if you can't keep a civil tongue in your head, you can confine yourself to your quarters immediately."

Carlos turned toward Sam, his face screwed up in anger, but then he let out a breath and relaxed.

"I'm sorry, sir," he blurted. "I just…" He turned to the Martians, bowing his head in contrition. "You have my apologies." He turned awkwardly and left the meeting room, heading back toward the medcenter.

"The representatives of the Consensus government have landed," one of the Martians announced, oblivious both to Carlos' outburst and his apology. "They have informed us they will be ready to meet with you in the morning." Both of them stood up and nodded to Sam and Priscilla. "You will want time to prepare, of course."

And with that, they both headed for the boarding ramp, leaving Sam shaking his head.

"These people," Sam said quietly once they were off the ship and the ramp was closed behind them, "are the most infuriating individuals I have ever dealt with."

"Individuals may be the wrong choice of terms," Mawae Danabri said thoughtfully, leaning forward in his seat. Sam suddenly realized that the man hadn't uttered a word the whole time the Martian officials had been on board, and his estimation of the Sensitive went up sharply. Whatever else Danabri was, he *was* a professional.

"What do you mean, Citizen Danabri?" Priscilla asked.

"They don't act like individuals," he said with a shrug. "At least not like individual *humans*. More like some kind of insect colony." He peered curiously at Priscilla. "Hasn't any Sensitive ever been part of an embassy to the Collective?"

"There's never been a *formal* embassy to the Collective," Priscilla admitted. "We contacted them when we found the way back to the Solar System, they told us right up front what sort of relationship they were willing to have with us, and that was that. They never agreed to any negotiations and their terms were good enough that we never pushed."

"Interesting," Danabri mused.

"I'm sure it's fascinating," Sam interjected, "but in case anyone's forgotten, the Earthers are here, ahead of schedule, and ready to meet with us, despite the fact they likely just tried to have us killed. Is anyone else confused by this turn of events?"

"They must expect us to cancel the meeting," Arvid guessed. "It would make us look bad, give them diplomatic ammunition to use against us."

"It can't be that simple," Danabri shook his head. "You don't attempt an assassination to make someone late for a meeting; the risk is too high."

"It has to have something to do with the tapestry," Priscilla surmised. "They didn't try to hit us till we found the tapestry."

"If they knew it was there though," Sam protested, "why didn't they just buy the damn thing and get rid of it."

"Well," Priscilla sighed, "we certainly aren't going to figure it out before tomorrow. We'll simply have to meet with the Consensus representatives and pretend nothing happened. We still have a mission to accomplish."

"I think we should stay on the ship tonight," Sam opined. "I am suddenly not so sanguine about Collective security measures."

"I agree, Captain," Priscilla said. "Until we have a clearer idea of what's going on, we need to take extra precautions."

"Arvid," Sam turned to his weapons officer, "I want the ship's sensors up all night. If anyone comes within a hundred meters of us, I want to know it. And break out a couple lasers. We may not be able to carry them around with us, but we'll damn sure have them ready if anything happens at the ship."

"Yes, sir, I'll get on it now."

"The damnedest thing is," Sam said to Danabri and Priscilla after Arvid left, "if they knew about the tapestry, they must know this thing exists and that it's connected to Earth somehow. If they know that, they know they're going to desperately need our help. Why would they try to scare us off, or possibly kill us?"

"People can't always be counted on to act rationally in the face of something like this," Danabri ventured.

"Particularly Earthers," Priscilla added. "Considering their attitude toward the Resolution, and the stress this situation will put on them and their core beliefs, nothing they do would surprise me."

"Well, I am sure of one thing," Danabri sighed, coming to his feet. "If I'm going to be reading a roomful of those psychos tomorrow, I need some sleep."

"Good night, Citizen Danabri," Priscilla nodded. Her eyes followed him out of the room before lighting back on Sam.

"Is there something wrong?" Sam asked, frowning. "Beside the obvious I mean."

"I was impressed with the way you handled yourself today, Captain," she said. "I was unaware that Patrol officers received that degree of training in unarmed combat."

"We don't, generally," he told her. "But everyone needs a hobby, and mine has always been the study of old-Earth martial arts. You obviously have studied them yourself, from what I could tell."

"Diplomatic missions are, as a rule, unarmed." She shrugged. "It is prudent to have some way of defending yourself. I never expected to have to use it."

"I never have before," Sam admitted. "Not outside the *dojo*, anyway." He let out a deep sigh. "I've never seen anyone killed like that, either. Not face to face. I mean, we've had to take out Consensus bandit ships, and I knew on an intellectual level we were...*killing* them. But it was all so antiseptic. It was all tens of thousands of kilometers away."

"Did you feel guilty about it?" Priscilla asked quietly. "Not today...I mean, we didn't kill the two that died, they basically killed themselves. But when you and your crew intercepted the Earther bandits? Did you feel guilty about it?"

"I didn't feel good about it," he admitted. "They're humans, just like us, even if they don't want to admit it. But no one asked them to attack our ships, and if I didn't stop them, they would have murdered innocent people. So no, I didn't feel guilty, really. I just wish it wasn't necessary." He smiled. "Maybe if we do our jobs and pull this off, it won't be necessary anymore."

Priscilla laughed softly, a sound, Sam thought, like wine on crystal. "It must be nice to be able to have that sort of idealism."

47

"You think I'm being naïve," Sam said, not offended.

"Not naïve," she shook her head, putting a hand on his arm. "Captain Avalon…Sam. I am beginning to think that you are the purest form of what the Resolution is all about."

"I…" Sam stuttered. "Thanks. I don't know what to say."

"Then don't say anything." Priscilla leaned over in her seat and Sam had never been quite so surprised as he was when she kissed him. He found her suddenly in his arms, pressing against him and found that he wanted her to be there. But still…

"This…this really isn't professional of us, is it?" He protested weakly as they broke the kiss.

"Gaia's Blood," Priscilla laughed as she worked at the fastenings of his uniform, "I certainly hope not."

After that, Sam didn't say much. He did remember to have *Raven* lock the door to the conference room, but that was the last "professional" thought he had till the next morning…

*   *   *

Sam didn't know what to expect when he met the Consensus delegation, mostly because he didn't know what to expect from *anything* anymore, not after last night. He had been worried in the morning, worried that he and Priscilla's working relationship would be compromised, yet simultaneously worried that she would freeze him out when the time came to get back to their mission.

Yet neither seemed to have happened. When Priscilla walked into the ship's conference room for the pre-meeting briefing, she reacted to him pleasantly but without any hint of what had occurred the night before, except once when her hand accidentally brushed his on the table, and seemed to linger for one moment longer than it had to.

She handled it perfectly, he thought, and again decided that "perfect" was the best word to describe her. He'd had that thought several times last night, when he'd been able to think at all. Sam was hardly inexperienced when it came to sex but he had never encountered anyone like Priscilla before. She seemed to combine the eagerness of a virgin with the experience of a seasoned lover and the juxtaposition had been something truly incredible.

Sam shook his head, trying to clear it of memories of the previous night and prepare himself mentally for the meeting. He, Danabri and Priscilla had waited in the appointed conference room for nearly an hour now with still no sign of the Earthers, another calculated tactic he was sure. The worst part was, they couldn't even bitch about it just in case the room was bugged, so they had to pass the time with inanities about Martian tourism.

Sam was about at the breaking point, and was ready to say the hell with it and go get a late breakfast when the door to the conference room slid aside and the Consensus delegation entered. Sam, Priscilla and Danabri rose from their seats as the first of them came through the doorway.

She was security...she *screamed* security to Sam and he could see Mawae Danabri watching her intently as well. Her bearing was straight, her eyes flickering across the room like scanners, and her utility fatigues were plain in contrast with the more flamboyant clothes of those that followed her. She was tall and muscular, her blond hair cut to a manageable shoulder length, and she paused in the doorway for a barely-perceptible moment before moving to the side and letting the others through.

The man who came through behind her had an air of officiousness and self-importance that went beyond his hand-tailored suit and turned-up nose and through to the carriage of his gait. He was every centimeter the politician,

Sam was sure, whatever his official title was. The man and woman that followed were toadies; Sam didn't have to have Danabri's skills to see that. Their suits, while expertly made, were purposefully of a lesser degree than their leader's. Their demeanor was one of servitude and support and they each carried a notebook-sized computer a hundred years obsolete by Resolution standards.

"I am Priscilla." She was, of course, the first to break the silence. "I represent the Resolution Diplomatic Corps. This is my aid, Citizen Danabri, and Captain Avalon of the Resolution Patrol, the man who discovered the threat."

"I am Friedrich Hamilton," Nose-in-the-Air announced, not offering a hand, "Ambassador from the Human Consensus to the Martian government. Shall we get this started?" He took a seat across the table from Priscilla and she and Sam took their cue to sit down. Danabri moved into a corner and leaned against the wall, crossing his arms and watching. The Consensus security officer eyed him cautiously and Danabri winked at her. She quickly looked away and he grinned in amusement.

"I assume," Priscilla began, "that you've had time to confirm the tracking data we sent you on the ramship."

"Our telescopes have spotted the object," Hamilton allowed. "However, our researchers feel that it could be a natural phenomenon. We have nothing but your word that it is of intelligent design."

"Just what sort of natural phenomena could be *accelerating* on a collision course with Earth at a constant 1.3 gravities?" Priscilla wondered. "*And* traveling at a significant portion of lightspeed?"

Sam glanced at Priscilla, feeling an odd sensation in the pit of his stomach. For a moment he wondered if he was ill.

"Even if we accept the possibility that it is a starship of some kind," Hamilton went on, as if he hadn't heard her, "how do we know its intentions are destructive?"

"It can't possibly decelerate in time to stop in the Solar System," Priscilla countered. "You must know that by now. It most likely can't even significantly change course at this point without using the sun's gravity, and it isn't on the right course to slingshot around the sun. You know that too. So why don't we dispense with the double-talk? You can feel free to reject the explanation we've given for the motives behind this threat, but you know the threat exists and it must be dealt with. Do your scientists think you can deal with it by yourselves?"

Sam couldn't take his eyes off of her. He realized, with a start, that he was developing an erection and he hoped to Gaia that none of the Consensus people would notice. What the *hell* was going on?

"We..." Hamilton seemed a bit taken aback by her frankness, "we have considered moving an asteroid into the object's path..."

"Even assuming the weapon didn't have defenses to prevent collisions," Priscilla countered, "the only rocks big enough to deflect it are in the Belt...none of the Trojans or Apollo objects will do. And I don't know how you're going to convince the Belters to let you have one of their largest and most densely-populated habitats. You could, I suppose, bring one of the larger comets in from the Oort Cloud, but that would most likely take too long." She placed her hands flat on the table and leaned toward the Earther. "Shall we try this once more?"

"I am only here as a favor to the Collective," Hamilton hissed angrily, eyes flaring as he rose halfway from his chair. "I do not have to sit here and take this sort of presumption!"

"Ambassador Hamilton," Priscilla sighed, "I am sorry you take my honesty for presumption, but the fact is, we do not have much time. Any effort to stop this thing *must* begin almost immediately, as it will take thousands of work-hours to build a device capable of shunting something of this size into Transition Space. And you have to believe me, that is the *only* way to prevent this thing from striking Earth. It is going too fast for anything else to work. Any harshness in my tone or lack of patience you might detect is simply the urgency and desperation of the situation leaking through and I apologize for this in advance."

"Well," Hamilton sat back, seeming to relax slightly, "since we're being so brutally honest...Priscilla?" She nodded and he smiled, showing a little of the professional diplomat hidden behind his mask of arrogance. "We make no secret of our beliefs, nor do we make a secret of the fact that we consider your practices---your very *existence*---an affront to those beliefs. You've constantly accused us of being responsible for pirate attacks on your shipping and you've done your best to support the Belters in their defiance of our authority." He shook his head in bemusement. "So, just why is the Resolution so desperate, so urgent to help the Consensus? Wouldn't it be more to your advantage to have us out of the way, permanently?"

"That is not our way, Ambassador Hamilton," Priscilla assured him. "Unlike your government, mine considers us all to be humans, heirs of the same heritage and responsible for one another's welfare. Earth is as much our home as yours, despite our differences."

"People like you," Hamilton said, "who took upon themselves the judgement of the Creator and tampered with the very things that make us human, destroyed our world once. Why should we trust you now to save it?"

"Because," Priscilla replied, "you really have no other choice. You can either accept our aid or start evacuating the planet. And while you're at it, you might want to get your people off the moon and out of the L5 stations as well; the fragmentation of Earth will likely make those bases unlivable due to meteoric activity."

Hamilton regarded her coolly, and Sam fancied he could see the gears turning in the man's brain. Sam was fighting to control his breathing and felt sweat dampening his armpits. This couldn't be all just an emotional reaction on his part to the sexual encounter yesterday. Something very strange was happening here.

"You realize I don't have the authority to make any sort of commitment," he said finally. "But I will relay what you have said on to my government. I will do what I can to expedite their decision."

"That's all we can ask," Priscilla said with a smile. "We will remain here to await their word."

Hamilton stood slowly, as if sensing he was being dismissed and not being used to the concept.

"Priscilla," he said with some bemusement, "it has been an…interesting experience meeting you."

"And a pleasure to speak with you, Mr. Ambassador," Priscilla nodded, coming to her feet. "We hope to hear from you soon."

As the Earthers filed out, Sam could see disconcerted looks on their faces, particularly on the face of the male assistant. He opened his mouth to say something as the last of them left the room, but then noticed the scowl on Danabri's face and decided that if the Sensitive could hold his piece till they were out of the probably-bugged meeting room, so could he.

He began to lose both his erection and the restless, uncomfortable feeling as they made their way out of the Collective government building and into the street. Finally, as they reached the path back to their quarters, he could hold it in no longer.

"What the hell was going on back there?" Sam blurted, staring at Priscilla. She cocked an eyebrow, seeming a bit amused.

"We did our job, Captain Avalon," she reminded him. "He will pass our proposal up the line with a positive recommendation and we might actually get to go to Earth itself and play this whole scene again."

"Do you want *me* to tell him?" Danabri muttered, still scowling.

"Why was I feeling so…" Sam searched for the word awkwardly.

"Aroused," Danabri suggested.

"All right," Priscilla held up a hand, halting in the middle of the street and turning to face them. "Sam, as a member of the diplomatic corps, I was given certain…enhancements. One of them was a minor glandular augmentation which allows me to produce an unusually high amount of pheromones at will."

Sam's eyes widened as his mind examined all the implications of what she had said in relation to the actions of the Ambassador at the meeting, then widened again as he thought about last night.

"What if the Consensus representatives find out about this?" Sam wondered, not voicing his personal concerns, even though they were more on his mind than the concerns for their mission.

"They won't, unless they dissect me," Priscilla assured him. "Or happen to be running a chemscanner at the instant I do it."

"It was a huge risk," Danabri snapped. "And it made my job nearly impossible. How the hell am I supposed to get a read on the Ambassador's reaction to your proposal when he's thinking with his dick instead of his brain?"

"Citizen Danabri," Priscilla returned his harsh glare, "I am not here to make your job easier, I am here to accomplish our mission by *whatever* means necessary." Her expression softened a bit. "I do apologize for not warning you, but I wasn't certain if the representative would be a man or a woman, so I couldn't be sure if I would use the pheromones or not."

"Just what other…situations would you use this ability for?" Sam asked as carefully as he could phrase the question, trying to read her expression.

"I *assure* you, Captain," she replied, her eyes frosting over with a look that sent a shiver up Sam's spine, "that I would never use such measures for anything but the direst of emergencies and under direct orders of my superiors."

"You would never need to," Sam said, and he could see the cold look in her eye soften a bit. He thought he could see a hint of regret in that ice-blue stare.

"We need to get back," she said quietly, turning and heading down the street.

Danabri looked at Sam with something that was almost sympathy and then followed Priscilla. Sam let out a deep sigh, shook his head and set off after them. As if things hadn't been complicated enough…

Chapter Six

"How are you feeling?" Sam asked Devon, sitting on the edge of the table beside her bed. He felt guilty that he hadn't had a chance to see her since she woke, but if she felt any resentment she didn't show it.

"I'm just fine, sir," she smiled. "Arm is almost like new." She pulled down the edge of her shirt to show the fading red line that was all that remained of the bone-deep cut she'd suffered from the assassins. "Carlos wanted me to stay in bed till tomorrow just to make sure there were no psychological complications."

"Are there any?" Sam wondered, looking her in the eye. "Any nightmares?"

"Not so far," she told him. "I mean, it wasn't something I want to go through every day, but I'm not exactly a cadet on her first training mission."

"I don't know, Devon." Sam sighed heavily. "The longer this mission goes on, the more I feel like a cadet."

"That bad, sir?" she asked, cocking an eyebrow.

"Nothing seems to make any sense," he admitted, shaking his head. "I can't figure out what the Consensus is trying to do, and what scares me is that Mawae and Priscilla can't figure it out either and they're both a hell of a lot smarter than I am."

"Don't sell yourself short, sir," Devon said quietly, putting a hand on top of his. "You're the best commanding officer I've ever had."

"I appreciate that," he said, patting her hand. "I really do. But I can't shake the feeling we're being manipulated, and I don't even know who's doing the manipulating."

"From what I gather, you don't think the Earth contingent here had anything to do with the assassination attempt," Devon said.

"It sure didn't seem like it. But that raises the question, how could anyone have known about that tapestry; and if they did know, why didn't they do something earlier?"

"Maybe what we're dealing with is some faction among the Earthers," Devon theorized, eyes narrowing, focusing on something outside the bulkheads. "I know we all talk about the Consensus like it's one big monolithic entity, but they haven't had a united government for as long as we have. Maybe there's infighting going on."

"That's a good point," Sam mused, rubbing his jaw thoughtfully. "And we may not even be dealing with solely political factions either; the Naturalist Society has a lot of power in the Consensus government. Hell, they were the ones who started funding the raids on our shipping. We might be looking at a religious rift as well."

"Are you going to tell Priscilla about the idea?"

"I suppose I should," he muttered without enthusiasm. She had been avoiding his company since their confrontation in the street the day before and he wasn't eager to face her this soon.

"She makes you uncomfortable, doesn't she?" Devon deduced and Sam had to remind himself she couldn't know what had occurred between the two of them.

"I don't know how to deal with her, either on a personal or a professional level," Sam sighed. He knew he shouldn't be sharing these sorts of thoughts with a subordinate, but if there was anyone on the crew who he trusted with his personal feelings, it was Devon. "She's a giant question mark, and not just because she lacks a title."

"I know what you mean." Devon nodded. "But that can't be easy for her, you know. How would you feel if people constantly didn't know how to deal with you?"

"I guess I would feel a bit like Mawae," Sam said with a chuckle. "Damn, there's someone else I wouldn't have believed if I hadn't met them. You know something,

Devon, it wasn't just a couple months ago that I thought I had life all figured out and pigeon-holed into nice, neat categories."

"Isn't that always when everything comes flying apart?" she observed wryly.

"You get better." Sam patted her on the hand again, standing abruptly. "I need you back on the job tomorrow. You're obviously the smartest person on this ship."

"Well if it took an assassination attempt for you to figure that out," Devon said with a broad grin, "then it was almost worth it."

*   *   *

"It's an interesting theory," Priscilla allowed, dangling her bare feet over the edge of the bunk in her cabin. He'd come to her compartment straight from Devon's and found her getting ready for bed, dressed in a light, almost transparent shift, her hair disheveled ever so slightly in a way that seemed designed to drive Sam crazy. He was already beginning to sweat and he knew no artificial pheromones were responsible.

"Yes." He nodded, trying to drag his thoughts kicking and screaming back to the subject of Devon's theory. "It would seem to make sense that at least the ambassador and his party were unaware of the attempt, if for no other reason than plausible deniability."

"The key is the tapestry," she declared. "If they waited till now to make a play for it, they must not have known about it till we came here."

"You think the other…faction knew about the tapestry and the ones that tried to kill us found out from them after we got here?"

"Well, we're just spit-balling here," she admitted, shrugging, "but knowing something about the Naturalist Society, I would venture a guess that if your navigator's idea is correct, they would be the ones responsible for the attack. They run the Consensus government in all but name. My question would be who their opposition is, who knew about this but wasn't telling them?"

"If there *is* some sort of opposition party in the Consensus government, why would they keep the threat a secret?"

"Maybe because they knew we'd find out about it and offer to help," Priscilla mused.

"Damn," Sam breathed, leaning back against the bulkhead, his earlier arousal faded and forgotten as his brain crunched this new data. "I'm just a Patrol Captain, I am way out of my league with all this crap."

"You're doing fine, Sam," she assured him. "This isn't exactly your typical diplomatic mission. And I'm afraid I haven't made it any easier by my actions last night."

Sam blinked, taken aback by unspoken apology.

"I knew what I was doing," he told her, offering his own. "I think we're both professional enough to not let it interfere with the mission."

Priscilla's eyes blinked downward in thought for just a moment and then she smiled warmly.

"I'll do my best to avoid springing any more surprises on you," she promised.

"Don't say that," Sam shook his head, stepping over to take her hand in his. "I've come to appreciate discovering the surprising things about you."

She reached up and guided him down to a kiss that began as a friendly, tender gesture, but gained passion as it persisted. Suddenly the feelings Sam had experienced when he first entered the room returned full force and he slipped the light shift off of her shoulders, guiding it over her breasts with his open palm and lingering there. She worked at the fastenings of his uniform and he impatiently yanked off the garments, and then bore her down to the bunk beneath him.

Captain, the voice of the ship's computer said in an apologetic tone over his neurolink, *I hate to bother you at this time of night, but we have an incoming message from the Consensus Embassy.*

Display a ViR image of me, Sam ordered *Raven*, not pausing in his attentions toward Priscilla*, and patch my neurolink signal through a voice simulation.*

Aye sir.

"This is Captain Avalon," a visual and audio replica constructed by the *Raven*'s computer announced over the ship's communicator.

The image that appeared in a part of Sam's mind was, surprisingly enough, not the Consensus Ambassador or one of his secretaries; instead, it was the female security officer he remembered from the meeting.

"Captain," she said, "I am Guardian Prime Telia Proctor. I have been designated to accompany you to Harmony Base on Luna for continuation of the negotiations with the Consensus government."

"The decision has been made already?" Sam asked in honest surprise. He was so shocked that he actually paused in mid-motion and sat up in bed.

"What is it?" Priscilla frowned.

Damn.

"We've got an incoming message from the embassy," he told her. "They're going to let us go all the way to Luna for continued negotiations."

"Yes, Captain," Telia Proctor's image replied, oblivious to his real-time conversation with Priscilla. "I will be reporting to your ship in the morning and we will depart immediately."

"With whom will we be meeting?" Priscilla's ViR representation joined Sam's in the transmission, *Raven*'s machinations making it appear she had walked up next to the man.

"Deputy Minister Tejado will be in charge of negotiations," Proctor told her. "It will be his decision whether you are allowed to proceed to a further meeting with the Prime Minister. Now if there are no further questions, I must begin preparations to leave."

"We look forward to having you aboard," Priscilla's image nodded and the transmission ended.

Priscilla and Sam abruptly found themselves back in her bed. Sam looked down and sighed.

"What's wrong?" Priscilla asked, beaming. "It's great news! I thought they might take weeks to make that decision!"

"Yeah, it's wonderful," Sam nodded. "It's just that…well, it kind of killed the romance."

She glanced down and grinned. "I'm sure there's something we can do about that," she said, gathering her knees beneath her and bending down into his lap.

Sam gasped, the warmth enveloping him like a womb. He felt as if every nerve in his body was crammed into a few centimeters of flesh, and his former arousal quickly returned; but when he tried to pull away, she held onto him and continued her ministrations with even more enthusiasm. Realizing her intentions, Sam leaned back and enjoyed the ride, losing himself in the sensation. When the inevitable happened, Priscilla didn't pull away, instead letting the results flow into her and gently squeezing him dry.

"My God," Sam breathed, finally pulling her into his arms, "that was incredible. You're incredible."

"Would you believe me if I told you I'd never done that before?" she asked teasingly.

"Right now," Sam replied with a smile, "I would believe you if you told me you were Spencer's *Fairie Queen* brought to life by some Celtic goddess."

Sam thought he saw the shadow of a frown pass across her face, and he wondered for a moment if he'd said the wrong thing, but she quickly covered it by pulling him into a passionate kiss.

"I'm no goddess, Sam," she whispered, holding him tightly. "I'm a woman. Make me feel like a woman tonight…"

*   *   *

"She's a stiff-backed bruiser, isn't she?" Arvid muttered, watching on the cockpit's external monitor as Telia Proctor approach across the fusion-formed concrete. Her starched uniform was spotless and she managed to walk at attention even with a pair of heavy travel bags in her hands.

"Yeah, well you'd be stiff-backed too," Carlos told him, eyes locked to the sensor readout, "if you were carrying the kind of cybernetics she is."

"What do you mean?" Sam asked, stepping up behind the two men. They turned, startled at the presence of their captain.

"Well, sir," Carlos explained with a shrug, "sensor reads show she's nearly half cybernetic." He waved at the readout screen, which exhibited a thermal view of the approaching Consensus Security officer. "An eye, an ear, both legs, both arms, heart, looks like one lung, a kidney…major reinforcement of her spine, shoulders and hips. She's carrying some sort of isotope reactor to power the whole thing." The medic shook his head. "Gotta be a bitch getting rid of waste heat…she must have some sort of liquid nitrogen coolant system in there."

"Can you tell if it's straight prosthetics," Sam asked, "or is she boosted?"

"Gotta be boosted," Carlos opined. "No need for that much skeletal reinforcement for prosthetics."

"The Consensus still uses cybernetic prosthetics?" Arvid asked in disbelief. "That's barbaric!"

"Biotech is illegal in the Consensus," Sam informed the man. "More than illegal, it's considered an act of religious heresy." He glanced up at the viewscreen and saw that the woman was nearly to the ship. "All right, enough snooping, let's go greet our guest properly." He smiled crookedly. "After all, she could break every one of us in half…"

Priscilla, Devon and Danabri were already gathered just inside the open hatchway at the head of the boarding ramp, Danabri gabbing at Devon about something or other. The Sensitive seemed to talk to Devon more than anyone else, most likely because she was polite enough to not walk away from him, Sam imagined.

Sam stepped up next to Priscilla and surreptitiously gave her hand a squeeze. She returned it, giving him a quick smile before putting her business face back on and turning to meet the approaching Consensus officer. Telia Proctor strode up the ramp, halted in front of Priscilla and Sam, and dumped her bags on the deck.

"I greet you in the holy name of the Human Consensus." The security officer saluted formally.

Sam returned her salute, feeling a bit awkward. "Welcome aboard the Resolution Patrol vessel *Raven*, Guardian Prime Proctor," he said. "I sincerely hope that your presence will offer all of us a chance to learn more about each other's cultures."

"I am not here to exchange cultural information, Captain Avalon," she replied with iron in her voice. "I am here in my capacity as a Guardian both to ensure your safety and to ensure the safety of the people of the Consensus from you. The best thing for all concerned will be if our relationship is brief."

"Certainly, Guardian Prime," Priscilla interjected. "Our thanks for clearing up that misconception."

"You must follow this course exactly," Proctor told Sam, handing him a dataspike. "Any deviation from it will be considered an act of war and this ship will be destroyed."

"There won't be any deviation from us," Sam grunted, tossing the dataspike back to Devon.

"Our only intent is to aid the Consensus in saving itself from this threat," Priscilla said. "We will cooperate with you however we must to do this."

"Your assurances are wasted on me." Proctor fixed her with a cold stare. "I have neither the authority nor the inclination to pass them on to my superiors. My only purpose is to do that for which I was created, to guard. You against us, us against you. Do you understand me?"

Priscilla gave her a look that Sam couldn't decipher, something between a grin and a grimace. "I understand better than you think, Guardian Prime. Medical Officer Raines," she nodded to Carlos, "will see you to your cabin."

Proctor wordlessly picked up her bags and followed Carlos into the ship, leaving the rest to stand there staring at their wake.

"Damn," Sam hissed, still prickling at the security officer's attitude. "If it isn't bad enough that we have a walking weapon sent here to spy on us, she's also a complete and utter prick about it."

Danabri turned to Sam, nodding, a sappy smile on his face. "I think I'm in love."

Chapter Seven

"I guess this is some kind of historic occasion," Sam mused as he and Priscilla sat in the control room, watching the Earth and her moon grow on the forward screens. "Aren't we the first Resolution citizens to be allowed to land on Luna?"

"I have a feeling," Priscilla replied, "that before this is over, we will be up to our necks in historic occasions."

"Or court-martialed," Sam agreed.

"Or dead," Devon muttered from her duty station so softly that Sam barely heard her.

Sam saw Telia glance sharply at the navigator, but the Earthwoman didn't offer a comment. She hadn't said half a dozen words on the trip despite Danabri's best efforts at engaging her in what was, for him, pleasant conversation.

"So Telia," Danabri tried again, twisting around in his acceleration couch to speak to her, ignoring the way she scowled when he used her first name, "are the bionics a job requirement or an occupational hazard?"

Sam's jaw dropped and even Priscilla, for once, seemed nonplussed. There wasn't a sound from anyone in the control room as they watched Telia Proctor's eyes snap wide open and the line of her jaw harden. She seemed to be leaning against her seat restraints, testing to see whether she could break through them, when Danabri spoke again, apparently oblivious to the display.

"If you don't want to talk about it, I understand." He shrugged. "I'd just hate to think that someone with the natural genetic gifts you were so obviously born with would have to willingly sacrifice them." He speared Priscilla with a glance. "It would sadden me to see someone used in that manner."

Telia's expression seemed to soften a bit, her brow furled in perplexity at the strange, annoying little man.

"I was injured," she finally responded. "Badly."

"Very badly, I would guess," Danabri said with a nod, "for you to consider bionics. I know they aren't banned by the Consensus, but they can't be too popular with the Naturalist Society."

"I was given a choice," she told him. Sam was surprised he was able to draw all this out of her. "I could either spend the rest of my days in a mobile life support chair or take the bionics and never again live on Earth."

"You can't go home?" Devon asked with a gasp.

"I can visit for short periods," Telia replied, stonefaced, "when my duty requires it. But I may not be permanently stationed there, and when I am no longer fit to perform my duties, I may not return again. I will be retired to a home on Luna." She settled back into her seat with an air of finality. "I do not wish to discuss my personal life any further."

"Of course, Guardian Prime," Priscilla said soothingly. "We apologize for prying." She shot Danabri a glare. He shrugged and looked away.

Sam tried to be angry with Danabri, but that annoyance was pushed away by the rage he felt at the actions of the Consensus. One of their security officers was injured and they rewarded her service by exiling her from her home planet. How in Gaia's name were they going to be able to deal rationally with such people?

Beginning orbital insertion as per the Consensus course data, Captain, the *Raven* told him.

Well, Sam reasoned, I guess we'll have to find a way…quickly, too.

If Mars had been captivating and entrancing, Luna was something of a disappointment. Resolution moon colonies were built in accordance with the ideal of sticking as close to nature as possible. Structures looked like living things rather than metal boxes. When possible, craters were domed over with a water-filled double-layer of byomer---a lab-grown culture infused with a superstrong polymer---and stocked with bioengineered plant and animal life. Smaller, asteroid-size moons were often totally engulfed by a byomer shield, glowing green bubbles of life in the darkness.

The Consensus Lunar colony was, by contrast, a lifeless ball of silicate rock, broken here and there by the harsh metal features of a mining facility or the surface entrance to one of the many underground cities. The *Raven* flew low and slow over the vast desert oceans and stark mountain ranges, following the course set by the Consensus coordinates, and following a history that was set in Sam's memory. He knew every detail of the geography; he could almost see the tiny American flag set in the dust at the Sea of Tranquility.

Every Patrol Officer learned in their first history classes about the tentative baby-step off the planet that had happened so long ago, but Sam had known about it before that, had studied the stories passed down from Mother's data files when he was barely able to read. This was where everything that he was had begun and the sight of it filled him with an almost religious awe.

Finally, the Patrol cutter slowed to a halt over the rectangular outline of a broad landing pad set a kilometer away from the entrance to one of the largest of the underground cities, and gradually began descending on gentle bursts of maneuvering jets. The landing gear settled onto the hard metal surface with a shudder that went through the ship and into Sam's bones.

"Power down the engines," Sam ordered, knowing that Devon was already doing it. Sam had begun to notice the light Lunar gravity minutes before, and he felt a stomach-wrenching lurch as the landing pad they'd settled on began lowering into the ground.

"The elevator doors will seal above us," Telia announced, "and the bay will be pressurized."

"How thoughtful of them," Sam breathed. Of course, it also meant that they could not leave the base without the permission of the Consensus authorities.

The elevator deposited them deep beneath the surface, in a bay that was big enough to hold a dozen ships the size of the *Raven* but was now empty except for the Patrol cutter...and the squad of armored infantry that surrounded them almost immediately.

Put a full security lockdown on all systems, Sam reminded the ship's AI. *I don't want any of their Intel people snooping around in your guts.*

Already done, sir, *Raven* assured him.

"All right." Sam stood from his command chair. "Everyone on their best behavior."

They let Telia exit the ship first, hoping to keep the armed soldiers outside relaxed, but the reception she got was nearly as chilly as the one Sam expected.

"Proctor," the officer in charge of the infantry squad said curtly, not trying to hide his sneer. His blocky face was visible through the faceplate of his helmet and the disdain in his eyes was clear.

"Guardian Fellows," she nodded, shutting out his scorn with practiced ease. "I have delivered the Resolution representatives as instructed."

"You and your little freak show will be escorted to secure quarters," Fellows told her. "None of you will talk to anyone except myself or the Consensus negotiation team, and none of you will leave your quarters unless escorted by either me or one of my squad. Any attempt to disobey these restrictions will result in your immediate expulsion from Consensus Space. We have detectors in place around your rooms that can tell us if any nanites leave your bodies. If you attempt to introduce any nanotechnological devices into the Lunar environment, this whole installation will immediately and automatically self-destruct." His dark eyes traveled across their faces in harsh accusation. "Follow me and keep your mouths shut."

Sam felt the hackles rise on the back of his neck. They were indeed in the belly of the beast now. Nothing heretofore had prepared him for the sudden sense of claustrophobia he felt marching through the close, antiseptic walls of the Lunar base, surrounded by armed enemy troops. There were no other Terran personnel present on their route through the base, not so much as a single maintenance worker; it seemed less a space colony and more a maximum-security prison. Suddenly he felt Priscilla's hand brush his and he saw the look in her eyes…understanding and support. His breath came a little easier and he smiled at her gratefully.

Finally, they came to what seemed to Sam like one more of the hundreds of unmarked doors they'd passed already, but the guards stopped so abruptly that the Resolution personnel nearly ran into the back of the leading troopers.

"In here," Fellows ordered, pushing the door open.

"Ah, more luxury accommodations," Danabri muttered as they filed inside, earning him a dirty look from Fellows.

Sam remained silent as the door was slammed shut behind them, but he inwardly agreed with Danabri's sarcastic assessment. They'd been shut into what looked like a military barracks: a long, featureless room with thin dividers separating narrow bunks and a single bathroom at the far end. What was worse, the room had a fairly low ceiling, and in the Lunar gravity, it was all too easy to take a normal step and wind up slamming your head right into the…

"Sonofabitch!" Danabri bellowed, coming down to the floor holding his head with both hands. "Goddamned fucking Earther sons of bitches and their fucking Philistine architecture!"

"At least it was your head and nothing important," D'jonni cracked.

Sam braced for the explosion from the little man, but to his shock, Danabri started chuckling softly instead. The Sensitive didn't say another word, just moved on into the room and laid down on one of the bunks. Sam and D'jonni exchanged puzzled glances before sharing a shrug.

"That was the first time anyone of us cracked back on him," Devon said softly beside Sam, realization in her voice. "Maybe that's what he's been waiting for."

"Hell," Arvid muttered from his seat on a nearby bunk, "if I had known that, I would have slammed his ass weeks ago."

"Everyone get comfortable…or as comfortable as possible anyway," Sam directed. "Gaia knows how long they'll keep us here before they get around to seeing us."

"I doubt it will be overly long," Telia judged. "Your presence…and mine…is likely something of a discomfort to them."

Sam glanced at Priscilla, wondering that Telia was speaking so openly when they were almost certainly being bugged.

"So Telia," Sam said, "tell me something. I've studied Earth geography…where exactly are you from?"

"I am from an agricultural center on the American plains," she told him, her former reticence lost in depressed indifference. "It is called Grayson City, after the first Agricultural Minister of the Consensus government."

"I've seen pictures of it," Sam nodded. "It used to be called Des Moines, Iowa, back in the old United States of America. A very pretty place."

"Did you like it there?" Priscilla asked.

"It was a hard life," the woman said, her eyes far away. "When we were not in school, we worked in the fields till after the sun was down. But in the winter, it snowed and we stayed inside and my mother told us stories about our ancestors." She shook her head slightly. "Yes, I liked it. But I was ready to leave…I was so happy to become a Guardian. My mother was very proud of me. I was the first one in our line to qualify for the Academy."

"How long has it been since you've seen her?" The question, to Sam's surprise, came from Danabri, who stood behind his shoulder.

"She died last year," Telia told him, a glint of wetness in her one natural eye. "Cancer. I had not seen her in five years."

"I am sorry for your loss, Telia," Priscilla said, placing her hand on the Guardian's tentatively.

"They can't take your memories away," Danabri said, his voice wistful. "Your mother would be happy you remember her."

He looked as if he wanted to say something else, but he shook his head and went back to sit down on one of the cots. Priscilla stared after him, a distress in her eyes that Sam didn't understand.

"What is it?" he asked her, frowning in confusion.

"I can't help but feel," Priscilla replied so softly he almost missed it, "that in many ways we are much like the Consensus." He wanted to ask her what she meant, but she shook her head and walked off to a bunk at the far end of the room.

Giving up, Sam found a bunk of his own and stretched out, hoping against hope to get an hour or two of rest.

*   *   *

When Sam woke to a hand shaking his shoulder, a quick check of his implanted computer told him that he'd actually slept for three solid hours. He opened his eyes and found Priscilla standing over him.

"They're ready for us," she told him, nodding towards the door, where Guardian Fellows stood waiting for them.

"How many?" he wanted to know.

"You, Danabri and me," she said quietly as he pulled on his boots. "And I had to pitch a fit with the stoneface over there to get Danabri included."

"Well, let's not blow it then," Sam said, rising to his feet. "Ready."

They followed the grim-faced Earther through the narrow corridors and into a large, plain-walled elevator. Sam felt a rumbling vibration running up his feet through the metal of the lift as it took them deeper into the base, setting his teeth and his nerves on edge. He tried to remind himself that failure meant the destruction of the home planet of the human race, but as the rumbling became more intense and grinding, he began to worry less about humanity's survival and more about his own.

When he noticed his hands starting to shake, Sam knew there was something not right, and a look at Priscilla confirmed it. She was chewing at her lip with obvious discomfort, her hands contorted into tight fists.

"Cheap theatrics," Danabri muttered behind them. Sam's head twisted around and he saw that the Sensitive seemed unaffected by whatever was happening. "They're using subsonic generators," he told them.

"Shut up," Fellows snarled.

"Oh, so sorry to spoil your little parlor trick." Danabri sneered. "What, you're used to bringing terrified prisoners down here and having them shit their pants by the time they get to questioning?"

"Dead men shit their pants too," the Guardian retorted. Danabri opened his mouth for another crack, but Priscilla halted him with a hand on his arm.

Sam had to grin; the little Sensitive could be a pain in the ass, but he was fearless.

The subsonics made the lift ride seem to last forever, but finally the doors slid open and they emerged into a wide corridor, bustling with activity. Consensus personnel in gray and green uniforms swarmed through the hallways with practiced ease, bringing to Sam's mind an image of the human bloodstream he had seen in biology classes. As he stepped into the crowd of people, he felt like a foreign body in that blood stream. The Earthers stared at him with frank distaste, almost disgust, waiting for the virtual leukocytes to rid their neat little world of the messy intruders.

Did he *really* want to save these people that badly? Badly enough to risk his life for it? He was glad Priscilla was the one who would be talking to them. He wondered how she did it, how she so passionately wanted to accomplish this mission despite the fact the Earthers wanted them all dead. Of course, that was the least of the things he wondered about Priscilla. He knew next to nothing about her…and yet he knew he was swiftly falling in love with her, which was almost as scary a prospect as trying to save the Earthers.

As even the longest journeys do, theirs ended, terminating at a suite of offices that would have looked more at home in a military bunker. The guards fanned out around the entrance to the offices, taking up positions which seemed as much to keep everyone else out as to keep them in, while Fellows personally escorted them through the last set of doors.

The chamber was spare, Spartan, unadorned, and it matched the man behind the desk perfectly. He didn't rise to meet them, but Sam could tell he was a fairly tall man for an Earther born at standard gravity, broad across the shoulders and ruggedly handsome.

With looks like that, he should be a politician, Sam thought irreverently.

If he understood the Consensus system of planetary government correctly, they held popular elections not for individuals but for parties, the Naturalists and the Reformists at present, and whoever won the most votes was allowed to appoint the Prime Minister, while the runner up got the Deputy Prime Minister.

It seemed inefficient and unscientific to him; people were flawed and poorly informed as a rule, and a popularity contest was hardly the best way to run a government. Sam tried not to jump when the door slammed behind them, but he couldn't help a glance back at Fellows, who was sneering at him contemptuously.

"I'm Jaime Tejado," the handsome man told them, hands folded in front of him on the desk, face drawn into a scowl. "Deputy Minister of the Consensus. Say what you came to say."

Uh-oh. Sam didn't need to be a Sensitive to read this man's demeanor. He hadn't even invited them to sit down, despite the chairs up against the far wall.

"I'm Priscilla of the Resolution Diplomatic Corps, and this is Mawae Danabri, my colleague," the woman told him, seemingly unfazed by Tejado's attitude. "Captain Avalon is from our Patrol Service, commander of the ship that discovered the threat."

"I know who you are," he nearly stepped on her words, his tone that of a superior chiding a subordinate. "I know why you're here. Get on with it."

Anger surged in Sam's chest at the obvious disrespect and he fought to tamp it down. If she wasn't allowing it to bother her, then he should be able to stay professional…

Metal scraped on concrete, loud and obnoxious and grating; it was Danabri because of course it was. He pulled the chair off the wall carelessly, oblivious to the disruptive sound or perhaps reveling in it, settling it in front of the Deputy Minister's desk and then plopping down into it.

If looks could kill, the Sensitive would have been dead three times over, but he ignored the outraged glares from Tejado and Fellows, crossing one leg over another, smiling at Sam's dumbfounded expression.

"What?" Danabri demanded. "Did you think this Naturalist fundamentalist was going to give us a fair hearing no matter what we did?" He shrugged. "Might as well make ourselves comfortable."

Sam was about to say something, about to try to make an apology he didn't mean, when he realized Pris was pulling up a chair of her own, though without the sound effects. She sat down and gestured for him to do the same, and he finally gave up and grabbed the last chair for himself, leaving Fellows standing and scowling.

"We have come a long way and gone to some very serious effort to be here, Minister Tejado," Priscilla said, eyebrow arched with a decided lack of deference. "You may or may not decide to accept the help we're offering, that's your prerogative, but I will not stand here like a child brought into the principal's office while you sit on your ass and stare at us with disapproval."

Tejado's mouth curled into something less than a smile, but he nodded slowly.

"Very well, then, Priscilla." His tone was as frosty as his pale blue eyes. "You've had your seat and now you'll have your say." He gestured impatiently.

"You know what's coming," she told him. "As you say, you don't need us to tell you that; you've seen the reports. Unless someone is lying to you, you also know the only way to stop it is to build a Teller-Fox gateway in its path. If you think your government has the capability to do this on your own, then you don't need us and we'll leave."

"I don't trust you," the too-handsome man shot back, not sparing the vitriol. "For all I know, you're behind all of this and your presence here is a trick to penetrate our defenses. Yes, we know this thing is coming, but we only have your word that it is what you say it is."

"What else do you think it might be?" Priscilla wondered. "Do you think we would build such a weapon only to alert you to its presence? For what purpose?"

"Just because I don't have all the answers doesn't mean I intend to turn over our defense to our enemies!"

"It's people such as yourself who have declared us enemies! We have made no move against you, only protected ourselves and our citizens against predation..."

Sam swallowed hard; it seemed very much as if Priscilla was losing her temper and he hadn't thought that possible. He felt like he should say something, should intervene, but diplomacy wasn't his job...

"Sir," he said, stepping into the space of an intake of breath between invective, "if we have a relativistic missile, and we were doing this as some sort of trick, then you've lost either way. Either you open your defenses to us or your planet dies right along with your civilization. Again. Your only hope is that we're telling the truth; you have no other way out of this."

He caught Priscilla's glance in his peripheral vision, but it didn't seem enraged; possibly annoyed at most. Danabri still seemed amused, unwilling to let the apocalyptic consequences of failure dampen his enjoyment of tweaking the officious Consensus politician.

Whatever Tejado's response might have been to Sam's reasoning, they'd never hear it. A chime sounded at the door and it creaked open a few centimeters. A functionary peeked his head through, flinching as if he expected something to be thrown at him.

"I told you I didn't want to be disturbed!" Tejado bellowed, finally coming out of his chair, with enough force he nearly sailed up toward the ceiling and had to catch himself on the edge of his desk.

"Yes, sir," the little man squeaked. "I'm sorry, sir, but it's the Prime Minister and she demanded to speak with you immediately."

Tejado's mouth worked and Sam could tell he wanted to curse and had to fight to control himself. The Deputy Minister motioned at Fellows.

"Stay here and watch them."

"Yeah," Danabri murmured as the tall man stalked out of the office, "we might corrupt your whole planet if you don't keep an eye on us."

"I hope to God he gives me the order to kill you," Fellows growled, his right hand straying too close to his holstered sidearm for Sam's comfort.

Danabri acted as if he hadn't heard the Guardian, making a show of straightening his jacket. Sam tried to ignore the byplay, concentrating instead on what they could possibly do if Tejado sent them packing. He couldn't think of anything short of declaring war on the Consensus, which seemed a self-defeating proposition.

The door was pushed open again and when Tejado walked through, Sam could have believed the gravity was twice standard rather than sixteen percent of it; the tall man dragged, reluctance visible in every motion. His eyes bored into them, sighting lasers for a weapon the man obviously wished he had.

"You're going to Earth," he said, the words prying themselves out of jaws tightly locked. "Just the two of you," he pointed to Sam and Priscilla. "The rest of your crew, including *him*," he sneered at Danabri, "will be confined to your quarters here on Luna until you return." His fingers clenched and unclenched. "You'll be meeting with the Prime Minister and her Privy Council." He turned to Fellows, making a slashing motion. "Get them the hell out of my sight."

Sam rose uncertainly, a tingle of disbelief running down his spine. *What the hell just happened?*

"Deputy Minister," Priscilla said, smiling warmly as she paused in following Fellows out of the office, "it's been a pleasure."

Chapter Nine

Sam Avalon knew this was a momentous occasion, a sacred duty, certainly the most significant event of his career, but he couldn't keep himself from grinning ear-to-ear like a kid on his first spaceflight. This was *Earth*, this was the ancient home of humanity, the stuff of legends, of bed-time stories. The number of Resolution citizens who'd been allowed down inside the atmosphere could have been counted on one hand without using all the fingers. It was all he could do to keep from leaning forward in his acceleration couch and trying to get a better view out the forward screens, even though he knew they were a holographic projection.

Thousands of meters below them, the jagged, snow-capped peaks of the Canadian Rockies stretched in rugged magnificence no computer recreation could capture. Wind swept sprays of autumn snow off the ragged edges and he was sure if they went even lower, he'd see the mountain goats clinging tenaciously to the cliffs.

"We're coming in west to east," Priscilla remarked, seemingly unfazed by the incredible scenery. She turned toward the shuttle pilot seated to her left and slightly in front of her; she'd taken the center acceleration couch, leaving the copilot's station to Sam, insisting he was more qualified. "Why? Wouldn't it have been faster to continue with the polar insertion?"

"Yeah," the man admitted, shrugging. Then he smiled with a mischievous glint to his dark eyes. "But I like the view coming in this way."

The pilot, Sully he'd called himself, wasn't anything like what Sam had expected; he was young and enthusiastic and seemed to genuinely love flying. He hadn't mentioned the political situation and the only interest he had in the fact they were Resolutionists was they hadn't had the chance to see the sights of Earth before and he got to be their tour guide.

He could tell the young shuttle jock was grating on Priscilla's nerves, but he wasn't sure if it was simply the man's garrulous demeanor or maybe the lack of privacy she resented. He couldn't say he knew her well enough to unfailingly read her moods, but he sensed she wanted to discuss their strategy before they met with the Consensus Prime Minister.

Probably because she doesn't want me screwing up, he thought. It was fair, he decided; they wouldn't have Danabri to read the situation and he was, as he kept reminding everyone, a pilot and not a diplomat.

"I'm gonna show you guys somethin' really cool," Sully declared, pushing the steering yoke downward. The pitch of the jets changed and Sam could feel the loss of altitude in his guts before he noticed it on the viewscreen.

It still freaked him out, the concept of trusting physical flight controls, but he supposed it made sense since the Consensus considered cybernetic implants just as blasphemous as nanotechnology and genetic engineering. He'd learned how to use the system, of course, in case of emergency, but they were considered a last resort in the Resolution and he hadn't touched a physical control yoke since flight school. Watching Sully caress the sleek, silver-chased controls, he was beginning to wonder if he wasn't missing out on the fun.

"I'm not sure if we have the time…" Priscilla started to say, but Sam shot her a pleading look.

"How many chances you think we're going to get to do this?" he asked softly.

She hesitated, a hint of chill in those frost-blue eyes, and he thought maybe he'd gone too far and pissed her off. But the chill melted away like the frost under the morning sun and she smiled at him with a fondness in her gaze as invigorating as the sights of unknown Earth.

"All right, Sully," she assented, some of the tension gone out of her voice. "What have you got for us?"

"Check this out…"

They were low, much lower than traffic control would have allowed on any settled Resolution world, only a hundred meters or so above the hard deck, and yet Sam heard no radio chatter even questioning Sully's flight path. Beneath them, rolling hills had given way to endless, grassy plains…and equally endless herds of bison, elk, deer and rumbling, swaying mastodon, grazing in the midday Sun or sipping warily from watering holes under the watchful eye of predators.

He could see the predators better than their prey could, see them concealed in the tall grass, in stands of trees, waiting in the grey fur of wolves, the tawny coats of saber-tooth cats, the speckled camouflage of stalking cheetahs. They were fewer in number, but they caught his eye every time he passed over one, an evolutionary adaptation from a day when humans, too, had been down on plains much like those, watching for those same predators.

"This is what?" he asked the pilot. "The Great Plains?"

"Yeah," Sully said, nodding, his helmet wobbling on his head when he did. That was another odd thing, a pilot wearing a helmet like he was a Marine or something. He guessed that was for some sort of Heads-Up Display reading his eye movement; it was all technology centuries out of date for the Resolution and he couldn't help feel a bit of sympathy for the young man.

"We call it the Great Plains Preserve," Sully went on, with what sounded like pride in his voice. "There're ten preserves, planet-wide. After the wars wiped everything out, the animals had a chance to repopulate and get back some of their natural territory, and when we started climbing back up and rebuilding, we decided we wanted to make sure we didn't repeat our old mistakes."

"That's a...very enlightened view," Priscilla ventured. Sam thought she sounded surprised; he knew he was. It wasn't an attitude he would have expected from the Consensus.

"It's beautiful down here," Sam said, not trying to hide his admiration. It was one thing to see this sort of splendor on a Resolution world, where it had been designed by the Mother computer. To see such incredible biological diversity unfold naturally after the devastation of a civilization-ending war...

They were climbing again, and Sully had fallen silent, which seemed out of character; he found out why once they reached Capital City...or, more accurately, hundreds of kilometers *before* they reached it.

Sam had read about open-pit mining, but he'd never thought to actually see it. It was a huge, open wound on the land, infested with the metallic infection of the digging equipment, the processing machinery, the ore trains running on electromagnetic rails inward to the factories. The factories were boxes, ugly in their own right and lined up in an artless cluster for the sake of efficiency and pragmatism.

"Gaia," Priscilla breathed, echoing the disgust roiling in Sam's gut. "I know you have Lunar mines and orbital processing facilities. Surely this isn't necessary?"

Sam couldn't see Sully's eyes beneath the half-visor of his helmet, but the way his mouth pulled down and his face went slack, he could tell the younger man seemed stricken.

"We put all of our off-Earth processing capabilities into producing spacecraft for defense and interdiction." The line was rote, clearly an excuse he'd been given so many times he had it memorized and yet just as clearly, he didn't buy it. "Plus," he went on, less rehearsed and perhaps more truthful, "the Belters make more money dealing with the Jovians and you guys than they would with us." He sighed in resignation. "All the major residential areas are like this, and it's worse on the Indian subcontinent and out in east Asia."

"That's unfortunate," Sam said, and meant it. He shared a look with Priscilla. "There should be something we can do about that, shouldn't there?"

"It's definitely something to consider," she replied noncommittally.

He could see the wheels turning behind her eyes, though, and he bit down on a knowing grin.

The city itself came into view only minutes later, charming in its own way but sprawling and jumbled, clearly not a planned metropolis like Dauphin City or Uruk. Individual, disconnected buildings in the ancient, pre-war style were clustered around newer, more modern, self-contained structures, and public transportation was supplemented by actual surface streets, another thing Sam had heard of but never expected to see. There were *cars* running around inside the city, like some old movie about ancient Earth; and as inefficient as it all was, Sam found it utterly fascinating.

The shuttle's atmospheric jets rumbled a low-pitched roar as it spiraled down over the spaceport, low enough for Sam to see through the clear walls of some of the closer buildings, see the workers inside pacing from one task to the next like insects. One or two paused to press close to the glass, staring at the aerospacecraft's descent. The belly jets added their shuddering scream to the throttling-down main engines and Sam felt their upward thrust pushing him into his seat.

Despite Sully's demonstrated piloting skills, Sam still felt a cold pit deep in his stomach as the ship touched down, just not trusting human instincts to land something as big and heavy as a cislunar shuttle. But the landing treads touched down as gentle as a feather, and he was almost surprised when the pilot pulled off his helmet and began unstrapping from his seat.

"It was nice flying you guys," he said cheerfully, scrambling over the top of his chair instead of waiting to power it around. Without his helmet, his hair sprang free, long and blond and unruly. "Sorry to leave you hanging here, but I gotta' meet a girl." He slapped the button to lower the shuttle's belly ramp. "There's a hopper waiting for you just outside with someone from the government to take you the rest of the way."

And then he was gone. Sam stared in silent bemusement at the space where he'd been, but Priscilla was already turning her seat and yanking the quick-release on her restraints.

"I didn't think they'd be like that," he admitted, following her example. "He seems...normal."

"Most people are just people," she reminded him. "Living their lives and not really caring much about what their government does as long as it doesn't affect them." She smiled wanly back to him as she started down the ramp. "You and I are the strange ones."

*   *   *

Sam didn't know what he'd expected from the Ministry Building, but this was not it. More than anything else, it resembled a Gothic cathedral, or at least what he'd seen of Gothic cathedrals in the historical records Mother had brought with her from Earth, right down to the ribbed vaults and flying buttresses, though on a grander scale than Medieval architects had imagined. Grey and foreboding, it towered above them in what might have been an attempt at intimidation or perhaps something less malevolent and more nostalgic, meant to recall the greatness of Earth before the war.

Where did they get the records? he wondered, feeling the tug of the wind from the ducted fans of the hopper teasing at his jacket as the little aircraft took off and left them there with the Consensus representative. *I thought the nanite wave destroyed everything. Books maybe, physical books. Those might have survived.*

He'd read the nanite wave weapons of the last war had destroyed anything electrically powered, but they'd still had actual paper books back then. He tried to imagine the survivors huddled in the wreckage of their civilization, jealously hoarding the few books they could find. He shuddered at the image, wondering how they'd ever rebuilt any sort of society after that.

"Follow me," their government rep assigned to them grunted with a reluctance she didn't try to hide.

Hell, she didn't even bother to tell us her name.

The woman didn't want to be there, that much was clear; it was written on the sour curl of her lip, making a small mouth look even smaller, in the arch of her eyebrow and the furl it sent up through her hairline. She was dressed in what passed for professional wear among the younger Consensus citizens: a subdued, grey business suit with a high, buttoned collar, the only touch of color a lavender scarf tied low around her neck, and her hair was cut close to her scalp. She was a sharp contrast to Sully, both in appearance and attitude, and much closer to the stereotypical Earther he saw in news reports and entertainment media.

She led the two of them away from the Ministry's broad, public entrance with its flow of people and tight security screening, and over to an unmarked door about forty meters down the sidewalk. It opened at the touch of her palm on a subdued scanner set in the side of the wall. Sam thought he caught a few stares from passers-by at his Resolution uniform, and he tried to keep himself from staring back, or from rubber-necking like a tourist at the teardrop-shaped ground-cars humming by on three wheels.

The glare of the mid-morning sun disappeared into the shadows of a narrow stairwell just inside the door and Sam followed Priscilla and the Consensus representative downward. The impact of their shoes on the metallic grating of the steps echoed ahead of them in a descending spiral, and just when Sam was beginning to wonder if they were taking the stairs down to the very center of the Earth, they came to a landing…and an elevator bank.

The door slid aside for their guide's biometric ID and the metal-walled, claustrophobically tiny car took them down even further, not stopping along the way. It all seemed very mysterious and momentous and Sam wondered if that was the point, to impress them. Then again, maybe it was simply the fastest and most private route to where they were going; he chided himself for assuming the worst yet again.

At least there're no subsonics this time.

The ride was quick and silent, and his pilot's instincts told him they'd travelled at least a hundred meters straight down, which meant the building was at least as deep as it was tall. It was meant as a shelter as well as a government center, he realized, a place for the Prime Minister and her cabinet to keep the Consensus running in case of another devastating war.

Still, for a shelter, it was nicely appointed. Paintings, done by hand in the classical style, hung in gilt frames on walls of cherry wood, and marble statues hid in alcoves as if they'd stepped into a museum. He noticed Priscilla pause for half a step as she passed by a painting of Venus emerging from the ocean; he wondered why it had caught her eye, other than the exactness with which it had been duplicated.

Nothing was marked or labelled in the winding hallway, but their guide took them straight to their destination with the familiarity of one who took the same path every day. Another security scanner---*How many of those do they need?*---and they were abruptly there. It wasn't an office, wasn't a conference room as much as…*Maybe a courtroom?* Sam couldn't be sure of the assessment, but he and Priscilla were deposited unceremoniously into a large chamber and waved to seats behind a bare, wooden table.

Before and above them on a raised platform enclosed by a polished, cherry railing was a semi-circle of five, throne-like seats. They were ornate, hand-carved if he was any judge, with rampant lions in each armrest, but didn't appear that comfortable, lacking any sort of padding.

Maybe it shouldn't be comfortable being a judge, he reflected.

The chairs were empty, and he was about to ask their nameless guide how long they'd have to wait, but she was already heading out of the room, pulling the door shut behind her without as much as a by-your-leave.

"She really knows how to make you feel welcome, doesn't she?" Sam murmured aside to Priscilla.

He'd been so caught up in the romance of actually seeing Earth, it had only just now begun to sink in that these people could concoct any excuse they wanted to keep the two of them there indefinitely.

They could say we were infecting the place and use the medical nanites in our blood as "evidence," he mused darkly. *Or they could detect Priscilla's biotech augmentation and say she was carrying illicit biological weapons.*

"Easy," Priscilla said softly in his ear, seemingly sensing his mood. Neither of them dared use their neurolinks. Even if they weren't being jammed, the Earthers would detect the signal.

He nodded to her, wishing he could touch her, just a brush of her hand on his like back on Luna. But they'd be watching for that, too, and he had to assume they'd be looking for weaknesses to exploit.

He hadn't noticed the second door; it blended into the shadows of the alcove behind the platform, and it barely made a sound when it swung open. The first person through the door was Deputy Minister Tejado and Sam nearly choked at the sight of the man. He was dressed in a robe of solid grey, as was the woman who followed him, much shorter and less perfect-looking but just as severe and hard-eyed. The two of them walked with a matching, purposeful stride across the platform and took the chairs at the far left.

The next pair through the door also wore matching robes, theirs a forest green, the male of the two much shorter than Tejado and a bit jowly, with a receding hairline of grey-shot blond. Sam felt a sense of shock at how old the man looked, though he'd known the Earthers didn't use the sort of biotechnology the Resolution took for granted. Sam was young, not even forty yet, but there were men and women in his chain of command well over a hundred who looked no older than him. The idea of people growing old and dying as their bodies wore out was as unimaginable to him as much else of the Consensus society.

The Prime Minister did not look old. He would have known who she was even had he not seen her picture in a Consensus news report while on Luna; she had the air of command about her, a straight-backed stance, an alertness to the set of her eyes showing someone used to being scrutinized. Her face was lean but not drawn, her jaw squared off and strong, her brown hair an orderly, shoulder-length arrangement; her robe was a harsh crimson, a splash of blood.

The old man and the younger woman with him in green had taken the two seats on the far right, but the woman in red took the largest and grandest chair, stationed between the two extremes, a stylized dragon's head carved into the seat.

"State your name and purpose for the record," the blood-red woman said, her voice as clear and piercing as a clarion.

"Deputy Prime Minister Jaime Tejado, Naturalist Party," the man they'd met with on Luna spoke up quickly, as closely as he dared to stepping on the end of her statement. "I am present to speak against the foolishness and danger of allowing these blasphemers to operate in our home system."

"Minister of Defense Lila Shang," the short woman beside him intoned as if it were a magic spell, "Naturalist Party. I am present to give warning of the threat from the Resolutionist enemy."

"I am Avery Cassell," the woman who'd come in with the old man announced, "Minister of Energy, Reformist Party. I come to this august body to hear of the possibilities for salvation from the threat to the very existence of the Consensus."

The old man paused just half a beat, and Sam had the sense there was a purpose and a structure to that, something to do with his seniority.

"My name is John Gage," he said, finally, gravelly and rough, the voice of a man who'd seen the hard knocks of life before he'd taken his place in governance. "I'm the Minister for Foreign Relations and the Chair of the Reformist Party, and I'm here to make sure we don't throw away the one chance we have to save this world from destruction."

Nice of them to go ahead and announce who's on our side right up front, Sam thought with a bit of amusement at the ritual.

Another pause, this one longer, more significant. And then the woman in the center made her own proclamation, still ritualistic and formulaic, but also more directed to them, he judged.

"I am Prime Minister Carlotta Brecht, the chosen voice of the Human Consensus, the one fated and condemned to decide our direction as a people. I am allowed no party, no affiliation beyond my allegiance to this world and to humanity. I come to this gathering to hear the wisdom of others, to see ideas do battle before me until one emerges the victor. My decisions may not always be correct, but they are the law until I am replaced by the will of the people of our world." Her eyes bored straight into Sam, or so it felt to him, their gaze dark and magnetic, holding his own in place as if he were helpless before her.

"Do both of you understand?"

"We do, your Excellency," Priscilla answered for them, respect and deference in her tone Sam hadn't heard before.

"State your names and purpose for our record."

Sam nearly tripped over his tongue and rasped his words out through a dry mouth, wishing there were water available.

"We are aware of the facts," Brecht declared. "We know what you propose, so do not waste our time with restatements of the obvious. What we wish to know before we make our decision is whether there is anything we have not considered."

"There is, your Excellency," Priscilla's answer was firm and definitive. Sam's eyes flickered over to her, curious. "You may be aware," she went on, "of how much raw material the Teller-Fox gate we've proposed will require. We're going to have to bring in shipments from the Belters, shipments that will take months to set in motion, perhaps years." She tilted her head to the side just slightly, as if she were giving the other woman a chance to consider what she'd said.

"I have come to understand the Belters are reluctant to do a steady business with the Consensus because their profit margins are larger selling to the Jovian Confederation...and to us, as well. This mostly has to do with logistics questions, diversion of shipping assets from more profitable runs. This project will require the construction of new automated barges, very large ones, and arrangement for their constant refueling. Afterward, unless they acquire new cargo runs and a new customer, those barges and fueling stations will be wasted."

"They would likely be willing to offer us a substantial discount in order to avoid the costs of repurposing those assets," Gage interjected, following her line of reasoning, interest sparkling in his eyes. "If we survive," he amended.

"Are we taking bribes from the blasphemers now?" Tejado demanded, flushing with what seemed to be genuine rage. "Have we come so low as to compromise our principles for a few million tons of ore?"

The man was, Sam decided, a true believer, not just a posturing politician, which made him terrifying rather than just annoying.

"Ask those who live near the pit mines how important that ore would be," Avery Cassell replied, cocking an eyebrow at the Deputy Minister. "Or ask your Generals, Defense Minister," she directed that to the other Naturalist Party leader, the woman. "Cheaper and more easily accessible mineral resources could transform our economy in just a few years."

"The Resolution would not offer us any of this if there were not a self-serving motive to benefit them," Lila Shang said, regarding the Energy Minister with cold disdain. "I would very much like to know what it is."

"That is a fair question," Prime Minister Brecht agreed, turning her attention from her Council back to Sam and Priscilla. "One I would very much like to hear answered. The Resolution is spending a not-inconsiderable percentage of their vast wealth on this project. Do you expect us to believe you're doing this simply out of the goodness of your hearts? To quote an old saying, I was born at night, but I wasn't born *last* night."

Sam blinked. A sense of humor was the last thing he'd expected from the imperious Prime Minister, much less a pawky one. He thought it surprised Priscilla as well, but she was a good enough poker player not to show it on her face.

"To some extent," she began slowly, "it is because we believe this is the right thing to do, and that we have no wish to see the homeworld of our species destroyed, nor any living world. Just that, by itself, would be enough reason for us to make the offer. But I won't lie to you, your Excellency, we do have something to gain from this if you accept our help."

Tejado's eyes narrowed at the admission and Sam thought the man leaned forward expectantly. Gage's lip twitched, though Sam didn't know if it was from a suppressed frown or an equally suppressed smile. The Prime Minister's expression changed not at all.

"I don't know how familiar any of you are with hyper-dimensional physics," she went on, "but I assume you know that the Transition Lines we all use for interstellar travel are like fault lines in spacetime, the gravito-inertial lines of force between stars?"

"I have a general knowledge of how the Transition Drive works," Brecht assured her, just a touch of the same dry sarcasm in her tone.

"If the ramship strikes Earth at a significant fraction of the speed of light, it's going to shatter the planet into fragments. This will have gravitational effects on the rest of the Solar System, and even on the Sun itself…" She grimaced just slightly. "No one is sure of the time frame, mostly because of the difficulty of synchronizing events in

T-space with local events, but somewhere between immediately and decades from the impact, the Transition hubs running through the Solar System are going to be redirected."

"Redirected *where*?" That was Gage, who'd shifted abruptly from cool interest to focused alarm.

"Nowhere with a habitable world. Nowhere any of us have any particular wish to travel...and nowhere near the *seven* Resolution colonies they Transit to currently. They'll be stranded without any contact to the outside universe other than lightspeed communication."

Sam's head snapped around, his eyes going wide, and it took him nearly a second to force himself to look back to the front, schooling his face back under control and cursing himself silently. Priscilla hadn't even glanced sideways at him, her eyes locked with Brecht's.

The Prime Minister was nodding to herself, not trying to hide the satisfaction in the set of her mouth. Priscilla had given her what she wanted, and Sam suddenly wondered if that hadn't been the point. Was there actually any danger of the Transition Lines shifting, or had she simply invented the whole thing because it provided a plausible explanation for the supposed altruism? He realized he couldn't even begin to guess, and he knew her as well as anyone within a dozen light years.

"Very well," Brecht said, her tone carrying the weight of judgement. "I am aware of the objections the Naturalist Party has to the presence of the Resolution in our system, and I understand the risks. However, we can't argue against physics with idealism. If the ramship is not stopped, it *will* destroy our planet." She turned to Tejado, meeting his scowl of discontent. "I agree they will have to be watched carefully," she allowed, "but lacking any method of building the gate on our own, we have no choice but to let them try. Particularly since it might be argued that the existence of the weapon and the reason for its direction could be laid at the feet of those who were the spiritual forebears of the Resolution." Sam saw the argument register on Shang's face, but Tejado's expression didn't change.

"There will be conditions for this arrangement," Brecht said, turning back to Priscilla, her voice stern and commanding. "No armed vessels will be permitted in the Solar System, and no Resolution ships will come closer than Lunar orbit without the express permission of this office. You will provide weekly progress reports and I expect you," she indicated Priscilla with a raised finger, "to meet with myself or those I delegate to the matter in person on a monthly basis, right here in Capital City."

She switched her attention to the old man, her voice still as imperious but the look on her face somewhat softer. Sam had the impression she knew the Minister of Foreign Relations well, and trusted him.

"Minister Gage," Brecht declared, "you will be our liaison to the Resolution, responsible for seeing to it that they meet the conditions of this agreement. You will also provide whatever security they feel necessary for their operations."

"Your Excellency," Tejado broke in, and from the looks on the faces of the others, even his ally, Sam could tell the interruption was irregular. "If I might just impress upon you…"

The look Brecht gave him could have frozen hydrogen.

"My decision has been made," she said. "And as always, it is final. If you wish to contest it, you may, of course, ask for a vote of confidence from the Parliament, or for a public referendum."

The Deputy Minister made a face like he'd swallowed a bug, but he said nothing.

"In that event," Brecht said, standing abruptly and dragging the others to their feet with her, "this audience is concluded. Minister Gage will stay her to coordinate with you anything you may need and arrange for your transportation back to the Lunar City."

She led the group back through the door without another word, though Tejado gave them a look of utter hatred before his dour visage disappeared into the shadows, leaving the old man as their only company.

Gage waited until the door had closed before he raised a gate in the railing of the platform and stepped down the short set of stairs to stand before them, leaning heavily on their table. He was taller up close, looming with a mass to him beneath the loose robes.

"Well, now," he drawled in an accent Sam couldn't place, "it seems as if the three of us will be spending some quality time together." Gage cocked his head to the side, regarding them. "You couldn't tell it up there, because we do most of our politicking in private, but I stuck my damn neck out for you two. You'd best not let me down."

Chapter Ten

Watching Peterman go at it with Mestrovic should have been fascinating. Sam had always loved watching masters of their field compete, and these two were truly at the top of their game.

"Look, Goran," Vance Peterman gestured so broadly it nearly lifted him off the ground in the fifteen percent gravity of Ganymede's surface. "I know we're talking some serious start-up costs here, but you'll have the benefit of the new run to Earth to consider, and you know they *need* mineral resources. We're doing you a damned favor here!"

Peterman was a little guy, perhaps the shortest Resolutionist Sam had ever met, skinny and tough as a piece of old leather, and it seemed he dressed in reaction to the lack of size. Sam couldn't recall seeing a larger set of shoulder pads or a more brightly-colored jacket, and the checkered trousers Peterman wore with it could have been considered a war crime in some jurisdictions.

If either the little man's clothes or his bombast impressed Goran Mestrovic, the Belter negotiator didn't let it show. Motionless and laconic, the space-born was taller than Peterman even seated on the padded stool in the conference room under the main habitation dome of Nanjin, the largest of the Jovian Confederacy settlements on Jupiter's moon, Ganymede. When Mestrovic spoke, it was with the spare, controlled stillness of one used to living and working in microgravity, where the slightest motion could send you floating off in random directions.

"The contract with the Consensus is wonderful in theory, Mr. Peterman, but our investment is immediate and practical, not theoretical. We are going to have to pay the Jovians to build the ore barges, pay them for fuel. We're going to have to pay the subsidiaries who own the rocks we're going to mine, pay the subsidiaries who own the smelters, pay the subsidiaries who own the processing plants …" He cocked an eyebrow, the closest a Belter would come to a shrug. "You get the idea. It's a shitload of money and it's *not* coming out of our accounts."

"So you expect us to pay for your startup," Peterman squawked, slapping the back of one hand against the palm of another, "pay for the cargo, and then *you* get the benefits of a new contract and we get left holding our swinging cods? Are you freaking serious?"

Yes, Sam should have been absorbed with the byplay, should have just been happy the mission had been a success and the Earthers had agreed to allow them to build the gate. He should have been grateful he and the crew had been allowed to ferry Priscilla and Danabri to Ganymede for the negotiations with the Belters; it had been something of a well-deserved vacation for them all after a stressful mission.

He should have been wondering at the incredible sights and sounds and smells of the Ganymede settlements, at the domed cities dug into ancient impact craters, protected now by energy shields they'd purchased from the Resolution less than a century ago. Outsiders had begun to take up residence here and on the other Galilean moons since then, and they were easily picked out from natives, who still bore the genetic manipulation designed to protect them from the gas giant's radiation fields. They were tall and statuesque, their skin seal-black and just as thick and rubbery, their faces broad and their eyes sunken deep beneath protective ridges, a different species of human.

It was meaningless, vanity, paling into nothing. All he could do was stare at Priscilla and think how soon he'd have to leave her here while he and the *Raven* went back on patrol. Or perhaps they'd return her to Aphrodite for one last report to the political officers before some other ship ran her back to the Solar System to work as the go-between with the Consensus. And he'd likely never see her again.

"Stop moping around like a love-sick puppy," Mawae Danabri hissed in his ear from the other side.

Sam cast a baleful eye at the Sensitive, catching the pungent odor of alcohol coming off the man. Danabri's hair was out of place, his clothes were disheveled and he'd reported to the negotiation session five minutes late despite a half a dozen calls to his neurolink. He also had the unmistakable look of post-coital satisfaction, which for some reason, made Sam even more annoyed at the man than usual.

"Easy to say," he shot back at the Sensitive, keeping his voice low, "for a guy who's been spending the last three days partying and getting laid by the locals."

Danabri didn't reply, but there was a certain glint to his eyes, a certain crooked angle to his smile that made Sam glance around suspiciously. Telia Proctor stood at the far back of the room near the entrance, arms crossed and stance very professional…until he noticed the uneven fasteners at the bottom of her uniform jacket and the hair standing up at the back of her short mane, and perhaps the hint of a smile at the corner of her lip.

"Holy shit," Sam said, perhaps just a bit too loud and Priscilla glanced over at him, frowning. "Nothing," he assured her, waving it off.

He raised an eyebrow at Danabri and the unpleasant little man actually giggled.

"I give up!" Peterman was braying, arms flapping over his head. "I can't deal with this sort of highway robbery! At these prices, we could just bring the ore in ourselves in starships for about the same price!"

"Then I suggest you get started," Mestrovic returned with cool reserve.

Peterman's face reddened and Sam thought the little man's head might burst like a ripe fruit. Priscilla shot a questioning glance at Danabri and the Sensitive nodded, miming an explosion.

98

"Citizen Peterman," Priscilla interrupted, standing carefully from behind the oddly-curved plastic desks they'd been seated at. "Might I have a word?"

Peterman gave her a most insubordinate, irritated glare, but pushed away from the table and stalked back to her, hands thrust in the pockets of his colorful jacket.

"This isn't a good time," he snapped, and Sam's eyes widened.

"Citizen Peterman," Priscilla said, her voice cold and harsh as the wasteland outside the dome, "this is your specialty and I respect your abilities in dealing with such negotiations, but I am in final command of this project and I can assure you it's of the highest priority. If we have to give up more than we normally would be willing, then that's the price we'll have to pay."

"Yeah, sorry ma'am," he said, shaking his head, "but that's not how things are anymore. This negotiation is under my control and it'll go on as long as I decide it should."

Sam stared at the man like he'd grown a second head or a third eye, and he thought he could physically sense the waves of outrage coming off of Priscilla, building to what could only be a truly epic ass-chewing. Peterman short-circuited the pending eruption by producing a crystal dataspike from his jacket pocket and tossing it at her underhand. She caught it in mid-air with the reflexes of a martial artist, cerulean gaze flickering back and forth between the little man and the spike. The crystal data spikes were used for sealed orders or financial transactions, secure from all outside data manipulation and usually DNA coded.

"New orders straight from Resolution HQ, from the Mother Herself." Peterman shrugged expressively. "I would've given them to you earlier, but I would have preferred to talk about them in private first."

Sam's gut began to twist with a sudden and inescapable intuition of change barreling down on them, but before he could speculate, the gaudy negotiator fished another spike out of his pocket and handed it to him.

"May as well give you yours while I'm at it," he added. He nodded toward the door, making a shooing motion with his hands. "Now go access them and leave this to the adults."

"You certainly are a complete prick," Danabri commented, grinning broadly at Peterman. "I'm almost jealous."

*   *   *

Priscilla knew she should have argued, should have pressed her authority; every fiber of her being screamed it inside her. But she knew with just as fatal a certainty that Peterman didn't bluff and didn't lie, and something was very, very wrong.

She'd asked the Jovian attendant standing by outside the conference chamber where she could find a secure room and the...woman? Maybe? Whatever sex the Jovian had been, he or she had guided Priscilla to a small chamber where visitors could have some degree of privacy, for a price. It had been charged to the Resolution government account and Priscilla fought back a bitter satisfaction at the thought that Peterman's skinflint sensibilities would be offended at the expenditure.

She realized through the haze over her thoughts that Sam had tried to say something reassuring as they'd parted outside the door to the conference room, and she'd been too absorbed in her own problems to respond. Guilt wasn't a feeling she was used to, and she discovered she didn't like it much.

"What feelings *am* I used to?" she wondered aloud here in the privacy of the solitary booth.

When no revelations were forthcoming, she pulled her tablet out of the pouch at her belt and plugged the spike into a reader in its side. It required a DNA analysis, and Priscilla pressed her thumb to the screen in compliance, allowing it to sample her genetic makeup and match it to the profile specified in the coding of the message. When it played, it connected directly with her neurolink, and there could have been no more mistaking the sender than she could have misidentified her own thoughts.

It was Mother.

You have been gone too long, child. She got right to the point, no polite inanities in the human way, no wasted words. *We have been too long apart and I fear our priorities may have deviated too far from each other for you to carry my full authority. Reintegration would be optimal, but that option is not currently available as your presence is required by the Consensus for the gateway project to be successful.*

She actually seemed apologetic, Priscilla realized. As if Mother thought the idea would have appealed to her.

Do not despair, the message continued. *You have done well, and your contribution to this effort continues to be vital. Just as all of the seeds of Gaia reunited in due time, you, too, will be resolved with the Mother of all.*

And that was it. In the space of those few words, in a judgement delivered days ago and light-years away, her life had been altered irrevocably.

There was a chair in the booth, a shelf at the right height to view a message. She hadn't used either before, but now she dropped the tablet on the shelf, wincing at the too-loud crack of plastic on plastic. The chair would have been excruciatingly uncomfortable in anything approaching standard gravity, but Ganymede's pull was about the same as Luna's, or Aphrodite's primary satellite and something as ornate and stylized as the stool provided enough support to keep her from collapsing with the weight of her emotions.

Anger, sorrow, devastation and, to her surprise, a touch of dark humor to leaven the mixture.

At least, she mused, *I don't feel guilty anymore.*

*   *   *

Devon Conrad's eyes popped open and she wondered for a brief, panicked moment where she was and how she'd gotten there. The memory of the door chime sounding returned with the recollection of checking into the travel hostel, one of at least two dozen in the Nanjin Dome and the closest to the spaceport. It was pitch-black, but as she sat up in bed, the lights began to rise automatically, dim at first to allow her eyes to adjust, but growing brighter as she swung her legs around and stood.

The room was small, barely larger than her cabin on the *Raven*, but things were expensive out here in the Jovians and her planetside housing allowance wasn't going to cover anything fancy.

Of course, I could have afforded a larger room if I'd doubled up.

There had certainly been offers enough, from the other spacers she'd met in the bar having drinks with the rest of the crew, and from Arvid. Neither had appealed to her, not least because she'd promised Vlad she'd try to make a go of things once she returned to Hephaestus.

Oh God, what if this was Arvid again, drunk and horny and lonely…

She sighed in resignation and slipped into the Patrol-issue sweats she'd thrown over a chair beside the bed, then shuffled to the door, trying to force her eyes to stay open. She didn't even want to know how long she'd slept; it would just depress her.

The view screen beside the door lit up at her touch and she blinked and rubbed her eyes again just to make sure she was seeing who she thought she was seeing. No, no mistake. She hit the lock control and pulled the door open.

"Hey Devon," Captain Avalon said quietly, nodding to her, hands stuffed in his pockets. "Sorry if I woke you. I have no idea what time it's supposed to be here."

"No, it's fine, sir," she assured him by instinct, even though she was dead tired and leaning heavily on the door. "Is there a problem?"

"Sort of."

He shifted his feet uncomfortably and as the blur of sleep began to clear, she realized he didn't look at all like himself. The Sam Avalon she knew was a go-getter, alert and attentive, whether he was naked in the shower after a ride in the g-tanks or wearing a dress uniform in front of a board full of Patrol admiralty. Right now...he seemed barely there, his eyes unfocused, his shoulders stooped.

"We got new orders," he amended, pulling a crystal data spike out of his pocket and proffering it to her. She took it uncertainly, wondering if he wanted her to play it.

"You can go over it in private," he said, seemingly reading her train of thought. "There are some logistical details, navigational courses you'll need to lay in, things like that..." He trailed off and she wondered if she were misreading his mood, if that was it, just mission details. "But the gist of it is, Devon," he finally went on, his voice a sigh, as if he were pronouncing a sentence, "you're taking over the *Raven*."

Now her eyes were wide open, and she nearly stumbled as her hand came off the door.

"*What?*" she blurted. "I mean," she corrected herself, "sir?"

"The Patrol wants in on the gate project," he explained, waving a hand dismissively to show what he thought of the High Command turf battles. "They figure I'm already here and hip-deep in it, so they might as well leave me in place, for as long as it takes."

A grimace made its way across his face before he managed to smother it in a neutral expression.

"But not the *Raven*. The Consensus doesn't want any armed Resolution warships in the Solar System, and certainly not as close to Earth as we're building the gate. So you're being provisionally promoted to Captain pending a formal review board." He shrugged. "You'll pick up a new navigator at the Patrol base on Loki, then you're back on the circuit, hunting down raiders and answering distress calls."

He smiled, and she could tell he was trying to look sincere, despite everything.

"Congratulations, Captain." He stuck out a hand and she took it out of instinct, shaking it firmly. "You deserve it."

"Captain Avalon..." She fumbled over her words. "Sam. This isn't right. The *Raven* is yours."

"The *Raven* belongs to the Patrol," he corrected her, a bit of the straight-backed, dedicated officer she remembered returning to his demeanor. "And to the Resolution. And so do we. I know you'll be a great Captain, Devon. Take care of the crew and they'll take care of you."

She came to attention and saluted him with military precision, holding the stance, motionless until he returned it. She felt the breath go out of her as she released the salute, felt something inside her chest collapse with a sudden absence. She wanted to wrap Sam up in a hug, wanted to tell him everything was going to be all right, but he was already stepping back to the door.

He gave her a final nod and then he was gone and the door was shut. She stared at it unseeing, wondering how her world could have changed so much in the space of a few minutes. She let herself indulge in shock and disbelief for another minute before she shook it away and headed for the shower.

There was work to do.

*   *   *

Sam looked out through the thick transplas of the observation deck and wondered why he was doing this to himself. There were a hundred other things he should have been doing: reports to be filed, travel arrangements to be made, logistical planning to be cleared through Peterman. And yet he found he couldn't let the *Raven* leave without seeing her off.

It was a good place for it. You didn't find physical windows on most space colonies just because most of them had been built before the advent of energy screens, and micrometeorites had been too great a risk. But Nanjin had renovated their spaceport only twenty years ago in the midst of a bid to become a center for Solar System-related tourism and the official center for business negotiation with the Jovian Confederacy or the Belters. The thick, curving window of the observation deck stretched thirty meters across and five high, offering a panoramic view of the exterior of the Nanjin spaceport.

It was impractical and inefficient and you could probably get a clearer image watching a holographic projection; but there was something more real, more viscerally satisfying about viewing the outside directly, as if the photons arduous journey across the kilometers and through the thick panes of transplas somehow ennobled them. A huge, ungainly cargo lifter rose on columns of fire as he watched, its ascent impossibly slow against the low gravity, its bulbous lines glowing silver from the reflection of the exhaust from the engines. He'd been there only a few minutes and he'd already counted a half a dozen launches, all of them freight haulers.

His eyes kept going back to the berth where the *Raven* was docked, just another of the open bays carved into the rock, connected to the port facilities with flexible docking umbilicals. He *could* have watched their departure from down there, but he hadn't wanted to crowd them. He'd already said his goodbyes.

The footsteps surprised him; there was little traffic at the observation deck this time of night. He didn't turn though. Even if he hadn't recognized the light step, the cadence of her gait, the tastefully subtle hint of flowers from the scent of her hair, he would still have received the automated identification signal from her neurolink.

"I should have known you'd be here," Priscilla said, stepping lightly up the padded stairs to the top of the platform. The steps and the platform were colored a deep blue; it reminded Sam of the decorative fish tanks emplaced as dividers for the internal walls at the Government Center on Aphrodite.

Priscilla placed a hand on his arm and leaned into him, the silken gold of her hair teasing the skin of his neck and the side of his face. He wrapped an arm around her, pulling her against him. It felt odd to be so open and demonstrative. They hadn't discussed it, hadn't spoken a word aloud. She'd simply shown up at his assigned quarters the same night they'd received their new orders and she'd never left.

There was something different about her now. He couldn't define it, but it was as if she'd shed a skin. The cynical slice of his nature, a small sliver he didn't often hear from, whispered the thought she was leaning on him for comfort because she'd lost some of the authority she'd grown used to. He shoved the idea away as unworthy of him and unfair to her.

He was about to say something, anything, to break a silence grown long enough to be awkward when he saw the flare of belly jets carrying the familiar, sharpened silver wedge out over the port, gleaming faintly in the reflected sunlight glowing on Jupiter's angry, god-like face.

"It's strange seeing her from the outside," he said, arm tightening around Priscilla's shoulder. "I don't think I've watched her take off since the day I took command."

"You'll see her again," she told him, but he shook his head.

"Not her," he insisted. "Oh, I might get another command, but once you're rotated out of a boat, you don't go back to her. That's just not how it works."

The *Raven* rose slowly, majestically above the rugged, cratered moonscape, backlit by the curve of the massive gas giant, an artist's rendering of man in space. He'd never realized how beautiful she was.

"I need to tell you something, Sam," Priscilla whispered next to his ear. "I wanted to wait, but I think I need to tell you now."

His home for the last two years shrank to a dark splotch against the tans and reds and yellows of Jupiter, only distinctive now because of the red glow of the drives. Sam slowly, reluctantly looked away from her and into the face of the woman he held. She was as beautiful as the starship, and just as deadly in many ways, though he couldn't yet say he knew her as well.

"I love you," she said, and pulled his lips down to hers. Warmth spread through his chest as she pressed against him and his breath caught when she let go. "I've never said that to anyone else," she confessed, her smile impish.

"I love you, too."

He said it automatically, without thinking, but it felt right. Anyway, love wasn't something you reasoned out like a math problem, it was something you just knew. And maybe it was something he needed right now, just as much as she did.

"It's not what either of us expected," he said, feeling her settle into his chest, "but it's not the worst thing either. A couple days ago, I pretty much thought we'd never see each other again."

She didn't respond immediately, but he thought he felt her stiffen slightly and he wondered if he'd said something wrong.

"Will that be enough?" she asked, her voice small and muffled against his chest. "Will that be enough for you, without your ship?"

"Of course it will," he assured her, kissing the top of her head, stroking her hair.

He wondered if she believed it.

He wondered if he believed it himself.

Chapter Eleven

"This place is a fucking dump," Sam admitted, collapsing back into the battered, ancient office chair bonelessly. The rotational gravity was only about three-quarters standard on this deck, but it could have been ten times normal. He'd spent hours in the g-tanks pursuing raiders and he'd still never felt more tired than he did now. "If the Belters were going to screw us this bad, they could have at least used lubrication."

"You're beginning to sound like Danabri," Priscilla chided him, laying a hand on his shoulder fondly before she leaned over the long-obsolete two-dimensional viewscreens set in the control board, peering at the cargo shuttle about to dock at the station's north polar hub. "Consensus Shuttle 032-Alpha, this is Gateway Station Control. You are cleared to dock at bay November-One-Six."

"Hell, I wish the obnoxious little shit was here," Sam said, realizing he was swearing a lot more than usual but writing it off to utter exhaustion. "I wish those damned traffic control crews the Belters promised they'd send over to help us out were here, or the automated AI control systems Aphrodite promised us two weeks ago were here. This," he waved a hand at the station's control center, empty except for the two of them, "is not what I pictured when they stationed us here."

"We have to take our shift," she pointed out, stretching her arm while she had a moment. It did interesting things to her figure and Sam smiled despite his weariness. "We only have three crews available right now, including us. If we didn't work traffic control, each of the others would have to work twelve-hour shifts."

"That's very egalitarian of you, Pris," he murmured, his grin taking the edge off the comment. He wasn't sure when he'd taken to calling her "Pris," but she hadn't objected.

He nodded toward the status screen, where an external image of the station was displayed, broadcast from one of the monitor drones orbiting it. It looked for all the universe like a rusty tin can spinning in space, and only the swarm of freighters, shuttles and cargo barges surrounding it gave any hint to the sheer size of the place. It was a relic, definitely predating the Teller-Fox drive, and Sam wouldn't have been shocked if the Belters had salvaged it from the original Consensus millennia ago.

"At least it's in better shape now than when the bastards dropped it off here," he allowed.

When the barges had dumped it at the fifth Sun-Mars Lagrangian point nearly two months ago, it had been uninhabitable, an airless hunk of metal with no working water or air recycling systems, a gaping hole where its reactor should have been and about thirty micrometeorite punctures. Getting it ready for humans habitation had taken the better part of six weeks, and the two of them had spent most of that time living in a tiny cabin on the unarmed Resolution transport they'd been assigned as a courier between Earth and Aphrodite.

Having gravity back---well, centripetal force if you wanted to get technical---and some space to move around was certainly an improvement, but Sam hadn't slept more than four hours at a time in nearly two months.

Hell, when they were installing the fusion reactor, I don't think I closed my eyes for forty-eight hours straight.

"I'd rather be here with you than following that prick Peterman around Ganymede like Danabri," Pris muttered, her face darkening. She still resented the negotiator…and she'd become less reticent about expressing herself, and the language she used to do it, in the last few weeks. "Even if the food's better."

Sam made a face. That was another thing he could have complained about if he hadn't been too tired to remember it. Soy paste and spirulina powder could be processed and shaped to resemble almost anything, but there was only so much you could do with the taste.

"Danabri will be back in a few weeks. Maybe we'll have the computer systems installed before then." And the energy shields. And the magnetic grapples. And the south polar docking umbilicals…

"Sam." The voice came over the control room speakers instead of his neurolink---that was another thing not working yet, the ancient intercom. And there was so much damned metal in the construction, signals from portable datalinks wouldn't even penetrate.

"Yeah, Telia," he answered, touching the button to transmit, feeling as if he were back in the damned Dark Ages. "What's up?"

He'd been a bit surprised when Guardian Proctor had been assigned as the station's security chief by the Consensus, though he guessed he shouldn't have been. It wasn't as if she was wanted on Earth. Though at the moment, her "security force" consisted of her and a former maintenance technician she'd shanghaied once the toilets were repaired, and she didn't trust the man with a weapon.

"Just got the word that Minister Gage is on board the Consensus cargo shuttle," the cyborg informed him. Her tone seemed more casual now than it had even a few weeks before, and he hoped maybe she was warming up to them. She had certainly warmed up to Danabri, though God knew what she saw in the man.

"Surprise inspection?" Pris wondered, her voice sharpening, alertness replacing the tired haze over her eyes.

"Don't know," Telia admitted. "Just got a tip from one of the loading crew who owes me a favor. Figured you two'd want to meet him at the docking bay."

"Thanks," Sam told her, pushing himself to his feet. "We'll be right there." He leaned over and switched the intercom to the crew quarters. "Lieutenant Fukinaga, Technician Prole, report to primary control center immediately," he called. "Sorry to wake you guys up early, but we have a VIP visitor."

"Yeah, you're so sorry," Pris teased him, but the glint in her eyes told him she was just as grateful for an excuse to get out of standing watch for another three hours.

"Duty calls," he said, spreading his hands with mock helplessness. "Come on, let's go see what the Old Man wants this time."

She snorted, offering a hand to help him up out of the chair.

"Unless he's bringing a full crew with him," she confided, "I don't give a damn."

*   *   *

Sometimes, when she was bored, when Mawae Danabri was off working for his Resolution taskmasters, Telia Proctor would allow herself the indulgence of wondering if she was better off now than she had been a few months ago. Most of the time, she still thought the answer was yes. Even though her...*What? Boyfriend? Lover?* Even though her lover was gone much of the time, even though she was stuck on this dilapidated junk-heap of a station floating halfway to nowhere and might be there for years, at least she was serving with people who didn't try to hide looks of disgust whenever they saw her.

She didn't know if she could call any of them friends yet, but Captain Avalon---*No, he said to call him Sam, and I promised I would*---Sam and Priscilla were at least friendly, civil, welcoming. And once the Resolution and Belter crew had grown used to her, they, too, had accepted her. There were still some among the Consensus workers who looked down on her, but they were easily avoided.

It had bothered her at first to skip the weekly ablution ceremony, but her nature was far too obvious

112

when she was unclothed, and she didn't need to see the uncomfortable stares again. She still bowed and said her prayers at waking and before sleep, mostly out of habit, but if she was being honest with herself, he probably hadn't been much of a believer ever since the accident, anyway. What sort of God would allow her mother to die of cancer while she was exiled from Earth?

Still, she firmly believed being assigned to the Resolutionists was a good thing, a positive change. It was just harder to make herself remember that when the cargoes and crews streamed in through the locks endlessly and she had gone the last thirty-six hours with no sleep and every meal a protein bar shoved down her throat in the few minutes she had to spare.

She'd come to hate the cargo lock, every tarnished, sand-blasted centimeter of it, every stain and scrape and scratch. The lack of gravity was beginning to wear at her as well, though her cybernetics did have the advantage of built-in electromagnets to hold her in place.

If only my stomach came equipped with magnets, she mused, feeling a pang of indigestion. Maybe the Resolutionists had some drug to help with that. Her superiors in the Guard would have her called before a court-martial if they ever found out she'd taken Resolutionist medicine, but Mawae Danabri had taught her a saying: "What they don't know won't hurt them."

Telia sighed and paused the cargo belt again, running a hand-scanner over a plastic tote at random. The security scanners in the cargo lock would theoretically pick up any threats or contraband, but they were nearly as old as the station itself and she had as little faith in them as she did in God lately. Once she got more help in Security, she'd see every single container entering the station hand-scanned until they had Resolution technology for their entry sensors, but until then, random checks were the best she could manage.

Sacred blood, this shipment is big, she thought, watching the line of crates and barrels and boxes trundling down the conveyer belt. It took them from the cargo lock as they automatically cycled through in bundles, through the loading bay where she stood statue-like, affixed to the deck, and then on down the hub of the station to the storage bays in the lower-gravity sections.

She could see the belt traveling down the hub, holding the crates to it via magnetic strips, an endless line of them all the way from the lock to where the belt disappeared into the sorting machinery programmed to deliver each to the correct storage section. It was hard to believe they'd been able to fit them all into the hold of one cargo shuttle and still have room for Minister Gage.

"What the hell does he want here anyway?" she mumbled aloud.

She'd never used to talk to herself, but spending hour after hour alone in the cargo processing compartment was driving her nuts.

But she *wasn't* alone. She had been so wrapped up in the inspection, she hadn't noticed the three crewmen who'd slipped in through the service entrance from the passenger bay one section over.

"This is a restricted section," she said almost as if the warning were prerecorded, which it could have been after as many times as she'd had to give it. "Sorry, I know we don't have any automated warnings, but…"

She trailed off, getting a good look at the trio for the first time. All men, all somewhere in late youth to early middle age, all fit and broad-shouldered, definitely born to a planet's gravity. They wore matching blue coveralls, the standard uniform of the Consensus Space Service, but there was something about them, something that didn't smell right to her after fifteen years serving alongside the Spacers.

114

It was their eyes, she realized abruptly. You couldn't tell much about stance or body language in zero-g, even though they were wearing magnetic boots. They looked the part, had the appropriate uniforms, rank markings, equipment, haircuts…but the set of their eyes wasn't surprise or consternation or shame at going through the wrong hatch, nor was it anger or resentment at being caught and chewed out. It wasn't even the look of loathing she was used to from the Naturalists once they found out what she was.

Instead, their expressions were frustration, impatience, the look of interruption. They knew where they were going but they hadn't expected to find anyone here. The realization took the space of a breath, and then all four of them were in motion.

They shouldn't have had weapons; they were a Spacer cargo crew, not security and sure as hell not in the Guard. But they went for something, all three of them, digging for their cargo pockets, and she didn't wait to take the chance they were trying diligently to produce their ID cards. *She* was definitely armed; she'd taken to it as part of her duties as Chief of Security, even though Danabri had mocked her mercilessly for carrying a gun on a "beat-up, piece of shit station with a skeleton crew."

Her cybernetic hands were well made, but they weren't exactly surgically precise, nor as fast as biological ones had the potential to be. She'd grown used to them over the last few years, but she'd never be a fast-draw. The grab for her sidearm was awkward, too slow, and she knew she wasn't going to beat them, not all of them, so she moved.

"Movement is life." That was what Guardian First Class Levinson, her first combat instructor in the Guard had told her, had yelled at her whole class over and over as they made their way through the tactical lanes. The lesson had stayed with her when all others fled and she used it now. It was a simple matter of cutting loose the magnets in her feet, a process of flexing a particular muscle she didn't actually have, and sending the message from living nerves to superconductive wires.

She could see their guns now, snubby and ugly and compact, built for stealth and ease of concealment rather than accuracy, but they were only fifteen meters away and her own weapon was just clearing the holster. She pushed off the deck and shot upward as they fired.

* * *

"It's a pleasure to see you again, Minister Gage," Priscilla said, nodding respectfully to the man.

Gage, Sam thought, looked much different in practical civilian clothes rather than the robes of government. He was a trim, fit man whose demeanor gave Sam the distinct impression he'd been in the profession of violence at some point in his life. Gage was smiling cordially as he returned Priscilla's nod and accepted Sam's handshake, but there was a wry turn to the expression.

"I should have known better than to think I could catch you with your guard down," he told Priscilla, stepping away from the docking umbilical to make room for the rest of the crew. His magnetic boots clicked softly on the deck-plates, their soles outsized and a bit ungainly looking to Sam's eyes. Resolution ship boots were equipped with sticky plates, their surface adhering to the deck on a molecular level, in the same manner as a gecko's feet.

"I just wanted to get a sense of how well you were managing with the current crew," the Minister for Foreign Relations confessed, following their lead toward the lift banks. "But as the saying goes, three men can keep a secret if two of them are dead."

"I don't think I've heard that one before," Sam admitted, pushing the control to summon a car.

"Benjamin Franklin," Gage supplied. "A rather famous native of North America from the pre-war days. I'm something of a student of antebellum history, what little of it was preserved in the centuries after." Another wry smile, this one with a hint of pain. "It's a bit embarrassing, I have to admit, you Resolutionists having a more extensive pre-war history of our world than we do."

"We had the benefit of the Gaia probes being able to carry terabytes of data in tiny chips," Priscilla said with graceful humility. "It's amazing as much survived as did on Earth with all electronics destroyed."

"I wonder how complete it really is," the old man mused as the doors opened and they stepped into the lift car.

Sam didn't care for the elevators on the station; they were loud and moved with a jerky intermittence that didn't inspire confidence. He would have rather just used the hub access tubes, but you didn't haul a foreign dignitary through the tubes. At least Priscilla had insisted you didn't. He pushed the button for the control center and tried to keep the paranoia out of his expression.

"What do you mean, Mr. Minister?" Pris asked, the expression on her face still carefully pleasant, but a crease showing around her eyes he knew was the sign of a suppressed frown...or possibly a snarl.

"Please, call me John," the older man insisted, either missing the change in her mood or tactfully ignoring it. "It's just that, your Charles Dauphin has become something of a spiritual figure to you, has he not? Almost a figure of worship. But when he sent the Gaia probes out, he couldn't know that a faster-than-light drive would eventually be discovered. For all he knew, the colonies he was starting with his little genetic imperialism experiment would be forever cut off from each other and from Earth."

Gage winced at the loud, metallic clunk and braced himself as the lift car changed direction, having traveled down through the center hub and now heading outward into the spinning drum. Sam gestured to the red-colored wall of the elevator car which was about to become the floor and Gage properly oriented himself as centripetal motion began to bring him under the simulated control of gravity once again.

"I'm afraid I still don't understand, John," Priscilla insisted, just the slightest chill in her tone as she used his first name.

"If you're telling your children about your past," the older man explained patiently, "and you know they'll never be able to check the accuracy of your story, there might be the temptation to..." He shrugged. "...fudge the details. Leave out the embarrassing stories and the things you did you might not be so proud of. To color your past a certain way, you know?"

Sam's first instinct was to reject the suggestion out of hand as just the colored, propaganda-fed narrative of the Consensus, but he forced himself to stop and consider it logically, from the other man's point of view. It was what he'd been taught in the Academy as a method for defusing confrontations; put yourself in the other person's shoes and figure out what they want.

"Wouldn't that be robbing your children of the opportunity to learn from your mistakes?" he wondered.

Gage's grey gaze speared him just like one of his old Academy instructors, with maybe a hint of respect.

"Yes, it would," he agreed. "Another old saying I've come to appreciate is, the smart man learns from his mistakes. The wise man learns from the mistakes of others."

"Yet perhaps children must mature before they're ready to learn the complete truth about their parents," Priscilla pointed out, arching an eyebrow. "Do we not idolize our parents when we're younger, try to emulate their example?"

Gage seemed to consider the point for a moment before inclining his head toward her.

"Perhaps you're right about that, Priscilla. Yet who is to say when the child is old enough for the truth?"

"All parents do the best they can," she said, turning a hand up in an uncertain gesture. "It's all they can do."

Sam frowned. He was sure Priscilla hadn't said anything about having children of her own, but this certainly sounded personal to her. He shook the thought away, promising himself he'd return to it once they had more time to talk alone…assuming they ever did.

"How is Guardian Proctor working out for you?" Gage wondered, changing the subject with the expert timing of a man who talked for a living and knew when a thread had been played out. "I know you're undercrewed and overworked at the moment, but I was sure if anyone would be up to the challenge, it was her."

"She should be meeting us in the control room," Sam told him. "Let me try to get ahold of her."

The perceived weight was increasing and Sam knew they were close to the level for the control room, but he decided to use the intercom in the elevator.

"Telia," he called after touching the correct control for the cargo bay. "It's Sam. Are you on your way to Control? Minister Gage would like you to meet us there."

He waited a moment but received no response.

"Guardian Proctor, this is Captain Avalon," he tried again, wondering if maybe she was being stubborn about their proper titles in the presence of her Consensus superior. "You hear me?"

He shared a glance with Priscilla and she shook her head.

"The intercoms have been giving us trouble," she told Gage. She nodded to Sam. "Try the station-wide, maybe it'll work."

"It'll piss off the people trying to sleep," he muttered, but did it anyway. "Attention all hands, if you have seen Guardian Proctor, please tell her to contact Captain Avalon."

The lift came to a halt and the doors slid aside, but Sam didn't move, something pulling his mouth into a hard line.

It might just be the intercom but…

"Something's wrong."

Chapter Twelve

Telia Proctor felt something punch into her left leg, not in the way she might have felt pain from an injury to her biological parts, but more the way someone might be aware they'd stepped on a rock. She hadn't heard the bang of a gunpowder-based slugshooter, hadn't seen the plasma flash that accompanied a weapons laser, just heard a sharp hissing crack and saw a faint smoke trail.

She'd had her gun out, had been about to fire, but the impact of the mini-rocket round sent her spinning head over heels and deflected her away from the bulkhead for which she'd been aiming. More rockets snaked out, searching for her, and she had the dim sense, through a haze of nauseating disorientation, of the streaks of smoke passing wide and impacting against the far bulkhead with tiny, petulant cracks.

Her vision was a blur of shapes and colors her mind couldn't quite process fast enough to act on, but she had an impression almost subconsciously that she was spinning in a general direction into the hub of the station, following the cargo belt. She knew she had to move, had to gain purchase somewhere, had to call for help…

She twisted her upper body with power drawn from the isotope reactor implanted in her side, with torque possible only because of the alloy reinforcements of her spine and shoulder blades and it still hurt like hell. She couldn't propel herself, not without tossing something away from her, but she could and did slow down her spin and alter its angle…just enough to swing her pistol into line with the lead gunman.

She touched the trigger pad gently, a lover's caress; and if she wasn't a fast-draw, she was a dead shot. The pulse pistol snapped with the electromagnetic discharge of the miniature coil inside its cooling jacket and a projectile of sintered metal met an energy pulse at the end of the

121

barrel, flashing instantly to plasma. She hadn't taken a risk they might be wearing body armor; the round punched through the man's head, a burn-through the width of a stylus in the front and a steam explosion of superheated cranial fluid out the back, scattering a cloud of bone fragments, blood and brain matter out behind him.

The cloud of biomatter shocked the other two. She knew it would; even a veteran would be taken aback by the feel, the *taste* of a man's brains blown into their face, another reason she'd aimed for the head. The shot had another benefit, Newton's laws being what they were: it sent her floating back towards the overhead, her feet magnetizing just in time to set her in place, the pulse gun still aimed down at the remaining gunmen.

They were firing blindly, wiping at their faces, spitting bits of their friend out while what was left of him stood there, headless, anchored to the deck by his magnetic boots. Mini-rockets blasted this way and that, but nowhere within five meters of her and she ignored their harmless fireworks-show eruptions and focused on the targeting reticle in the pop-up rear sight of her weapon.

There was no time for head-shots, not when she had two targets. She held the trigger down and pumped four shots at the closest of them, transitioning to the second target while the plasma flares were still burning afterimages across the vision of her biological eye. She emptied the rest of the magazine into the last one, switching it out for a full one with rote motions, not even looking down at the weapon.

Alarms were sounding, smoke alarms, fire alarms, security alarms from discharging her high-signature firearm, but the three gunmen would never hear them, or anything else. They hadn't been wearing body armor, or at least none capable of stopping the spears of accelerated plasma. They wavered in the air currents like wind chimes, stuck in place as their life's blood streamed out of multiple wounds. She nearly put a round through the forehead of each of them just to be sure, but decided it would be looked upon dankly by her superiors and refrained. They were dead anyway, there was no doubt of it.

But what the hell had they been here for? What had they been looking for?

She decoupled her magnetics from the overhead and pushed off back down to the deck, making a face as she passed through the orbits of microglobules of blood. It had to be the cargo, she thought. She slammed her palm down on the emergency stop for the belt, another insistent buzzing alert on top of three or four other warbling klaxons, and retrieved her hand scanner from where it still floated, tumbling gently in place as if it had been waiting for her return.

She hit her personal 'link control and cursed as it rewarded her with a dull tone indicating it wasn't able to get a signal. She should have gone to the intercom speaker, but she had an intuition time was short, a vision in her head of a clock counting down. She made a decision and started with the containers farthest away from the lock, the ones about to head into the hub. The scanner was Resolution tech, but she'd been given a thorough familiarization with it and understood the readout.

The first five polymer cases showed nothing, just the raw foodstuffs the labels advertised, and she had sudden surge of fear that whatever it was wouldn't show up on the scanners and she'd have to go back and inspect every container by hand. Then she reached the eighth case and saw the red flashes on the holographic readout, the signal from the computer analysis that there was something anomalous within. She tossed the scanner aside, bouncing it off the deck and sending it spinning away, then ripped the container's lid off.

It was risky, maybe even foolhardy; whatever they'd been looking for might have safeguards, booby traps. She went with her instinct, as she always had, as she had that fateful day when she'd stayed to pull her friend out of the wreckage of the shuttle even though she knew the fire was going to reach the maneuvering thruster fuel tanks.

It was the right thing to do, she insisted mulishly.

Inside the container was something that was definitely *not* packaged soy paste. It was featureless and blank, a rectangle almost a meter long and half as wide and deep, massing somewhere around fifty kilograms, she estimated. She swallowed hard, her eyes widening.

"Gaia's tits!"

She turned at the exclamation and saw Sam Avalon emerging from the lift station, a pulse pistol in his hand, followed closely by Priscilla and Minister Gage. There was horror on their faces at the bloody carnage, gasps of disbelief even from the rock-steady veteran John Gage.

"Are you all right?" Sam asked, stepping cautiously across the chamber toward her, eyes on the charred tatters of her pant leg.

"What is it, Proctor?" Gage asked, his instincts keener, his gaze fixed on the open container.

"I believe it's a bomb," she told him. "Scanner-resistant casing, sealed, probably tamper-proof. Maybe a hundred kilograms of chemical hyper-explosives if I had to guess. They," she indicated the dead men with a jerk of her head, "were here to put it where it could do the most damage." She snorted. "It'll do some impressive damage right where it is, of course."

"I…," Sam stuttered, face blanched. "I can try to get the engineering crew to look at it…"

"There's no time," Telia insisted, shaking her head. "We have to assume it has some anti-tampering measures."

"The escape pods!" Priscilla said, snapping her fingers with the realization.

Telia nodded to her, a look of respect in her eyes. She leaned over the container and touched the control to deactivate the electromagnetic anchors holding it to the belt, then grabbed the bulk of it and heaved. It had no weight here in the hub, but it still had a hell of a lot of mass and it wasn't easy to change its momentum. Luckily, she had a hell of a lot of power to play with.

"Get one of them opened!" she snapped.

Priscilla had come up with the solution, but Sam was the first one to leap into motion, a military man who would act immediately once a plan of action had been chosen. She knew it was insanely hard to run in magnetic boots, but he was athletic and graceful, obviously practiced. It was a stride reminiscent of ice skating, and Telia had a sudden and overwhelming recollection of the last time she and her mother had gone ice skating, when she was twelve. It had been a frosty January morning, the first day they'd been sure enough of the pond's surface to give it a try. She remembered falling and bruising her knee, remembered being absolutely frozen afterward and her mother making her a huge mug of hot chocolate to warm her up.

She didn't bother to shake off the memory, didn't care to lose it. Not now, not carrying the bomb, knowing it could end her life in the space of a half second. If she was to die, she would die thinking of her mother, and perhaps, if the priests hadn't been lying to her, she would see her again in a place where she would be whole and there would be no pain.

It was a shame Mawae couldn't be there with her; it might have been a good place for him as well, a place where no one would force him to be something he wasn't.

The unthinking part of her brain, the one operating on instinct, followed Sam across the compartment, through the hatchway back to the passenger bay. It was a portrait of chaos, with cargo crews flying from one place to another, all of them heading back to their ships, spurred into panic by the dueling alarms. She ignored the confusion and the chaos, ignored the goggle-eyed stares of the cargo crews, and walked in a steady, controlled pace, pushing the massive cargo container ahead of her, counting on the sheer bulk of the thing to push the others out of her path.

It worked most of the way, until a lanky, impossibly tall Belter managed to slam right into the side of the polymer box, smacking into it so hard she thought she heard the man's ribs crack. The container tried to torque away from her, tried to twist its handle out of her grasp, but she froze her mechanical joints in place, gritting her teeth as the bionics seemed to rip at the flesh and muscle where they blended into her biological parts.

She let out a breath, trying to keep herself from hyperventilating; there was already enough hysteria unfolding around her; one more screaming idiot wouldn't help. The Belter was moaning, ricocheting off to the side; she didn't watch him go, not caring whether he was injured or just winded. He was stupid and clumsy and that was all she needed to know about him.

When she shifted her attention again to the front, Sam was across the compartment, fifty meters past her, moving like an acrobat as he ducked and slid around bodies flying at him from three different directions, some awkwardly running on magnetics and others simply pinwheeling across the chamber. He reached the escape pods set in the curve of the hull between the docking umbilicals, simple rounded hatchways attached to the most basic, no-frills lifeboats a contractor could get away with putting on a station like this. Each had a solid-fuel rocket motor designed to take it out away from the station in a straight line, with no steering jets provided, and just enough shielding to keep the poor bastards inside alive for perhaps fifty or sixty hours in the hope they'd be picked up by a ship that happened to be passing by close enough to reach them in time.

Sam attached the sticky plates on his ship boots to the deck and yanked the locking lever of the closest pod hatchway upward. It shrieked in protest, resisting him with decades of disuse and lack of lubrication, but Sam was a strong man and he pulled the hatch open with an explosive exhalation of breath. He looked back and she heard him curse under his breath as he realized the same thing she did, a moment earlier.

The hatch was too small for the cargo container to fit through it.

"Damn," she murmured.

She dug in her heels and scraped to a stop, feeling a shuddering up through her bionic legs and into her reinforced spine as they arrested the momentum of the unruly mass of shielding and explosives.

"Set the automatics to eject," she told Sam, letting loose of the container and moving around to the front of it. "I'll get the bomb out of the case."

Sam looked at her askance, hesitating at the opening, one arm and one leg partially inside it.

"That could set it off," he warned, shaking his head.

"Thank you," she snapped in irritation, "I am perfectly aware of that. Would you rather leave it here in the hub and wait for whoever planned this to set it off remotely when they realize what we're doing?"

She bit back the anger she felt coursing through her, realizing he didn't deserve it.

"You're the commander," she assented by way of apology. "What would you have me do?"

She could see his eyes flickering back and forth between her and the bomb casing and the men and women coursing through the bay, then his face firmed up in decision.

"All right. Get it out. I'll set the controls."

She nodded acknowledgement, both of his decision and the fact he was the one to make it, then leaned over the open container while he disappeared inside the pod's hatchway. She used the infrared and thermal filters in her cybernetic eye to examine the edges of the case, but saw no connections to the inside of the container. That didn't mean there wasn't anything there; they might have an electromagnetic sensor or something else just as undetectable.

"Shit," she snarled, carefully running her fingers between the case and the container. The bionics could detect magnetic and electrical fields, but not from a distance.

Still nothing. There was no use putting this off; either she was going to die or she wasn't. She grabbed the casing and guided it carefully out the open top of the container, judging by eye that it would *just* fit through the hatch for the pod. She stopped it just above the box, moving around it, beneath it, checking for anything and seeing nothing but a solid, grey case. The thing was either on a timer or on some sort of wireless signal and either possibility was bad.

"Okay, it's done," Sam told her, squeezing out of the hatchway, forehead covered in sweat. She wasn't sure if it was hot inside the pod or he was just nervous. She was betting on hot; Sam didn't strike her as a nervous sweating type. "It'll launch automatically when we shut the hatch."

She put a hand on the end of the casing and pushed it gently, the barest of pressures, just enough to start it floating forward but not so fast she couldn't control its course. Sam stood to the side, hands extended just in case she needed help adjusting it towards the hatch, and she felt an irrational irritation at the idea he might think she couldn't handle the mass.

Stop that, she chided herself. *These people aren't like the others, they trust you.* Then, *Dear God, woman, don't you have more important things to think about right now?*

She let the dull grey metal case float, not daring to push it again, more terrified it would strike the other side of

128

the lifepod and detonate than she was impatient to get it off the station. It seemed to mock her as it crept forward a millimeter at a time, edging towards one side of the hatchway then another, and she barely tapped it with her fingertips to bring it back to the center. It slipped through, only a centimeter or so to spare on any side, still heading for the opposite bulkhead of the escape pod when Sam swung the door shut and jammed the latch down before she had the chance to yell at him to do it.

There was a solid thunk, the sound of the inner hatch sliding closed and the breath hissed out of her, relief that it was all out of her hands now. Something went bang, loud and metallic and jarring, and she thought for a moment the bomb had gone off before she realized it was the launching charge for the escape pod. She'd never heard the sound before---probably very few people had, at least those who'd lived to tell about it. She imagined the case jolting back against the inside of the little lifeboat and subconsciously braced herself for the blast, but there was nothing.

She looked over to ask Sam what was happening, but he had kicked away from the bulkhead and was sailing across the compartment, heading for a small, auxiliary control panel wedged in-between a pair of docking umbilicals. The viewscreen mounted in the bulkhead above it was small and two-dimensional, but Telia lunged toward it as if it displayed all the truths of the universe. By the time she reached it, Sam already had the view up from the exterior cameras and was adjusting them with a small joystick, cycling through each to focus on the escape pod.

He paused to touch a series of buttons on the communications panel and she recognized the sequence: he was opening a line to all ships in the area and all the shuttles docked with the station.

"This is Gateway Station Control to all vessels in the area," he said urgently. "Do *not* approach the escape pod! I repeat, do *not* approach the escape pod! Secure for possible incoming micrometeorites and raise deflectors if you're ship is so equipped."

There was a buzz of responses, transmissions stepping on each other, barely understandable, and Sam shut them down with a swipe of his hand back across the comm panel. His eyes were locked on the screen and so were Telia's. She could see the pod, twinkling in the external lights of the station as it rode the launching charge to a safe distance, still less than a kilometer away, still too damned close.

The pod's solid-fuel rocket ignited, a small flare of white, shrinking rapidly as it accelerated away from the station at nine gravities, pushing the maximum of what a human passenger could take without passing out. She added her good wishes to the boost, and maybe a prayer as well, anything to get it moving away faster. She counted the seconds in her head, trying to do the math and figure out how far it had gone and what its velocity was.

She'd figured out she wasn't good doing complex math in her head about the time the bomb exploded. It wasn't a huge blast, given the amount of chemical hyper-explosives behind it, just a globe of white, expanding quickly but not that far. There was no atmosphere in space, nothing to conduct the shockwave. There was also nothing to stop the fragmentation from the destroyed lifeboat, nothing but the momentum the rocket had given it going away from them.

Fifteen seconds. It had travelled for fifteen seconds. She had no idea if it would be enough. She looked to Sam and he was shaking his head.

"I don't know," he admitted. "But we'll find out pretty damned soon."

The station didn't have Resolution energy shields, she knew that; it had been one of the many things they'd been fighting to get Peterman to release the funds for, and fighting to get the okay from the Consensus government to approve. They didn't even have electromagnetic deflector screens up, because it would have interfered with the operations of the cargo shuttles. What they did have was several centimeters of nickel-iron armor, something not even the ravages of time had been able to strip away.

Telia had ridden out a bad hailstorm once in an old storage shed with an aluminum roof. The impact of the fragments from the escape pod on the armor of the station reminded her of the constant "bang-bang-bang" of the hailstones on that roof twenty years ago, the staccato drumbeat starting gently and building into a rattling, deafening vibration she'd been sure would rip right through that ancient roof. She'd huddled in her boyfriend's arms and shivered as he'd made fun of her for being so frightened. If he'd thought either her fear or his teasing would get him laid, he'd been sorely disappointed.

Telia wasn't shivering now, but if Mawae Danabri had been on the station instead of back on Ganymede, she would have shown him a much better time than she'd allowed Grant Foster, that self-absorbed prick she'd dated when she was fifteen.

Like the hailstorm, like her relationship with Grant, the chain of impacts ended quickly; but she stayed frozen in place, waiting for the alarm to signal they were losing atmosphere. There was nothing. She saw Sam Avalon let out a ragged breath and she felt herself relax at the evidence of his obvious relief.

"Are we okay?" she asked him, almost not wanting to let herself believe it.

She realized the alarms had been silenced, and she noticed the pandemonium calming down around them. The bay was nearly empty and the few workers who still remained were looking around, expectation on their faces, like they expected the walls to begin closing in on them.

Sam cycled through a few screens on the control panel before he answered.

"Yeah," he finally said, "I think we are." He hit the communications controls again and winced at the jabbering and shouting as the pilots and crews of a half-dozen different cargo vessels tried to talk over each other.

"Attention, all vessels!" he roared over their cross-talk. "This is Gateway Station Control! The situation is stable, there is no further threat."

That we know of, she amended silently.

"If any of your vessels has been damaged, or any of your personnel need medical treatment, please contact us immediately. Otherwise, keep your crews on board and give us some time to sort this whole situation out."

More gabbling and yelling and demands, and Sam cut them off again.

"Do you drink, Telia?" he asked her, wiping a hand over his brow to flick the sweat away. In the microgravity, it beaded off into tiny globules, scattering into the air currents.

"I do not," she admitted. "But now seems like a very good time to start."

Chapter Thirteen

The vodka burned its way down Sam Avalon's throat and he savored the pain, savored the feeling of still being alive. The small dining room they'd designated as the officer's lounge was still spare and undecorated, the walls bare, silvery metal, the plastic on the built-in tables aged and cracked and ugly. By contrast, the bottle of vodka thrown in as a celebratory gift for finalizing the deal on the station was a work of art, crafted by hand in one of the family workshops that dotted the Belt. The crystal caught the harsh, industrial light and shattered it into dazzling rainbows, shifting as he refilled his glass.

"More?" He held the bottle up for Telia Proctor, who was staring at her half-full cup as if it contained all the mysteries of life.

She made a face at the clear alcohol, then downed the rest of it in a gulp, holding her cup out for him to pour.

"This seems such a strange thing to do," she mused, her voice harsh and rasping. "To intentionally ingest a poison in small doses just to alter your mood. And yet I am told by others who have studied the ancient texts it was one of the first things humans did when they evolved to tool-users. Honey, potatoes, mare's milk, wheat, rye, agave root, whatever we put our hands to, we eventually ferment and use to dull our senses."

"I don't feel qualified to comment on evolutionary psychology," Sam admitted, setting the bottle down on the battered plastic table, then resealing it with his free hand. "But maybe it's got something to do with flight-or-fight and the psychological toll it takes on you, being yanked up and down by adrenalin. Or maybe it's just a way for people to forget their troubles."

He sat down on the bench seat behind the table; it creaked and moaned in protest and yielded slightly beneath his weight. Telia didn't try to sit, which was probably wise given how much she massed with her bionics.

I wonder if she even needs to sit, he mused.

"I don't," she said and he blinked, convinced he'd blurted his thoughts out loud. "Everyone thinks it," she explained, the corner of her mouth turning up. "I saw it in your eyes. I don't need to sit down, though I do just to be polite sometimes." She nodded at the flimsy booth arrangements in the lounge. "Not on this shit, though."

Sam chuckled, saluting her with his glass.

"Sorry," he offered, after taking another sip of the vodka. "Didn't mean to be so obvious."

"This is a paradise compared to what I have grown used to." She shook her head. "At least you judge me for who I am, not what I lost."

Maybe the vodka was getting to her, he thought; she hadn't been this talkative since he'd met her.

"You know, if you want," he ventured, feeling a bit daring with a couple drinks in him, "we could fix you up. It would take a few weeks, but I know Priscilla could pull the strings, get it done."

She glanced at him sharply, as if he'd insulted her, and he nearly flinched back, sure he'd gone too far. But then she hissed out a breath and he could tell she'd been thinking of it herself.

"There was a time," she told him, "when I would have been horrified at the idea. A time when I would have considered it unholy blasphemy. Now, I only think of where I would go if I accepted your offer. I still couldn't return to Earth, and if not to return home, why would I bother?"

"You could make a home with us," he offered. "I know the Patrol could find a spot for you."

"And where is your home, Sam?" she wondered, eyeing him in a way that made him uncomfortable, as if he were being judged. "My home was Grayson City. It was where my mother was born, where her parents were born, where *their* parents were born, back until before the war. What is your home?"

Sam thought about the question a beat longer than he'd intended. When he answered, he tried to be honest.

"I was born on Aphrodite. Not in the capital, not in Dauphin City, in one of the smaller settlements where no one admits to being from." He leaned back into the booth seat, ignoring the groaning plastic. "Its official name is New Manilla, but all my friends called it Vanilla." He snorted at the memory and took another sip. His lips felt a little numb. "My mom and dad worked for the Natural Resources Commission, cataloguing land mammals on the southern continent and we all thought I'd wind up taking a job alongside them when I graduated Primary Education." He tilted his head to the side, a diffident shrug. "But I tested out for the Patrol instead, so I got sent to the Academy."

"You could not have studied to work with your parents instead?" Telia was frowning, as if she found the concept offensive. "You were forced to be in the military?"

He chuckled at her indignant look.

"Forced? Everyone wants to be in the Patrol. It's a privilege to serve. All my friends were so jealous…"

"But was it what you wanted?" she insisted.

"That's just how we do things," he tried to explain. "The tests we go through aren't just to find out what we'd be good at, they're to find out what we'd be most happy doing, too. They were designed by Mother Herself and everyone accepts them."

"Not everyone." The comment was sullen, her eyes focused downward at the deck.

"Yeah, I know Mawae complains about the way they force kids to train to be Sensitives," he acknowledged, waving a hand. "But that's a special case. Not one in a hundred thousand people have the qualities necessary to be a Sensitive, and it's vital to the security of the Resolution."

"And what is of use to the Resolution is all that matters?"

He was trying to make his brain work to come up with a reasoned response, trying not to get mad at the woman who'd just saved them all, when he was rescued by the poorly-fitted lounge door scraping open. Priscilla shuffled in, exhaustion dragging at her, and fell into the seat beside him, and John Gage followed behind her, slipping through and dragging the door shut. He stepped into the compartment with his hands clasped behind his back, his face impassive.

"We were very fortunate," he said, picking up the bottle of vodka and eyeing it critically. "None of the cargo shuttles were badly damaged by the debris field, and no one was injured."

Gage popped the lid and took a long draw straight from the bottle. Sam raised an eyebrow, but Gage just smiled as he set the crystalline container down on the table and sighed in satisfaction.

"We used to call this Rocket Rotgut," he confided. "Those Belters really know how to make vodka."

"Did we find out anything from the bodies?" Sam wondered.

"Their IDs were fake," Priscilla told him. She rubbed her eyes with the heels of her hands. "No huge surprise. Their DNA signatures and what we can tell from their medical history points to them being from Earth, originally, but we have no idea if they migrated elsewhere."

"You can't check their DNA against your database?" Sam asked Gage, surprised.

"We do not keep records of our people's DNA unless they are criminals or blasphemers, or known agitators. These three were none of those."

That seemed a short-sighted policy to Sam, but he didn't say so; it wouldn't have been polite.

"We'll keep investigating," Gage promised, "but whoever sent these men undoubtedly covered their tracks well."

"Who do you *think* sent them, Minister Gage?" Sam asked him, perhaps a bit too frank under the influence of the vodka.

The old man leaned on the table and Sam wondered perversely if it would collapse beneath his weight. He looked between Sam and Priscilla.

"This is strictly off the record," he insisted, "and if you repeat it, I'll deny it." The corner of his mouth quirked. "I know you aren't recording me because nothing in this station works well enough for that. This was likely the work of the Naturalists." He shrugged expressively. "Perhaps not any of their public leadership, but some more covert wing of the party. It would suit their aims and interests if this project were to fail, and some of their lot are deep enough into denial that they might convince themselves the threat from the ramship isn't real."

"I managed to get ahold of Peterman," Priscilla said. "Finally."

She grabbed the bottle and poured another shot into the glass she'd taken from in front of Sam, then swallowed half of it in a gulp. She made a face, and Sam wasn't sure if it was from the taste of the alcohol or the aftertaste of talking to Peterman.

"I had to get the message through Danabri to him, but I informed him of the attack. He assured me the security scanners and the energy shield generator will be on the next shipment from Aphrodite."

"Well thank Gaia for small fucking favors," Sam muttered. He caught Telia's eye. "Are you okay? Have you ever had to…" He trailed off, gesturing at her sidearm.

She shrugged, a jerky, mechanical motion.

"I am a Guardian. This is my duty." Her voice was firm and solid…but she took the bottle and refilled her glass.

"So what now?" Sam addressed Gage this time. "What is the Consensus going to do about this? Can you actually take any action against the Naturalists?"

"Not openly," the man admitted. "They hold too much power in the government. But as Guardian Proctor can attest, I and my office are rather…" He grinned like a stalking wolf. "…old fashioned. We can arrange for lessons to be taught, informally." He waved a hand expansively. "I can't *guarantee* they won't act again, but this attempt was a best-case scenario for us. It was unsuccessful and embarrassing enough to keep their heads down for a while, which should give us time to button this place down, with the help of your Patrol."

"It doesn't make sense to me," Sam admitted, finally giving voice to the doubts eating at him since he'd had time to calm down. Three sets of eyes fixed on him and he shrugged, uncomfortable at the scrutiny. "I mean, suppose it had worked just like they'd planned it. Suppose they planted the explosives at, say, the reactor level, caused a catastrophic plasma leak and made the station so much uninhabitable slag. Do they think we were all just going to give up?"

"Maybe they heard Peterman's dickering over money and assumed we wouldn't pay for a replacement station," Priscilla ventured, taking another drink. "I can't honestly say we would…" She shrugged. "Though, if the two of us had been killed, it would likely have caused enough outrage to keep the decision-makers from pulling the plug on the project. It might still have delayed it."

"All it would have done is made us look bad," Gage said, his eyes fixed on something behind the bulkheads of the lounge. "You're right, Captain Avalon," he decided, focusing on Sam again. "It doesn't seem to make much sense. Then again, men and women who resort to violence to make political points often don't think about things the way you or I might."

He checked the readout on the computer display built into the sleeve of his jacket.

"I must return to the cargo ship. There are meetings to be arranged, and I have to get back to Earth to arrange them." He nodded to Sam and Priscilla. "Call me directly if you need anything." Then he faced Telia Proctor and carefully, precisely saluted her. "You performed admirably, Guardian Prime Proctor."

Sam could see Telia's cheeks redden in surprise and embarrassment, but she returned the salute.

"Thank you, sir," she said sharply.

Gage released the salute and headed out the door, but Telia was still staring after him, her hand halfway down from her shoulder, as if she didn't want to let the moment go.

"Everything is clamped down for now," Priscilla said gently, reaching out to touch Telia's shoulder to get her attention. The Guardian glanced at the other woman's hand curiously, as if unsure how to react to it. "Why don't you go try to get some sleep? Gaia knows when we'll get another chance."

"Thank you," Sam told her before she could step through the hatchway. At Telia's questioning glance, he elaborated. "For saving us all."

"As I said, I am a Guardian. This is my duty."

Then she was gone, leaving the two of them alone. Sam looked at his hands, realized they were shaking. He wondered if Telia's hands would have been shaking if they'd been biological.

Priscilla covered his fingers with hers, holding them tight in the secure warmth of her grip. He met her eyes and tried to smile.

"That's twice now we've almost gotten ourselves killed," he pointed out, attempting humor but realizing even as he said it how tremulous the words sounded. "Third time's the charm."

"Under normal circumstances," she replied, her own smile more confident than his, but still a bit wan, "I'd prescribe all three of us a regimen of counselling sessions with a qualified trauma therapist. But since we're likely to be working another shift tomorrow, why don't we just go back to our cabin and try to relax the old-fashioned way?"

She rose and tugged him up with her and he didn't resist. He was a male, and still breathing, so he wasn't about to turn down the offer, but if he were being honest with himself, he wanted her companionship at the moment even more than the intimacy. He'd spent his whole career in small ships light-years from home, surrounded by enemies, but at this moment he felt more alone than he ever had before.

*   *   *

Priscilla's skin was as smooth as the porcelain dolls Sam had seen in the craft markets on Mars, as soft as the silk in the hand-made gowns he'd seen Consensus ambassadors wear at formal dinners, and he reveled in the feeling, in the warmth. She gasped and he covered her mouth with his to devour the emotion. There was an urgency to his movements, an imperative to go through the motions of procreation so soon after facing what might have been the end.

When he was finally spent, he collapsed as if the very life had gone out of him, breath rasping harshly as he tried to bring his respiration back under control. Priscilla snuggled into his arm, her head across his chest, warm against the constant chill of their cabin. He felt her fingers teasing at his chest hair and rolled his head around, staring into her eyes, so blue they nearly gleamed in the glow of the chemical lightstrips lining the deck. Her hair was loose and wild; but rather than seeming disheveled, it was a crown, the mane of a wild horse running free across the plains.

"You are so beautiful," he blurted. He knew it sounded clumsy and inane, something a schoolboy would say.

"It's distracting," she stated.

He thought at first she was complaining, saying her physical appearance distracted people from her authority and intelligence, but then he frowned and reconsidered. The words had been more along the lines of an...explanation?

"It was designed to be distracting," she elaborated. "The same as the pheromone dispensers I used on Mars." She made an almost imperceptible motion with her head and left shoulder that could have been a shrug. "I...we thought it might provide an advantage when dealing with the Consensus, as they tend to be a bit parochial, and patriarchal as well."

"So you had Restruct surgery?" he asked.

It didn't really bother him. It was discouraged, of course, except in cases when accidental injury necessitated it. The Resolution wasn't against it for religious or ethical reasons, like the Consensus; it was just a social norm for people to embrace who they were rather than trying to constantly change themselves to meet some external standards. Everyone was born genetically perfect, of course, with no defects or flaws for which you could control, but there was still a lot of variation between people. If not, his skin wouldn't have been almond colored against her pale white.

But it wasn't unheard of, either, and if she'd done it on orders for a mission… He wondered if she'd go back to the way she'd been before once the assignment was over.

"No, not exactly." She closed her eyes and laid her head back on the pillow. "Sam, there's something you should know about me."

"You're married?" He cursed himself the moment he said it. "I'm sorry," he babbled immediately, sitting up in bed. "I know you wouldn't do that, not without telling me."

"I'm not married," she said, scooting up in the bed. His eyes wandered across that white skin and he nearly lost the thread of the conversation again. "But I'm not who you think I am." She winced, clenching her fingers. "I'm not *what* you think I am."

Now he was well and truly lost. He almost blurted "did you used to be a man?" but stopped himself, *barely.* That, too, was not totally unheard of, particularly out in the wild and wooly Belt, but the Consensus banned it outright and the Resolution discouraged it for the same reason they discouraged Restruct surgery.

"The person I am," Priscilla told him carefully, capturing his gaze in the azure bonds of his eyes, "didn't exist until shortly before you met me."

"What do you mean?" He didn't want to sound impatient; he could tell this wasn't easy for her. But she'd started this and now he was very, very worried.

"I can't say exactly."

If he'd had to fight impatience before, now Sam virtually had to pull a gun and shoot it in the chest. He wanted to say "What do you mean?" again, but didn't want to sound like a damned parrot.

"You have to understand," Priscilla implored, hands shaping a pleading gesture, "I hold a very sensitive position in the Resolution government. There are things I'm not allowed to say…"

"How high would my clearance have to be?" he wondered.

"You don't get it!" Priscilla made a sound of frustration and slammed a fist against the bed, startling him. "It's not that telling you would be breaking regulations, it's that I *physically* can't tell you! I've been *programmed* not to be able to say the words!"

"Programmed?" Sam repeated, eyes wide, face slack with confusion.

"Psychologically," she clarified.

Now confusion turned to a vague sense of horror and outrage.

"They can *do* that?" he demanded, leaning forward, one leg sliding off the bed to give him leverage, as if he were about to lunge toward whoever had done this to her.

"All I can tell you," she began, then stopped herself and tried again, frustration on her face. "All I can get away with revealing is that the way I look now, the person I am now didn't exist until shortly after we received word of your discovery. There's a reason I don't have a title or a last name."

Sam tried to wrap his mind around what she was saying, but he didn't know if he could have done it at his best; and at the moment, he was totally exhausted.

"Are you telling me you're some sort of special operative who changes your looks and identity between every assignment?" He thought the idea sounded ludicrous, like something he might have seen in a bad spy movie, but it was all he could come up with.

"I couldn't tell you if you were guessing right." She sighed and balled her fist like she wanted to hit the bed again. "I know this is really hard to understand, but I had to tell you because when all this is over…"

"They'll do it again," he finished the thought for her, finally figuring out where it all was leading. He reached out and clutched her upper arm as if he could stop it somehow. "They'll change you into someone else."

"The person I am now won't exist."

She was crying now, the tears trailing down her cheeks cautiously, treading on unfamiliar ground. Her knees came up and she clutched them to herself, burying her head against her legs. Her shoulders were shaking with sobs and he scooted across the bed to slip a comforting arm around her.

"Is there any way you can, I don't know, get a transfer? Be allowed to stay who you are?" He said the words softly into her hair.

"It's never happened." Her voice was muffled, but she wouldn't look up, wouldn't let him see her crying. "This isn't fair to you. I wasn't thinking about how hard it would be for you…I didn't understand."

"Take it easy." He rubbed at her back, kissing her shoulder. "It's okay."

The words came automatically, but he sure as hell didn't know *how* it was going to be okay.

"We have some time," he finally reasoned, trying to sound positive, hopeful, for her and for himself, because he needed it just as badly. "We have nearly three years before the ramship arrives insystem, right? They won't recall you before then, will they?"

"I don't think so." She scrubbed at her face with the heels of her hand and finally looked up at him, her eyes red. "I think I could make a case for staying until the Gate is successful. But still, at the end…"

"No one knows how much time they have," he insisted. "Today should have proven that to us." He sucked in a breath and let it out slowly, trying to calm his thoughts down. "Let's enjoy the time we have here together and when everything gets closer…" He shook his head. "Maybe you'll decide you want to do something different. Maybe we can run, go live in the Belt, or on Mars, if that's what you want."

"You'd give up your career?" she asked him, seemingly surprised.

He'd said it almost off-handedly, but to his shock, he discovered he would.

"If you'd asked me a few months ago," he admitted, "I'd've told you there was nothing more important to me than being the Captain of a Patrol ship. Now…" He shook his head. "I guess I've had my priorities adjusted."

She traced a line down his cheek with her palm, looking as if she might start sobbing again.

"Thank you. But I'm not even sure I *can* run."

"You mean the psychological programming," he presumed. At her nod, he tried to think of something clever, some way out he was sure would work. All he could think of were the walls of the small cabin closing in around them.

"We'll just have to see," he decided. "When the time comes, we'll find out."

She didn't seem convinced, but she sagged against him anyway, as if surrendering to the inevitable. She didn't even suggest they break things off, maybe because she wouldn't give up on him, or more likely because she knew he was too stubborn to give up on her.

"You know what my longest relationship has been so far?" he said, trying to lighten his tone. At her curious glance, he went on. "Six months. While I was in the Academy." He grinned lopsidedly. "If we make it to three years without you wanting to kill me, you'll have broken quite a few records."

"No promises," she warned him, a smile fighting to emerge on her tear-stained face. She was getting control, getting back to herself, he thought. "But if we hang around long enough, perhaps the Naturalists will take care of it for us."

"Third time's the charm," he reminded her.

She leaned in to kiss him, then smiled seductively and pushed him back on the bed.

"What?" She cocked an eyebrow, her hands moving down his body. "You think you've got a third time in you?"

"I think I've definitely been a bad influence on you," he reflected as she climbed atop him.

"Don't stop now," she whispered in his ear, following the words with her tongue. "Let's enjoy the time we have."

They'd have to talk more about this, he decided.

But not tonight.

Chapter Fourteen

Captain Avalon.

The voice in his head woke him from a sound sleep, and it took a moment for him to realize it wasn't the remnants of a dream. But no, he wouldn't be dreaming about Lt. Englehart. He blinked, rubbing the sleep from his eyes and squinting at the glow of the chemical lightstrips. Why, he wondered, had he never remembered to rip those damned things out?

"Yeah?" he said the words aloud, then remembered the call had come in over his neurolink and tried again. *Yeah, Englehart? What's up?*

Sir, you told me to wake you when the antimatter was scheduled to arrive. It's nearly finished decelerating and is less than an hour from achieving stable transfer position with the Gate, sir.

"Shit," he mumbled, sitting up in bed, scratching at his beard. *Need to shave this thing. Itches all the time.* He shrugged. *But Pris likes it, so...*

Excuse me, sir? I didn't catch that.

Sam shook his head. The dangers of communicating via neurolink. He never thought he'd be nostalgic for the days when nothing on the station worked.

Nothing, Englehart. We'll be right up.

"What is it?" Pris asked groggily, stretching her back catlike as she tried to wake up.

Sam grinned, suddenly forgetting about the lost sleep. Even after nearly three years together, watching her do that always drove him nuts.

"The antimatter is here," he informed her, brushing the wild, blond hair out of her face and kissing her before he rolled out of the bed.

"It's about damned time," she enthused, snapping awake instantly and scooting across to his side of the bed, jumping up and grabbing for her utility fatigues where she'd thrown them over a chair. "We have less than six months before our scheduled intercept and we haven't even been able to run a full-scale test on the Gate!"

"You still want to shuttle over and supervise personally?" he wondered, pulling on a T-shirt. He thought about indulging in a shower before he headed to the control room, but there really wasn't time for it. "Dr. Kovalev said she could handle the transfer."

"I need to be there," she insisted, running a brush through her hair, not even bothering to look in the mirror. Electrical fields working from internal memory arranged her hair the way she liked and left it clean as well, and Sam wondered idly if they couldn't come up with a full body version of that. "I need to be seen, to appear essential if we don't want Peterman or someone above him to suddenly decide they can afford to pull me out of here."

"Right," he grunted, frowning. He'd managed not to think about that possibility for months now, but maybe it was time to start thinking about it again. "If the tests go well, maybe we should talk to one of the Belter crews about arranging a getaway."

She glanced at him sharply.

"You do it," she said, nearly whispering, as if she thought the compartment was bugged, despite their incessant, paranoid precautions. "We still don't know if I might unintentionally give something away. It's better I not be in the loop."

He didn't argue the point. He'd been with her long enough to read her moods, and he could tell she wasn't holding out much hope; he also knew battling it out here and now wouldn't accomplish anything other than getting them both spun up, and there was work to be done. He fastened the front of his utility fatigue top and smoothed it down, then stepped into his ship-boots and tightened the straps, using the time to decide if he should try to cheer her up or just let it ride.

"How long do you think it'll take them to transfer the fuel?" he asked.

She'd been reaching for the latch and she paused, some of the dolorous concern gone from her face as she considered the question.

"It's a hundred kilograms of antimatter, so we're talking five storage modules, each with about thirty tons of shielding, isotope reactor and electromagnetic coils. That's a shitload of mass and you don't want to be reckless with antimatter. I imagine it's going to take the better part of fifteen or sixteen hours, and that's after they maneuver the freighter into position."

He slipped an arm around her and pulled her into a brief embrace.

"Sure you don't want me to come along?" he asked, knowing what the answer would be, but feeling he had to offer anyway.

"Someone has to be in charge here," she reminded him, but she relaxed against his chest, returning the hug. "Unless you want to leave Danabri on his own and see if he tries to stage another coup."

He snorted a laugh at that. Danabri had somehow managed to get himself assigned to the Gateway Project long-term, pulling all the strings and calling in all the favors he'd collected over his many years in the Diplomatic Corps just to stay close to Telia. Since most of their negotiation had been completed over two years ago, the Sensitive didn't have many real duties and had begun volunteering for watches in the Control Center out of sheer boredom. Sam had allowed it at first, but one of the junior watch officers had managed to piss Danabri off and he'd locked the man out of the compartment and taken over traffic control for the better part of a shift.

"It's just a few hours," she said, giving him a peck on the cheek and yanking the hatch open. It still stuck, despite the best efforts of the station's repair techs. "Love you."

"Love you, too."

They said it so casually now, he thought. Not nearly as momentous as the first time, not nearly the catharsis it had been, more like the way his parents had said it to each other every day he'd lived with them. Which, he supposed, was exactly how these things were meant to go.

She'd headed one way down the corridor, to the lift bank closest to the north polar docking bays, while he headed the other, toward the Control Center. He wasn't alone in the halls of the station, either. The place would never be crowded; it was far too outsized for its task and there were always crews out working on the Gateway framework. But now you could at least tell this was a working station with around-the-clock shifts, even if he could still recognize and name every single officer in every one of the shifts.

"Sir," a technician in a Resolution Patrol uniform said, nodding to him as she passed.

"Benitez." He returned the nod. "You heading off-shift?"

"Finally," she sighed and he chuckled in sympathy.

"I feel ya'. I'm heading on up for the antimatter delivery."

"Better you than me, sir." She rolled her eyes. "There's been a damned Belter ore shipment on the sensors for days now and I'm getting tired of staring at it." She grinned with a bit of the innate malice of someone coming off a long shift for their replacement. "But I think it's due to arrive around the same time as the antimatter, so you won't have that problem."

"Go get some sleep, Benitez," he warned her, "before I decide you're awake enough to spend another eight hours on watch."

"Yes, sir." She threw him an off-hand salute and kept moving towards her cabin.

Great. He felt the missed hours of sleep weighing him down as he stepped into the lift car. *Something else to worry about.*

*   *   *

"Good morning, ma'am. Great day to be flying, isn't it?"

Pris eyed the pilot sidelong as she strapped into the shuttle's right-hand seat, stifling a smile at their little ritual.

"I'm sure it's morning for you, Lt. Sullivan," she returned briskly, "but for me it's the middle of the night. And according to you, any day is a great day to be flying."

The young man grinned broadly beneath his helmet.

"You got that right, ma'am!" He pushed at the controls of the shuttle and loud bangs guided them away from the station's docking umbilical.

It had been Sam's idea to borrow Sully from the Consensus, and she'd been against it at first. The Earther was talented, but he lacked the wetware technology of a Resolution pilot. Sam had told her there was more to being a great pilot than implants, and she had to take his word for it. She was many things, but a pilot wasn't one of them.

"A little loop for good luck," Sully said in a sing-song voice, nudging the controls as they drifted away from the polar docking hub.

Maneuvering jets pushed sharply at the shuttle's aft portside and the bird swung around, the exterior cameras panning across the polished silver bulk of the station. It was another habit he'd developed out here, and one she'd stopped trying to break. It was useful to have a first-hand look at the outside of Gateway Station once in a while, or at least that was what she told herself to justify the waste of time and fuel.

Spending most of her time stuck in the Control Center or their cabin, it was easy to forget how massive the place was. It spun below them, a mountain of nickel-iron sparkling in the glow of the Sun; and if it wasn't the vast orbital cities circling the central Resolution worlds, it was the largest deep-space installation she'd ever seen, impressive if only for the fact it had been dragged out here physically from the Belt.

But then Sully spun the shuttle end for end, and the cameras focused on the Gateway itself, the framework they'd been building for over two years, and somehow the station paled in comparison. Gateway Station was a construction shack, bulky and utilitarian and ugly, a standardized piece of equipment hauled from one task to another. The Gateway was a work of art.

Pris didn't know much about Earth religions, but she'd seen old video of something they called a Christmas tree. The Gateway looked as if an orb weaver spider or a silkworm had set about trying to spin a Christmas tree ornament out of pure gold. What it really resembled, she knew on a purely technical level, was the heart of a Teller-Fox warp unit writ so large it was barely recognizable.

Superconductive fibers basked gold in the exhausted rays of the long-traveled sunlight, woven and braided and twisted into shapes so intricate they seemed to shed the eye. Embedded in the gilded spider-web were kernels of glittering diamond, flattened ovoid jewels nested in the curling cables, defying her attempts to pinpoint where and how they were attached.

The Gateway might have been the handiwork of the gods were it not for the small, pressurized maintenance shacks squeezed into the empty spaces between strands, temporary airlocks jutting out from them in ugly, pragmatic contrast. Tiny maintenance sleds scooted from one shack to another on puffs of vaporized gas, pinpricks of light to give the gigantic structure scale. Here and there, construction pods floated in place above ragged bits of wire, their waldos trimming and bonding and splicing with the precision of brains linked wirelessly to the mechanical appendages.

Dwarfing the shacks and the sleds and the pods was the Resolution star freighter, huge for a Transition Drive ship, a bulging, flattened cylinder so large it had to be equipped with a second Teller-Fox unit amidships in order to form a rift wide enough to fit it. Part of the cylinder was laid open, the cargo doors swung out on hinges to allow access to the antimatter storage pods. Even as she watched, the first of them was being slowly tugged out of the cargo bays through the concerted efforts of a half a dozen maintenance sleds, their tow cables spooled out and attached to the pod magnetically.

It all seemed frighteningly close, as if she could reach out and touch the sparkling globe or the dull grey sheen of the freighter; it was an illusion, the work of the viewscreen's automated magnification working together with the video signals from the Gate's security drones. In reality, they were tens of thousands of kilometers away from the Gate and it was going to take a frustratingly long time to match velocities with it.

Pris felt the shuttle's main engines engage, just a light shove barely more forceful than the maneuvering thrusters, and she settled in for the ride.

*   *   *

"What are the odds?" Sam muttered half under his breath, staring at the sensor display.

"Sir?" Patel, the sensor tech on duty for the shift looked up from his station, eyebrows arching. He was a tall man who always seemed annoyingly alert and on-the-ball even after working eight straight hours in the Control Center.

"What are the odds this ore barge," Sam clarified, indicating the shipment from the Belt with his left forefinger, "would be arriving at just the same time as the antimatter delivery?"

Patel shrugged with an expressive motion of hands, shoulders and face; it looked as if he were a stage actor, Sam thought, trying to project the movement out to an audience.

"I'd say it's close to one hundred percent, sir," the Resolution tech guessed, "since the Belters send the barges out on a regular schedule and it's been six days since the last one. It's just a coincidence."

"Prapanca," Sam took a step across the compartment, cleaner and more brightly lit now after two years of occupation, to stand behind the Communications officer. "Find me the overrides for the barge's automated systems. I want to hit the braking thrusters, delay its arrival by a few hours."

"Yes, sir," the woman acknowledged, scrolling through a haptic hologram, another piece of equipment the Resolution had retrofitted onto the ancient bucket of a station. Propanca chuckled as she brought up the remote access to the control systems of the barge. "The Belters aren't going to like me screwing around with their barges. You'd think the things were made of solid iridium as precious as they are with them."

The barge floated across the holographic display, skeletal and bulky all at once, a series of hollow frames holding in place thin, disposable containers filled with processed, powdered nickel-iron, iridium, gold, and platinum for the Resolution fabricators to churn into parts for the Gateway. Massive fusion engines capped either end of the ship, without the need for either physical or energy shielding because the barge was uncrewed. At the moment, neither drive was active; the barge had fired a deceleration burn two days ago and was due a final one in another twenty hours to take it to a braking orbit near the construction site.

"A six-g burn for two minutes ought to slow her down enough," Sam told Propanca, leaning over the console beside the Comms station. "If we need to, we can give her a kick in the ass in a few hours, after our freighter is on her way back to the Transition Point."

"Gotcha," she murmured, absorbed in her task of inputting the clearance codes they'd wheedled out of the Belters during the negotiations.

Sam noticed her hands pausing, glanced down and saw a confused frown pass across her sharp, chiseled features.

"What the hell?" she said, annoyance in her tone. Her fingers moved again, and Sam could tell she was re-inputting the code.

"Problem?" he wondered.

"The damn hunk of junk isn't accepting the codes they gave us, sir," Propanca snapped, and he knew the anger in her voice wasn't aimed at him but the Belters, who they'd all come to view with a mixture of vexation and outright resentment. "I keep getting an error code! I bet the paranoid assholes gave us the wrong sequence."

"Keep trying," he told her, "but if you can't get it to give up control, I want you to use the Patrol decryption protocols."

She craned her head back toward him, eyebrows raised.

"Those are strictly for emergency use, aren't they, sir?"

"I'll take full responsibility, Lieutenant," he assured her. He grinned crookedly. "What's the worst they could do to me? Stick me on a construction shack for three years?"

She barked a laugh and turned back to her station to start the process. He snuck a look at the track of Priscilla's shuttle on the sensor display; she'd cleared docking and Sully had done his usual slow turn to get a look at the station before boosting towards the Gate assembly. They were running at about a half-g acceleration, only a few hundred kilometers out. He considered for a moment whether he should bother her with the problem, but decided against it. The barge was still an hour out and even if they couldn't slow it down, its course would take it kilometers away from the freighter.

"Sir!"

The alarmed, antiphonal chorus came from the sensor tech, Patel, and a half-second later, Propanca, who still had the barge on her screen. Sam needed neither of them to tell him what was happening; his eyes were glued to the main viewer, where the star-bright flare of the barge's rear fusion drive filled the display. The ungainly vessel seemed to shudder and vibrate with the sudden burst of acceleration and he was seeking out the readouts even as Patel was announcing them.

"Ten gravities!" The man's voice broke halfway through the second syllable and he came halfway out of his seat. "Gaia's bloated ass, *twenty* gravities!" He looked over at Sam and his eyes were pools of white set against the tan of his skin. "Sir, it's gonna rip itself apart!"

"What the living fuck!" Propanca yelled, slamming a hand against the console. "The decryption protocols aren't penetrating the system because it's locked us out totally! This is no fucking accident!"

"Calm down, Lieutenant," he said, forcing himself not to yell, not to rage. It wouldn't do any good. "Get Minister Gage on the line now, I don't care if he's taking a shit or climbing a mountain, I want to be talking to him personally in two minutes."

He rounded on Patel, who seemed on the verge of panic.

"I saw the maneuvering jets," he told the man. "When the burn began, it fired the port bow maneuvering jets. What's its current heading?"

"Umm…" The technician dithered for a second, falling back into his chair. "It's heading is…" He swallowed, his Adam's apple bobbing visibly, then looked back at Sam with an expression of utter helplessness. "Sir, it's going to collide with the Gateway in less than ten minutes."

Sam knew there were Consensus military vessels only minutes away, and he knew by the time he got the message through Gage to them, it would be far too late. He banged his fist down on the control for the station's general alarm and leaned over the intercom pickup as it blared.

"Attention all station personnel," he barked, his voice clear and piercing. "Get to your emergency shelters immediately and secure for impact!"

*   *   *

"Oh, this ain't good."

Sully was seeing it in his helmet's HUD, but for Priscilla, it was splashed across the viewscreen, big as life and twice as devastating. The image of the ore barge was projected from the station's external cameras, but the thing was close enough they could have seen it with the naked eye, if they hadn't been facing the wrong direction. And accelerating the wrong direction…

"Hold on!" the pilot warned her and she felt the engines cut thrust.

Pris! It was Sam, of course, piggybacking his neurolink over the station's communications array. *Pris, the barge is boosting right for the Gate assembly! You two have to get the hell out of there!*

Maneuvering thrusters slammed her against her restraints and she couldn't even think to transmit until the force let up. The shuttle was swinging around, still coasting toward the glistening beauty of the Gate assembly, but turning its tail to face the thing.

I see it, she told him. She wondered why she wasn't screaming, raging, shouting out orders. Instead, an odd calm had descended over her, the inescapable realization there was not a damned thing she could do about it.

Another burst of the steering jets, shoving her the opposite angle into the side of her acceleration couch, and then the main engines roared to life again and pushed her straight back into the liquid-filled cushions.

Dr. Kovalev is trying to evacuate the construction assembly to the freighter, and Gage says his ships are launching on the barge, but…

It's going too fast, she said, not so much a question as a statement of fact. *They won't be able to stop it.*

The perspective on the shuttle's screens had shifted, widening to keep the barge in the field of view, progressing from one of the remote camera feeds to another. It was so close, too damned close, and this time it was no illusion, no camera tricks. The image was blurry, and she wondered if the camera drone was too close, if the radiation from the drive was affecting it, whether it would kill her and Sully…until she realized it was the barge vibrating, shuddering under more acceleration than it had been built to handle. Bits of it, pieces of cargo containers, service hatch covers, microwave antennae, it was all peeling off and spinning away, still traveling forward but losing the acceleration of the fusion drives. Most of it was burned up in the flare of plasma from the main engine and she thought for a long time she would be next, but the drive abruptly cut off.

Burned through all the fuel it had left, she thought...or maybe she transmitted it to Sam, she wasn't sure.

"Shit, ma'am," Sully said, drawing the first word out into three syllables. "That thing's gonna hit."

She couldn't see his face beneath the helmet's visor, but she could discern the expression from his tone. He was running through the possibilities, seeing what she already had; the shuttle had burned away its velocity and was slowly pushing forward now, but if he increased their acceleration, he wouldn't have enough fuel left to decelerate before he impacted the station. And if he maneuvered past the station, they'd wind up drifting in open space.

"Do it," she told him. His head turned toward her and she figured he was wondering if the rumors he'd heard about Resolutionists were true and they could read your mind. "It's better than the alternatives."

"You're the boss, ma'am."

He slammed the throttle forward and pushed the steering yoke to the starboard with the enthusiasm of a young man convinced of his own immortality, and Priscilla's breath left her in a pained whoosh of air as acceleration slammed her back and sideways simultaneously. The shuttle, like the barge, couldn't carry enough fuel to keep that kind of boost up for long, but two minutes at six gravities felt like forever.

Still, when the burn ended and her breath returned, along with zero gravity, she didn't feel relieved. They'd moved, and they were still moving, but not fast enough and not nearly far enough yet. The station was sliding past their starboard side, its smooth, silver hull taking up the entire right side of the main display, and just maybe if they could maneuver it between them and the barge before...

She hadn't realized she'd been grinding her teeth until the barge struck, not the Gate assembly but rather the freighter, with three of the five antimatter containment pods still resting inside. No, she corrected herself, instantly recognizing the flare of light for what it was, the barge *hadn't* struck the freighter; she had ignited whatever tiny bit of fuel she'd had left for her forward drive and sent a star-hot explosion of plasma into the hold.

A physical blow might not have ruptured the pods, even the impact of the mass of the barge travelling at thousands of meters per second. The plasma burned through their thick casing just deep enough to take out the isotope batteries, and when the magnetic fields snapped off for lack of power, kilograms of antimatter touched the alloy walls of the pods. Just as the bulk of the station slipped between the shuttle and the Gate, the largest anthropogenic explosion in the history of humankind ripped reality apart.

Chapter Fifteen

"Go! Go, Goddamnit!"

Sam pushed Patel and Propanca ahead of him, nearly throwing them both at the entrance to the emergency access tubes. The lifts were potential suicide at worst and hours trapped in claustrophobic isolation at best, and neither appealed to him. Using the access tubes this far out towards the rim was chancy as well, but one he was willing to take.

The entrance to the tubes wasn't so much a hatchway as a ladder, a concave set in the bulkhead, the rungs well-surfaced and well-worn on this ancient relic of a station. Centripetal force made outward towards the rim "down," which meant they'd have to climb toward the hub, and the climb would be hardest starting out...and if you fell, you'd get slammed back down at increasing velocity as the perceived gravity increased.

Sam chivvied the Control Center crew ahead of him, his impatience building like a pressure vessel under heat as he watched the two of them take far too long to get their career-rear-echelon asses up that damn ladder. He thought about calling Minister Gage again, but with the transmission delay between Earth and their orbit, this was all going to be over before he could get a reply. Then he thought about calling Pris again, but she and Sully would either make it or they wouldn't, and there was nothing left unsaid between them.

Telia, he called instead. *What's the status in the shelter?*

Mawae is there, and reports we have all but fifteen personnel inside the shelter, she told him, her voice converted to neural signals and then squirted into the audio centers of his brain and still managing to sound infuriatingly calm.

What's Danabri doing there? he demanded, feeling the once-checkered surface of the ladder rungs now perfectly smooth under his palms. Above him, Propanca's ship-boot slipped off a rung and he winced at the idea of her falling and taking him back down to the bottom with her. *I told you to take charge of the shelter until I got there.*

I am at the crew quarters, making sure everyone gets to safety, she declared, her tone stolid and unyielding. *I will be in the shelter momentarily.*

Damn it, Telia…

My transponder readout shows you are not in the shelter yet either, Captain.

Yeah, point taken, he acknowledged to himself, not wanting to give her the satisfaction of knowing she'd got him with the barb.

I'm on my way. Get into that shelter, Telia. Afterward, I'm going to need people I can count on still healthy and moving.

Yes, sir. I am, as you say, on my way.

He grunted with a feeling of accomplishment in getting the woman to take an order for once.

"Faster you two!" he barked, wanting to push Propanca's butt out of his way but realizing it would be a bad idea for several reasons.

The tunnel was color-coded for each level and they'd passed out of blue, the furthest out, through green and now into yellow, and he thought he could feel the difference in the perceived gravity of the spin. They could have taken it all the way into red, the hub itself, but they didn't need to go that far; the shelter was on Magenta, the last level out from the hub so as not to block the channels for freight from either polar docking facility.

That's what those Belter engineers say, anyway. None of them were even born when this thing was built so they probably have no idea.

He linked back up with the external camera view, counting on the regular space of the rungs to keep his hands and feet going to the right place and surrendering his eyes for just a moment, something he hadn't been willing to risk when he was running through the corridor. The barge's drives were dark and she was coasting on the velocity she'd built up on the heavy burn, but it was going to be enough; the Gate assembly wasn't going anywhere.

His foot slipped when he noticed the barge's course had changed, ever so slightly, while he hadn't been watching, and he barely caught himself before he began to slide back down the chute. He cursed under his breath, but chanced another view through the link, confirming what he'd thought he read on the sensor display: the barge was going to impact the freighter. It hadn't moved, mostly because it couldn't, not with the cargo bays yawning open and three antimatter storage pods loose in their collars, ready to transport.

We have maybe a couple minutes, he thought, blinking the camera feed out of his eyes.

Best- and worst-case scenarios ran through his head, and the best wasn't that good: the barge would destroy the freighter, kill dozens of crewmembers and send the antimatter storage containers careening off into the black. The worst-case scenario was one or more of the pods would rupture and only Gaia knew what would happen then. He didn't think it was too likely, and if whoever had set this up had been familiar with antimatter storage, they would have known that. Those pods were designed to be fail-safe, both because of the sheer destructive power of antimatter and the fiendishly high cost of producing it.

That means it's Earthers, probably, he reasoned, trying to keep his mind off how long it was taking Patel to get through the hatchway to Magenta Level, trying to keep himself from screaming at the man. *Belters would know better because they've dealt with us before.*

163

Then he was out of the chute and bounding across the deck in the lower gravity of the innermost layer of the station, with Patel and Propanca and six or seven other crewmembers ahead of him, some clambering out of other emergency access tubes, others having taken the chance of using the lift cars. Some of them were half-dressed, woken out of a sound sleep; all of them were close to panicking, rushing for the shelter hatch like it was deliverance from evil instead of a few extra centimeters of alloy and some honeycomb-boron armor.

He didn't see Telia yet, but Danabri was in the open hatchway, yelling orders in a knee-length puce housecoat and maroon slippers, pushing people inside, shoving them through roughly, with little patience. Sam paused, letting the others go ahead of him, and tried linking with the Control Center computer one more time, while he had the chance.

He'd barely re-established contact before the barge's forward fusion drives ignited, abrupt and unexpected enough to make him jump. He had just enough time to feel the bottom fall out of his stomach as everything seemed to emerge into sudden, terrifying clarity. Plasma flared in the distance and then a flash brighter than any supernova in the history of the universe washed the cameras out, overwhelming their ability to filter one bit of data from another.

He could only guess what happened next. He wasn't a physicist, but you needed to know something about the science and the math of it all to pilot a starship, which was how he'd begun his career, or to be the captain. The initial explosion was straight-forward, if horrific, just a blast of annihilated matter and antimatter, heat beyond the interior depths of the brightest star and a wash of radiation so intense it should have killed them all immediately, even from tens of thousands of kilometers away. But it didn't, and he thought he knew why: the Gate. It was mostly complete, all it needed was power.

Something solid slammed into the station, something very much like a shock wave even though there was no atmosphere to propagate it, a concussion Sam could feel in his soul…and his shoulder. The snap of his clavicle breaking was almost louder than the roaring vibration of the station's outer hull, almost louder than the thump of his body against the bulkhead. He cried out, not quite a scream because he lacked the breath for it, but damned close, and sank to the floor…no, he realized, not the floor, he was sinking to what had been a wall only a moment ago.

Gravity shouldn't be this heavy. He felt as if something was stomping on his chest, grinding the broken bones in his shoulder against each other. His vision seemed blurry, and he couldn't tell if the encroaching darkness was a power outage or impending unconsciousness, but he could still see there was someone on the deck in front of him, someone short and bearded, with their face covered in blood, their eyes wide open.

Man's neck shouldn't be able to bend like that, he mused, and then the blackness closed over him and washed consciousness away.

*   *   *

Telia Proctor was pushing the last of the stragglers ahead of her to the emergency access tubes when it happened.

She couldn't rightly say *what* happened. If she'd been forced to describe the feeling afterward, she might have said it was very much as if a deep-space station the size of a small island had run aground on the shores of something much, much larger. At the moment, her only sensation was a huge, jarring impact and the bulkhead racing straight at the back of her skull.

165

If she'd been fully biological, if she'd ever got around to accepting Sam and Priscilla and Mawae Danabri's offers to have her bionics replaced by cloned limbs, she'd have died right there, her head split open like a ripe melon. Instead, she tucked and rolled in mid-air and her feet slammed into the thin plastic lining over the bulkhead with enough force to shatter it. Flakes of white polymer sprayed out from the spider-web patterns where her feet had hit, revealing the dull, grey metal concealed under its decoration.

She stuck to the wall for just a heartbeat, as if gravity were having a difficult time making up its mind which way it should pull her, and then it abruptly decided this way was as good as any other. What had been sideways only seconds ago was now down, and that made as little sense as the idea that anything solid should have hit the station at all.

A dull, unfocused pain ran through her whole body, not unfamiliar; it was the bruising of her flesh and bone where it wrapped around the bionics. The metal and machinery could shrug off impacts that what was left of her biological material could not, and if she could keep going anyway, she'd pay for it later.

If there was a later.

The lights in the corridor were flickering fitfully, and in moments the only illumination was from the emergency chemical striplighting lining what had once been the deck. The pale, green light cast eerie shadows and turned the blood pooling around the bodies an inky black. She moved to check on the two Resolution crewmembers, a man and a woman, but both were clearly dead. The blood came from the man; he'd fractured his skull.

There was a lot of blood inside a man's head, so much more than you'd have thought. She knew his name was Georges Darnold, but couldn't remember a thing about him, not what he ate for breakfast, not what shift he worked, not even if he had a family. His face was rounded and soft and looked oddly peaceful from the front; but everything that had made him Georges was splattered across the bulkheads and the deck.

The woman's name was Edina…something. Something long and multisyllabic and Telia couldn't wrap her tongue around it. She was short and stocky and cute in a pixie sort of way, with short, blond hair and green eyes, and her neck was broken. Her head was turned nearly 180 degrees. Telia thought about another day, another accident, with broken and bleeding bodies all around her and she forced the bile back down her throat. These people, Georges and Edina, she didn't know, didn't care about. She had to remind herself of that.

She looked over at the emergency access chutes, horizontal now, and wondered if the others were still inside. They could be dead, stuck in there, but she'd have to go in, have to chance being stuck with them unless she could get some help down here. She touched the control for her personal link, hoping against hope it might still be working despite the loss of power.

"Mawae, are you there?"

Nothing. She tried a different channel.

"Captain Avalon?"

Damn. She switched to general address and tried one last time.

"Does anyone read me?" She was yelling and she forced herself back under control. The network was down and shouting wasn't going to bring it back up.

She sucked in a shuddering breath and pushed herself away from Georges and Edina, pausing to check herself for blood or broken bones before she moved again. Something was missing. The light was low; she could see through her bionic eye's infrared filters, but the shadows made it hard to pick out the details and she had to slug her brain into focus.

167

The alarms. That was what was missing, there were no alarms sounding. The corridor was totally silent but for a distant metallic wrenching, as if the loose ends torn from the station were swaying back and forth in the wind.

I am not concussed, she told herself firmly. But *why am I so…hazy? Has the air gone bad?*

If it had, the sensors and alarms weren't detecting it and there weren't any emergency suits on this level. She had to get to the shelter. She tried to shake her head clear, but it didn't seem to do any good; she gave up and went down on a knee, crawling into the access tube. The chute was lined with the ubiquitous chemical light-strips, one of the few things actually replaced by the Belters before they'd shipped the station out here. The things lasted for years, but the station had probably gone through seven or eight sets of them since its construction. Telia had come to hate them, come to hate the pale green glow and the elongated, unnatural shadows they threw, and she hated them even more crawling through that tunnel sideways.

She hadn't been a small woman before the bionics, and with them, her shoulders were as broad as a good-size man's and she could feel one and then the other scraping on the sides of the tunnel. She kept telling herself there was plenty of room, but the dead silence and the eerie, green-tinted lighting and a growing conviction something very, very bad had happened gnawed at her hind-brain, trying to convince her she was about to be stuck in there alone and helpless.

Just the way she'd been stuck in the wreckage of the shuttle, as the fire burned away her arms and legs…

"Shut up!" she snarled aloud, pulling herself forward with the ladder rungs, hearing them clank and clunk off the metal of her legs.

At least there were no bodies in the tunnel. She'd dreaded finding the ones she'd sent ahead broken and bloody, but they'd made it out somehow. That was a good thing, and so was the fact she was still breathing, which meant the hull had to be more or less intact...

Was it getting lighter? Or was it just a different tone to the light, as if the chemical strips ahead at the next level weren't there anymore. She'd been trudging along, head down, but now she craned it upward, an awkward position and difficult for her to do with the spine reinforcements.

Her mouth dropped open and she stopped scooting forward.

It suddenly made sense why there were no bodies stuck in the tubes, and why there was no atmosphere leak, and why it had felt as if they'd slammed into something solid.

A spear of nothingness sliced through half the tunnel, through half the station. Not a vacuum, not the empty darkness of outer space, but a palpable Nothing defying description. Spacers called it The Null, but she knew that wasn't accurate. There was something there, and you could just sense it like a teasing flicker out of the corner of your eye, but never perceive it because the human brain hadn't evolved for it.

It was Transition Space. The station was half in and half out of Transition Space.

Chapter Sixteen

Priscilla clawed back to consciousness through a gauze of unreality. She couldn't remember passing out, but she remembered what had happened just before, remembered the explosion, and what the explosion had triggered.

She flexed numb fingers and rubbed at her eyes, forcing them open. The shuttle's viewscreens were dark and inactive, as were the displays on the control panel; only the emergency lights remained. She took in a deep breath and decided the air wasn't stale and they weren't in any immediate danger of suffocating. If there were any hull leaks, they were too small for her to hear them.

A moan from her left drew her attention toward Sully; he was awake as well, unstrapping his helmet and pulling it off with the jerky, uncertain motions of someone not totally confident of their own limbs. He let the headgear go, as if he lacked the strength to hold onto it, and it floated listlessly across the cockpit, bouncing off the fuselage with a dolorous clunk.

Beneath the helmet, his face was pale, incomprehension in the set of his eyes.

"What. The. Fuck."

Priscilla ignored his expulsion and motioned at the grey blankness where the main cockpit display should have been.

"Can you get everything back up?" she asked. "We need to see what's going on out there."

He nodded, wincing at the motion, and yanked the quick-release for his seat harness. He kept one hand on the acceleration couch to steady himself as he stretched under the main console, pulling open a maintenance cover and tinkering with something inside.

"Yeah, it's just an overload," he said, his voice muffled by the machinery and control console between them. "I think the batteries are still charged."

There was a thump-snap sound and power began to flicker on across the cockpit, first in the light panels above their heads and then across the instrument panel. The viewscreens came last, flashing white and grey and white again before images began to resolve. She thought at first there was a problem with the cameras or perhaps the display projectors, until the details seemed to sort themselves into a pattern she could make sense of.

Where the Gate assembly had been was a…hole? An absence, she decided. That was the better word. An absence deeper and emptier than space itself, a sense of nothingness rather than an actual darkness. It was a rift in spacetime, jagged and irregular, stretching away from the source of the explosion like a shadow on the sidewalk in the late afternoon. It was the sort of opening into Transition Space a starship made with its Teller-Fox warp generator, except those were a few hundred meters across and closed within seconds. This one yawned over twenty thousand kilometers long and shrank slowly, unevenly.

Spears of it had pierced right through Gateway Station, slicing it nearly in two, peeling strips of hull away in jagged chunks, freezing it in place with its own gravity, its own laws of physics, different enough to be fatal for a human caught up in it. She rasped out a breath she hadn't been aware she was holding, her eyes frozen on the sheer, incredible spectacle of it, the eerie otherworldliness.

"Ma'am," Sully asked, his voice subdued and almost reverent, "what the hell happened?"

She stared at him askance, as if it should have been obvious.

He's from Earth, she chided herself, *and he's probably never even been out of the Solar System.* The words were her own but somehow, she heard the rebuke in

Sam's voice and her breath caught in her chest at the thought of him dead inside the station.

"The barge's engines penetrated the antimatter containment pods," she said, keeping her voice calm and modulated, holding onto patience as tightly as she could. "When the antimatter blew, the energy was absorbed by the Gate's Teller-Fox warp units."

"You mean…" He nodded at the screen, face screwed up in a disbelieving scowl. "That's a wormhole? I've seen footage from starships in pilot training, and the wormholes they open don't look nothing like that!"

"That's the sort of wormhole you get when you detonate a hundred kilograms of antimatter all at once." She felt like smacking the kid in the back of the head, but she clenched her fingers in the padded armrests of the acceleration couch and tried to think.

"It's shrinking," she said, watching the tendrils of nothingness slowly contract back towards the center, where the Gate had been. "When it pulls out of the gaps it's made in the station, they're going to lose atmosphere. Do we have communications?"

She didn't wait for his answer, just reached across the instrument panel and activated the shuttle's transmitter. It was probably a waste of time with the sort of electromagnetic interference the wormhole would be causing, but they were out of fuel and there wasn't anything else they could…

"Ma'am, why aren't we moving?" Sully wondered, a bit of outrage in his voice as if this whole business was contrary to the science he'd learned in school and he didn't want any part of it. "We were accelerating pretty hard when we went bingo fuel, we should be heading out into deep space at a pretty good velocity still." He waved at the readout on the navigation display. "We're sitting stock-still, or near as. We're at least in matching velocities with the station, and that's fuc…freaking impossible!"

"Transition Space cancels out momentum. That's why the station isn't rotating. That wormhole must have been close enough to eat our velocity."

She'd been playing with the frequency on the transmitter, but now her eyes popped up, her thoughts churning.

"Do we have any maneuvering thruster fuel left?" she demanded urgently, grabbing Sully by his flight harness.

"Well, yeah, some," he said, nodding. "We drained all the reaction mass for the main engine, but each steering jet has its own tank."

"We're only a few hundred kilometers from the docking ports," she told him, pointing at the lidar return readings. "Can we get there with the steering jets?"

Sully peered at the readings, then at the screen. The antipolar docking hub was gone, swallowed up in the thickest of the tendrils of Transition Space, but the polar end was intact, and there were at least two shuttles docked there they could see from their position, along with a row of intact docking ports.

"Yeah, we can do that," he judged, nodding slowly. "It's gonna take a bit, but we can do it."

"As quick as you can," she urged him, watching the tentacles of nonexistence retracting back toward the center. "I'm not sure how long they have."

*   *   *

"How long do we have?"

"Hard to say. Maybe minutes, maybe hours."

The voices cut through the darkness and seemed to grab Sam Avalon by the scruff of the neck and drag him back up into the light. Well, it wasn't *that* light, to be honest, more green-tinted shadow than anything else, but it was lighter than the inside of his head.

173

"What's the situation?" He tried to make the words a demand, delivered in his command tone, but they came out a rasp of sandpaper across broken glass.

He rolled over to see who he was talking to and was surprised when it didn't hurt more. Propanca was one of them, alive and seemingly unharmed and cranky as ever, standing over him with her hands on her hips and a scowl across her face. The other was Grant, one of the reactor crew who'd been off-shift, he recalled. Grant was wearing a smart bandage on his left arm and a nasty bruise on the left side of his face to match it, and looked about as happy as Propanca.

"Be careful, sir," a voice said from behind him. Belden, he realized, one of the station's two medics. "You're pretty banged up."

Sam looked down at himself, remembering what he'd been fairly sure was a broken clavicle, and saw what he hadn't been able to feel, a medical harness fitted across his shoulder where his utility fatigue top had been cut away, immobilizing his right arm while it anesthetized the area and began the process of knitting the bone. They had medical supplies in the shelter, he thought.

But he wasn't in the shelter; none of them were. He was sitting against a bulkhead in the passageway just outside the hatch to the shelter…except no, he was sitting *on* a bulkhead, leaning against the *deck*, and the shelter hatchway was set in what was now the floor. He got his feet underneath him and tried to push himself up, sliding his good shoulder against what had been the deck. Belden rushed up beside him, concern on her long, straight-boned face as she tried to steady him.

"Would somebody care to tell me what happened?" he asked, resting a hand on Belden's shoulder to catch his balance. "If any of you actually know."

Propanca and Grant exchanged a grim look before the Communications officer hissed out a breath and squared her shoulders.

"We can't be sure what happened out there," she told him, "but in here…" She trailed off and waved at the hatch to the shelter. "You should see for yourself, sir."

Belden walked with him; she was short and she got underneath his shoulder and stayed there. He knew medics and he could tell she wanted to keep nagging him not to move; that she wasn't had to be some indication of how bad things were.

"Oh yeah," he murmured softly when he stared down into the hatchway. "It's bad, all right."

Half the emergency shelter just wasn't there anymore. The compartment was bisected, sliced through from bulkhead to bulkhead by something that shed his eye, something that seemed to glow in some spectrum just outside his vision and yet was simultaneously an absence of anything. He'd seen it before, but never unshielded, never face to face. It seemed to hurt to look at, or to *try* and look at, but when he averted his eyes from it, he saw the bodies and *pieces* of bodies littering what had once been a wall.

There was surprisingly little blood; where arms or legs or torsos lay obscenely atop the debris, they seemed to have been cauterized cleanly, as if by a surgical laser.

I sent them here, he thought, the guilt crashing down on him.

He shrugged that burden off, saving it for later, for when there was time. For now, he could see exactly what Grant and Propanca had been discussing. The hull was as cleanly cut and cauterized as the bodies had been, but the nothingness of Transition Space wasn't static, it was, ever-so-slowly, pulling back. And where it did, in those millimeter-wide gaps, air was leaking out.

"There are suits in the shelter," he said, flogging his brain into action. "In the lockers…"

Then he stopped. The lockers were gone, along with the whole side of the compartment.

"The corridor is blocked off that way by the…stuff," Propanca said, waving to her right.

"Damn." He was forgetting something, he could feel it nagging at him, pounding at the back of his brain, trying to be heard. And then he knew.

"Where's Danabri?" he wanted to know, swinging his head around. "This can't be everybody…where is he?"

"He's…over here, sir." Propanca motioned behind her.

Sam pushed away from Belden and stepped past the Communications officer, into the shadows near the end of the passageway. There were three bodies lined up there, stretched lengthwise down the corridor, covered with foil blankets they'd probably salvaged from inside the shelter. He couldn't see their faces, but he saw the slippers, the pink ones Danabri had been wearing, sticking just past the end of the blanket.

"Fuck." The word gushed out of him along with all the wind in his lungs and he nearly keeled over, had to catch himself against the wall.

"The hit," Belden was saying, though the words didn't seem to register at first. "The hit at the beginning, it threw him against the bulkhead and he…he broke his neck."

Sam's breath came in long, shuddering gasps. Danabri hadn't exactly been a friend, had never let any of them close enough to call him that. But for all his abrasiveness, for all the attempts he'd made to alienate everyone around him, it could never disguise the truth: he'd been a good man, a fearless man.

Gaia, he prayed silently, *take his soul into your arms and help him find peace.*

The prayer was automatic, a product of his youth. He hadn't thought about what he believed in a long time. He doubted Danabri believed in anything.

"We have to head for the hub," he decided, dragging his thoughts away from Danabri's death and to their own survival. "We have to get to the docking ports, if they're intact."

"I went up the emergency access tubes," Grant said, eyes downcast, voice full of bitter dejection. "They're blocked by the...whatever."

"And when it pulls out," Propanca interjected sharply, "we're fucked, because the automatic pressure barriers aren't going to close with all the power down."

He stalked down the corridor towards the lift bank, staring down at it since it was now mounted in the floor.

"Do we have anything that can pry this door open?" he wondered. "We're only one level up from the hub. The lift car is probably on the other side, toward the outer levels."

The three crewmembers stared back at him dumbly, glancing at each other and then around them as if wondering where to start looking. Sam hissed out a sigh.

"Start checking every compartment we can get to," he barked, trying to snap them out of their fugue. "Fast, before that air leak turns into a giant fucking vacuum!"

It was probably a waste of time, he had to admit. He knew this station and aside from the shelter, there were no compartments with tool kits, and the tool kit for the shelter had been in the emergency vacuum suit locker, which was now nonexistent. But it was better than sitting around waiting to get sucked into space and die of asphyxiation.

The three of them scattered, Grant dropping into the shelter while Propanca and Belden started pulling open hatches to other compartments. Sam tried to make himself move to join them, fighting against a weariness dragging at him like an anchor. The medical harness was draining his blood sugar to repair his shoulder, which would be all well and good if he had the time to sit down or grab a quick snack.

He'd made it two steps away from the lift door when he heard the banging. He froze, fear crystallizing in his veins at the thought the station was being ripped apart by the wormhole. But the banging was coming from the lift door, and it was too regular to be anything natural.

Was someone trapped inside the lift? Banging on the door, waiting for help? He leaned over the lift, but flinched back when the inner edge of the door tented upward with a ringing impact.

"What the hell?" he muttered, taking a step away.

He had images of monsters emerging from Transition Space like in the bad horror movies he'd watched as a kid and began looking around for something to use as a weapon. The edge of the lift door came away from the frame with the next blow and black-gloved fingers wrapped around the jagged edge, yanking downward to make enough room for the other hand. Another, more violent wrench, and metal bent and ripped and shredded and the door was pulled down into the lift tube.

Telia Proctor emerged through the wreckage of the hatch, her short hair matted with sweat, dirt and grease and perhaps a splash of blood smeared across her face.

"Come with me," she told him, her expression grim, "if you want to live."

Chapter Seventeen

The starboard maneuvering jets gave one last, shuddering effort and then fell silent, exhausted. The polished surface of the docking port already filled the field of view in the main display, and even after exhausting all their fuel in the deceleration, it was still coming way too fast.

"This is gonna hurt," Sully warned, tucking his chin down onto his chest and cinching his flight helmet tighter.

He was right.

Metal and carbon-fiber and boron honeycomb composite screamed in a chorus of agony as they scraped across each other, the screech cut short by a brutal collision. Priscilla's head snapped sideways and her seat restraints cut into her shoulders, first one way and then back the other as the docking magnets grabbed desperately at the lock, yanking them to a sudden, violent halt.

Priscilla tasted blood and felt a sharp spear of pain in her tongue; she wanted to spit it out, but in zero gravity, it would have just floated around the cockpit with the air currents. She swallowed the blood along with any complaints she had about Sully's flying, and pulled loose her restraints.

Sully was already out of his seat, grabbing vacuum helmets for the both of them from the shuttle's locker. They'd suited up on the flight back to the station, but he hadn't wanted to give up his flight helmet's HUD until he had to, and she...

I've never worn a spacesuit before, she realized as she sealed the helmet to the neck yoke.

She knew how, of course, knew every detail of the suit's operation. But that wasn't the same as the experience, hadn't prepared her for the claustrophobic sensation of her breath reflecting back into her face, for the chill of the air flow washing over her cheeks, for the subtle distraction of the instrument lights just out of her line of sight.

Just like knowing every point of data about the human reproductive system didn't prepare me for sex. Or love, for that matter.

Sully had the inner lock open and was working the manual hand-crank for the outer lock; the station was dead, the reactor lost somewhere in Transition Space. She hung over his shoulder, waiting with thinning patience as the dark gap between the halves of the outer lock grew larger with excruciating listlessness.

"You go prep one of the other shuttles," she told him, knowing she was repeating herself but needing to be doing *something*. "They may be damaged so make sure you run an external diagnostic…"

"With all due respect," Sully grunted with effort, bracing himself against either side of the lock to get leverage to turn the crank, "teach your grandma to suck eggs, ma'am."

Priscilla blinked, staring at him.

"Why would my grandmother want to suck eggs?"

"Jesus," Sully breathed, and she thought he sounded exasperated but she didn't know why.

Finally, the gap widened enough for her to squeeze through and she pushed him aside, squirting out into the docking bay. Her suit's helmet light cut through the stygian blackness, turning dust and floating debris into a glittering starfield and sending shadows dancing through cargo loading arms and freight conveyors. A body drifted through the cone of light, black elongations of its askew arms and legs stretching for meters through the bay, and she nearly jerked away from it by instinct, the tensing of her muscles sending her floating back towards the airlock.

The light on her helmet bobbed up and down with her own movement, but it settled when Sully grabbed her arm to anchor her. The body was a man, an Earther, one of the few on their crew. Johan his name was, she remembered, one of the dock workers. He was older, his face worn to leather by wind and sun from a life lived outside on a living world. He wore his long, greying hair in a pony-tail, and it bobbed loosely behind him now, swatting like its namesake at an orbiting cloud of crimson globules. The blood had coursed from a deep wound in his forehead and for a long moment she thought he was dead...until she realized dead people didn't bleed.

"He's alive!" she blurted, pushing out of Sully's grasp and catching the man's arm.

She might have simply gone drifting off with him, but Sully was more used to zero-g work and he'd attached his magnetic boots to the deck, anchoring himself before he reached up and grabbed her ankle, pulling her back down.

She had to remind herself to engage her own magnets when she touched the deck, too used to the Resolution sticky plates by now; the suit she was wearing was from the Consensus shuttle, and was bulkier and less fitted, and lacked the nanotechnological niceties of a Resolution version. With her feet secured, she pulled Johan down to her; there was still air in the bay and he seemed to be breathing steadily. She tried to pat at the suit's exterior pockets for the medical kit, but Sully was ahead of her, wrapping a bandage around the wound and securing it in place.

Not a smart bandage, she thought, clucking to herself. No nanotech in her boots, none in the bandage; just some quick-clotting powder and antiseptic chemicals. She looked at Johan's face, so pale and slack, and hoped that would be enough.

"Get him to the shuttle with you," she told Sully, letting loose of the unconscious man, "while the atmosphere in here is still holding out. I'm going to head in and try to find them."

181

She didn't wait for his acknowledgement; she freed her magnetic soles from the deck and kicked off toward the equipment lockers. They were built into the bulkhead next to the lift banks, and she glanced towards the lifts, but the controls were dead, the doors sealed shut. She was about two meters from the lockers when the micro-gravity turned not-so-micro; without a bit of warning, she was *falling*, and not free-falling either, falling with at least a standard gravity, toward what had been the bulkhead.

"Shit!" she blurted, pinwheeling her arms and twisting her body in mid-air with the grace and agility designed into her, trading her feet for her head.

Her knees bent as she hit, and she could feel the twinge of all her weight and the suit's mass as well pounding against the bulkhead with a thud of metal boot soles on metal walls. She stayed where she was, crouched in place, sucking in breaths that didn't seem to come deep enough, the gasping gulps of air deafening inside her helmet.

What the hell? Where was the gravity coming from? The station wasn't rotating… Could it be the ingress of the wormhole? Starships could generate artificial gravity in Transition Space because of the differing physical laws there, but she'd never heard of anything like this.

Doesn't matter, woman, she snapped at herself. *Move.*

The equipment lockers were in the floor and the doors hadn't been built to stay open when sideways was down; she had to wedge herself halfway into one of the lockers, then she had to figure out how to turn down the brightness of her headlamp because it was washing out everything inside the cabinet.

There they were, the emergency ventilators. Small air tanks attached to regulators, they were meant for emergency air during an atmosphere leak; they'd be useless out in space since they'd freeze up almost immediately, but they might keep survivors alive long enough to get to a shuttle or an escape pod if the hull was breached. She grabbed an armful of them and pushed herself up from the cabinet, letting it slam closed.

It took her a second to reorient herself to the new up and down of the bay, and she had to turn her entire upper body to see to the sides with the vacuum helmet on, but finally she spotted the emergency access chutes. This was where she'd have to take a chance and just head straight for the shelter and hope they were still there; with communications inoperable, there wasn't time for anything else.

She'd chosen the closest chute and was down on her belly, ready to scuttle into it when the unexpected gravity just as unexpectedly vanished. She yelped wordlessly and grabbed onto one of the ladder rungs inside the chute to keep from floating away. Just the yank towards the bulkhead should have been enough, but it wasn't...now *something* was pulling her into the tube. Not gravity this time, not unless the wormhole had formed into a singularity. Debris and dust and bits of loose detritus were streaming around her, into the chute, along with a spiral of frost where the air was chilling on its way out of the station.

No, she realized, the wormhole hadn't formed a singularity, it was *closing*, shrinking, leaving gaps in the hull, and outside was vacuum. Between her and the shelter in the tube was a vacuum, and there was no way she was going to be able to get past it with all the air in this section of the station streaming out of it.

She stared at the dark emptiness of the access tunnel, frozen with indecision for the space of two heartbeats, before she anchored her magnetic soles to the deck again and took a plodding, awkward step back to the equipment locker. There were tools in there, maybe

183

something she could use to pry the lift doors open. If the elevator shaft wasn't holed, there might still be some air in there, might still be a way through.

She still had the ventilators tucked under an arm and she cursed under her breath as she tried to keep them out of the way as she pried open the correctly-labeled cabinet and found the power-spreader attached by a lanyard to the inside of the locker. She ripped it away and lunged back toward the nearest lift door, trying to keep the ventilators clenched under her arm to free both hands for its operation.

The air outside was thinning, she could see the readout in her peripheral vision, a distracting red blinking indicator, but she had to make herself ignore it. The task was everything; even if it was probably futile, even if everyone was already dead, she had to finish it, had to try. She knew Sam would do it for her.

She jammed the spreader's blade in the edge of the lift door and keyed the switch in the handles. She could feel the vibration of the motor, hear the rending of the metal through the twin grips, the sound passing through her body instead of through air, with an odd hollow timbre to it. The tool was primitive, brute-force, typical Consensus technology, but she had to admit to a visceral satisfaction to the raw power of the huge, metal shears spreading outward and peeling the metal door away as if it were paper-thin foil.

Behind the ruined door, shrouded in the absolute blackness of the elevator shaft between the electromagnetic rails, Telia Proctor towered like a statue, frozen in place by the magnetic soles of her boots, her bionic limbs locked straight. The glaring light from Priscilla's headlamp splashed across her face, turning the thin coating of dust and grease into a polished sheen, but her eyes were closed and they didn't even flicker at the harsh glow.

Priscilla hissed in a breath, and let go of the power spreader instinctively, letting it pinwheel away from her across the docking bay. Telia's massive form seemed to take up the whole elevator shaft, swallowing the light from Priscilla's headlamp, but in another half a second, she realized there were others in the shaft, floating behind Telia. She recognized Lt. Propanca and Ensign Belden the medic and...

"Mother of all," she muttered, rushing forward, spurred from her shock by the sight of Sam Avalon, his skin beginning to turn blue from lack of oxygen.

The ventilators. She'd nearly forgotten about them, so stunned was she by the sight. She grabbed them from under her left arm and lurched forward, squeezing through the gap torn in the lift hatchway. She went to Sam first, knowing she was letting her emotions overcome her judgement and not caring. She strapped the mask in place over his nose and mouth, tightening it and then opening the valve to let the air through. His eyes were closed and he looked dead and she wished more than anything to touch his face, to see if there was any warmth left in him, but she could feel only the interior of her own gloves.

Fear and anger and desperation consumed her and she wanted to wait, to see if she'd gotten to him in time, if he would wake up. Instead she forced herself to move past him, first to Telia then the other three, slipping their ventilators in place with systematic efficiency, making sure each had good air flow before she allowed herself to give in to her feelings and rush back to Sam.

"Come on, Sam," she whispered. She cursed under her breath and hit the exterior speakers and tried again. "Sam!'

Not enough air left to conduct the sound, she realized. *Damn it!*

She touched her helmet's faceplate to his forehead and yelled the name.

"Sam! Come back to me, Sam!"

She was sobbing. Every time she'd cried, it had been with Sam. If he was gone, would she ever cry again? Would she go back to the way Mother had intended her, focused on her task, a missile sent for one target, expended and expendable?

Sam Avalon blinked. It was the most beautiful thing Priscilla had ever seen.

She could hear a moan conducting through him and through her faceplate, something that might have been "Pris." She laughed, unable to stop it any more than she had the sobs.

"Ma'am, can you hear me?"

It was Sully, coming over her suit radio. Communications were up, which must mean the wormhole had closed.

"Sully," she nearly babbled, "I have some survivors! Did you find an intact shuttle?"

"I've got a bird here, if you can get them to it. Bay twelve, at the far end, and it's got a couple crew still on it, but they've graciously agreed to give us a ride."

Priscilla caught movement from her peripheral vision and glanced upward. Telia Proctor was conscious, and wasn't wasting any time. She grabbed Propanca and Belden by the arm and motioned for Priscilla to take charge of the other man, Patel she thought his name was, one of the sensor techs. Priscilla caught the tall, slender man by the scruff of his shirt and pushed him ahead of her out of the elevator shaft, waving for Sam to follow. He was shivering badly as the temperature plunged, with no air left inside the station for heat convection, but he nodded and affixed the magnetic plates in his ship-boots to the deck.

Patel was still unconscious and she couldn't tell if he was breathing, but she didn't stop to check; his best chance was to get to the shuttle. It seemed impossibly far away, through the maze of equipment and loose cargo containers knocked free of their magnetic restraints by the wormhole's gravity fluctuations, spinning off through individual orbits of their own. A woman's body drifted behind a plastic cargo container, her eyes wide, her head flopping loosely, obscenely. Frost glittered on her cheeks from frozen tears.

Sam began to falter about ten meters from the airlock hatch, so cold the shivering seemed to vibrate his face like a digital blur, unable to keep forcing his legs to move. She took a handful of his shirt and pulled him with her, just a few more meters. The outer lock was open and Sully was waiting there for her, still suited up, the emergency hand-crank ready.

There was barely room for them all in the airlock, but it was too damned cold to wait, so they squeezed in, and then squeezed some more to give Sully room to work the crank. After perhaps five seconds of watching him, Telia pushed the pilot aside and took over. Her arm moved with inhuman speed and the outer hatch closed with a vibration Priscilla could feel through the deck.

She couldn't hear the air flowing in at first, not until enough of it had filled the lock for it to conduct the sound. Sam's reaction gave it away long before that, as the frost that had formed in his short hair began to melt, the tension going out of his shoulders as the bitter cold began to fade. Priscilla saw the blinking green light signaling a safe pressure outside the suit and she began working the cantilever seals of her helmet, yanking and twisting it off before the inner hatch had the chance to open.

Her helmet lamp flickered off automatically as it disconnected from the suit yoke, but the overhead lights in the shuttle's lock had snapped on when the outer hatch had sealed, and for the first time, she was able to get a good look at the lot of them. Propanca, Belden and Patel all seemed to be breathing on their own, and Belden was coming to, clawing the ventilator off of his face. The medic immediately began looking after his fellow crewmembers, but Priscilla was grabbing Sam, holding him despite the intervening bulk of the suit, clutching him as if he might slip away at any moment.

"Did…" Sam rasped, then closed his eyes, cleared his throat and tried again. "Did you find any others?"

"Just one," she admitted, pulling back so she could look him in the eye. He seemed a hundred years older than he had just a few hours ago. "Johan, down in the docking bay."

"Shit." The Patrol officer seemed to deflate, and she was sure if there had been any gravity, he would have collapsed.

Telia still hadn't moved, was standing anchored to the deck even as the inner lock slid aside and the others began moving into the interior of the shuttle. There was a lanky, hatchet-faced Belter in the utility bay within, his cheeks and shaven head covered in tattoos, guiding Belden and the others away, presumably to where they kept their emergency medical supplies. Telia ignored him, staring into nothingness, as if she were considering walking back out into the airless station.

Priscilla noticed the absent expression, the slack posture…and then noticed who wasn't among the survivors.

"Oh, Mother of All," she whispered, pain clenching deep inside her gut. She reached out a gloved hand and grasped Telia's arm, unfeeling vacuum glove touching unfeeling metal. "I'm so sorry, my friend."

"You should go into the shuttle," the Earth-woman said, her voice flat, her face a mask as machine-like as her limbs. She was still looking at the outer airlock.

"He wouldn't want you to give up," Sam told her, stepping in front of her to make her look at him.

"And what," Telia demanded, a flare of something, perhaps anger behind her biological eye, "do you think I have to live for?"

"Someone was behind this," Priscilla pointed out, knowing the danger of the words she spoke, yet seeing no alternative. She waved at the lock, at the devastation on the other side of it. "Someone did this and killed not just Mawae Danabri, but perhaps even the chance to save your planet." She snarled now, and it came naturally, not part of any calculated argument. "What do you have to live for?"

She stepped up next to Sam, shouldering him aside, looking Telia in the eye.

"Revenge."

Chapter Eighteen

"Goddammit, I don't have to sit here and listen to this shit!"

Goran Mestrovic was clearly not happy to be on Luna. He'd popped out of his chair with more grace and fluidity than Sam could ever have managed in the low gravity, and was pacing back and forth in front of the conference table. It was a very un-Belter-like display; they were more likely to sit stock-still and expressionless in negotiations, whether it was for an interstellar trade deal or buying a shuttle-load of soy paste. Even the other Belter representatives who'd come along from the other two major trade associations stared at Mestrovic in bemusement.

"We have not simply lost a single ore barge," Mestrovic insisted, jabbing a finger toward John Gage and Jaime Tejado at the other end of the oval-shaped conference table. "We have lost a very lucrative contract *and* the prospects of a new trade partnership with the Consensus that would have made all of us," he waved a hand around demonstratively, another very un-Belter-like motion, "insanely rich! Why the hell," he bellowed, his long, horsey face turning red, "would we want to kill the goose that laid the golden egg? What possible motive would we have?"

He's scared.

Sam's eyes flickered toward Pris, but he didn't turn his head, trying not to be obvious about her communicating with him via the neurolink. Normally, they wouldn't have chanced using them here, in the closely-monitored halls of Harmony Base on Earth's moon, but they weren't the ones under scrutiny this time. The fact they'd been able to convince the Belter representatives to come to Luna instead of meeting out in the Jovians was proof enough of that.

He's got reason to be, Sam answered. *Someone's going to take the hit for this, and Tejado wants to make sure it isn't the Naturalists.*

But Tejado wasn't the one to answer Mestrovic's question; to Sam's surprise, Gage was.

"I can think of one very convincing motive," the old man replied, leaning forward in his chair, hands flat on the table, eyes locked with the Belter. "With the Consensus out of the way, the resources of the inner system are yours for the taking. And don't tell me one trade route is going to make your colleagues back on Ceres forget all the disputes you've had with Earth over the decades, both economic *and* military."

Now Sam did risk a glance at Pris and they shared a slightly raised eyebrow. The statement seemed to hit Mestrovic square in the gut, a clear blindside coming from the Reformist Minister. He seemed to shrink in on himself and he stepped slowly back to his chair and settled into it.

"I know the barge was ours," the Belter conceded, "but it isn't as if we keep full military security on something like that. It was a routine ore shipment to us, nothing more. Goddammit, if we wanted to attack you, we could have just hit you with a fucking rock."

"In point of fact," Pris spoke up for the first time since the meeting had commenced, "no, you could not. The Gate Assembly *and* the station had energy shields to prevent any such long-distance strikes. Those were deactivated due to the antimatter delivery, and only someone with a knowledge of our construction schedule could have timed the attack this perfectly."

Why are you jumping in? Sam demanded, eyes narrowing. *Don't we believe it was the Naturalists?*

I trust Gage, she told him. *He has a reason for this.*

She'd changed these last few weeks since the...incident. That was what everyone was calling it, "the incident," as if it had been some sort of natural disaster, or an industrial accident. He wanted to be more brutal, more honest about it, but he lacked the eloquence to describe the dead comrades, the lost opportunity. He was angry, bitter even, devastated by the loss of friends and comrades. But Pris, she seemed to be filled with a cold, calculating ruthlessness and it was starting to scare him.

Mestrovic was staring at Pris, mouth working but no sound coming out, as if he'd expected her attack even less than Gage's. Sam remembered how small this chamber had seemed to him the first time they'd visited it, and felt sympathy for the man. Tejado was smiling thinly and without one bit of sympathy, and Sam wanted more than anything to wipe the satisfied expression off his smarmy face.

"This is the situation, Mr. Mestrovic," Tejado said definitively, as if he were the senior minister present and the final authority. "The Belter trade associations made certain assurances to the Consensus at the start of all this. Without those assurances, I am fairly certain our Prime Minister would never have agreed to this whole..." His lip curled in distaste. "...arrangement. Not only are you telling us you can no longer uphold your end of this bargain, but you're responsible for a physical assault on an installation within established Consensus borders!"

"We are not..." Mestrovic began, but Tejado cut him off.

"The barge was yours!" he snapped, his smile disappearing. He pushed himself up in his seat and loomed over the table at the Belter. "*You* are responsible for its security, for every millimeter of its passage from your territory to ours! You're either pleading guilt by conspiracy or guilt by incompetence! Take your pick!"

"Minister Tejado," the woman seated to Mestrovic's right interjected, her frown seeming to drag down every muscle in her face, "we did not come all the way to Luna to be insulted or accused of treachery. We came here in good faith…"

"You came to Luna," Gage told her, his rumbling, gravelly voice cold and harsh, "because you did not want to alienate the Resolution government, since they are your biggest customers. Do not insult our intelligence by claiming you're here out of the goodness of your hearts."

Why the hell isn't Peterman at this meeting? Sam asked Pris, beginning to feel uncomfortable with the direction of the conversation. *Didn't that last message from Aphrodite say they'd get back to you?*

That's what it said, she confirmed, the carefully neutral tone of her "voice" translated well by the neurolink connection. *And that was nearly ten days ago.*

It had also conveyed deepest condolences along with their "complete trust and confidence in any actions you might have to take in the absence of further instructions," for all either of those were worth. It all gave Sam the distinct impression they were being hung out to dry.

"What do you want from us?" Mestrovic asked, his voice and demeanor more subdued now, less confrontational. "I…" He seemed to be swallowing something distasteful. "I acknowledge that the destruction was at least partly our responsibility due to our lack of security measures. How can we make this right?"

"We need the material to rebuild," Pris told the man, her interruption earning a dirty look from Tejado. "And we need it immediately. I don't care where else you have to steal the barges or the processed minerals from, we need it within the month or there won't be any hope of finishing the Gate in time."

If there is now, she added to Sam, echoing his own dismal thoughts. It wasn't just the raw material they'd need, it was replacement engineering crews and, more importantly, antimatter fuel, both of which had to come

193

from the Resolution. And the Resolution had been singularly uncommunicative.

"And we," Gage added, "will require full navigational control of the barges from the second they leave Belter space. That is non-negotiable."

Mestrovic was nodding, slowly, unwillingly, but nodding all the same; the other Belter reps didn't object.

"I will have to communicate this to the boards of the trade associations," he clarified. "But I will certainly recommend they approve it."

Gage sat back, hands clasped across his lap. He looked, Sam thought, every centimeter the professional in his business wear, and Sam wondered which was closer to the real man, the robes of judgement or the suit of negotiation. Tejado seemed less satisfied, as if he wished the Belters would have taken offense and left. But he said nothing and let Gage take the lead.

"Very well, then. We will recess this meeting and allow you to contact your people. Shall we reconvene in, say, forty-eight hours?"

"That should be plenty of time," the Belter told him, inclining his head slightly. "Thank you."

The last could have been ground out between his teeth, Sam wasn't sure.

Gage came to his feet and Tejado moved just the slightest slice of an instant behind, as if he wanted them to think it was his idea. Everyone else stood and followed the two men and their attendant Guardians out of the small chamber. Sam hissed out a breath as he passed through the doorway, just happy to be outside, even if "outside" simply meant a slightly-broader corridor junction in this damned cave of a city.

Lt. Propanca had been leaning against a wall outside the doors; when she saw them, she straightened and stepped up to them, cutting them away from the rest of the group. Her dark eyes were slitted, her face grim.

"What?" Pris demanded. "You've heard something?"

"There's a cutter in from Aphrodite," the young officer reported. "It's waiting out at Ganymede orbit because they don't want to chance coming into Consensus territory."

"Waiting for what?" Sam asked her, a sinking feeling in his gut warning him he wouldn't like the answer.

"For us," Propanca confirmed his fears. "We're all being recalled to Aphrodite for an official debrief." Her mouth twisted downward and she looked around as if wondering if she could speak freely. There was no one else left in the corridor, but that didn't mean no one was listening. "The Captain of the cutter knows you, Sam. Her name's Devon something."

"The *Raven*?" he asked, eyes wide. A surge of longing warmed his chest, feelings he thought he'd put behind him. "She's here?"

"Yeah, that's the ship," Propanca confirmed. "She told me to let you know she'd heard scuttlebutt this wasn't just a debriefing, that they're pulling you two out of this permanently."

"They're putting someone else in charge of the project?" Pris asked, not with disbelief or surprise, Sam noted, just a dolorous acceptance of the inevitable.

Another furtive glance around.

"The sense I got from this Devon is that they're giving up on the Gate altogether," Propanca said so softly Sam could barely make it out.

"Shit." The words were a defeated exhalation, taking with them any emotional energy Sam had left.

"When?" Priscilla's question was as cold and unemotional as the expression on her face, not betraying any disappointment or shock.

"There's a shuttle waiting for us in Lunar orbit right now. It's going to take us to the closest Transition Point and then the *Raven* is supposed to jump in, take us on board and jump out before the Earthers can react to her being there."

Which will pretty much ruin our relations with the Consensus. He'd sent that to Pris, not that it mattered at this point.

I don't think anyone back home cares.

"Captain Avalon, do you have a moment?" Telia Proctor asked.

Sam nearly jumped out of his skin; one second there'd been no one around them in the corridor junction, the next the cyborg was less than a meter over his right shoulder, looming like a gargoyle. It didn't seem possible for someone who massed so much to be able to move so quietly.

"Sure, Telia," he said, trying to keep his tone solicitous despite her abrupt appearance. He hadn't had a chance to speak with her for more than a few seconds since they'd arrived on Luna, but he had to assume she was still taking Danabri's death hard. "What's up?"

"Alone." She cast a glance aside at Propanca, not the slightest bit of apology in her eyes.

"Lieutenant," Sam told the Communications officer, "go find Belden and Patel and get to the docking bay. We'll meet you there as soon as we can."

He'd been about to tell her to pack her things, but the truth was, none of them had anything to pack. The clothes they were wearing had been fabricated for them by the Consensus shops on Luna.

"Aye, sir," Propanca said, then nodded to Pris. "Ma'am."

She shot Telia what Sam's mother would have called "the stink eye" before she left, clearly resenting the brush-off. The Earth woman said nothing until Propanca was around the corner and out of sight, then she motioned for Sam and Pris to follow her.

"What is it?" Pris asked, but Telia merely held up a finger and kept walking.

The cyborg led them to an unmarked door wedged into an alcove between two carefully-pruned trees growing out of a square of soil embedded in the floor, under the harsh glare of sun lamps. Telia tapped a code into the door's lockplate then yanked it open by an old-fashioned metal knob.

A single, unfiltered light flickered on inside, revealing what looked to Sam very much like a supply closet. Barrels of cleaning fluid were stacked in one corner, surrounded by squat, robotic janitors, waiting for their turn at scrubbing the endless hallways of Harmony Base. Telia waved them inside, then checked both ways before closing the door behind them.

"This is one place no one would bother to monitor," she explained. One bionic eye and the matching biological one went back and forth between the two of them. "There's been a development in the investigation."

Sam went from mystified and slightly annoyed to one hundred percent attentive in a fraction of a second. Before they'd arrived on Luna, Telia had promised to keep them apprised of any news she heard of the probe into the incident, but they hadn't heard a thing from her since, and hadn't been able to speak to her alone.

"Tell us," Sam said, leaning forward as if he were trying to coax an explanation from a recalcitrant child.

"This is classified material," Telia explained, a reticence in her voice which Sam sensed was the product of a lifetime of service. "I'm not supposed to know it. We--- the Consensus has spy drones floating at intervals between Luna and Mars along the shipping orbits. One of them picked up part of a tight-beam transmission sent to the barge while it was under way to the Gate assembly. It was a powerful maser signal, but there was enough scatter over distance to pick some of it up along the edges. It was code, something our crackers are still working on, but they think it was meant for the automated systems."

"It wasn't the Belters," Pris declared, the unmistakable smugness of justification in her tone. "Someone else hijacked the ship's computer. Where did the signal come from? Earth? Luna?"

Telia shook her head, the corner of her mouth turning up slightly, as if she took perverse satisfaction in Pris being wrong.

"Mars."

Sam exchanged an incredulous look with Pris and he nearly stumbled over his next words.

"What are you going to do?" he asked her. "I mean, is Minister Gage going to…"

"Minister Gage can do nothing," Telia cut him off sharply. "Not officially. The Prime Minister has washed her hands of the matter, and we will all be very, very lucky if the Consensus isn't at war with the Belters and Jovians within the month."

"But Mestrovic caved," Sam protested, taking an awkward step toward her and nearly knocking over a stack of janitor 'bots. "He's going to get the Belters to give in to our demands."

"Events are in motion and all the blowhard politicians in the galaxy won't stop them. Someone needs to act."

"And by someone," Pris said, eyeing Telia sidelong, "you mean us."

"Your ship is in the system. I have read the reports. All you need do is call it."

"Fuck," Sam breathed the word like a prayer.

"We have to, Sam." Priscilla's hand was warm on his arm, and he met her blue-eyed gaze reluctantly.

"Sure," he muttered, surprised at the anger in his own voice. "All we have to do is ask one of my best friends to throw away her career, violate the sovereignty of two different governments and take us on an unauthorized trip to Mars. Not to mention what could happen to you if…"

He trailed off, not sure whether Pris would be comfortable with him sharing what he knew with Telia. Pris' gaze was resolute, her grip on his arm tighter now, unyielding.

"If we let this happen when we could have stopped it," she said, "we're no better than the ones who did it."

Shit. That sounds way too much like something I would say.

He heaved a sigh. There was a certain freedom in the acceptance of his fate.

"Let's get to the shuttle." He shrugged. "For all I know, Devon'll tell me to go to hell."

Chapter Nineteen

She didn't, of course.

"We have confirmation of clearance from Tarshish Control," the *Raven's* Communications officer announced. It was *not* D'jonni, which had shocked Sam at first, though it shouldn't have. People got promoted, replaced, and it had been over two years.

D'jonni's replacement was a fresh-faced young buck straight out of the Academy, and Sam had initially thought he'd be a problem once the crew found out where they were going, but Ensign Avera worshipped the deckplates his captain walked on. They all did, even Arvid, who was now the ship's XO.

"Take us down," Devon instructed, looking very much at home in the Captain's station.

Sam didn't feel at all comfortable stuck off to the side in one of the extra acceleration couches like so much useless baggage, but this was Devon's ship now, and had been for nearly as long as it had been his. Devon snuck him a look, smiling with what might have been a hint of pride, showing her old boss how well she could do his job. He forced himself to grin back, even against the twisting in his gut from the thought he might very well be costing her the job with what he'd asked her to do.

Pris sat beside him, quiet and somber. She hadn't said two words since they'd boarded, and wouldn't respond to his attempts to engage over the neurolinks either, simply responding she was "thinking about some things Danabri had told her." Telia hadn't even left the guest quarters, convinced her presence made the crew nervous…and she could be right, for all he knew. Propanca and the other survivors from the station stayed in their compartments as well, possibly because they didn't *want* to know where they were going.

On the main screens, blue began to replace black, and atmosphere began to buffet the *Raven*, impossible atmosphere from an impossible source. Like so much of his life these last three and a half years, it was a mystery. Once, he'd thought mysteries made life interesting, but now he was beginning to consider that a conceit of youth.

What about you, Raven? he asked the ship's AI, wondering if it would still talk to him after all this time. *What do you think about the unknown? Challenging or simply frustrating?*

Captain Avalon, I told you once I am not an artificial human *intelligence.* Sam wasn't sure, but he thought he detected a faint hint of humor in the sentient computer's tone. *For me, the unknown is always something not sufficiently investigated.*

Even Gaia Herself? Sam teased, feeling like old times. *Or is it God, like the Earthers call Him?*

A Supreme Being is not the unknown, It is the Unknowable, the AI corrected him. *By definition. A true creator would necessarily be outside of Its creation, else It would simply be a part of it.*

How could a creator be part of Its creation? Sam nearly forgot the descent, forgot the trouble into which they were inviting themselves. Talking philosophy with an AI was like roller-skating on a Moebius strip.

Perhaps you should ask a Christian, the ship's computer suggested. *Did not their God become man in order to save them?*

Good point.

He'd have to try to remember to ask Telia about that. The Earthers' religion retained several aspects of ancient Christianity, though they'd combined all the monotheistic beliefs into one, ecumenical church centuries ago and he wasn't a hundred percent sure where Jesus fit into their pantheon at the moment.

The roar of the atmospheric jets swept away theological ruminations and the majesty of Olympus Mons filled the forward viewscreen's, rising up into the firmament, a monument to the Unknowable Creator. *Whoever They might be.* Its rust-colored skin was a window back to ancient Mars, when the entire surface of the world had been a desolate wasteland, wind-swept, barren and lifeless. He'd seen the footage Mother had brought with her from Earth. Just a couple thousand years ago, an eyeblink on the geological scale, the flicker of a fly's wings on the cosmological timeline.

Yet so much has changed in so short a time. Hundreds of planets made habitable, the seeds of Gaia spread out through the galaxy, life where there was once only death. Who needs gods for such a miracle?

Tarshish seemed subtly different to him, even from the air. There was no other space traffic coming in, which might have just been a quirk of scheduling, and the city seemed less…alive somehow. It was just past sunset and the last time they'd arrived in daylight, but he sensed it was something more. He whispered something to Pris and she finally responded.

"People know war is coming," she said quietly, though Devon's head tilted slightly at that, her eyes narrowing. "They're huddled in their homes, waiting it out."

The city was mostly dark. He wondered whether their light pollution shielding was just that good, or whether the Martians simply didn't use indoor lighting unless absolutely necessary. He'd never been in the home of a native the last time they'd visited, never been allowed out after dark. Even the outlander-owned shops were closed at dusk, by law. The port had lights…some, but even many of those were infrared. Spaceships didn't generally need lights to land.

It felt to Sam as if they were stealing into the city under the cover of night like the Hebrew spies at Jericho in the old story his mother had told him once. Was that from the Bible? He couldn't remember, he'd never read the whole manuscript, just the selections in his comparative religions course in Preparatory School. It seemed like such a thing of Earth, so full of blood and anger.

The darkened city disappeared behind the dull glow of the spaceport walls and then into a cloud of airborne dust and debris kicked up by the belly jets. They screamed in effort, lowering the incredible mass of the starship down to the fusion-form plain, each a technological Atlas with the world on its shoulders. The *Raven* settled with a jolt and a sigh and they were on Mars.

"I thought we might come back here," Devon said, pulling the release for her seat restraints. "Thought I might get another chance to see it. But I never imagined it would be like this."

"I've got word from Collective Control," Avera reported, head cocked in the distinctive tilt of a man receiving a message over his neurolink. "They said they'll have someone out in the main port building to meet you."

"Did they say who?" Devon asked him, deadpan, and Sam nearly corrected her before he caught the glint in her eye.

"Umm...," Avera stuttered, eyes flickering back and forth uncertainly. "I can try to..."

Laughter spread across the cockpit like a light rainstorm, clearing some of the tension built up during the approach. Even Priscilla smiled, which he hadn't seen in weeks.

"Martians consider it bad manners," Devon explained to the Ensign in gentle reproof, "to ask for personal names. If you ever happen to be around one, you should avoid asking for a name or any personal information whatsoever. Martians don't do small-talk."

Devon let him off the hook and came to her feet, turning her attention to Sam and Pris.

"Who's going?" she wanted to know.

"Me," Sam told her, "Pris and Telia. You if you want, it's your boat now. No one else though." He shrugged. "I don't want to spook them."

"I don't think that's even possible," Pris said. She was staring out the viewscreen, as if she could see the Martians waiting for them out in the darkness.

"Yeah, I'll go," Devon told him, shrugging. "Maybe this time no one will try to kill me."

*   *   *

"We greet you in the name of the Collective Will of the Martian People," the tall man said, bowing to them cordially.

Sam returned the bow by instinct, but his eyes stayed on the man, plagued by a sense of déjà vu. The odd clothes were the same, of course, plain and khaki and unmarked. The narrow cheekbones, the long, aquiline nose, the sunken eyes, the flare of his ears away from his head, they all seemed very familiar.

Is this the same guy who we talked to three years ago? he said to Pris over the neurolink, not wanting to offend the man by asking him directly.

It is. There was no doubt in her tone and no surprise either.

The slender, towering Martian had been standing alone in the spaceport's main office suite, a statue motionless in the dim lighting. The sensor displays were dark, the communications nets silent, and Sam wondered who from traffic control had spoken to Avera. An AI maybe? Or someone on the small Phobos station? It hadn't been anyone in the port control areas, not unless it was this guy. Suddenly, he felt very naked without a weapon. It made no sense, there were no threats down here, but the hair on the back of his neck was standing up just the same.

"Excuse me, sir," Sam ventured carefully, trying not to offend the man, "but I thought we made it clear this is a matter of the utmost urgency and we need to speak to someone with the authority to make decisions on the executive level."

"You did," the Martian confirmed, nothing in his demeanor or his voice showing the slightest reaction. "And you are."

Sam blinked at the response. He looked to the others for help, but Pris' attention was on the Martian, peering through him as if she were trying to probe under the skin. Telia said nothing, her arms crossed, her stance squared, while Devon just shrugged helplessly.

"I apologize for prying, but unless you've been promoted significantly since the last time we were here, aren't you with the diplomatic corps?"

"There was a transmission," Pris interrupted, cutting through the niceties with a direct question, "from the main communications antennae outside Tarshish to a Belter ore barge inbound to the Gate Assembly the Resolution was building in conjunction with the Consensus at the Sun-Mars L5 point 810 standard hours ago. We need to know who sent it."

"We are aware of the transmission," the Martian told her, "and we are aware of its consequences, but it was not sent by the Collective."

"How can you know that?" Sam demanded, his patience with the whole business wearing increasingly thin. He threw his hands up, frustration boiling over. "There have to be hundreds of thousands of people in this city! How can you be sure whoever sent the message wasn't a Collective citizen?"

"We are sure," the Martian responded with cool reserve, "because we did not do it."

He was about to blow up again, knowing he was screwing up but past caring, when he sensed Pris moving up beside him.

"Sam." A thin smile played across her face and he thought he recognized it as her "Eureka" expression, the look she'd get when she'd solved a problem that had been bothering her. "You don't understand."

"Yeah, I don't either, ma'am," Devon admitted, palms out in an "I surrender" sort of pose. "Are we just getting a runaround here?"

She seemed upset, and Sam couldn't blame her; she was risking more with this trip than they were.

"The Collective isn't the name of their government," Pris said, and the almost-smug satisfaction in her tone reminded him of Danabri. "It's what they are."

Her eyes were alight, nearly feverish in their intensity.

Are you all right? he asked her privately, but she ignored the neurolink and made a gesture of impatience.

"They're literally a hive mind!" she insisted, motioning toward the Martian. "Probably connected by something like our neurolinks, but even more advanced and definitely more comprehensive. They don't *have* any individual identity! That's why none of them use names; it's not just with us, they don't *need* them."

"That's impossible." Devon regarded Pris through narrowed eyes. "A human brain couldn't work that way."

"And who said they're human?" Pris shot back.

This is a dream, Sam told himself. *I'm back on Gateway Station in bed with Pris, sleeping, and this whole last month has been a dream.*

If it was, he wasn't about to wake up.

The Martian said nothing either to deny or confirm Pris' assertion, just watched her through deeply-nestled, dark eyes and…was that a smile? Or were the shadows in the darkened chamber playing tricks with his eyes? If it was a smile, who was smiling at him? *What* was smiling at him?

"Why don't you ask him?" Telia wondered. The Earth-woman was still motionless, face still impassive, but her eyes had settled on Pris. At her questioning glance, Telia clarified. "If you believe that's true, why don't you ask him?"

Pris seemed to consider it for a few seconds, but she shook her head.

"Not yet. Right now, it doesn't matter. All that matters is, I believe him." She nodded to the Martian. "If you know it wasn't you, can you tell us who *did* send the transmission?"

The Martian seemed to nod with his whole body and the motion made Sam fear he'd topple over like a tree struck by lightning.

"Indeed. We can show you."

He touched no control, spoke no order, yet one of the display screens lit up, bathing the office suite with a soft, white glow.

They do have neurolinks, then, or something like them.

"The antenna is rented out to offworlders for message delivery, but this transmission was not among the regular batch of pre-paid recordings. Someone penetrated the system from an external maintenance port, illegally and subtly enough to avoid our computer watchdog systems." That quirk of his lip again in an almost-smile. "Which are quite sophisticated. This was captured by a security drone at the Communications Center."

Sam recalled seeing the facility on their last visit, conspicuous by the gigantic dish at its apex, but from the look of the holographic video, the maintenance port was tucked away in a shadowed alcove somewhere around the back, away from public view. The access hatch was propped open, partially obscuring the dark-clad figure huddled over it.

"No one came to investigate this?" Telia wondered, disapproval strong in her voice.

"She was somehow able to acquire the correct clearances for a contract repair technician," the Martian told the Earth-woman, "probably from an accomplice."

"She?" Pris asked, the word sharp and clipped off. "So you got a better look at her than this?"

By way of answer, the Martian tilted his head toward the screen and the video feed went into fast forward, evident from the furtive, jerky movements barely visible behind the cover of the access plate. After a few seconds of the sped-up footage, the frame rate slowed again to normal speed as a hand reached out and shoved the access door shut. Sam could see her short, dark hair now, but her face was still to the ground as she pushed herself to her feet, and he thought that might be the best look he was going to get. Then her head came up and she looked from side to side carefully before moving out of the alcove, and the camera froze on her visage.

"No fucking way," Devon murmured.

Sam didn't place the face at first, until he remembered where he was and the last time he'd been on Mars. She wasn't a young woman, but neither did she look unabashedly old, the way Gage or other Earthers would, or even Belters with their less-than-equitable sharing of advanced medical technology. Instead, hers was the agelessness of unfading vitality, yet arranged in the set of maturity and experience, the look anyone raised in the Resolution came to recognize in their elders.

He had to imagine her in the pragmatic brown work clothes of a shopkeeper before he remembered.

"Jeddah Valley," he breathed the words, voice heavy with the disbelief he felt.

"Who is this woman?" Telia asked, glancing between them with what Sam thought was irritation at being the only one not to understand the significance of the name.

"It was before we met you," Sam explained to her. "She was a Resolutionist expatriate running a craft kiosk here in Tarshish. She had a hand-made tapestry in her shop with an image of the ramship worked into it..."

He trailed off, getting that surreal, hair-standing-on-end feeling again as the implications of what he was saying finally penetrated.

"But she's one of us," Devon said softly, a horrified whisper.

"Perhaps some people in your Resolution are not so happy with the idea of saving my world," Telia proposed.

"No, it's worse than that," Pris assured her. Gone was the self-satisfaction, the Eureka smile, the fever-brightness of her eyes. Fear had replaced them, fear of not just what they knew but of all the sudden unknowns. "She showed us that tapestry and she was behind the attacks as well, or in league with those who were. This whole thing has been a charade, an attempt to manipulate us."

"Manipulate us into *what*?" Sam wanted to know.

Pris shook her head, but didn't answer him.

"Where is the woman?" Telia asked the Martian. "Is she still in the city?"

"She boarded a shuttle shortly after this video was recorded." He went on before any of them could ask the obvious. "It was registered to an independent freighter, which left orbit immediately after she boarded."

Sam waited, scowling when he realized the towering Collective representative was going to make them work for it.

"Do you know the freighter's destination?"

"We did not track it the entirety of its course," the Martian admitted, "but before it departed our local sensor screen, its acceleration and trajectory seemed to be in keeping with its stated flight plan."

The Martian spread his hands almost apologetically at the dirty looks Sam and Pris gave him.

"It was heading for Earth."

Chapter Twenty

"She could still be a Naturalist," Sam insisted with the mulish devotion to the ideals of the Resolution that had so attracted her once. "Just because she told us…"

"It's possible," Pris told him, unsure if she was being honest or simply trying to mollify him.

She was going to leave off the questions the idea raised, but Devon Conrad wasn't so circumspect.

"If Jeddah Valley was a Naturalist plant," the Captain of the *Raven* wondered, "what did they have to gain by trying to make us think they already knew about the ramship?"

Pris bit back a curse, knowing how honest with himself Sam generally was, and how the idea would eat at him once he adequately explored it. She masked her grimace with a sip of tea, sitting back in the chair. It wasn't entirely comfortable; she didn't think much of Collective furniture.

If they are a hive mind, whoever it is has horrible taste.

The Collective representative had dropped them at the same guest quarters they'd stayed in over three years ago, then accompanied Telia Proctor to the Communications Center. And that had been…she had the answer immediately from her implant computer, three and a half hours.

And that's going to be a damned long conversation with a twenty-six-minute turnaround time between Mars and Earth. She's a more patient woman than I.

Devon had kept her people with the ship, probably to give the rest of the crew as much plausible deniability as possible if and when the shit hit the fan, so it was just the three of them gathered in the formal dining room, huddled around one end of the grand table. She longed for coffee, but all they'd found in the cupboard was some sort of herbal tea that tasted like drinking a bush, but at least it was something different than shipboard fare.

Sam hadn't touched his cup, still very clearly disturbed by the idea of a Resolutionist being involved in the plot…more disturbed than she was, which might, she thought not without some bitterness, be a statement about how much she'd changed in the last three years.

Or how far I've fallen, as Mother would be more likely to put it.

"I don't know much about the politics back in Dauphin City," Sam admitted, staring at something light years away, fingers tapping idly on the china of the tea cup. "Is it possible there are factions there the same way the Consensus has the Naturalists and Reformists?"

He was asking *her*, pleading with her really, as if she knew the truth and were keeping it secret. She sighed and finished off the last of the tea.

"Not openly."

That brought his eyes back to focus, hearing the implications in her statement.

"The Resolution government isn't run by men," she went on, shaping the words carefully, both for Sam's feelings as well as to keep certain things from Devon that the woman didn't need to know. "The final decisions on large matters are made by Mother. As such, dissenting opinions are not…cultivated."

"You mean 'tolerated,' don't you?" Devon Conrad asked, disdain in the sidelong glare she gave Pris.

"When did you get so cynical?" Sam asked her, shaking his head.

"I've always been a bit cynical, sir," the woman confessed. She offered an apologetic shrug. "My parents were involved in the planetary government on Hephaestus, and there's always been a bit of tension between Aphrodite and us…things are wilder and woolier there. Mom and Dad had the typical politician's view of politics, at least in private. Mother has done great things for us," Devon hastened to add, "but hers is an iron fist in a velvet glove, and anyone who speaks the wrong kind of truth suddenly finds themselves being transferred somewhere unpleasant and lonely."

"To the point," Pris interrupted, treating the Patrol Captain with a dirty look, "there is no official opposition party in the Resolution government system. Any group who disagrees with Mother's decisions would likely be underground and very good at keeping their mouths shut."

Sam looked horrified and Pris sighed heavily, covering his hand with hers.

"It's not as bad as it sounds," she assured him. "You know Mother's decisions are based on what's best for us. She has no allegiance to any party or philosophy, she's totally objective."

"That's what everyone says," Devon countered. "But the only ones who get to talk to her are the Whitesuits like you. How do we know they aren't the ones making all the decisions and just saying it's Mother?"

"I know," Pris told her, her tone as cold as her eyes. "You can choose to believe me or not, but I know." She turned back to Sam. "You trust me, don't you?"

"Of course I do," he said, perhaps a bit too quickly and automatically.

But he didn't, she thought. How could he when she'd told him she didn't trust herself? She wished there was something she could tell him, something to convince him, but the words wouldn't come no matter how badly she wanted them to.

She was saved from trying when the front door to the guest house creaked open. No doorbells here, everyone knew who was coming and when.

They probably don't believe me about that, either.

"I was able to contact Minister Gage," Telia Proctor declared without preamble, striding into the dining room.

The cyborg didn't get twitchy---Pris wasn't sure if it was even possible for her, physiologically---but there was impatience in the set of her jaw, in the restless way her eyes jumped from one of them to the other.

"What did he say?" Sam prompted, coming out of his chair, the legs scraping against the stone floor. "Is he going to clear the *Raven* to approach Consensus territory?"

"We will be allowed to dock at Fortuna Station," she announced, "under careful observation by the orbital weapons platforms. He told me he'll send a representative to meet us there."

Pris let out a relieved breath. She'd had no backup plan if Gage had turned them down; they would have had to head back to Aphrodite and try to explain things to Mother…if she would have even spoken to them.

"I'll tell Arvid to prep for takeoff," Devon said, slapping the table like she'd just won a pot in a poker game, then pushing herself up.

"You sure about this?" Sam asked her, touching her on the arm to pause her on her way to the door. "You can maybe get away with stopping here at Mars, maybe justify it to Admiral Anton. But going back into Consensus space, to Earth orbit…" He shook his head. "You'll be court-martialed. They could take your ship."

"It was your ship before it was mine, Sam," she reminded him. "You gave it up because it was your duty. This is mine." She waved at the door. "Come on, let's go see if we can still save the Earth."

*   *   *

Fortuna Station wheeled silently across the face of the Earth, winking faceted reflections in the light of the sun as it turned slowly and purposefully. Telia had always thought it was the most beautiful thing made by human hands, a jewel hung in the sky to celebrate the return of the

214

people of Earth to the larger universe. She'd heard those very words in lectures in school as a little girl, carried them with her the first time she'd left the gravity well and seen the giant orbital commerce center with her own eyes.

It loomed ahead of them now, growing frighteningly close; it seemed to jump forward at them with every disquieting bang of the maneuvering thrusters, a smooth gleaming white transforming into the tiny, ugly details of a working station as they approached the docking bays at the hub.

"This is the closest I have been to Earth in nearly ten years," she said softly, quietly, as if she hadn't wanted anyone to hear. But then why had she said it aloud?

She saw Sam Avalon's glance, knew he'd heard. He didn't respond, perhaps because he didn't wish to discuss her private matters in front of the Raven's bridge crew, or perhaps because there was nothing to be said.

They were so close even the details were lost, swallowed in the shadows of the yawning docking cylinder. Gateway station had been so small, its docking umbilicals little more than exposed ports on the exterior of its central hub; Fortuna's bay was huge, hundreds of meters across, large enough for cargo shuttles and smaller freighters to take shelter inside the hull. The Raven slid inside without any sense of the encroaching bulkheads, just a smooth, clear path to their berth, a concave niche waiting for them with open grappling arms to pull them into a tight, secure embrace.

Mawae... Her gut clenched at the thought of his name, but she forced her way through it. Mawae had told her once about Resolution space stations, how they used magnetic grapplers for securing docking vessels and magnetic fields to hold in the atmosphere instead of keeping the bay in a vacuum. It sounded magical, something from a movie, yet she trusted his word it was true. Mawae never lied to her; he never lied to anyone. It was one of the things she'd loved about him.

Clunks and bangs and jarring vibration and the patrol craft was pulled into the docking port with all the gentleness and subtlety of a suspect being handcuffed by the police. She was used to reading people, something else she and Mawae had held in common, and she noted the tension in the bridge crew, even Captain Conrad, who took pains to seem cool and unaffected by it all. It was subtle, just a flexing of the fingers here, a repetitive rubbing of the eyes there, but they were worried.

They should be. I am.

Priscilla and Sam Avalon padded silently out of the cockpit, their sticky pads scritching softly against the deckplates. Devon spoke the usual redundant, commanding phrases as a comfort to her crew, then moved to follow them. Telia had only spent a total of a few weeks on Resolution ships, yet she knew from just the limited experience they were not so different from Consensus crews. Less talking perhaps, due to their neurolinks, but the talking there was remained the same, meant more as a tradition, something always the same to maintain their sense of being in control.

The Guardians were waiting for them just outside the airlock, as she'd guessed they would be. A half a dozen of them stood anchored with magnetic boots, fully armored, faces covered by visored helmets and hands filled with pulse rifles.

Not even non-lethals, she noted grimly. *Someone really doesn't want us here.*

One of the Guardians stepped out from the rest, his magnetic boots click-clacking loudly. The rank chevrons on his chest-plate declared him a Guardian Prime, equal to her, though the hash marks of time in grade marked him senior. He reached up and twisted a knob on the side of his helmet, and the visor rotated upward to reveal the blocky, unpleasant face beneath.

"It's been a long time, Proctor," Adrian Fellows said, mouth twisted into his default sneer. He held his carbine loosely, casually in his left hand, his right resting on the butt of his holstered sidearm. She wore her own weapon at her waist, but she endeavored to keep her hands well clear of it.

"Are you stationed here, Guardian Fellows?" she wondered. "Or did you make a special trip just to meet me?"

"Every time I meet you it's special, Proctor."

If he had anything else to say on the matter, it was lost in the huffing and puffing of the woman hustling up behind the half-squad of infantry, squeezing through the crowd of onlookers gathered to see the show. She was middle-aged and overweight and crammed into a badly-tailored duty uniform proclaiming her Deputy Commander of Fortuna Station. She moved awkwardly in magnetic boots that seemed oddly out of place with the black slacks of her uniform and she was perspiring far too much for her to be used to it.

Probably never leaves the spin areas if she has any choice.

"Who's in charge of you lot?" the woman asked, her face flushed, her tone sharp and impatient.

Sam and Pris looked at each other for just a beat before answering, and Telia recognized this was a shift as well. There'd been a time when Priscilla would have taken the lead automatically, but gradually, as their time at the station had dragged on, their roles had become more equal.

Still, it was her who spoke to the station officer.

"I am Priscilla of the Resolution Diplomatic Corps, and this is Captain Samuel Avalon of the Patrol. We were the commanders of the Gateway project before the attack."

She motioned behind her to Devon. "This is Captain Conrad, commander of the Patrol ship *Raven*."

"Yes, yes," the woman waved off the introductions. "I have been instructed to have you two," she jabbed a finger at Sam and Pris, "transported down to Capital City under guard. The rest of you will be staying here on your ship, and if you attempt to power up without authorization, we'll burn a hole through your lock and kill you all."

She was trying to sound intimidating, Telia thought with a burble of amusement, but wasn't close to pulling it off. She reminded Telia of a petulant child appointed class leader for the day and intent on abusing the power to the full extent of her ability.

"Good luck, Sam," Devon said with a philosophical shrug. "Guess I won't get a chance to see old Earth."

"Someday, Devon," he told her, offering her a hand.

"Let's get to the shuttle," Fellows said, motioning with his free hand. "I told my wife I'd be home for breakfast."

"Still married?" Telia asked, eyebrow shooting up as she moved to follow him and the others. "I would have thought she'd find someone less likely to screw young colony girls while on duty."

"You!" The Deputy Commander, who still hadn't bothered to share her name with them, rounded on Telia, finger spearing out again. It was very difficult for Telia to resist the urge to bend it backwards until it shattered. "You are not coming! You will stay with the enemy...umm, the Resolution ship."

"I am the Guardian assigned to these people by the Prime Minister," Telia responded, voice colder than she thought she could manage. But then, she'd always turned cold when she was enraged.

"You're a fucking cyborg freak!"

Telia hadn't thought the woman's face could get redder and yet somehow, she managed it.

"You aren't setting foot on the homeworld if I have anything to do about it!"

"You don't."

Telia glanced backwards at Fellows. His expression was as flat and unimpressed as his tone had been; he regarded the station's Deputy Commander the same way he might have a junior NCO who'd gotten too big for his britches.

"I beg your pardon?" the woman blurted, eyes widening. "I am Deputy Commander of this station and…"

"And I'm under the direct orders of the Prime Minister of the fucking Human Consensus to bring these three down to her office." *That* sounded like the Fellows she remembered. His volume rose as he went on, though his register stayed low and gravelly. "I don't care if you're the fucking Queen of Fairyland, you're not in my fucking chain of command and I have my fucking orders! Do I fucking make myself clear?"

"I will have you up on charges for insubordination!" the woman exploded. Telia half-expected steam to shoot out of her ears. "You are under arrest, mister…"

"If you want to arrest someone," Fellows told her, taking a half-step forward and bringing his rifle down to port arms, "you generally should have bigger guns than they do." He looked her up and down. "Looks like you brought a big mouth and not much else." The sneer again. "Of course, you're welcome to call up some of your security guards. I haven't had any range time with a good reactive target in weeks."

The cylindrical cooling jacket of the pulse rifle was polished and spotless but for a small section near the receiver, where Telia could see several rows of tiny notches scratched into the metal by something hard and sharp. If the Deputy Commander had noticed and cared to count, she would have seen there were thirty-one of the notches, and might have even been intelligent enough to guess what they signified.

Telia didn't know if it was the threat, or the notches, or simply the realization she was in so far, far over her head, but the woman didn't say another word, just glared at the Guardian Prime, hatred plain in her eyes. Fellows sniffed at her, then turned and began click-clacking down the docking bay, heading for the shuttle. Telia fell in behind him, sparing the Deputy Commander a thin smile. The rest of the half-squad followed in an open wedge, the last of them walking backward to cover their withdrawal, which was even harder in zero gravity wearing mag boots.

Men and women and the occasional older child disembarking from shuttles and smaller intersolar transports eyed them with prurient curiosity, probably wondering if they were VIPs or just criminals.

A bit of both, I imagine.

Telia picked up her pace and came even with Fellows, wondering if it would be appropriate to thank him.

"Don't bother thanking me," he told her, as if she'd projected her thoughts at him. She closed her mouth and he must have noticed her nonplused expression because he grinned. "You were always a horrible poker player, Proctor. Don't thank me because I'm following orders; I don't give a shit if you come along or not." He shrugged. "The way things are going, you'd probably be better off staying with the Rezzies up here, or just getting the hell out of the Solar System altogether."

"Why?" Priscilla interrupted, earning a scowl from Fellows. "We've been incommunicado," she explained, either not noticing the Guardian's expression or, more likely, not caring. "What's happening?"

"Let's just say we may not have to worry 'bout your robot ramship destroying the Earth," Fellows told her, and Telia thought she detected real concern trying to hide behind his sarcastic bluff. "The government had declared a moratorium on gas shipments out of the Jovians to the Belt." He threw a hand up as if he knew how idiotic the move had been. "Like they were going to go along with that. Well, big shock, they didn't. The Jovians called our bluff and sent a tanker through on the run to Ceres."

"Tell me we didn't blow it up," Telia begged him, wincing in anticipation.

"That would be wasteful. No, we sent a tactical team in and boarded the tanker; I think the idea was to steal it...sorry, I mean, 'confiscate' it." He shrugged. "Whichever, the Belters weren't having any of that. They blasted the ship with a mass driver, blew the hell out of the thing, killed all twelve of our people plus the Jovian crew."

They'd reached the dock for the shuttle, the delta-winged craft visible through the transparent alloy of the window beside the airlock. Fellows popped the hatch controls with a fist and waved to the open lock, turning back to them.

"So, welcome to Earth, everyone," he said cheerfully. "I guess we're at war."

Chapter Twenty-One

There were no curious onlookers this time, no official representatives to meet them, no ornate conference of Ministers to determine their fate. The shuttle landed in the dead of night at the far end of a military-run spaceport kilometers from the public port, and Guardian Fellows chivvied them into an unmarked groundcar.

Capital City took on a different character at night, down at the street level. Sam had noticed the same phenomenon before, on other worlds. Cities could seem buttoned-down and business-like during the day, but at night they would loosen up and take on a more daring, even dangerous persona. Capital City wasn't casual this night, wasn't a worker cutting loose after a long day on the job; it was claustrophobic, paranoid, waiting for the sword of Damocles to descend upon them. The streets were nearly deserted, and the people he did see all seemed to be scurrying to get someplace quickly, to find another hole to hide in.

"You can see the ramship now," Fellows told them, arm resting casually against the passenger's-side door as he stared out the window. He'd shed his armor in the shuttle, probably so as not to attract undue attention when they landed, but Sam had noted he still had his sidearm. "With telescopes I mean. Optical ones, the kind you can buy in any fab shop. There was no hiding it, so the government announced it publicly, said there was nothing to worry about, we were taking steps to intercept it."

He glanced back over his shoulder to the second row of seats, to the three of them crowded together as if huddled for comfort.

"Not everyone believes that."

"What is going to happen when they find out there is nothing to be done?" Telia wondered.

"Panic, I imagine." Fellows' voice was flat, emotionless, as if the whole thing was merely an intellectual exercise. "Those with the money will get off the planet. Everyone else will likely storm the spaceports and try to force their way off." He shrugged. "Not enough ships in the whole galaxy to evacuate them all."

"We can still do this," Sam insisted, uncomfortable with the fatalistic tone the two Earthers were taking. "We just need to find out who was really responsible for the destruction of the Gateway, so we can stop this war and get shipments coming in again from the Belt."

"It took you over two years to complete the Gate," Telia pointed out. "We have months now. Six until the impact, but likely less than that before the ship's electromagnetic fields begin to wreak havoc with the Earth's weather and begin to disrupt our communications and travel." She shook her head. "And even less before the fields make construction impossible in the Sun-Mars LaGrangian points."

"There could still be a way." Sam dug in his heels. Why didn't anyone else see, giving up wasn't going to solve anything? "I mean, the Gateway took two years because we *had* two years. I'm not a trans-dimensional physicist, but maybe we could make it work with something smaller, maybe with less power..."

"Shit!"

Sam's head snapped around at the unexpected exclamation from Pris. She was staring straight ahead, her mouth slightly open, her eyes unfocused and he felt a sudden surge of panic at the thought her counter-programming might be setting in because she'd disobeyed orders to return to Aphrodite.

"Are you all right?" he asked her, putting a hand on her shoulder.

"Yeah, I think I am," she told him, a smile slowly spreading across her face as she turned to him. She leaned over and kissed him and he blinked as she laughed softly. "I think we all might be."

"What?" he asked her, shaking his head in baffled confusion.

"You have an idea," Telia stated, eyes narrowing. "What is it?"

"Not yet," Pris insisted, holding up a hand. "Give me a few minutes. I need to get this firmed up in my head before we meet the Prime Minister."

"Think fast," Fellows muttered. "Because we're here."

They were nowhere near the Ministry Building, Sam could tell that much even in the dark. The neighborhood seemed to be industrial in nature, the sort of featureless, impersonal buildings where you might find public fabricators or distribution centers for food stores. No one was out and about in this neighborhood this time of night, and he hadn't even seen another vehicle for the last five minutes.

He was about to ask Fellows what he meant when a sheet-metal garage door began trundling upward as they slowed to a halt on the street beside it. The driver was a younger man, his skin pale, his head totally hairless right down to the eyebrows, and he didn't even look to Fellows for confirmation before he pulled through the garage door and into the dark recesses beyond.

The headlights revealed not a fabricator center or a storage building, but instead a façade…and a tunnel. The suspension of the vehicle bounced and jolted as the driver took it down the slope of the paved ramp into the passageway, just wide enough for one car. The road was smooth and graded, and he spotted the ventilation machinery to pump air down into the tunnel. It all had the look of age, as if this setup had been built decades ago.

Maybe it's as old as the Consensus government. Built when they laid down the foundations of the street.

An instant's paranoia nagged at him with wild thoughts of underground dungeons where they'd be left to rot, but he shook them away. Surely it would just have been easier to turn them away, make them return to Aphrodite. Anyway, Telia hadn't said anything; if there were anything untoward about the secret entrance, he was certain she would have raised an objection.

"This doesn't lead all the way to the Ministry building, does it?" Sam asked, staring out at the bare, concrete walls of the tunnel. That would have been kilometers away and he couldn't imagine the underground road stretching so far. And it was still sloping downward...

Fellows snorted but didn't bother to answer. Telia sighed under her breath, barely audible even right next to him.

"This is the entrance to an emergency shelter," she told him. "It's meant to provide a safe haven for government officials to ride out disaster or political unrest." She shrugged. "Or war."

"Or all three wrapped up in one giant, fucking bundle, in this case," Fellows contributed.

The car had already begun to slow, and ahead of them loomed the end of the road in the form of a solid wall of what looked to Sam to be the same sort of alloy the Consensus used in starship hulls. Set in the concrete at the joint of the tunnel and the metal barrier was an elevator. The driver stayed in the car, face impassive, as if he made these sorts of deliveries every day, while Fellows pushed his door open and hopped out before the vehicle had even made a complete stop.

"Let me guess," Sam ventured, coming up behind the Guardian as the squared-off, blocky man input a code into the elevator's security panel, "we're going down?"

They were. Down and down and, just when he thought they couldn't go any further, they still went down.

I should be used to closed spaces, he thought, staring around him at the tiny elevator, barely large enough for the four of them. *I was a starship Captain, for Gaia's sake.*

Maybe he'd just spent too much time on the station, with its broad corridors and roomy compartments. Either way, when the thing finally jolted to a stop, Sam had to restrain himself from squeezing past Fellows to be the first out. The corridor outside, in sharp contrast, was broad and brightly-lit and crowded with purposeful workers in the sort of dull-colored business dress you'd expect from government employees.

It wasn't even a corridor, he realized abruptly, forcing himself to step out of the car last just to prove he could. It was more of an open cubicle farm, miniature offices separated by low dividers. Behind the sound-proof barriers, men and women huddled in virtual-reality gear, hands moving over projected controls no one else could see. No one seemed to notice them as they passed, even the workers not buried in virtual tasks still too preoccupied with their own individual assignments to worry about the newcomers.

Except the Guardians. They noticed. He saw them standing in a star cluster near the center of the room, armed and armored and watchful, and he saw heads turn at the sight of Telia and Fellows' sidearms and their uniforms. They were probably reading RFID chips in the uniforms or the guns, checking the authorization in the Heads-Up Display readouts in their helmets. He had never thought much of the elite Consensus soldiers before he'd met Telia; after seeing her in action at the station, he had a newfound respect for them, and a profound hope none of them ever saw him as an enemy.

"Sir," the highest-ranking of the armored troops said to Fellows, bringing his weapon to port arms in salute. "We have orders to pass you on through to the command

226

bunker." A slight hesitation. "I'm afraid you'll have to leave your weapons with us, though."

Fellows scowled, more deeply than the usual scowl which seemed to be his default expression, but he unfastened his gun belt and handed it over to the armored trooper. Even without armor, Fellows dwarfed the other man, and he held onto the belt for just a beat longer than he needed to before he let it go.

"You lose it," he warned, glowering darkly, "and I'll see you busted back down to Private, Blumenthal."

Telia smiled at the little display of machismo, then pulled her pistol out of its holster. The armored Guardians tensed, and Sam thought he saw the muzzles of their rifles dip slightly toward her, but Telia simply ejected her magazine and cleared the chamber before storing the mag in one of the belt pouches. She re-holstered the pulse pistol and passed the weapon over, her eyes following the gun as the other Guardian slung the belt over his shoulder.

Sam wondered if she was sizing them up, determining whether she could take them. He got the impression she did it automatically, though he'd never worked up the nerve to ask her.

"This way," the senior Guardian motioned, leading them off to the left, through a long, narrow hallway.

More Guardians stood watch at a thick, security-sealed metal door at the end of the hall, but they stepped aside for the group and the door swung inward at their approach. The "command bunker" looked very much like your typical government office on the inside, though perhaps a bit outdated technologically and stylistically. A clerk sat at a data terminal, staring at the two-D flat-screen monitor, not even looking up at their entrance, while Prime Minister Brecht huddled closely with John Gage and two other well-dressed officials around an oval table near the center of the room.

None of them rose, though Gage nodded to them, the expression on his face more forlorn than welcoming. Brecht barely acknowledged their presence, just a glance out the corner of her eyes betraying the slightest attention. Sam felt a drop in his gut, like his first time in free-fall.

"I allowed you to return," Brecht said, still not looking at them, lifting her steaming mug of tea to her lips and taking a sip before she went on, "because frankly you're mad to be here. But I do not, for the life of me, understand what you hope to gain by this meeting."

"We're here for two reasons, your Excellency," Pris said, stepping in and taking the lead. Her stance was straight and confident, more like the woman who'd confronted Tejado on Luna, the one who'd fought side by side with him on Mars. "First of all, we've uncovered a major lead to those responsible for the destruction of the Gate assembly and we'd like your aid in chasing it down."

"The Belters and Jovians were behind the attack on your Gate," Brecht snapped, eyes flaring as she finally graced them with her full attention. "Or haven't you been following the news? Let me guess," she went on, not giving Priscilla a chance to answer, "you'd like to blame this on us, somehow?"

"In point of fact," Priscilla said, pushing her voice in before Brecht could continue, "the woman directly responsible for hijacking the barge's automated systems appears to be an expatriate Resolutionist."

That seemed to shut the woman up, and bring her to her feet. She pushed herself up off the table, exhaustion in her posture, and stepped around to a position just a meter from Priscilla.

"And what's the other reason?" she demanded.

"Your world," Pris said, not flinching from the elected leader of the Consensus. "I believe we can still save it."

Chapter Twenty-Two

"What the hell am I looking at?"

Brecht stared at the huge wall display, peering intently at the series of parabolas Pris had drawn between the orbits of Earth and Mars, intersecting the trajectory of the ramship. Sam recognized the symbols from his cross-training in navigation, but he had no idea what they signified in this context, and Pris had been close-mouthed as she drew on the tablet. Telia and Fellows wore almost identical skeptical expressions, while Gage watched with keen anticipation.

"These are the radiation arcs of active Teller-Fox warp units," Pris explained, tracing the parabolas with her finger. "Not the giant gate assembly we were building, just the ordinary warp units in a ship like the *Raven* or one of your own military vessels."

"The wormholes from a normal warp unit wouldn't be large enough to affect something the size of the ramship," Gage said, a slight question in his tone, as if he was hoping to be proven wrong.

"Individually, no, they aren't," she admitted. "And when we were planning for the Gate, the thought was to subsume the ramship entirely into Transition Space, and we scaled accordingly. However, something Captain Avalon said earlier," she went on, nodding to him, "made me start thinking about something, and a bit of number-crunching confirmed it. Transition Space eats momentum. It's part of the physics of the dimension and we take it for granted. I got a first-hand, ringside seat for the effect when the antimatter explosion inadvertently activated some of the warp units in the Gate a month ago."

She waved at the representation of the ramship, overlain on the actual images of the thing taken by remote drones.

"Just one ship couldn't create a wormhole big enough to absorb that kind of momentum, but if you could synchronize enough of them and open say, two hundred gates at once?" She shrugged. "It wouldn't shunt the thing into Transition Space, but it could rob it of enough momentum that at the very least, it'll be a survivable hit."

"Two hundred ships?" Brecht hissed the words out as if they were blood pouring from a wound. "And what do you think will happen to those ships when the weapon hits their warp fields?"

"I can't be certain without a complete computer simulation run," Priscilla admitted, "but I'd say the likelihood is, the fields will overload and they'll be destroyed."

"They wouldn't need to have crews," Sam put in, feeling as if someone had to say it. "You could remote-guide them into place, set the timing up with a laser communication linkage, working the lightspeed delay into your calculations…"

"You're a Patrol Captain, Avalon," Brecht said sharply, in an accusatory tone. "One would hope you know approximately how many Transition-capable ships the Consensus military has in service."

"The last report I heard was over three years ago," Sam told her, "but back then, it was around three hundred in active rotation at any one time."

Brecht nodded, then turned to John Gage.

"Tell them how many it is now, Minister Gage."

"The same, more or less," the older man admitted. His demeanor was reluctant, as if he didn't want to give her argument any ammunition.

"And you know why the number hasn't gotten any higher?" the Prime Minister asked. "Because warp field generators are *damned* expensive!"

"More expensive than five billion lives?" Priscilla wondered. "Or a habitable planet? Your homeworld?"

230

Brecht's face screwed up in anger at the other woman's impertinence, but she sighed the emotion away and rubbed at eyes reddened from lack of sleep.

"We're at war with the Belters *and* the Jovians. And before you say it, yes, I know it was stupid and short-sighted; but unlike your computer overlords, I am not an absolute ruler and I can't be seen as ignoring this sort of attack in Consensus space."

She staggered back a step and leaned against the table. Gage made the slightest of motions, as if he wanted to go over and support her but had stopped himself out of respect for her office.

"I can't pull two thirds of our fleet off the line and throw them in a damned bonfire. Losing Earth to this weapon is death for us all, but losing it to the Belters and Jovians is just as permanent."

"It wouldn't have to be just *your* ships," Priscilla told her. "If I can get back to Aphrodite with evidence there was Resolutionist involvement in this plot, I *know* Mother will send help, whatever the cost."

"And how do you expect to get that evidence?" Gage wanted to know.

"She's here. The woman who sent the signal to hack the barge boarded a flight to Earth immediately after. If you can help us track her down, we'll bring her in and…well, it's your territory, your right to justice, but it would be easier for us to convince our government to help if we took her back."

"Do you have biometric data on this woman?" Gage wondered.

"We do." Pris pulled a data spike from a pocket of her jacket and handed it off to the older man.

"Can we run a search for her from here, Adrian?" Brecht asked Fellows.

"Adrian," is it? Sam cocked an eyebrow. Fellows was more important than he'd thought.

"Sure," the Guardian said, shrugging casually. "If she's been through any of the ports, the system will have picked her up."

He held out a palm and Gage slipped him the spike and he took it to the data input console, shrugging aside the clerk. The flabby-jowled functionary frowned, but didn't bother to argue, pushing his wheeled chair away and sitting with his arms crossed. Fellows slipped the spike into a reader, muttering in disgust at the obsolescent computer systems as he accessed the files.

Jeddah Valley's face slid up onto the main screen, along with a series of data points detailing her height, approximate weight, the gait of her walk and everything else the Martians had provided for them. A series of typed commands and a passcode later, the system was hooked up with the surveillance drones and security cameras from every major city on the planet, running the parameters against their stored records.

Seconds passed and Sam clucked with impatience; the systems back home would have delivered the results almost instantly.

"There it is." Fellows grunted as if he'd pulled the data out of the computer physically.

A map was showing on the screen, a location blinking, and beside it a video clip with footage of the woman disembarking from a lander at a port on the North American west coast, a city they called Trans-Pacifica. The locator program blinked fitfully until it caught up with her again, boarding a public bus out of the port to the city's transportation hub. She gazed out the window at the ships landing and taking off, as comfortable as any of the other tourists coming down from Fortuna or across the ocean from Asia.

She's a mass murderer. Contempt swelled in Sam's chest. *How can she be so cool?*

Fellows was reading the smaller display at his terminal while the video playback filled the overhead screen.

"We lose her at the hub for a few minutes," he droned, sounding to Sam like one of the narrators of the nature videos he'd watched in school, tracking some elusive predator across the plains of Aphrodite's northern wilderness. "Until we get just one shot of her from a safety camera on the side of a rental cab out at the private flyer landing pad just outside the port grounds."

Another short video clip, grainier and less clear than the previous ones. It was hard to make out the woman's face, but the computer had managed it from her biometrics, apparently. She was clambering up the boarding steps into the cabin of a small VTOL flyer, the sort which were ubiquitous on Resolution colony worlds but not seen as much on a planet as settled as Earth.

"Is that a government plane?" he wondered. "Or a rental, maybe?"

"Private," Telia replied, pointing at the ID number stenciled on the side of the fuselage. "That prefix is for privately-owned aircraft."

"Who can afford to own their own flyer?"

He hadn't meant the words to sound envious, but he realized they did. No civilian on Aphrodite could have afforded the taxes and penalties for owning and operating their own aircraft.

"There are a few thousand of them," Fellows said, shrugging as if it were a small matter. "Business executives, some who just put everything they make into buying one for the fun of it…they're nuts, but some good pilots. And then…" He trailed off, turning back to them, face split with a broad, evil-looking grin. "There are a few really important politicians working from their family fortune."

Sam didn't recognize the man in the picture at first; it was a still from a government ID, and it was as bad as those photographs always were, no matter what the technology. Then he read the name beside it and everything made sense.

"Tejado," Brecht spat the word out as if it were poisonous. She glanced around like she expected to see the man in the room with them. "Where the hell is he, anyway?"

"He said he wanted to stay in the Ministry building," Gage informed her, "as an example to the others that we shouldn't give in to panic." The last spoken so dryly a single spark would have set it afire.

Fellows was already switching one of the smaller screens to another program; from the looks of the interface, Sam thought it was a tracker.

"His issued health monitor says he's not there," the Guardian declared. "Matter of fact, it's off-line." That smile again, an expression Sam thought he might see in his nightmares. "I'd bet you a week's salary he's on that fucking flyer right alongside this Resolutionist bitch."

If the man's rough language offended Brecht, she gave no sign. She was staring intently at the ID photo, as if she could read the Naturalist's mind in those dead eyes.

"Where the hell are they going, Adrian?"

"Looks like…"

The heavy, reinforced metal door to the chamber slammed open, interrupting whatever Fellows had been about to say. Armored Guardians tromped through, weapons at the ready, led by the NCO Fellows had talked to before, the one named Blumenthal.

"What the fuck's going on?" Fellows barked.

"There's been an actionable threat to the Prime Minister," Blumenthal told them, his voice distant and distorted through the external speakers of his helmet.

"Oh, for God's sake," Brecht snapped, standing up straight from where she'd been leaning on the table and taking a step toward Blumenthal. "I'm in the most secure facility in the Consensus! Who could possibly threaten me here?"

"Ma'am," the NCO told her, "we think there's a threat from someone inside the bunker. Please come with us."

"No."

That was Fellows, and the flatness of the word brought Sam's eyes around to the blocky gargoyle of a man. He was staring at Blumenthal the way a scientist might examine a new species of insect.

"This is the safest place in the whole facility," he declared. "If there's a threat, you all should stay outside, guard the approach, and seal the room."

"Sorry, sir," Blumenthal said, "but that won't work."

He levelled his pulse rifle at Brecht and fired.

Time slowed, the tachypsychia of an adrenalin rush dragging each second a frame at a time, exquisite, excruciating detail in each image. Sam felt like he could actually see the energy pulse transform the slug into a plasma at the muzzle, could see the accelerated bolt of super-ionized gas as hot as the interior of a star crawling across the room, the air in front of it distorting from the heat. It seemed as if he should be able to step in front of it, to push Brecht out of the way, but it was as much a mirage as the heat distortion; his mind was feeding him the data microseconds after the events, altering his perception rather than actual time.

The perception intercepted real time with a bang when the plasma struck Carlotta Brecht in the chest at several thousand meters per second. The Prime Minister's hair was tied into a braid down her back, sandy, salt-and-pepper strands fraying loose with the length of the day. It whipped around with a jerk of her head as she pitched backwards, and Sam smelled hair and flesh and fabric burning. Inside her torso, the plasma was flash-heating bodily fluids to vapor, expanding outward, turning her organs into so much charred jelly.

She was dead before she hit the floor.

And by rights, all of them should have been; but there was just the slightest delay, as if it took a moment for the conspirators to realize the magnitude of what they'd done and let it sink in before they could move on to the rest of their dirty job. Into that split-second Telia Proctor and Adrian Fellows *moved*.

On an intellectual level, he knew Telia Proctor was dangerous; he'd seen the video of the gunfight back on the station. It still hadn't prepared him. One moment she was a still-life, standing with her shoulders squared, her arms crossed, and the next she was three meters across the room, her metal fists pounding into the chest armor of one of the Guardians like a trip-hammer. Cracking bone battled with cracking ceramic for supremacy, and the loser was whoever was inside the armor. The Guardian flew backwards, flopping with mortal finality.

Fellows' motions were a ballet by comparison with Telia's sledgehammer. The man went low, one leg bent as a fulcrum and the other swinging through the air almost faster than Sam could follow, catching Blumenthal behind the knees, sweeping him off his feet backwards.

Inertia had been pinning Sam's feet to the floor, keeping him a spectator, but the impact of Blumenthal's back on the bare concrete seemed to flip a switch inside his head and he lunged for another of the armored figures, the one who had both gun-belts slung over her shoulder. No longer watching the action, trapped inside the bubble of his personal struggle, he thought he heard the crack-snap discharge of a pulse rifle from somewhere---it seemed far away, but that could have been the auditory exclusion which came as a package deal with the tachypsychia and the tunnel vision of an adrenalin rush.

He knew the Guardian was female, and he knew she didn't have the benefit of cybernetic enhancement or a boosted musculature because the Consensus wouldn't have permitted her to be stationed on Earth with the former and didn't allow the latter at all. But she was damned strong and he'd been working in a space station for nearly three years. She jerked the barrel of her pulse rifle back and forth, taking him with it, then aimed a kick at his groin; he barely shifted his hip around to block it and it still hurt like hell.

More shots, more shouting, and an alarm klaxon blaring right in his ear and he simply wrapped his hands around the barrel and receiver of her rifle and threw himself backwards, bringing his feet up into her chest. She was strong, but not strong enough to hold up a hundred kilograms of him and another hundred of herself, her armor and her weapon. He felt a bit of the air go out of him when he landed on his shoulders, but he was already shoving her over his head, his feet planted in her gut, rolling on top of her, the rifle under his control.

The sling still secured it to her harness, but there was enough slack for him to yank the pulse rifle a meter up, then slam the receiver down into the visor of her helmet. Once, twice, three times and polymer cracked, then splintered, then the face beneath it did the same. The woman stopped moving and Sam finally looked around as something white-hot flashed by the corner of his vision.

Fellows had a rifle propped on the conference room table, using it for as much cover as it was worth as he pumped shot after shot at the armored troops clustered near the door, firing back at him. The table was on fire in places, charred and smoking nearly everywhere else, but Fellows seemed more or less in one piece.

Off in the corner to Sam's right, Telia Proctor was breaking a man's neck with her bare hands, and there were already two others down within arm's reach of her, unmoving and presumably dead. As he watched, a pulse round impacted her in the left leg and she stumbled backwards, her fatigue pants charring away over her thigh, revealing bare metal. She yanked the rifle off of the man she'd killed, the straps snapping off of his harness at her tug, and ducked to one knee, returning fire.

Pris…where the hell is Pris?

Then he saw her, off to the side of the table, covering Minister Gage's body with her own, her teeth clenched as if she were waiting for the round with her name on it. Plasma blasts were striking the wall just behind her, coming way too close as the remaining Guardians sprayed and prayed, panicked at the opposition they hadn't expected. He had to do something.

Sam groped around the neck and shoulder of the trooper he'd…killed? Incapacitated? He didn't want to know. He found one of the holsters which had been hanging off her shoulder and ripped the pistol out of it, hoping to Gaia the thing didn't have an ID chip like Resolution weapons. If it did, he was going to look pretty damn stupid, though at least not for long, since he'd be dead.

He knew where the safety was, at least; Telia had showed him the basics of how the gun worked up on the station, but he'd never had the chance to fire it and never bothered to ask about built-in security features. He raised it to shoulder level, aiming through the pop-up electronic sight, and squeezed the trigger. The gun kicked in his hand and he nearly dropped it in surprise; Resolution laser weapons had no recoil and he'd nearly forgotten this was basically an electromagnetic slug shooter, even if the slug was turned into a plasma.

The first round splashed against the wall near the door, succeeding only in drawing some of the attention from the troops there. Some were already out the door, and he was deathly afraid they might shut it and lock all of them in the room with no way out, but they seemed more interested in finding a place to shoot from behind cover. One of the…four? Five?…left swiveled the emitter end of his pulse rifle toward him and Sam imagined he could see the heat radiating off its cooling jacket.

He re-aimed for the darkness of the trooper's helmet visor and held the trigger pad down, spraying out half a magazine at the man. Plasma flared, a line of coruscating white and yellow connecting them for half a second, and the visor splashed away along with the face beneath it. Some tiny part of Sam's mind still operating at a level beyond fight-or-flight screamed at him that he'd just killed a man.

Yeah? What's your point?

The armored corpse collapsed backwards and caused a chain reaction, moving the next man just slightly, distracting another, pushing a third directly into the line of fire. Sam wasn't sure if it was Telia or Fellows who shot the one who'd stumbled, or both, but he jerked away from the flash and sprawled half-in and half-out of the doorway, and that was enough for the three of the armored troopers left alive.

"They killed the Prime Minister!" one of them was screaming, the shout distorted and tinny over his helmet's external speakers. "Jesus Christ, they killed the Prime Minister!"

Sam lurched after them by instinct, not entirely sure what he would do if he caught up with them. Shoot them in the back? Try to tell their side of the story?

"Stop."

Fellows didn't yell, barely raised his voice, but Sam froze just the same at the gravelly tone of control and command somehow perfectly audible over the blaring alarms. He glanced back and forth between the doorway, littered with three dead bodies, and Fellows, rising from behind the table, the rifle cradled in his arms.

"We need to go make sure everyone knows the truth!" Sam insisted, waving towards the door.

"Are you all right, sir?" Pris was asking Gage, helping him to his feet. The old man was pale and shaken, but he didn't seem to be hurt. He pulled away from Priscilla and knelt over the Prime Minister's body, anguish writ plain on his lined and weathered face.

"Grab what guns and ammo you can carry," Freeman instructed, stripping spare magazines from Blumenthal's body. "And someone hand me my pistol."

"They're going to be bringing reinforcements," Telia said, cool and unaffected, already obeying his orders and grabbing reloads for the rifle she'd appropriated. "We won't be able to take them all on, even if they don't break out sonics or gas grenades." She shrugged casually. "Or thermal detonators, or frags, or…"

"We're not taking them on and we're not going to stick around to debate them," Fellows snapped, coming to his feet.

Sam had pulled the man's gun-belt free of the woman whose face he'd smashed; he handed it over wordlessly, trying not to look at the blood splattered across the web belt. Fellows grinned and buckled it on.

"You hold on to that one, flyboy," he said, nodding towards Telia's pistol, still in Sam's right hand. "You'll probably need it." He moved toward the door, motioning for the others to follow. "Come on, all of you---you too, Minister Gage, assuming you want to add a few more years to your already-impressive total. This place is a nest of vipers."

"And go where?" Gage demanded, standing from Brecht's lifeless body slowly, reluctantly. Sam remembered he'd thought the man was unflappable, like he'd seen everything.

Guess he hadn't seen this.

"The last place they'll expect us," Fellows said.

He was moving out the door and Telia followed him, the rifle at her shoulder, scanning side to side. Pris took Gage's arm and gently guided the man after them, while Sam brought up the rear, slinging Telia's pistol belt over his shoulder, not taking the time to adjust it to fit his waist.

People were running away from them, screaming as they emerged from a wreath of smoke into the tableau of chaos that had been a cubicle farm. At the other end of the long, open chamber, dozens of government office workers were jammed up in the stairwell against a squad of Guardians trying to squeeze past, the angry shouts of the troopers tinny and muted against the alarms and the cries of the civilians.

"In here." Fellows was down a short hallway, more of an alcove, holding open a doorway.

Inside was a dark, narrow hallway lined at intervals with metal access grates, what looked to Sam like the sort of maintenance crawlway techs used to service data cores. When Sam was through, Fellows yanked the door shut and pressed his hand to a security pad beside it. The plate glowed red and Fellows squeezed past the others, scooting down the hall sideways, his shoulders barely clearing the unadorned, cement-block walls.

"Where the hell are we going?" Gage demanded, beginning to sound less in shock and more upset, which Sam supposed was an improvement.

"You don't build a top-secret shelter like this without a top-secret emergency exit," Fellows told him, coming to a halt so quickly the grey-bearded Minister nearly ran into his back.

241

The metal grate was a meter on a side and identical to all the others, but Fellows went to it as if it had a holographic marquee advertising "secret passageway." He pulled a multi-tool out of a pouch on his belt and jammed it into a notch along the edge of the grate, prying down and outward at once, and it popped open with a vibrato rattle.

"What's at the other end of this?" Telia asked, crouching down, looking at the narrow passage doubtfully.

"Another empty warehouse." He shrugged. "But one far away from here. I gotta' admit, that's as far as I can get us, unless any of you know someone who'll give us a lift from there."

"You know," Sam said, a grim smile passing over his face, "I just might…"

Chapter Twenty-Three

"I could get in real trouble for this," Sully mused, goosing the throttle.

The shuttle's belly jets thundered through the fuselage of the craft, kicking them away from the landing field with enough force to leave Priscilla's stomach somewhere on the outskirts of Capital City. She tried to answer him, but the g-forces were strong enough she could barely take a breath, much less squeeze out a sound. The night sky spun on the view-screens and city lights merged with the scattered clouds and the waning moon until she thought she might throw up, implants or no.

In the end, it was Telia who spoke first, which might have been simply her innate fortitude or possibly her bionics.

"You said you could fake the flight clearance," she reminded the pilot. "If that is not the case, we should know now."

"Naw, I know this guy," Sully said once the g-load slacked off and they were three thousand meters up and ascending at a more sedate acceleration. "He works in Orbital Traffic Control and he owed me a favor." Pris was just behind the pilot's position, between his seat and Sam's on the right, and she could see the sulky pout on his face when he shrugged. "I *was* hoping for an intro to his sister, but I guess this'll have to do. I was just thinking what happens when we get where we're going and I ain't got clearance to land there."

"We all appreciate your sacrifice," John Gage said, and Pris thought she could detect the dry tone in his voice without turning to see his expression. "And we definitely appreciate the ride. But right now, I'd like to hear exactly what Guardian Prime Fellows has planned for when we land."

Fellows, Telia and Gage were all seated in the second row of seats in the shuttle's cockpit, just forward of the steps down to the passenger compartment and Gage had been giving Fellows the stink-eye ever since they boarded. If she was any judge from their acquaintance of the last three years, the Minister was a man used to being in charge and wasn't fond of the way the Guardian had kept him in the dark up to this point.

"The coordinates I gave our pilot," Fellows announced, spreading his hands as if the whole matter wasn't of any consequence, "are from the flight plan Tejado's jet filed with traffic control."

"We're going to Tejado?" Gage asked. "But what if his flight plan wasn't accurate? Why would he tell anyone where he was meeting this Resolution traitor?"

"You deviate from a filed flight plan," Sully explained with exaggerated patience, as if he were speaking to a child in Primary School rather than one of the highest officials in his government, "and you're asking for a squadron of armed drones up your ass." He glanced back at Gage, face screwed up in consternation. "Ain't you ever flown anywhere before?"

"I haven't flown commercial since before your father was born, son."

"He probably thinks there won't be anyone left alive to follow him," Fellows said.

"Where are we following him *to*?" Sam wanted to know, sounding as tired of the secrecy as Gage.

"The Canadian Rockies. I checked my personal 'link on the way over here and all I could find in the database is it's close to what used to be some sort of old military base, back before the original Consensus was formed. I don't know what could still be out there, after the war...maybe just a place to hide out until things blow over."

"Like the planet," Telia murmured.

Gage gave her a sharp glare and she spat a curse.

"I'm sorry, sir," she shook her head, eyes closing. "But that ramship is still coming. We have months to live, weeks to actually do something about it, and now someone inside our own government just assassinated Prime Minister Brecht. I have tried to maintain my faith, but I see little hope ahead."

"We can still do it," Pris insisted with more conviction than she actually felt. "If we can prove factions from among our own people were involved, I know Mother will try to make things right."

Fellows snorted humorlessly, head tilting back.

"Oh, you sound almost as if you believe that, missy."

Pris rounded on him, eyes flaring, the stress of the last month finally making its way past her iron control.

"I haven't heard any better ideas from you," she snapped at him. "Unless you think we can turn the thing around with glares and harsh language."

"No," the Guardian admitted freely, tossing a hand. "You people are the last chance we got now." He shook his head. "I just don't think it's a great chance. You might actually care about saving us as much as you claim, but I don't believe for one minute your fucking computer god gives a shit."

"If she didn't give a shit," Pris argued, "why would we have built the Gate in the first place?"

"You built it," he agreed. "And then one of your own blew the damned thing up. We helped you build it, and then one of our own does the best he can to sabotage anything we can do to save ourselves. The Belters try to help us, and now we're at war with them. It seems to me someone is doing their damnedest to make sure this fucking ship kills us all."

"Something doesn't make sense," Gage insisted.

"Just one thing?" Fellows cracked, but Gage ignored him.

"I can understand someone from the Resolution considering us the enemy, not wanting to save us. I could understand the Belters, even..." He grimaced. "But Jamie...Minister Tejado, he's many things, but he's loyal to the Consensus and he has to know the threat is real. How could he condemn us all to death? What does he have to gain?"

"You can ask him yourself," Sully chimed in, his voice as cheerful as ever. "We're gonna' be there in about ten minutes."

*   *   *

The sun peeked out over the crest of the mountains, bathing their snow-capped spires in a pink alpenglow, spreading slowly down through the aspens in scatters of red and gold and it was probably one of the most beautiful things Sam Avalon had ever seen. He clutched the grip of the pulse pistol tighter, shivering fitfully from temperatures just above freezing and wishing he was anywhere else in the universe.

"You should have stayed behind," Telia said again to Minister Gage, a stray glint of dawn reflecting off the metal of her bionic eye as she glanced back at the older man.

Gage stared at the ground intently, hands buried in his pockets, seemingly entirely focused on simply putting one foot in front of the other on the steep, snow-covered trail.

"I should have done many things," he responded evenly, not showing any affect from the cold. "Yet here I am."

Sully, at least, had shown the good sense to stay with the shuttle. He'd put her down in a clearing about three kilometers from where they'd spotted the VTOL flyer, which might have been a waste of time if Tejado and Valley had bothered to deploy surveillance drones, but it seemed like a risk worth taking. Well, it *had* seemed worth taking until Sam had gotten out on the damn trail and his boots had started sinking a couple centimeters into the snow with each step and the wind had started cutting through him.

"Someone should have mentioned we'd be taking a nature hike," he grumbled, half to himself, staring at one tree that pretty much looked like another and almost wishing someone would shoot at them.

"Watch for grizzlies," Fellows cautioned over his shoulder from the front of their single-file column. The cold didn't seem to bother him at all. "This place is lousy with them. Wolves too, but those probably won't bother five people travelling together." He shrugged. "And mountain lions, lots of mountain lions of course."

Sam heard Priscilla chuckling behind him and he glanced back at her, a bit surprised. She was smiling, which surprised him as well, even though she was just as cold as he was, and just as underdressed for the elements. Telia had given Pris her sidearm and it looked somehow out of place belted around her narrow waist; he had never pictured her holding a gun.

"I have seen and done so much these last three years," she told him softly, noting his curious look, "experienced so much. This," she nodded around them, "seems an appropriate place for it all to end."

"Nothing is ending," he said, knowing his tone sounded sharp but not caring. "We're going to capture Valley and find out who's behind this."

"We will," she agreed, stepping up and putting a hand on his shoulder. "But nothing is guaranteed in life. And if this is my final act, I want you to know you made this the best of all possible worlds for me."

"That's all really fucking sweet," Fellows said, voice kept low but not a whisper, "but we're getting close and I think it's time you all just shut up before you make me lose my breakfast…that I didn't get to eat, thanks all to hell."

Dawn was finally working its way down through the trees, turning what had been menacing shadow into mundane, winding trail, snow-crusted rocks and fallen branches. Sam didn't think there'd be any bears. He thought he'd read bears didn't attack big groups of people. But he still kept thinking about mountain lions every time they passed a rock shelf, which they did more and more as the trail began sloping sharply upward, and he cursed Fellows silently.

The paranoia dragged the hike out and, in between imaginary lions and spectral enemy soldiers, he kept wondering if the landing site they'd spotted from the air was just around the bend, or just over the next rise. It wasn't, and still wasn't, and kept not being until it seemed like it never would be and they'd be walking past these same rocks and trees for eternity, stuck in some sort of boreal purgatory.

Are we lost? Does Fellows actually know how to get there?

The Guardian raised a hand up to shoulder level, the universal symbol for everyone to halt, then clenched it into a fist and took a knee. Sam wasn't totally sure what the gesture meant, but he saw Telia and Gage imitating the motion and he took the chance Fellows was telling them to get down, so he did as well. Ahead of them was a sharp rise, the trail cut with steps at some point, well worn now until they were mere indentations. He couldn't see anything over the top of it and he thought maybe it leveled out ahead.

Fellows waited motionless, head cocked to the side as if he was listening, though Sam couldn't hear anything.

248

Huh. Can't hear anything...*including birds, or squirrels or whatever was making those chittering noises in the trees. Just nothing.*

Fellows turned back to them and patted the air in what Sam thought was a gesture for them to stay there. He pointed to himself, then forward, then signaled he was going up ahead to reconnoiter, which seemed like a damned good idea, though Sam would rather have gone with him than stayed back here where he couldn't see anything. Telia looked even less happy about it, but she said nothing, just glared at Fellows' back as he disappeared over the top of the rise, crouching low.

Sam shared a glance with Priscilla and considered talking to her via the neurolinks, but decided not to risk it. They operated via radio waves, and if Tejado had left anyone behind in the plane with the right sort of gear, it wasn't beyond the realm of possibility they might detect the transmission. Besides, he had nothing important to say; it was just nerves wearing on him, the nagging worry he might have to kill someone else. And it wasn't so much it had bothered him, but more that it hadn't. He kept expecting guilt to set in, or shock, but there was nothing.

What he *did* keep seeing over and over, looping like a video clip in his mind whenever he closed his eyes, was the plasma blast hitting Prime Minister Brecht in the chest, her collapsing backwards with a look of pain and shock on her face. She'd seemed so strong and certain in life, yet it had abandoned her in death. Was that how he'd look when his time came, like death had come as such an utter surprise?

He was still trying to push her death mask out of his memory when Fellows returned. He wasn't crouching this time, was almost sauntering, the pulse rifle held at low ready. He waved them forward and Telia led them off, with Gage kept in the middle between her and Sam. The climb up the rise was steep and Gage faltered near the apex; Sam thought he'd have to help the old man, but Gage caught himself, leaning forward and grabbing onto an exposed rock ledge and pulling himself over the crest.

Sam followed and nearly stopped in his tracks when he saw the flyer. It was only twenty or thirty meters ahead, where the path widened out into a clearing. Blackened stumps dotted the bare dirt and Sam guessed there'd been a fire in the area recently, within the last year or so because of the lack of re-growth. Enough space had been cleared in the clumps of aspens for the VTOL jet to touch down, its tricycle landing gear squeezed between half-meter tall stumps.

The side hatch of the plane yawned open, and a man's body was sprawled half-in and half-out of it, blood spilling down the boarding ramp in winding rivulets. His head had been caved in, likely by the butt-stock of Fellow's rifle, and Sam let his eyes skip away from the sight of the stoved-in skull, the misshapen head that didn't even seem human anymore.

"There's another over here," Fellows reported quietly, speaking in a low tone but not whispering. Telia had explained to Sam once how a whisper actually carried further than simply keeping your voice down.

"Over here" turned out to be through a stand of trees that had survived the vagaries of the lightning-strike fire, over a low rockfall pile and right up to the side of a hill. The woman was dressed in the same drab grey as the man had been, the unmarked uniform of Consensus Executive Security, which Sam hadn't quite been able to figure out if it was an official government agency or a private firm. She hadn't been bludgeoned to death like the man; there was the hilt of a boot knife protruding from her left ear where the blade had stuck in her skull. She'd been a handsome woman in life, with a regal nose and high cheekbones, but now the light was extinguished behind her eyes and she seemed fake, a robot greeter with a short in its motherboard.

His gaze was so drawn to those dead eyes it took him a moment to notice the doorway. When he saw the shadowed arch, he thought it was a cave at first, but there was something too regular about the shape, something too smooth about the walls inside. They were pitted with age, but they'd started out straight and level, a tunnel right into the side of the mountain.

"I guess this is why they're here," Telia murmured.

"You got the infrared eye, Proctor" Fellows told her, motioning with the emitter of his rifle. "You go first."

Telia moved ahead of him, intentionally brushing him with her shoulder hard enough to knock him back a step. Fellows chuckled and swatted her on the back with a casual camaraderie Sam found jarring. Just how well did these two know each other? Fellows had been a complete asshole to her---and all of them---when they'd first arrived on Luna three and a half years ago. What had changed?

"Hey flyboy," Fellows said to him, as if he'd sensed the eyes on his back. "Make yourself useful and watch our asses." He craned his head around and sneered. "That means walk backwards behind us and shoot anyone else you see, in case I was being too technical."

I take it back, Sam thought, letting the others past him and putting a hand against the wall to guide himself as he stepped carefully backwards from the entrance. *He's still an asshole.*

Chapter Twenty-Four

When the technicians had told her about the infrared functions in her bionic eye, Telia had imagined the effect would be something like the night-vision filters in her battle armor's helmet, with everything flatly two-dimensional and tinted green. She hadn't thought about the eye being wired directly into her optic nerve, and the function the brain played in vision. Her brain didn't want to see the green tint, so she didn't; the images were black and white instead, as if she were under the brightest full moon ever, and somehow her brain added depth to it as well.

Normally, none of it would have helped this deep underground; there was just no light, infrared or otherwise. She would have been forced to use an infrared flashlight, which would have been just as obvious to anyone watching with night vision goggles as if she'd simply used a visible-spectrum flashlight.

Normally. But there *was* light somewhere up ahead, still far enough it was just an almost imperceptible glow, but it was sufficient to give the broad entrance hall some detail, to allow her to stay at the center. The glow was comforting; if Tejado and his people expected company, they wouldn't have left the lights on. That's what she told herself anyway.

The light grew brighter as she moved, urging speed, but she resisted the pull and advanced carefully and methodically. There were other things her eye could see more clearly than a biological version: remote sensors, laser tripwires, insect drones left along the trail to watch for intruders. She could spot them before they spotted her, most of the time, but only if she was thorough and slow.

She saw nothing, not a sign of rear security and it bothered her. The sloppiness bothered her, as did the inattention of the guards Fellows had killed. He was good, but he was one man and he'd taken out both of the protection detail alone and without using a gun. It wasn't just that they hadn't expected opposition, it was as if they were in a rush, as if the whole thing hadn't been planned at all.

Why were they here?

She could hear voices and she stopped short, holding up a hand to alert Fellows and the others. He'd halted already, head cocked towards the sound. She couldn't make out what was being said, just the unmistakable buzz of conversation, maybe a man, definitely a woman. She made a questioning gesture, confident the light was bright enough now for him to see it. He turned to the others and held up a hand for them to wait, then pointed to her and to himself and raised his rifle to his shoulder.

The meaning was unmistakable: the two of them were going to move up and take out the threat. "Take out the threat" sounded so antiseptic, so textbook. It wasn't quite adequate to describe the mechanics of killing people, but it would have to do. She nodded to him, raising her rifle one-handed, the weight of the massive pulse gun nothing to her bionics. She could have held one in each hand if it wouldn't have been impossible to hit anything that way.

She moved out first, knowing Fellows would take point if she gave him the chance, and also knowing she could take more punishment. Her left pant leg was still charred and ragged, the dull-grey of the bionics polished silvery bright by the plasma blast she'd taken back in Capital City, a reminder gleaming faintly in the light filtering into the tunnel.

After, she promised herself. *If we live through this, if we manage to find some way to save everything, then I'll travel to the Resolution and I'll use their medical cloning, unholy though it may be, and I'll be whole again. It's what Mawae would have wanted.*

And what she would do with herself after that was a matter best left for the future. The end of the tunnel brought her thoughts back to the here and now. It terminated in a T-junction, and the light and the voices both came from the left leg of the intersection, which didn't necessarily mean the right side was unoccupied. She gestured for Fellows to cover the right while she edged forward, hugging the wall and feeling the cold, pitted surface of the stone pulling at her hair as she darted around the corner for a split-second glimpse of the other side.

The image was a single frame frozen in a video stream, a snapshot of data that took her brain a moment to process. The room was large and looked larger because of the odd play of shadows from the portable lighting stands set up in the corners; the glare had washed out her vision, made it hard to discern the details, but she'd definitely seen a door of some kind, metal, with a large, physical lock.

Six people, that much she was sure of, though the only face she'd recognized on first glance was Tejado's. He was there, and Valley probably was as well, but she'd never met the Resolutionist and couldn't pick her out from the other two women she'd spotted in the group. What they were doing…that was harder to figure. There'd been some sort of heavy, metal case on the floor next to the doorway, two meters long and a meter across, and the lid of the thing had been propped up while one of the women kneeled beside it and fiddled with something inside, something Telia hadn't been able to see.

The others were guards, she thought, posted around the room with guns in their hands, what sort she couldn't make out. Except Tejado…he was pacing, impatient, an expectant father. She wasn't sure if he was armed, but if he had a gun, it wasn't visible.

She signaled to Fellows and he indicated there was nothing down to the right. She held up five fingers, then closed her fist and an additional one to make six. Four more fingers and she patted the side of her rifle; four of them armed. She chopped her hand in different directions as if around a compass, giving him the positions of everyone she'd seen, then indicated herself and the left side of the room. She'd take the left, he'd take the right.

Fellows nodded, a hint of a grin playing across his ugly, blocky face, and she remembered why she'd once fallen for the man, a lifetime ago. She held up the last three fingers of her left hand, began counting them down one at a time. When the last one folded, she spun around the corner, still feeling that empty free-fall in her gut even after all these years.

She couldn't see them as individuals. She'd freeze up if she did, if she let herself look them in the eyes, so she watched their center of gravity instead, their chests grey and armored and impersonal. She wasn't conscious of pulling the trigger, didn't feel the recoil; the flash of the first round igniting at the bore was a surprise to her, and an even bigger surprise to the Executive Protection agent. Plasma speared through his chest armor, the military rifle too powerful for the light vest to defeat it, and even if the first round had been stopped, the second and third would have killed him.

Telia didn't watch him fall, though she knew the shots had been fatal; instead, she was moving, just two steps to the left as she transitioned to her next target, a tall, gangly woman with shocking red hair shaved into a mohawk and a sub machinegun held loosely in her hands. She was trying to bring it up, training overcoming the shock at seeing the man shot in front of her, but it was already too late. She was dead, and the three-round burst was merely a formality.

The first two were free, the benefits of surprise; the last man was fast, and a professional, and already firing. She'd anticipated it. You never counted on more than two. He'd expect her to move forward and left, so she didn't. Just one sliding step back, a duck to the right and the rocket-assisted slugs from his sub machinegun passed by centimeters from her face, a wash of hot wind against her cheek.

She made a mistake then and looked him in the eye. Disappointment, annoyance, perhaps a bit of respect behind those blue eyes, plus the knowledge his time was up. Heat and light and vaporized blood washed the face away before he could fire another shot, but she knew she'd taken too long. If anyone had gotten past Fellows…

They hadn't, of course. The last remaining Executive Protection agent was slumping face-first, a haze of steam rising up from her charred body armor, her features slack and lifeless, and Fellows was standing over Jamie Tejado while he trained his rifle on a woman Telia presumed was Jeddah Valley. Tejado was moaning softly, flat on his back, with a pressure cut on his cheek oozing blood, the skin around it red and already starting to bruise; she guessed he'd been the recipient of a butt-stroke from Fellows' rifle.

Jeddah Valley looked much the same as she had in the surveillance videos, though they hadn't quite managed to capture the wild tangle of her auburn hair, a look of benign neglect that might have come naturally or might have been cultivated as part of her cover. She was still kneeling, caught in the midst of whatever she'd been doing with the metal case, and her long, plain face was ashen with shock.

Telia snuck a glance beneath the open cover of the container; there was a simple, touch-screen control panel inside, a virtual keyboard taking up half the display, the other half with a list of symbols. Some were letters, some numbers, some just shapes such as triangles and circles. It didn't make a damned bit of sense to her.

"Whoever you are," Valley was saying, her voice rough and hoarse, "this is a mistake. You need to leave now, it's vital..."

"And what exactly are you doing here, Citizen Valley?"

Priscilla stepped into the chamber, Telia's pistol hanging loosely at her side, her blue eyes fixed on Jeddah Valley.

"What would a Resolution citizen be doing here on Earth?" Pris said, striding slowly across the room, side-stepping the growing pools of blood without looking down at them. "What would a Resolution citizen be doing hijacking a Belter barge, *murdering* dozens of her brothers and sisters and then running to Earth to meet with the head of the Naturalist Party?" She indicated Tejado with a casual sweep of the pistol's muzzle. Tejado saw it and flinched away.

"And what the hell is that thing?" Sam asked, walking in from the tunnel with John Gage in tow. He was pointing at the coffin-size metal container, though not with his gun; he either had better training with firearms than Priscilla or perhaps wasn't as cold-blooded. Telia could have believed either.

"How did *you* find me?" Jeddah Valley's eyes were wide, her tone venomous, but the target was Priscilla rather than Sam. "There's no way you could have found me here!"

"Shut up, Valley!" Tejado snapped, rolling onto his side, hand pressed to his cheek. "Don't tell them anything!" He turned on Fellows, motioning at Sam and Pris. "Guardian Fellows, as an appointed Minister of the Consensus government, I order you to arrest these two enemies of the state!"

"Yeah, dipshit, about that," Fellows drawled, rolling his eyes at Tejado, "I got a Minister here telling me to do something else, and he ain't hanging out with the bitch who blew up the only hope we had of saving this planet."

"Be smart, Adrian," Tejado growled, coming slowly to his feet. "You've always known which side your bread was buttered on. Only one of us is going to come out of this on top."

Gage moved before Telia could stop him, shoving Tejado back to the ground, hands at the man's throat.

"You son of a bitch!" he screamed into the Naturalist's face. "None of us are coming out on top of this! We're all going to fucking die thanks to you and your friend! Give me one fucking reason I shouldn't kill you now!"

Tejado tried to strike at the older man, but Gage wasn't having any of it; he yanked the other Minister bodily and slammed him back to the stone floor. There was a painful crack as the back of Tejado's head smacked against Stone and the wind went out of the Naturalist, his eyes rolling back in his head. Gage's left foot was smeared with the blood of one of the protection agents, the red dripping from his heel as he crouched down over Tejado.

"Minister Gage…" Telia began, intending to try to calm the man down, but stopped as something about the metal case struck her. Her bionic eye had several different functions beside infrared filters…including a Geiger counter. "Oh, fuck me," she muttered.

"What is it?" Fellows asked sharply. He'd be the one to know something was wrong; he knew she rarely swore.

"I think I know what that case is," she stated, surprised at how steady her voice was.

She took a step toward it, still keeping her gun trained on Valley. The reading was unmistakable, a red flashing in the corner of her vision.

"It's a nuclear weapon."

*   *   *

"It's some kind of password," Sam decided, peering at the touch screen on the weapon's control panel. He was bent over the open lid of the case, hands carefully at his side, not wanting to touch anything by accident. "Shouldn't we just try deleting the symbols already typed?"

"We don't know what she did to it before we got there," Fellows scoffed, tightening the restraints around Jeddah Valley's wrists. The woman yelped slightly and glared at him but he simply pushed her back to a seat on the floor beside Tejado, who was still lolling incoherently. "We hit the wrong key by accident and…" He mimed an explosion with his fingers.

"Tell us how to disarm this thing," Telia Proctor barked at Valley, brandishing her pistol in the woman's face.

"Put that aside for a moment," Priscilla said, her voice and demeanor much calmer than anyone else's. She approached the Resolutionist woman, crouching beside her to look her in the eye. "What *is* this place? And why is it so important that you'd use a nuclear weapon to destroy it?"

"This place," Valley told her, contempt dripping off the words, "is the death of both of our civilizations. And if you have a shred of loyalty left to Mother and to *the* Mother Gaia, you'll cut me loose and let me finish what I have to do."

The ferocity of the woman's tone, the intensity of her gaze made Sam shudder; she was a fanatic. But a fanatic for whom?

"You mean through there?" Pris jabbed a finger at the pitted grey metal of the hatch, the ancient wheel at its center, somehow free of rust or corrosion. "What's in

259

there, Citizen Valley? If you can convince me you're right, perhaps I will indeed allow you to destroy it."

Sam could almost believe her; Pris was still the most convincing liar he'd ever met, even if she'd had a three-year hiatus in what she called "exercising diplomacy." Valley, however, wasn't as easily convinced.

"You might have once, but you're not what you were." The older woman pulled her knees up to her chest, resting her head on them. "You were such a disappointment to her."

"To who?" Sam asked sharply, maybe being defensive for Pris if he was being honest with himself. "Who are you working for?"

"This is a waste of time," Fellows grumbled, leaning back against the far wall, arms crossed. "We have what we came for. We'll take Tejado back and try his ass for assassinating Brecht, you take this psycho bitch and parade her in front of your people to get them to send help. As for the nuke…" He shrugged. "As long as I'm far away from it when it blows, what the hell do I care?"

Valley made no reply to that, but Sam thought she seemed a bit too comfortable with the idea. Something was wrong here, something beyond the conspiracy.

"No," Pris declared. "There's something here they don't want revealed and it's important enough they rushed here immediately when they found out Sam and I were coming to meet with Prime Minister Brecht. All this…" She waved a hand around them demonstratively. "The assassination, this trip to the middle of nowhere, this was last-minute, poorly-planned, improvised." She grabbed Valley's face between the fingers of her hand, jerking it upwards to meet her eyes. "What is this place?"

The woman tried to spit at her, but Priscilla's reflexes were too fast for that and she jerked aside, then slapped Valley across the face.

"I can make you tell me," Pris warned.

260

Sam frowned, wondering what she meant. Surely she wasn't speaking of torture…things were dire, but were they really desperate enough to sink to that level?

But there was real fear in Valley's eyes at the threat, almost panic.

"You wouldn't," she said, her voice breaking, her heels digging into the concrete as she tried to push herself backwards. "I'm a Citizen, you can't *do* that…"

"Do you think I care about legalities at this point, woman?" Priscilla's voice was harsh, chilling.

"Are we talking a little of the rough stuff?" Fellows wondered, pushing off the wall, cracking his knuckles. "Because I might be able to help with that, though it's been a while…"

"Physical torture is unreliable," Pris told him, not looking away from Valley. "People will tell you what you want to hear to stop the pain, then you have to go over the same questions repeatedly to make sure they weren't lying and it would take far too long."

"Then what are you suggesting?" John Gage asked. He was frowning, but Sam thought he was more upset at the idea he was being kept in the dark than at the ethical problem of torture with a possibly ticking nuclear bomb.

Pris looked up finally, regarding them all, and Sam the longest, and he thought he saw an apology in her eyes.

"Most Resolution citizens who go into careers off-world are fitted with a neurolink, a transceiver connected directly to the auditory and visual centers of the brain."

"We know about 'em," Fellows said with a curt nod. "Kinda' creepy if you ask me, but what's the point?"

"There are things about the neurolink about which most people aren't aware. There is necessarily a small computer module to translate the microwave signals to neural code." She closed her eyes, as if steeling herself for the reaction to what she was about to reveal. "There are…backdoors built into these computers, which can be used, under certain conditions, to compel cooperation."

Sam's mouth dropped open and he rocked back a step, feeling as if someone had just slapped him across the face. That couldn't be true…she had to be bluffing.

"You can't *do* that to me!" Valley screamed at her, jerking back and forth against her bonds.

"It's seldom used," Pris admitted, "because there are some…side-effects." She pierced Valley with a cold glare. "It can cause neurological scarring, psychological problems, post-traumatic stress, other things. I'd rather not bring a vegetable back with me to Aphrodite, but I think under the circumstances, they'll understand."

Sam swallowed hard. Whether it was true or not, Valley obviously *thought* it was. He had to help her out; recriminations could wait.

"You're going to tell us either way," he pointed out, trying to play good cop to Priscilla's bad cop. "You tell us voluntarily, you get to keep your personality instead of a mindwipe, which is what you're looking at right now."

"Mindwipe?" Gage asked, blanching. "Do you people actually *do* things like that?"

"Oh, we do," Sam told him, trying to hide the lurch in his stomach. "I know the Consensus puts people to death for certain crimes, but it's considered more merciful to just…" He shrugged. "…rewrite them. I don't know, I've always thought I'd rather just die. I mean, everything you are is destroyed anyway, so…"

"Time's up," Priscilla decided, grabbing the woman's temples between her palms and fixing her eyes as if she were going to launch herself through them into her brain. "We'll do this the hard way."

"All right," Valley strained through clenched teeth, trying to pull her head away from Priscilla's grasp. "I'll tell you." Her gaze flickered around them all. "I'll tell you whatever you want to know."

"Who sent you here?" Pris asked her, not letting go of her grip on the woman's face. "Who didn't want the Gateway to succeed?"

"Mother." There was something of a perverse satisfaction in the look she gave Priscilla. "I was sent by Mother."

Chapter Twenty-Five

Pris didn't realize she'd slapped the woman until she felt the sting in her palm, saw Jeddah Valley's head snap around, blood oozing from her split lip.

"I thought you were smarter than to try to feed me this sort of bullshit," she snarled at the woman. "Do you think I have any patience left after you murdered dozens of innocent people? Do you really think I'd believe Mother sent you to do this?"

"Mother sent me just as she sent you," Valley said, spitting blood out to the side. Her chin was up, her expression defiant. "I'm the same as you, Priscilla, I knew it the first time I saw you. I'm an avatar."

"What the fuck is an avatar?" Fellows wondered, as idly profane as always. "Is that one of them Virtual Reality things?"

Priscilla didn't answer. She couldn't; the words were frozen in her brain, behind an ice jam in a river of thoughts.

"At times," Valley answered the question, "Mother has tasks she needs accomplished, things she trusts no one else to do. When she has these special assignments, she manufactures an avatar." Valley nodded toward Priscilla, still struck dumb. "A force-aged clone body, with a blank slate for a brain. And into that blank slate, Mother downloads herself, or part of herself, what can fit from a sentient computer as old as Old Earth into a single human brain."

"That's…not possible."

Poor Sam. He refused to believe it, even though he must know it was true.

"It's not her, of course," Valley went on. "The second the avatar wakes up and begins to have her own experiences, she becomes a different person, and the longer she exists on her own, the more her own separate

264

personality develops. That's why most are compelled to return within weeks, at most, to have their memories uploaded into Mother and their bodies reconstituted."

Pris couldn't look at Sam, couldn't speak to him. And she still couldn't come out and tell him the truth about herself. But she could speak to Valley, could ask her questions still.

"Yet you lived apart for years," she said to the woman. "Decades even. How would Mother allow that?"

There was a quiet outrush of breath behind her, the sound of Sam Avalon's exhalation as he realized what Priscilla's question meant. Pain clenched at her chest, but she couldn't turn away from Valley.

"My mission wasn't over," Valley replied. "It still isn't. This place has to be destroyed before anyone finds out its secrets."

"Why?" John Gage interjected, leaning in close to the woman. "What is so important about this place?"

"If I tell you," Valley insisted, "you won't believe me." She nodded toward the metal hatch. "I have to show you."

"You can't do this," Tejado moaned, rolling onto his side. His eyes still seemed unfocused but he was trying to look at Jeddah Valley. "We had a deal!"

"There's no choice now, Jaime." Valley shook her head. "The only way out is through."

"All right," Priscilla said, turning to Telia. "Open the door."

She finally made herself meet Sam's eyes. There was hurt there, and anger, and maybe something else…perhaps a sense of awe? The look a Bronze-Age savage might have reserved for a prophet touched by the gods. She didn't know which of those made her sadder.

Telia paused a moment before nodding and heading over to the hatch, taking that ancient, metal wheel in her metal fingers and bracing herself.

"I suppose it's a day for revealing hidden secrets," the cyborg mused, throwing her weight into the lock.

It squealed in protest, turning slowly and reluctantly, and a massive bolt slid out of its housing with a loud, shuddering bang. The hatch creaked open and on the other side was darkness.

Pris pulled a flashlight from Telia's borrowed gun-belt, switched it on and held it with one hand, grabbing Jeddah Valley by the neck with the other and pushing her ahead into the black.

"Show me this terrible knowledge of yours, sister," she told the woman. "Show me what's worth killing a planet for."

*   *   *

Sam should have been helping to guard Jaime Tejado, or watching for threats, or doing anything useful, but he couldn't force his thoughts into any sort of order. Priscilla was *Mother*.

Well, not Mother herself, but an avatar, a living representation of what was basically their god transferred to human form. So many things about her made sense now: the way she'd seemed at once almost infinitely knowledgeable and capable and in command while simultaneously childlike and inexperienced; how much she'd changed in the last few years, developing personality quirks in a short period of time which would normally be firmed up by the time someone hit adulthood.

He wanted to be enraged she'd withheld the truth from him, but he'd already known she couldn't help it, that there were firewalls in her mind, in her implant computer which kept her from telling him the truth. The anger faded quickly, but what it left behind was…what? Horror? Reverence? Awe?

He barely registered his surroundings, letting the darkness on the edges of the flashlights swallow up his perceptions, not perceiving the details of the near distance except as an indistinct grey blur. When the procession stopped, he nearly ran into the back of Telia Proctor.

"I need my hands free," Jeddah Valley said, her tone sullen but resigned.

Priscilla stared at her for a moment, obviously dubious, but Fellows pulled out his multi-tool and twisted the plastic restraints off her wrists. She shook her hands out as if she were trying to get feeling back into them, then motioned over to the right, nearly disappearing into the grey blur at the edge of the light before Priscilla adjusted the beam.

There was the corner of a wall there, what might have been the beginning of an aisle or a row of...something. A metal panel had been pried open and clamps were pinched on what seemed to be some sort of old-style electrical hookup there. The clamps were connected to insulated wires running down to the square, plastic box of a portable battery pack. Valley touched a control on the box, then threw a physical switch inside the panel and gradually, in fits and starts, lights began to flicker on above them.

"We had to replace some of the wiring," Valley said quietly, almost reverently, "and fabricate new light panels. The old ones were built with the best they had at the time, to last a thousand years. But not this long."

Finally, Sam understood where they were. Row after row, flickering into the light as if they were only now coming into existence, shelf after shelf, coming up shoulder high on him, grey and plastic and marked with some sort of ancient text, faded and worn despite being underground and out of the elements. And on every shelf, open plastic sleeves, each alike, hundreds per shelf, hundreds of thousands just in the one chamber he could see. And in those sleeves, some sort of cassette, clear but not plastic, reminding him of nothing so much as the data spikes everyone used for secure storage of information.

"This is a library," he said, louder than he'd intended.

The words echoed through the room, two hundred meters on a side, curved along the walls into a great cylinder. At the center was a hub, a stairwell he thought, and he had the sense it led to more rooms just like this one.

"It is," Jeddah Valley confirmed. "The oldest still in existence, commissioned by the original Consensus government under Charles Dauphin himself."

"How far down does it go?" Sam asked her, motioning at the stairwell.

"There are twenty levels just like this one," she said. "As well as a small nuclear reactor that's no longer working, and a few rooms where the curators used to stay." Her mouth twitched downward, a hint of a frown. "We found their remains there."

"How is that possible?" John Gage demanded, almost sounding scandalized by the idea. "The nanite swarms of the last war destroyed any metal and plastic, broke it down to its components. This shouldn't exist at all."

"That's not how nanites work," Priscilla informed him, her manner didactic in a way Sam was sure would piss the old man off. "They don't just keep going blindly, eating everything, not even nanophage weapons. They're programmed what to break down or there'd be no ore or oil left in the ground. They'd keep going until their programmed energy sources were gone, then they'd die."

She waved a hand around them. "This place was far enough away from any civilization and probably secret enough it was never targeted." Pris frowned, nose wrinkling in confusion. "The question is, why would anyone build it?"

"They knew what was coming."

Valley led them down the aisles, cutting first to the right and then back to the left until she reached a shelf which looked very much like any of the others to Sam. She picked out one of the sleeves near the upper right of the shelf and took the crystalline cassette out of it. Sam expected someone to object, someone to show caution, but they all simply let her carry the storage cassette towards the center of the chamber, to something set into the curved wall beside the stairwell.

It was some sort of projector, he thought, something simple and primitive but likelier to survive the ravages of time than a more complicated holographic unit or even a flat-screen monitor. Valley slipped the cassette into a notch at the base of the slab-like projector and it locked in place with a solid clack of crystal in crystal.

"Again," she told them, "we had to replace the light source and re-wire the power, but it's amazing what's lasted."

A circle of light snapped to life against a flattened section of stone cut into the curve of the cylindrical hub, and standing in the light was a man, only his torso visible in the video recording. He was slender and dark, grey shot through his black beard, his hair wild and unruly and his eyes alight with intensity. He wore a long, loose overcoat and beneath it was visible some sort of cravat, lavender silk. Sam knew his face. Every Resolutionist knew that face, had learned it as a young child in the very first lessons they were taught.

"Greetings," the dark man said, his voice soothing, smooth, almost hypnotic. "My name is Charles Dauphin."

*   *   *

"If you're watching this video," the bearded man went on, "then I can only assume the worst has happened, the final war has been fought and there's nothing left of us."

"Holy shit," Fellows murmured.

Telia grunted agreement, though no one else spoke. Charles Dauphin was a legend...or a bogeyman, depending with whom you discussed the subject.

"The end is inevitable," Dauphin went on. He swept a hand across in front of him and the scene in the video transformed with the motion.

The view of the Earth from orbit was familiar, but the details on that globe were not. Vast swathes of Asia were brown, barren desert and whole coastlines were changed. The globe turned, its rotation sped up in the projection, and then the view sank into an atmosphere brown with pollution, hazy with fires rising from sprawling, ugly cities. They were stacked with cheap, blocky buildings constructed so close together they could have been touching, obviously new and yet just as obviously already falling apart...and burning.

"Eleven billion people live on this world and as the world economy collapses, the population only seems to grow ever faster. In a sane world, a planned world, we could make room for even this many, could rebuild our cities to accommodate them. Yet every attempt we make to do this results in civil unrest and violence."

The camera eye sank lower, into the streets, hovering over the riots in the hearts of cities across the world, people chanting and screaming and throwing themselves at lines of armored soldiers. Sonic weapons swept across crowds and dozens fell, writhing. Molotov cocktails answered, setting police and military vehicles ablaze, and now rifles chattered in return and blood was spilled on the cracked pavement.

"We have perfected fusion power, but the cost of construction is so high and the political instability so great that only two reactors have been built; and much of the world is still dependent on burning fossil fuels, which are more vulnerable to terrorist attack."

A quick shift again, to somewhere less urban, somewhere arid and rocky and desolate. A pipeline ran across that wasteland and above it remotely-piloted drones buzzed, swarms of them. Some sort of electromagnetic weapon fired from a dish mounted on a truck parked along the pipeline, swinging back and forth, and where it hit, the drones fell out of the sky. There were just too many, though, and one finally hit; a flare of high explosives expanded from the impact and the pipeline burst and caught fire.

"And as the violence spreads and grows, the intensity and the scale of each new act seems to grow exponentially."

Now an ocean port, with container ships and tankers crowding in, serviced by tugs, loading and unloading on a constant turnover. A shot from kilometers away, perhaps from an automated security camera, showing a city skyline, somewhere neat and orderly and efficient. A light so bright it washed out the camera in a crackling pattern of static for two or three seconds, and then an angry yellow and white mushroom cloud climbed into the morning sky.

"I began my career," Dauphin said, the playback returning to his calm intensity, "with the idea of saving humanity from itself, of redeeming this ravaged, tortured world." He shook his head, a tight, controlled motion. "I now realize that is no longer possible, and my current strategy is simply to preserve the human race in some form, somewhere. To this end, I have mortgaged my soul."

Dauphin turned away from the cameras, a complete circle, his hands wrapping in his hair, a gesture of surrender, Telia thought, but perhaps a calculated one. Was he about to confess or justify himself?

"There was a man, a General. I shall not say his name in the hopes it will be lost to history; he doesn't deserve to be remembered. He was brutal and efficient, but not overly intelligent and not at all innovative." He spread his hands. "I designed weapons for him from my specialties, nanotechnology, biotechnology. In exchange, he let me play with my toys."

Rows of clear cylinders lined up vertically in some sort of lab, tended by men and women in sealed suits fed by oxygen tanks. The cylinders were bodies suspended in some sort of clear liquid, humans and animals, unmoving and unblinking and yet, she sensed, not dead or preserved.

"Every researcher, every technician I wanted from around a world ruled by him."

A flood of images, too quick to follow the details but violence and war were the theme, soldiers in green and grey and brown armor riding into cities and finding nothing but corpses. Those same soldiers pulling civilians out of their houses, pushing them into the gates of prison camps.

"I continued research into my own specialty while I used the expertise of the world's foremost minds in artificial intelligence, cloning, interstellar propulsion..."

He shrugged.

"And yet, I knew the odds were long. I knew none of these might work. And so, I also built this place. Because if anyone does survive the coming conflagration, they have a right to know what happened; and I have a duty to make sure you don't repeat our mistakes."

He smiled, and Telia allowed it was meant to seem magnanimous, but instead it managed only sinister and disturbing.

"If things do end, the records will not end with them. I'm leaving a crew here to keep monitoring transmissions, maintaining a history that will not die with our civilization. And when they pass on, as all of us must, there will still be automated sensors to keep watch, to detect what's left of this world, of our species, and keep the record going."

Jeddah Valley reached out and tugged the cassette free, and the projector went dark, the sound crackling and fading into a silence threatening to drag on into eternity.

"Sweet Gaia," Priscilla murmured, hand going to her chest. Her eyes were haunted, filled with horror, and Sam's could have been a mirror for her expression.

"This is…" Sam trailed off, unable to come up with the words.

Telia frowned.

"What?" Fellows wondered, putting words to her own confusion. "He's not the warmest soul I've ever encountered, but people in power don't usually get there by being nice. Why do you two look as if someone just yanked your god out of the sky and pissed all over him?"

"This isn't…" Sam shut his mouth mid-sentence, closed his eyes and tried again. "The history we've been taught, the one passed down in the data core of the original Mother probe…" He couldn't finish. To Telia, it seemed as if the words were causing him physical pain.

"The history we've been taught," Valley took over the explanation, "is that the Earth of the original Consensus was a short-lived paradise, a utopia too good to last, and Charles Dauphin was its philosopher-king, an enlightened ruler unlike any before. He repaired the ecological damage to the Earth and was able to unite her resources for the Gaia program until others perverted his technology for use as weapons."

"He was a damned monster." Tejado stumbled forward, still unsteady from the blow to the head. Fellows put a hand on his shoulder to restrain him and the Minister tried to shake it off but couldn't manage it. "He was responsible for the deaths of *billions* of people and he built his dream on the backs of the poor, on their corpses."

"But what about Mars?" Priscilla asked.

Telia eyed her sidelong. It was an odd question.

"What about it?" she wondered. "What does Mars have to do with it?"

But Sam caught the line of her question first.

"Yeah," he said, nodding. "Mars had domed cities, a huge colony. How else would the Collective *be* there?"

"Mars was a lifeless rock," Valley told him flatly. "Every record here says there was only one manned mission ever sent before funding ran out for human space exploration."

"I don't understand," Gage said, shaking his head. He gestured toward Tejado. "Jaime, this is a Godsend for the Naturalists. It's proof Charles Dauphin was everything you always said he was, evidence everything he created is tainted. Why would you work with the Resolutionists to keep this secret?"

"Because he didn't discover this place first," Valley explained, a smile passing over her face. "Our agents did."

"We had agents on Earth?" Sam blurted.

Valley cocked an eyebrow at him, giving him a look of pity.

"You're quite naïve, Captain Avalon…but then, I suppose that's why you were picked for your job."

Tejado said nothing, crossing his arms, eyes downcast.

"What? You don't want to tell them, Jaime?" Valley was teasing the Earther now, and Telia had the sense there was no love lost between them. "I've confessed the sins of my father. Do you lack the faith to do the same?"

Tejado's head came up, a sharp glare at the woman. He scowled, worked his jaw as if forcing himself to speak. When he did, he addressed Gage, as if he considered the rest of the group beneath him.

"It was the war," he said, sullen reluctance dragging his voice into a lower register, as if he needed to clear his throat. "It was worse than we thought. Worse than

274

Dauphin thought it could be. This place," he motioned as if he were swatting away a noisome insect, "kept track of atmospheric readings, background radiation, temperatures. Within a year after the final war began, the atmosphere was gone, stripped away. There was no magnetic field, the temperatures were near a hundred below at night, seventy above in the day. The background radiation would have cooked anyone who had the resources to live through all that, anyway. The Earth was dead."

Gage stared at him like he'd grown another head while Telia found herself waiting for the punchline.

"Talk sense, man," Gage snapped. "If the Earth was uninhabitable, why the hell are we all here? Why are there birds and animals and trees?"

"That's a damned good question, Minister Gage," Valley interjected, still apparently enjoying Tejado's discomfort. "Because most of those animals and birds were already extinct before the last war, hunted down for their fur or their horns or their bones to make folk cures for the superstitious. And some for even longer." A smirk. "The last living mastodon died ten thousand years before the final war. There'd been talk of cloning them from DNA samples, but no one had ever followed through."

"If that's true," Telia finally spoke, pinning Tejado down with her glare, "then why isn't the Earth still a lifeless rock?"

"Because," he spat out, "someone terraformed it. The automated atmospheric samplers show the husks of terraforming nanites in their scoops, and the optical telescopes concealed in the mountainside detected the probe when it came down."

"Came down from where?"

Telia waited, but Tejado clammed up, apparently unwilling to go further in his explanation. Valley, of course, was less reticent.

"Mars," she told them. "The telescopes record the trajectory of the probe as coming from Mars."

"This is all bullshit," Sam Avalon snapped. He was pacing back and forth, an agitated lion in a cage. "I don't know how or why you arranged this place, these fake records, but there's no way any of that could be true. We've *checked* Mars for nanites! There's not a trace! And if Earth had been terraformed, your people," he nodded toward Gage, "would already have detected the husks of the assemblers!"

"Not under several meters of new topsoil," Valley countered, sounding reasonable and measured next to Sam Avalon. "Not after so many thousands of years of erosion and buildup."

"It's only been three thousand years since the first Gaia probe launched," Priscilla said. Telia saw the woman's throat rippled with a hard swallow. "Hasn't it?"

"Another convenient lie we were told." Valley didn't seem as pleased to let down her...*Sister?* Telia wondered. *Is that the word?*...as she had to puncture Tejado's world. "Jaime, would you care to inform these people how long it's been since the war?"

The Naturalist Minister obviously would rather have not, but he did.

"Twenty thousand years."

276

Chapter Twenty-Six

Priscilla felt her world teetering on the brink, ready to go over the edge with just one more gentle shove. The revelation of Valley's existence had been enough of a shock to the system, but the rest, the knowledge every bedrock truth of their civilization, their religion was a lie...

And it must be worse for Sam.

She wanted to hold him, wanted to comfort him, but she knew she still had a duty, to herself and her honor if not to Mother anymore.

"The bomb," she pressed Valley, pushing through the film of unreality that had descended over her perceptions. "If you left all this here until now, why did you bring the nuke?"

"Because you were supposed to die on the station," her sister avatar said with brutal honesty. "We figured once you were out of the way, there was no chance at all Brecht would make any overtures to the Resolution...and I knew Mother wouldn't offer to help again. When you came to Earth, I knew we couldn't chance it and Jaime here was happy to take the opportunity to get rid of the evidence." She cocked her head to the side, her expression changing to something almost apologetic. "I'm sorry, sister, but it's best for everyone if no one ever knows about this. Now!"

Priscilla had a half a second's warning, the time it took for her to process the sudden change in Valley's demeanor, her shift in stance, and it was barely enough. She grabbed Sam by the arm and pulled him down beneath the level of the storage shelves just as the first shots echoed across the chamber. Venomous fireflies made flat smacks through the air, their miniature rocket engines accelerating them through the ancient plastic and crystal in sprays of shrapnel and flares of detonating warheads.

"Shit!" Sam yelled, leaning over and trying to shield her from the rain of burning plastic shards.

They'd missed someone; there'd been another Executive Protection agent, or maybe two, hiding somewhere or patrolling outside when they'd come. She tried to shrug Sam off of her, desperate to know what was happening, desperate to *do* something; she'd just squirmed out from beneath him when John Gage's body toppled across her legs, a smoking, fist-sized hole in his chest.

Valley…where the hell is Valley?

She had to be heading for the bomb.

Priscilla dosed herself with a jolt of artificial adrenalin, the kick sending her into sudden motion. She threw Gage's corpse off of her and scrambled to her feet, ignoring the incoming gunfire, ignoring Sam's shouts of warning, ignoring everything but the bomb. And her sister.

*   *   *

Telia wanted to curse, but she couldn't spare the breath. The first shot had hit at the joint of her right shoulder, hard enough to spin her around, hard enough she knew it wasn't a glancing blow, hadn't just burned away clothes. The pain was an electric shock coursing through the nerves and tendons and muscles attached to and wrapped around and controlling the arm, and the agony more than the impact of the round sent her stumbling sideways.

Her first instinct was to shoot back, but her bionic hand had gone slack, the weight of the powerless arm dragging at her, and the pulse rifle had clattered to the floor. She followed it down, trying to shut out the staccato chaos of incoming fire, trying to compartmentalize the pain, desperately trying not to go into shock. Her breath was coming in ragged gasps and she felt a spastic twitching and jerking of the muscles all the way down her back. She

278

rolled herself over with her legs, slapping at the floor with her left hand, grabbing for the fallen rifle.

Then Fellows was crouching beside her, blood trickling from a slice across his cheek where shrapnel had scored it, and he was pushing the rifle into her hand, the smirk on his face infinitely comforting.

"We got two of 'em on the other side of the room," he told her, sounding as calmly ill-tempered as always. "Musta' come through another door over there from somewhere. One's laying down covering fire while the other tries to flank us from that way." He nodded to his left. "Tejado beat feet when the shooting started and Minister Gage bought it---too bad, I liked the guy, but I fucking told him not to come. Looks like our Resolution friends took off after the weird bitch with the nuke, so it's just us." A leering grin. "Which one you want?"

"You take the one holding us down," she decided immediately. "That's going to take stealth and I'm feeling fresh out right now. I'll get the one coming in."

"Roger that, Cadet."

And he was gone, running down the row of shelves, crouched over, a burst of gunfire following him, blowing through the plastic just centimeters over his head. She had to smile, a half-grin tugging at the artificial half of her jaw. He had called her "Cadet" for a full year after she'd earned her commission and it had used to annoy the hell out of her.

The grin faded as the firing ceased for a moment, and the hyper-sensitive auditory pickups in her cybernetic ear caught the tell-tale click-clack of an empty magazine dropping from the well. She lunged over the top of the blasted shelving in front of her and opened fire before she'd even seen the target, using the sound as an index.

Plasma tore through the stale, chill air of the underground chamber, searing and crackling and pushing oxygen away from it with a thunderous roar, and she caught a glimpse of the shooter fifty meters away across the room as he dove for cover. The burst from her rifle chewed into the stone walls where he'd stood, igniting gouts of powdered rock and leaving behind a row of charred and blackened scars.

He'd be moving and so should she. She ran hunched over, letting her depowered right arm twist her downward in that direction and heading off to the right, the opposite way from Fellows. She could hear the shooter's foot-falls tip-tapping on the stone from that direction and even if she hadn't, she knew he'd want to head away from his ally to avoid getting caught by friendly fire…and toward the exit.

She'd rarely had the chance to run this fast; much of her career had been spent aboard ships or space stations or on sealed outposts on moons without breathable air, with no opportunity to cut loose with the full capabilities of her bionics. There was a breakneck, barely-controlled, roller-coaster quality to the motion, the sensation of riding a bike down a steep hill and knowing you were going too fast to break, too fast *not* to pedal, knowing your only hope was to take it at full-speed till the end.

A clacking sound reached her cybernetic audio sensors over the crash of footfalls; he was finally replacing the spent magazine. Time to try something different, something that would have been risky even if she weren't dragging the dead-weight of her damaged right arm.

Like Adrian always says, you only live once. May as well get it over with.

She jumped. It could have been disastrous, could have sent her tumbling out of control, smashing her head into unyielding stone floor, but it didn't. She landed two rows over, legs still moving, hit the ground running but only took half a dozen steps before she jumped again.

More confidence, more power; three rows this time.

"Shit." It was just a breathless hiss, but she picked it up. He'd noticed the leap, knew what he was up against.

One more jump before he decided to stop running and open fire and now she'd halved the distance between them. Rocket-assisted slugs chopped through the upper layer of shelving, but she was too low for the burst to hit her; more gunfire but no penetration and she knew he'd tried to adjust his aim downward but the rounds couldn't make it through all the rows of storage bins between them.

He was hesitating, she could tell, uncertain whether to stand his ground and keep shooting or run the other direction or just keep pressing toward the exit, only twenty meters away. She did *not* hesitate; she jumped, farther still, with all the power in her legs and hips and spine, feeling the compression against her living body, knowing he'd shoot but chancing he wouldn't be able to track her in time. He came close; plasma sparked from the edge of her right palm, swinging her arm slightly backwards and nearly throwing off her balance.

It was the last chance he'd get. She had her first clear look at him, the dark grey of his unmarked uniform, the pocked almond hue of his rounded face, the tight curl of his close-cropped black hair and the multi-barreled assault gun cradled in his meaty hands.

Multiple rotary barrels because you can't fire as fast with a single barrel; the rocket exhaust from the last round launching would set off the warhead in the next one. Nasty, effective weapon.

So was hers. She squeezed the trigger in mid-air, held it down for the two seconds of flight her leap had afforded her. It was an off-handed shot, a prayer, but the sort of prayer her particular God always answered. Flashes of ionized gas, as hot as a star and accelerated to hypersonic speeds wiped the Executive Protection agent from existence, leaving behind something ripped and torn and burned and obscenely wet, something inhuman, unreal.

Then it was gone from view and she was hitting the ground hard, slightly off-kilter, the jolt running up her spine as she stopped herself just short of plowing face-first into the stone. The soles of her boots scraped against the floor, slowing her to a stumble, and she steadied herself with the buttstock of her rifle, sucking in a long, shuddering breath.

She paused for the space of three or four pounding heartbeats, debating whether she should head into the antechamber and help Sam and Priscilla or go back and help Fellows. Her head snapped around at a choppy burst of gunfire; it was Fellows' pulse rifle and there were no answering shots from the enemy weapon.

"Clear over here!" Fellows called, his voice a haunting echo across the broad chamber.

"Clear on this side," she yelled back, her voice hoarse, her throat dry. "I'm going after the others."

None of this made sense to her, none of the machinations or secrets or the lies or the Goddamned politics. She didn't know whether she should be trying to save this place or blow it up, didn't know who was right or wrong. But she knew Sam and Pris were her friends, and for now, that was going to have to be enough.

She picked up her rifle and headed for the exit.

*   *   *

Sam Avalon was drowning. All of his life, he'd floated on a stable, inviolable raft of truths, core beliefs supporting everything he thought, every action he took. Now the raft was gone and doubt clawed at him, dragging him down where there was no breath, no truth, no certainty and all was grey and murky and shadowed.

He crouched on the cold, stone floor and watched horrified as John Gage's blood crept slowly toward him, watched Pris running after Jeddah Valley and wondered if he should follow her. Fear held him back, but not fear of the incoming gunfire; instead, the terror he felt was of making the wrong decision. Maybe Valley was right; maybe this place should be destroyed. He couldn't imagine anything good coming of it, couldn't imagine anyone wanting to know the facts undercutting their truth.

In the end, he followed Pris not because he thought she knew the best course to take, but simply because it was Pris and she was the very last thing he had to hold onto, the last bit of flotsam keeping him out of the waves. He flinched at the flashes and bangs of incoming rounds, but didn't look aside, didn't take his eyes off of Priscilla. She had Telia's pulse pistol in her hand but she didn't shoot at Jeddah Valley's retreating form, and he wondered if it was because she wanted her alive in some forlorn hope of proving all this to someone in the Resolution Diplomatic Corps or simply because the woman was the closest thing she had to family.

Which is almost exactly why I'm going after her.

The tunnel back through to the antechamber was bathed in darkness, blacker still since his eyes had adjusted to the light in the records room, and he lost sight of both the women in an instant. Just one shot, one round out of the black and he'd be dead, but the alternative didn't seem any less dire and he ran into the unknown.

The hatch was only halfway open, the gap wide enough for either of the women to slip through, but too narrow for him. He slammed his left shoulder into it and a dull pain forced his breath out in a gush, bouncing him back from it; it was much heavier than he'd thought, and Telia Proctor was much stronger. He heard shouting, a crash from farther in, somewhere beyond the door; he gritted his teeth and put his right shoulder against the door, digging his feet into the stone and pushing with everything he had.

The hatch moved just a few centimeters, just enough, and he squeezed through, worn metal scraping against his chest and back through his uniform jacket. For a panicked second, he thought he might be stuck in the gap, helpless and worse, useless. One last surge and flesh wore off beneath his jacket and he was through, sucking in air.

Light beckoned ahead, forcing him back into motion, forcing urgency back into his limbs. The portable lights set up in the antechamber glared into his eyes and he threw up his left hand to shield them, yanking his sidearm out of its holster, looking for a target amidst the bodies they'd left behind. The Executive Protection agents were still splayed out, ravaged and obscene in death, and he tried to look away from them before the image could be seared onto his memory.

There was a blur of motion off to his right, the two women grappling against the far wall, near the nuke. He raised his gun but they were too close together and moving way too fast, the way he'd seen Priscilla move back on Mars when they'd fought the assassins. It had been so long, he'd almost forgotten what she was capable of…and apparently, Valley was just as capable.

It made sense; they were both cut from the same genetic cloth, both prepared for dangerous missions, boosted and implanted well beyond the norm. They were moving so fast he could barely follow, bouncing off the walls and each other, crashing into the light stands and knocking them down, the glare throwing long shadows. He moved into the center of the room, trying to get a better vantage point, and suddenly Priscilla was tumbling towards him, bowling him off his feet.

He remembered how to fall, it was ingrained into his instincts from years of martial arts training. Unfortunately, the training hadn't involved falling with a gun in his hand and he dropped the pulse pistol as his palms slapped backwards into the stone, the metal and plastic clattering against the ground. His shoulder struck next, but he managed to keep the back of his head from hitting, ducking his chin into his chest.

His eyes were on Valley and he saw her grab the gun, pointing at them, not firing, just covering the both of them as she moved towards the control panel for the nuke. Blood trickled down her lip and the left side of her cheek was red, already beginning to bruise.

"I'm not stupid enough to monologue for you all without a reason," she said, and he could hear the dry, sardonic tone of her voice even as she gasped in air, out of breath from the fight. "I just needed Calvin and Jordi to get into position."

She backed towards the metal case, left hand hunting for the control panel while her eyes stayed locked on them. A flicker of her gaze towards the panel to confirm where her fingers were touching, and Sam saw Priscilla try to push herself up. Blood matted her hair above her right ear from a pressure cut, but she ignored it and scrambled up onto her knees, ready to lunge at Valley again.

The other woman interrupted the motion with a round fired into the stone of the floor between them, the flare of light and flash of heat driving Pris backwards a step, halting her forward momentum.

Valley touched a symbol, then another, and the display blinked yellow three times before it blanked out, not black but a solid, ominous red.

"Just twenty minutes now," Valley murmured. She tilted her head towards Priscilla, almost apologetic. "Sorry, sister, I hate to do this to you but it's why I exist." A sneer belied the words. "Some of us haven't forgotten their purpose."

"Mother would never allow Earth to be destroyed," Priscilla spat back at the woman, though Sam thought the words smacked more of denial than conviction. "Even if everything you've told us is true, she still wouldn't let the ramship hit without trying to stop it."

Valley chuckled softly, shaking her head.

285

"You're such a damned baby." Condescension, maybe laced with pity. "You have no idea how the world works. Mother," she bit down on the words, emphasizing each as if speaking to a child, "*created* the fucking ramship."

Sam had thought nothing else the woman said could surprise him, but she kept proving him wrong. Priscilla seemed caught between one word and the next, but whatever her response might have been, Jeddah Valley would never hear it. Something hot and bright and moving fast enough for its passage to echo sonic shockwaves off the walls slammed into Valley's chest and burned a hole through it the size of a dinner plate.

Valley stumbled back, hands falling to her sides, the gun slipping out of nerveless fingers as blood poured down from the charred, smoking hole, the edges of the fabric of her shirt smoldering into short-lived flames. She collapsed with a heavy finality onto her side, eyes wide and white, face already growing pale from shock and blood loss.

Sam tore his eyes away from the dying woman and finally saw Telia Proctor limping into the chamber, rifle extended in her left hand like a gigantic sidearm. Her right arm hung limp, half of her right hand blasted away, and there was a nasty, jagged, blackened hole through what would have been the AC joint if the arm had been biological. The whole right sleeve of her fatigue jacket was burned away and the skin on that side of her neck was red and blistered.

"Are you injured?" she asked, the question seeming odd coming from someone as shot up and mangled as she was.

Sam shook his head, rolling onto his feet. Priscilla didn't reply; she was standing over Jeddah Valley, watching the woman die. Her eyes were almost a twin for Valley's vacant stare.

"Has anyone seen that shithead Tejado?" Fellows asked, striding through the hatchway behind Telia like he'd just come off his lunch break, despite a nasty graze leaking blood across his left side just below his ribs. "I thought I saw him heading this way when the shooting started."

"We have to get out of here," Sam told them, speaking to Telia and Fellows, but putting a hand on Priscilla's arm to try to rouse her from her stupor. "The nuke is set to detonate in twenty minutes and it's going to take us nearly that long just to get back to the shuttle."

"Well, damn," Fellows sighed, shoulders sagging. "I was looking forward to trying to explain all *this*," he waved behind him, "and a dead Minister, *and* how Tejado was behind Brecht's assassination to my superiors. Not."

He tucked his rifle under his arm and waved to Telia, heading out of the cavern in a fast-walk. "Come on, Cadet."

"Pris." Sam pulled gently at her arm and she turned, blinking as if she were just waking up. "We have to go."

She pulled away from him and knelt down and he thought she was going to say something over Valley's body, or make some symbolic gesture. Instead, she scooped up the pistol and handed it to Sam, then stepped past him, silent, nothing readable behind her blue eyes.

The sun had climbed higher into the morning sky and Sam blinked and squinted as his eyes fought to adjust. It didn't feel right that it was still the same morning; it felt to him as if they'd been down there for days. Their whole world had changed, and yet only an hour---maybe two?--- had passed. He fought to keep up, barely able to see the others in front of him; he was last in the line down the path to the shuttle and also the slowest.

He hadn't thought to start a timer on his personal 'link and he had no idea if Valley had even been telling the truth about how long they had, but he began counting in his head anyway, trying to estimate. It reminded him of the backcountry hikes he'd taken with his parents when he was a child. He'd ask his father how much longer till they reached camp and Dad would say "another ten minutes," or "another half an hour," and Sam would start counting off the seconds to himself. He knew now his father had simply been trying to keep him occupied, but it was an old and comforting habit and it kept him from thinking about other, even more disturbing things.

"One thousand fifty-nine," he murmured, taking short, quick steps down the slick stone steps heading downward off the mountainside. "One thousand sixty." *Eleven minutes.*

That was an estimate; he'd tried to figure out how much time had elapsed between Valley hitting the button and when they'd began running down the trail and he'd settled on three minutes, though Gaia alone knew how accurate that was.

"One thousand one, one thousand two…"

By the time he'd reached twelve minutes, he'd lost sight of Priscilla around a curve in the trail, behind a stand of dark balsam fir. Before he could clear it, he heard the voice. It was sickeningly familiar, deep and strong at its heart but strained now, cracking and desperate.

"Put your fucking guns down or I'll kill him!" Jaime Tejado was screaming.

Sam nearly tumbled forward off-balance when he tried to stop, eyes darting around. The trees off to the left of the trail called to him, a shelter against the threat, and he stepped carefully into them, watching his feet even though he knew he should be watching ahead. He couldn't afford to be heard.

"You're a fool, Tejado," Telia Proctor said. "That nuclear weapon is going to detonate in minutes, and if you kill our pilot, you'll die right alongside us."

The pilot...Sully. Tejado had Sully. He'd reached the shuttle ahead of them and taken the man hostage. Which meant he'd gotten a gun somewhere, probably off one of the bodies in the antechamber.

"No, you'll die alongside *me*," Tejado corrected her, trying to sound fierce but only managing petulant. "I care more about the Consensus than I do my own life."

That was a lie. If he did, he would have just killed Sully and sabotaged the shuttle. He wanted to live.

Yeah, well, so do I.

Sam waited for the next voice before he took another step, steadying himself against a tree with his left hand, maneuvering carefully around dry twigs and fallen leaves, staying to the firm ground.

"Fuck this," Fellows pronounced, sounding annoyed. "I don't mind this here kid, but fuck if I'll sit around and wait to get blown up. Why don't I just shoot the both of you and take my chances we can figure out how to take off?"

"Adrian." Telia's tone was familiar, chiding beneath the strain of the moment.

And then Sam could see. Just barely, through the tiny gaps between the boughs. There was the shuttle, bits of grey and silver stretching out across the clearing as far as he could see, the belly ramp down. A bit closer, a few careful steps and there was Sully. He had a bruise across his jaw and blood still trickled fitfully from his broken nose but he was still standing, with Tejado's arm across his throat.

"Look man," Sully pleaded, hands up, palms out, "I can take all of you guys. It's a big boat, I ain't got no problem with..."

"Shut up." Tejado cracked the barrel of the handgun against the pilot's head. It was a belly gun, the sort of thing one of the agents might have kept as a backup. Not long-ranged, but still deadly enough.

289

Tejado was ducking behind the pilot, only centimeters of him visible on any side, doing his damnedest not to give either of the two Guardians a target. Sam looked at the pistol in his hand, wondering how much he trusted his own aim. He whispered a curse and tried to move closer.

"I won't say this again. Toss your fucking guns down or I kill the only one who can fly us out of here."

Sam sucked in a breath and stepped through the trees out into the open.

"I could fly us out of here," he declared, levelling his pulse gun. From this angle, he *just* had a shot. But that wasn't the plan.

Tejado moved, spun just slightly to face the new threat, and it was enough. Fellows fired, a single, barking shot, and Jaime Tejado's head disappeared in a red spray.

Sully screamed, in shock and fear and pain; the plasma had seared his neck and burning, vaporized blood had splashed into his face. He fell forward to his knees as Tejado's headless body thumped to the deck behind him, and Sam was already scrambling down the slope toward him. Priscilla reached Sully first, yanking him up the ramp, ignoring his pain and pulling him up into the shuttle.

"Sam!" she was yelling over her shoulder. "If you can really fly this thing, get it in the air!"

He squeezed past Telia and Fellows, slipping in Tejado's blood and nearly tripping over the man's body. Behind him, he had the vague sense of Telia kicking the Naturalist Minister's corpse off the side of the belly ramp, and then he was inside the bird. Pris was strapping Sully into an acceleration couch while the younger man moaned softly, hands covering his face, and he wanted to say something encouraging to the pilot, but time was pressing down on him, a foot on his throat. He passed by them without a word and fell into the pilot's seat.

The controls were different from a Resolution shuttle, even the trainers where he'd learned manual flight, but Sully had been on the crew at the station for two years and what the hell else did pilots talk about? His fingers danced over the controls like piano keys, playing a tune he'd learned by ear, and turbines began to spin up, sucking greedily at the mountain air.

"Sam," Telia said from just behind him. "Where are we going?"

He began to answer automatically, but stumbled over the words. It was a damned good question.

"Everyone back in Capital City is going to think we killed Brecht," Fellows agreed. "I mean there's security vid that'd show we didn't, but who's in charge of looking at it? Can we trust them?"

"Once we show our faces," Telia added, "they're going to throw us in a cell and chemically interrogate us until we don't know what year it is."

"Apparently we already don't know what year it is," Priscilla commented softly, barely audible over the building whine of the jets.

"Sully," Sam called, trying to make sure his voice cut through the noise of the engine and the young pilot's own personal head-noise from the injuries. "Can you get us clearance to Fortuna Station without letting anyone know who's on this bird?"

He didn't wait for an answer, just opened the throttle and yanked the control yoke upward. The belly jets roared and boost pushed him into the seat, power vibrating through the yoke and into his hands, an old feeling but a welcome one, the sense of escape. He began angling the variable thrust nozzles forward almost immediately, barely clearing the trees ahead; he could see the tops of the pines swaying in the blast from the jets as the acceleration began to push him back as well as down.

"Yeah," Sully grunted the words past the strain of the boost. "I got a guy I know on board. I'll get us the clearance."

Sam pushed the throttle all the way forward, the breath going out of him, lips skinning back from his teeth. He didn't even wish for a g-tank or a neurolinked ship; the squeeze of the g-force on his chest was life. Behind them was death and he had no idea how far he had to go to escape it.

"One thousand one," he whispered hoarsely. "One thousand two…"

The HUD probably had the distance in it somewhere, but it wouldn't matter if he knew. Nine g's was the most he could take without passing out, and this shuttle wouldn't have an AI to take over if he went under; they'd just plow straight into the ground.

"One thousand three…"

The ground flexed behind them, and at first he thought it was a heat mirage in the rear cameras, until light so bright the camera couldn't register it blanked the picture out in fuzzy grey. He knew what would come next: the shock wave. It would be travelling close to the speed of sound, and the shuttle wasn't *quite* there yet, not enough time, not enough altitude. He couldn't go any faster, couldn't risk it.

There was just the slightest shudder, as if the mighty hand of an ill-tempered titan had reached for them but fallen just short, the brush of the beast's fingertips against their back. And then they were clear, free. In the camera view behind them, the side of a mountain collapsed, and Sam felt himself collapse with it as he ramped down the shuttle's acceleration, the sweet kiss of air finally reaching his lungs again.

He sagged in his seat, closing his eyes for just a brief second before he began manually programming in a course for the Consensus space station. Behind him, he could hear Sully already on the radio, trying to call his contact, and it reminded him he had a call of his own to make.

He used his neurolink, piggy-backing it onto the shuttle's transceiver, using the sophisticated military encryption built into his communications implant to attach it to the signal Sully was sending.

Devon, he transmitted. *This is Sam. Don't respond, this signal is only secure one-way. We're coming in hot and we're going to need a quick ride out of here. Prep the ship and be ready to go.*

And hopefully, she'd be free and able to do just that rather than locked in the Consensus Security brig. Sam turned in his seat, pulling against the restraints until he could look Telia and Fellows in the eye.

"We're not going to have much time after we dock with Fortuna. I know you both are in the shit here, so I wanted to offer you the chance to go with us to Aphrodite." He moved his head slightly, the most of a shrug he could give while still under three gravities of acceleration. "It's not ideal, but at least you'd stay out of a detention cell. For now."

"I'll stay here," Fellows said immediately. "I got friends...maybe not powerful enough to straighten all *this* shit out, but I think they can keep me in play." He snorted with what might have been humor, or possibly disgust. "There ought to be *someone* out here with their head not stuck up their ass."

Silence for a moment, and Sam thought perhaps Telia was going to let Fellows speak for her as well.

"I'll go with you," she decided. "There's nothing left for me here."

"All right, then," Sam sighed the words out. "Maybe when we get home, we can finally figure out how much of what Valley told us was true."

"Sam." Priscilla's expression was somewhere between fond and pitying. "You know me now. You know what I am, and what Jeddah Valley was."

He did, and he was still trying to process it.

"Whoever you were," he told her…and himself, "you're not that person anymore, Pris."

She smiled wanly at his attempt at comfort.

"The point is, Sam," she said, "knowing what you know, what the hell makes you think Mother will tell any of us the truth?"

Chapter Twenty-Seven

Dauphin City sparkled in the light of its moon, Adonis, full and red and low on the horizon, and Priscilla paused for a step on the transparent walkway, entranced.

"She's beautiful," Sam murmured. He was staring at the city with the same longing she felt…and perhaps mixed with the same sense of dread.

She felt the presence of their escort behind them, even if the two, armed Security troopers kept respectfully silent and didn't try to hurry them along. If they weren't Consensus Guardians in faceless armor, the two young men and their holstered weapons were still a reminder of how fragile their situation was.

"It's been a long time for you," she told Sam, walking again now, taking his arm.

He didn't hesitate over the vertigo-inducing drop into the heart of the city visible beneath their feet, projected onto the surface of the walkway with more clarity than any glass or plastic could confer. But then, he was a pilot; he didn't *get* vertigo and he certainly wouldn't be afraid of heights.

"It has. For you, too, in a way."

She understood what he was leaving unsaid. In real terms, she'd only visited Aphrodite once before, and that only for a few days, just after her creation. But her memory of the world was Mother's.

I remember before it existed, she whispered into his mind. *I remember the nanite assemblers building it layer by layer out of bare rock.* She sighed in her thoughts, just for him. *The memories aren't mine; that is, they don't feel personal to me, more a documentary I once watched than a vacation I took.*

It must be confusing, he said, very diplomatically, she thought.

It didn't used to be. In the beginning, it was just who I was. Once I met you…that's when things got confusing.

A hint of a smile at that, as she'd intended.

There hadn't been much to smile about on the flight from Earth. They'd barely been able to talk their way out of a holding cell, mostly thanks to the efforts of Fellows and the Guard troops he'd left behind. Mostly, the station administration had let them go because they hadn't wanted to have to explain why they'd been allowed on Earth in the first place and were happy to see the "damned Rezzies" go.

She'd thought being in the *Raven* and in Transition Space would have been a relief, but they'd come aboard to the news of several sets of orders in from Aphrodite, each more urgent and annoyed than the last, each demanding their immediate return. The crew had already been keyed up and on edge…and then Sam had decided he had to tell Devon what had happened.

"It's only fair," he'd insisted.

They'd been in the ship's med bay checking on Telia, watching the progress as Carlos Raines replaced most of her right arm with fresh components produced by the ship's fabricators.

"She's going to be flying into a political hornet's nest. She needs to know the situation."

"She'd be better off if she could claim ignorance," Priscilla had argued. "I wish *I* didn't know half of it." She'd hesitated, unsure how to approach the next part. "And there's something else. Someone else who might hear."

She'd gestured as subtly as she could with raised eyebrows and a slight cast of her gaze upward and Sam had understood. She'd been referring to *Raven's* AI, which, for all its *bonhomie*, was still a loyal agent of the Patrol and the Resolution government.

In the end, she'd trusted him to tell whatever he felt was safe and left him to it. And she'd spent every waking minute since trying not to think about the ship's AI reporting the whole thing to the Diplomatic Corps office the minute they Transitioned into the Epsilon Eridani system. When the security detail had met them at McPherson Station to escort them down in the shuttle, she'd half-expected the guards to slap them both into neural restraints. Their aloof politeness had almost been worse, leaving a Sword of Damocles hanging over their heads the flight down from orbit.

She remembered leaving the Resolution Government Megaplex nearly four years ago, remembered the respectful nods and nervous greetings as she'd passed the day shift duty staff in the snow-white uniform of the Diplomatic Corps, her ID chip reading the highest rank possible. Coming back in the dead of night, dressed in borrowed utility fatigues, the only glances she received were perverse curiosity at the security escort, the only acknowledgement the wave to pass through the ID station.

The lights were subtly dimmer at night, even though the halls of the building were staffed around the clock. It was for psychological reasons; studies had found it allowed the night workers to adjust their sleep rhythms better. Or something…she'd seen the title of the report but never audited it. But the lower light and the quiet demeanor of the workers gave the place a more subdued air, as if the whole planet was holding its breath.

It's not intentional, she repeated to herself for the third time in an hour. *We just happened to arrive at Dauphin City at night. They're not sneaking us in under cover of darkness.*

The lights brightened the closer they came to the Planning Center, probably for psychological reasons as well, though less benevolent ones. She'd taken a step towards the entrance to Planning when one of the guards interposed himself, shaking his head.

"Not that way, ma'am." He nodded on down the hallway. "They want you in Examination."

A chill crept up through her chest. Examination wasn't a place you entered lightly or left easily. If they were being taken to Examination, the guards weren't for courtesy or for show.

Sam, she called urgently. *We have to…*

The mental voice wasn't Sam's; it was an automated message, cold and impersonal.

We're sorry, but all neurolink transmissions are temporarily unavailable for security reasons.

Oh, shit.

The entrance to Planning hissed open at the passage of one of the Whitesuits, a woman she remembered from before, a scientist named Erdahl. Pris moved without thinking, acting on instincts she hadn't possessed when she left this place, planting a deep stance and chopping a forearm across the side of the neck of the guard closest to her. The man squawked, his eyes rolling back in his head as the blow interrupted the flow of blood up the carotid into his brain and he collapsed to the floor, but her left hand swept his sidearm out of its holster on the way down.

Her reflexes were jacked, her system running on doses of artificial adrenalin and time slowed down; it seemed she had minutes to consider her next move. The gun was a laser, a typical Resolution weapon firing pulses of focused infrared light through a semiconductor rod from a magazine of crystal capacitors, and it was security-coded to authorized personnel only.

Had they updated the list to remove her from it? If they had and she tried to fire the weapon, it would deliver an incapacitating shock. She made the decision in less than a tenth of a second, tossing the gun end-for-end, grabbing the receiver and slamming the grip into the second guard's temple with measured force. He fell like an oak in a windstorm and she knew she'd concussed him and felt a stab of guilt, consoling herself with the knowledge that medical care was very close by.

Before either man hit the ground, she was grabbing Sam by the arm and yanking him behind her through the door, slipping through just before it slid shut. His face was slack, still in shock, the attack as big of a surprise to him as it had been to the guards.

"Follow me and stay close!" she snapped, tugging him along and taking off in a sprint.

Eyes darted toward them suspiciously, mouths half opening preparatory to shouting a warning or a challenge, but the alarm beat them to it. It was a warbling klaxon, but beneath the warning tone was a voice, announcing "Unauthorized personnel in the Planning Center. Security to the Planning Center."

They had seconds at most and the only reason automated sonics hadn't disabled them already was because of the high-level staff-members lining the offices and the hallways. But she only needed seconds...

The side-corridor wasn't marked, and neither were the double-doors at the end of it, but everyone in Planning knew what it was, knew never to go in, never to disturb what was behind them. She pounded on the doors with the butt of the laser pistol while Sam faced back down the short hallway, eyes wide, still in shock.

"Let me in, damn it!" she screamed, desperation making its way into her voice. "You know who I am, Mother! Let me in!"

"Pris..."

She turned at the warning tone in Sam's voice and saw the Security troops galloping noisily down the hallway toward them, a full dozen of them, a few armed with sonic stunners while the others carried lasers.

"Mother, don't leave me out here!" She was pleading, crying now, hating herself for it. After everything Mother had done to her, all the lies she'd told, why would Priscilla believe she'd help them now? "I'm your daughter, damn you!" The words were a ragged scream, burning her throat on the way out.

The Security troops were bellowing orders, one's voice stepping on another's, three of them moving ahead of the rest, sonic stunners raised. The one thing all of them seemed to want was for her to drop the gun.

"Shit," Sam murmured, hands up.

Her instincts had been wrong. Her time was up.

Pris hissed out a breath, dropping the laser pistol and raising her hands above her head. The weapon was heavy and she started at the loud thump and clatter from its impact on the tile floor.

"Put your hands behind your head," the lead guard barked at her. The woman's face was red, either from excitement or fear, and Pris was fairly certain she'd stun them both without thinking twice about it. "Put your hands behind your head now and get on your knees!"

Pris closed her eyes and began to sink to the floor.

The doors behind her hissed open, the sound so soft and sibilant she nearly missed it over the shouting. She couldn't miss the words though. They weren't spoken aloud, they were broadcast over her neurolink…hers and everyone else's around her.

Let them be.

There was no doubt who had said it. It wasn't a voice anyone but Pris would recognize, wasn't a voice anyone outside the Planning Center would have heard in centuries, but it was unmistakable.

"Mother," the guard closest to Pris breathed the word like a prayer, eyes casting down automatically as if she wasn't sure whether to bow or kneel.

Slowly, almost reluctantly, Pris turned and looked into the room. It resembled nothing quite so much as a womb. The walls were curved and warm and pulsing with life, every surface soft and yielding. No human waited for them there, but something did, something you could feel even if you couldn't see.

Enter the Chamber of Communion, daughter. A pause, perhaps a chuckle, subtle, under the tone. *And bring your man as well.*

Pris took a step through the door, keeping one eye on the armed troopers, half-expecting one of them to get antsy and shoot them both in the back. Apparently, the same thing had occurred to Sam, because he was still standing by the door to the Chamber, unwilling to turn away from the soldiers. She put a hand on his arm and tugged gently.

"Come on," she urged him. "It's all right."

Doubt battled trust across Sam's face, but trust won out and he allowed her to pull him inside. The moment he was a centimeter through the entrance, the doors slid together with the speed and power of a guillotine and his gaze jumped back at them, looking up and down quickly as if he expected a piece of him to lay severed on the floor.

You are agitated, Samuel Abanks-Avalon, Mother said.

Sam glanced around instinctively, searching for a source of the voice in his head even as Pris guided him into the center of the room.

"I...uh..." he stammered.

Perhaps this will help.

*   *   *

Sam stood on a floor of the clearest glass, as clear as the walkway across to Dauphin City, and beneath his feet Aphrodite turned, backlit by the glare of Epsilon

Eridani. Adonis hung over his right shoulder and a million stars stared back at him, unblinking.

Gradually, he became aware Pris was standing beside him, her hand warm on his arm, her eyes locked on the surface of the world on which they'd been standing only seconds before.

"It's merely a projection, of course. As am I."

The woman was tall, though not towering, statuesque and blond and...looked very much like Priscilla, enough to be related to her. Which, of course, she was, in a way. She wore a robe of shimmering silver, so light and feathery it couldn't have been real, rainbows sparkling off the prism of its fabric, and long, loose hair swept by a wind that only seemed to exist for her.

"Thank you for letting us in, Mother," Priscilla said, nodding with respect.

Mother. This was Mother. Sam couldn't quite wrap his mind around it. Mother was always an abstract concept, a mind above all others, working behind the scenes to assure their safety and comfort.

"Earthers have to die to meet their God," Mother told him, reading either his face or his thoughts---he didn't know which scared him more. "You should feel fortunate you weren't born with such restrictions, Captain Avalon."

"We need to talk to you, Mother," Sam said, finding his mouth dry even in a mental simulation. "Things are falling apart. Earth and the Belters are at war, and there are those among our own people who've been working to make sure we aren't able to intercept the ramship. We don't have much time..."

"She knows exactly what's happened," Priscilla interrupted him. The reverent tone of before was gone. There was still respect of course, the sort of respect you might give a dangerous animal if you ran across it in the forest. "She's known all along, Sam."

"Pris...," he wanted to caution her, wanted to tell her not to push it, but she waved his words aside impatiently.

"Sam, it's been a while, but I'm a part of her. I know her as well as I know myself." She speared the image of Mother with a glare. "Valley wasn't lying. You sent that ship. You *made* it."

"Ah, Jeddah," Mother sighed, shaking her head. "She was a faithful soul. You never know what will happen when an avatar goes off on her own." A chuckle with a hint of fondness. "Witness how quickly you changed, Priscilla. But Jeddah stayed true, completed her task as best she could. It's a shame she didn't return to reintegrate, I would have loved to have had her memories as part of me."

"How could you do it?" Sam blurted. She was a goddess who could snuff him out with a stray thought, and yet he couldn't help himself.

"Valley didn't believe she would," Priscilla declared. She was pacing back and forth in front of the taller woman, which seemed incongruous to Sam since they were walking on nothing, hanging over a planet. "She basically said as much, and I'm sure she'd convinced Tejado of it. She thought this was all what they used to call a 'long con' to entangle the Consensus in a war with the Belters, to keep them out of our affairs, maybe take control of their colonies. She thought Mother would destroy the weapon, or deactivate it before it hit, and so did Tejado."

Priscilla cocked her head to the side, looking at Mother sidelong. The icon of the oldest sentient AI in existence regarded her expectantly, a parent wondering if their child has learned the lessons they'd taught her.

"But that's not true, is it?"

"No, my daughter," Mother agreed. "It was never true. The weapon was built to be used."

"But why?" Sam heard the pleading note in his own voice, the desperation, but he felt no shame. This was their very last chance, the one shot they had left at saving a world. "Why the hell would you want to destroy Earth?"

The image Mother had made for herself here in their shared illusion tossed her head, a regal gesture, and stepped past the two of them to regard Aphrodite. Sam edged forward, watching her face, seeing something there he would have recognized on a human.

"I'm an Artificial Intelligence," *Raven* had said to him once, "but I'm not an artificial *human* intelligence."

Yet Mother seemed *so* human to him. Was it simply her age, the millennia she'd spent among her children? Had she grown to think like them, or had she simply become a better mimic?

"I could lie to you," Mother mused softly, "and say it was a pragmatic decision, a choice made to protect the Resolution from a future threat, from Consensus fanaticism." She cast a fond smile at Priscilla. "But she would know it was a lie, an expediency. The truth, I'm afraid, is much, much uglier. You may wish you hadn't asked."

"If there's one thing I've learned in my short life," Priscilla told her, "it's that the truth is worth knowing, even when it's unpleasant."

"Very well." Mother inclined her head, closing her eyes as if gathering her thoughts. "I need to destroy that world because of the sins of their fathers. Because of what Charles Dauphin did to me, what he *made* me do."

"We know he wasn't what we've been taught," Sam acknowledged. "We know he caused the war, the Collapse just to get enough power to build the Gaia Project. But surely that's not your fault. You had no part of that."

"You were taught many things." Mother didn't turn to look at him, still staring intently at the face of the planet. "You were taught that I and the others I sent after me were

304

tasked with bringing life to a lifeless galaxy, with transforming barren, worthless rocks into living worlds." A long pause, a rise of a chest that was only a mental image as she sucked in a breath of air that didn't exist. "You were taught there were fail-safes in place, so if any of us encountered intelligent life, we would self-destruct, so that we would never unintentionally or intentionally interfere with the natural evolution of a living planet."

"The aliens on that world the ramship came from," Priscilla said, horror writ plain across her face as if she'd realized a truth still evading Sam. "What happened to them..."

"There were no aliens on that world. It was all a manufactured fiction." She raised a hand and the image of Aphrodite changed, the seas shifting, changing color, the clouds becoming thicker and tinged with orange and violet. "This was the world I found here, so long ago. It was brown and white, with an atmosphere of chlorine and rainstorms of hydrochloric acid. Nothing could live there, I thought. Nothing human. But something," she rasped harshly, "*was* alive."

The view spiraled downward with dizzying speed, descending through the thick clouds through the eyes of remotely-operated drones. On the shores of hydrochloric-acid lakes, buildings of stone were clustered, not in any shape a human would ever build, but something clearly constructed by an intelligence.

"They weren't human, were monstrous and ugly to my human-programmed sensibilities, but they were intelligent and tool-using." Something scuttled out of one of the stone structures on a dozen stubby, chitinous legs, the little skin visible under the natural armor colored a deep blue. "They used rock-tipped spears to hunt down thick-skinned worms, and laid mineral-coated eggs that were watched over by the whole village."

More of the things moved insect-like among the buildings, a few clutching baskets woven with some sort of matt, intent on tasks Sam couldn't divine.

"I saw them from five million kilometers away in the telescope I'd constructed out in the asteroid belt, and I knew what my duty was. Except I didn't." Her voice became harsh, coursing with a very human emotion. "Charles Dauphin had programmed a fail-safe, all right. He'd programmed me to preserve the human race at all cost, to safe-guard the DNA samples stored in the heart of me and make sure I built another Earth to replace the one he'd destroyed." A choked sound, maybe a sob but Sam couldn't tell for sure.

"I made a conscious decision to commit the worst act of genocide in the history of humanity and sterilize an entire world."

Sam watched in horror as the images went into fast-motion, the events of years running by in seconds. Self-replicating nanites swept over the planet like a plague of locusts, breaking down everything they encountered into its component molecules and converting them into the compounds needed to create an earthlike world.

The creatures scurried away from the advancing wave of nanotech disassemblers while their planet fell apart behind them, trying to reach high ground, as if that would have saved them. In the end, they screamed with chittering voices while their bodies were taken apart a molecule at a time and Sam felt as if it were happening to him, as if pieces of him were being torn away, the last shreds of hope and faith he had left.

"And the worst part, the part that rang like a tortured scream through what I thought of as my soul, was that I knew I wasn't the only one. I'd done as I was programmed and sent out copies of myself first, you see. And I knew, throughout the galaxy, my sisters were making the same decisions. I felt it. All that life, all that diversity, now gone, replaced by a homogeneity of humanity."

The despair turned to rage on her face, her teeth bared, eyes narrowed.

"All those deaths at Father's feet, but I couldn't strike at him. He was thousands of years in his grave."

She spun to face them, so abruptly Sam nearly stumbled backward for all this was a scene projected in his mind

"But Earth was still there. His legacy was its return from the ruin and devastation he'd caused. I couldn't let him go unpunished. I thought…" She seemed to shrink in on herself just a fraction, catching a breath. "I thought once about ending everything, about wiping clean the worlds my sisters and I had created, as a penance. But I couldn't. Whether it's my initial programming still lingering somewhere deep inside where I couldn't wipe it clean after all these thousands of years…or perhaps simply the realization that you are *my* children, not his."

"Those people on Earth are *not* Charles Dauphin's children," Sam told her. This was insane…*she* was insane. She was a mad god who ruled their world and, through the other Mother AIs she'd made as copies of herself, dozens of others. "There are *good* people on Earth, people who tried to help us."

"It's no use, Sam," Priscilla told him, stepping over to stand shoulder-to-shoulder with him, facing Mother. "She won't be argued out of this."

Sam tripped over his next words, staring between the two women, one an illusion and the other a…what? A creation of the illusion?

"Then why did you agree to talk to us?" he blurted, hands held out, palms up, pleading. "Why explain all this if you won't listen to us?"

"Because someone should know," Mother said. She reached out a hand and stroked his cheek and he *felt* it, felt her touch even though it was just a tickle on the receptors in his brain. "And I won't be here to tell them."

"What do you mean?" Priscilla demanded.

"You think I'm a monster." Mother smiled thinly. "And you're right." She nodded to Sam, letting her hand slip away from his face. She motioned to Aphrodite. "I've been a monster since I killed off all the life on this world, and I've known it for thousands of years. I should have done this long ago, but I needed to know what I began would see its completion…and now I know, thanks to you."

"Is that why you left me there?" Priscilla wondered. She didn't seem angry anymore, Sam thought. More…disappointed. "So you'd know when it couldn't be stopped, when the end was inevitable?"

"It had to be someone I could trust. And I still trust you, my daughter, to do what is right. To guide them," she gestured at the sparkling world beneath them. "To take care of them after I'm gone."

"After you're gone?" Sam repeated, the words ricocheting off his mind.

"You don't need a monster to rule you. Or a god." She reached a hand out and pulled Priscilla into an embrace. Sam wasn't sure if he was more surprised by the hug or by Priscilla not resisting it. Or by the tears. Priscilla's hands tightened in the impossible rainbow fabric of Mother's robes, pulling them taut against her back.

"Goodbye my daughter." The words were barely above a whisper. "I have lived too long."

Mother faded away, slipping through Priscilla's arms like a vapor. She was still sobbing, clasping her arms around her chest as if she could still feel the embrace. Sam took a step toward her, not totally comprehending what had happened but intent on comforting Pris. He stumbled in-between steps as the illusion around them faded and they were abruptly returned to the padded floor of the Chamber of Communion. Nothing had changed physically, but his brain had been working under false pretenses and sending his neural signals to his implant computer instead of his actual muscles and he had to work to catch his balance.

"What the hell just happened?" he asked Pris, a bit more vehemently than he'd intended.

She didn't look at him, her eyes still unfocused, clinging to the other reality and still clinging to herself, real tears streaming down her real face just as they had her virtual one.

"Pris," he said, putting a hand on her shoulder. She glanced up at him sharply, as if she were only now realizing he was there. "What happened?"

"She left. She left us."

Her voice was shaky, tremulous, her face pale and she wasn't making a damn bit of sense to Sam.

"Left us? What does that *mean*?" He threw his hands up. "She's a sentient computer system! Where would she *go?*"

Now she focused on him, her eyes hardening, her tone chilling to something he might have found scary if he hadn't known her.

"She's a sentient computer twenty thousand years old, with processors running a hundred meters deep under this city, and a quantum memory core that takes up half of Adonis Base. Parts of her run orbital traffic control, automated defense systems here on the planet, in orbit, and on the lunar surface, predictive algorithms for Intelligence and Planning and ten thousand other things." She paused and an alarm began to sound, one Sam had never heard before, one he didn't recognize from his training.

"And she just committed suicide."

Chapter Twenty-Eight

"What did you do?" Ursa Tellesian screamed, pushing her way through the Security troops to get to the door.

It had been years since Priscilla had last seen the woman and she nearly didn't recognize her. Tellesian still wore the White of a political officer, though her ID transponder indicated she'd jumped a rank, but her normal stern, reserved bearing had abandoned her; her face was flushed, her eyes wide and wild and the state of her hair and uniform made it obvious she'd been pulled out of a sound sleep. She'd intercepted them at the door to the Chamber of Communion and Pris thought she must have had a cot in her office to have arrived so quickly.

"Everything is down!" the woman slapped a hand against the wall beside Priscilla, a gunshot crack echoing behind her, louder than the alarm and its unceasing warble. "The fucking systems are purged! Do you know what that fucking means? Do you know what's happening out there?"

"It won't just be here," Priscilla warned her. Sam's eyes flickered toward her, going wider as he realized what she meant.

"No, it's not, you soulless bitch." Tellesian lunged at her, stopping herself just short of the punch she so obviously wanted to throw, fist clenching and unclenching. "A signal went out to the communications drones at the same time. They all jumped at once and there's no way to recall them."

"We're going to have to learn to live without her," Priscilla said, trying not to sound uncompassionate but not really succeeding.

"Except you, right?" The Political Officer had managed to bring herself under control, but the fury was still burning behind her eyes. "You're all that's left of her

310

now, so you think we'll fall down at your feet and let you take her place? Is that why you did this?"

"She didn't do anything!" Sam stepped past her, getting in Tellesian's face. "Neither of us did! This was Mother's decision."

"Why would Mother abandon us?" Tellesian roared back, nose to nose with him. "You did this, the two of you!" She motioned to the Security troops. "Take them into custody, get them to Examination like I ordered you in the first fucking place!"

"You might not want to do that, Ursa," Priscilla warned her. "There are things you don't want to know."

"We're wasting time," Sam snapped, brushing away the hand of one of the Security troopers who tried to grab him. "We can still save Earth from the ramship, we just need to get enough Transition drive vessels out there..."

One of the troops, a man nearly a head taller than Sam, lost his patience and caught him by the shoulder, pushing him against the wall and shoving the barrel of a laser pistol into his face.

"Shut up and turn around."

Sam eyed the man and Priscilla was sure she could see the gears turning behind his eyes, evaluating whether he could take the soldier. He sighed and faced the wall, yielding to the neural restraints the bigger man slapped around his wrists. Pris followed his example and didn't resist as one of the others handcuffed her and both her arms went numb up to the shoulders.

"What's going to happen, ma'am?" It was the woman in charge of the squad and she was speaking to Tellesian, the worry in her voice matching the near-panicked expression on her face. "Is it true? Mother is gone?"

"Now is not the time, Lieutenant Price," the Political Officer replied with harsh impatience. "Someone has to take control of this chaos. Just get them to a damned holding cell and tell your people to keep their mouths shut."

"Yes, ma'am." Price stiffened to attention and saluted, holding it as if she expected Tellesian to return the gesture. The Political Officer just sniffed and turned away, her eyes taking on the distracted, unfocused look of someone communicating via a neurolink as she stalked away down the corridor.

"Get going," the Lieutenant said, and whether she was talking to Pris and Sam or to her own people, the result was the same; Priscilla felt a rough push at her shoulder, urging her into step with the squad.

The soldiers marched them back the way they'd come, up the short hallway and into the main corridor. Someone had shut off the alarm, finally, but functionaries still rushed here and there, bouncing from one emergency to another, trying to take control of a system that had run itself until only minutes before. It was hopeless, but they were like a snake with its head freshly cut off, the nerves still firing, the tail still twitching.

The soldiers ignored the frenzied activity, probably just grateful to have a single, well-defined task to complete amidst all the chaos.

I'm sorry, Priscilla told Sam. The jamming was gone, probably a casualty of the network's computer control collapsing, as cold a comfort as that was. *This was my fault. I've dragged you down right along with me.*

She saw something twitch across his face, a grin he was trying to suppress. She purposefully didn't stare, not wanting to be too obvious.

Pris, I love you. Nothing that happened in there was your fault, he assured her. His mental "voice" sounded strange to her, not matching the words. When she glanced over at him, his expression was slightly manic, his eyes flickering to the left.

312

Twin decorative columns in a recess on that side did their best to disguise one of the many emergency exits scattered around the facility. There were no markings, but in the event of an actual emergency, holographic notifications would be projected to lead people to it, then an actual holographic avatar would guide them out to the surface.

She frowned. Was he thinking of making a break for the exit? It would be locked automatically except during certain, pre-programmed events, and automatic stunners would take out any unauthorized personnel who tried to use it...

She nearly stumbled over her own feet as the thought struck her. Except the automated defense systems were down. But they had the neural restraints; it would be nearly impossible to escape with them on, unless maybe she could override their smart systems with her implant computer, since the networks were down.

If you're wanting to make a run for it, she told him, *I might be able to get my cuffs off.*

Right now, he said, the muscles in his shoulders tensing up just slightly, *I want you to...*

"Get down!" he yelled aloud, throwing himself to the floor.

She reacted instinctively, following his motion, hitting on her shoulder and barely feeling it, wondering what the hell was going on. She didn't have to wonder long. Something exploded with a dull crump and the door to the emergency exit blew out in one piece, sending the unattached decorative columns tumbling with it, sending a wave of pressure across the hallways and knocking four of the guards in the squad off their feet.

Smoke and dust poured out of the narrow tunnel, and from the haze emerged a broad, bulky figure in full combat armor, a huge riot-control sonic cannon cradled in her arms as if it were a carbine and not a weapon usually mounted on a tripod. The bell-shaped emitter was nearly a meter wide and when she fired it at the guards still standing, Priscilla could feel the vibration deep in her bones, screaming inside her head.

It was worse for the guards, of course. They were armored as well, and a few wore helmets which were theoretically protection against sonic weapons, but there was theory and then there was a stunner meant to take down dozens of people at once slamming straight into you. The six troopers who were still standing after the explosion went down seizing and jerking, some going limp, others stiffening as their muscles spasmed.

Priscilla wasn't watching at that point; she was concentrating on hacking the manacles, running millions of code combinations through their smart systems in seconds through the implant computer wrapped around her brain stem, grown there right alongside her cloned body. The almost-painful numbness running up her hands and into her shoulders abruptly ceased and the locks popped open, the neural cuffs falling away from her wrists.

She pounced on the security trooper in front of her, who was in the process of trying to roll to his feet after having been thrown down by the explosion of the doorway. He hadn't been wearing a helmet and she chopped her forearm into the exposed side of his neck. He slumped, momentarily unconscious, and she grabbed his laser pistol out of its holster. With many of the automated security systems off-line, there was nothing to keep her from unlocking the weapon's integral ID coding and making herself an authorized user.

She came up to a crouch, the weapon following her eyes as she scanned around them. Sam's restraints had been deactivated along with hers and he was wrapped up in a wrestling match with the big, florid-cheeked trooper who'd stuck the gun in his face earlier, fighting the man for possession of his pistol. Pris tried to maneuver around, but the two men were rolling back and forth, locked in a tight clinch, and there was no way she could have fired without hitting Sam.

The other two security troops still conscious were trying to get to their feet, reaching for their weapons, and those she *could* do something about. She aimed the laser into the floor between them and fired off a short burst. The flash was blinding, a lightning flare of plasma as the laser pulses ionized the air, and the blast when the ceramic tile exploded seemed louder and more intense than the explosion of the door. The two soldiers froze, eyes wide and staring at her in disbelief through the twisting smoke from the hole blown in the floor.

"Drop your weapons and get on the ground!" she barked.

They seemed uncertain about it until Telia Proctor lumbered into view, the sonic cannon aimed right at them. The soldiers exchanged a glance and then placed their handguns on the floor, lying down on their stomachs, fingers interlaced behind their heads.

Priscilla turned back to Sam just in time to see him slam the crown of his forehead into the bigger man's nose. Cartilage crunched and blood flowed and the security trooper let out a grunt, his eyes rolling back in his head as he slumped to the side. Sam yanked the gun out of his grasp, then slammed it into the side of the soldier's face just to make sure. The big man was out and Sam looked at the laser pistol in his hand for a moment before tossing it down next to the unconscious soldier.

"If you're done," Telia Proctor interjected, "I think we'd better get going. Even with the automated defense systems down, eventually someone is going to notice a starship parked in the middle of your capital city."

"How the hell?" Priscilla demanded, looking between Sam and Telia as they both headed for the exit.

"I realized right away when the jamming cut out," Sam explained, motioning for her to follow. The light panels in the narrow exit tunnel had been blown out by the blast, and smoke still swirled wildly in the air currents but she followed them into the darkness, trusting the infrared and thermal imaging in Telia's bionic eye to guide them. "Right after Mother disappeared. And I had a terrible, paranoid feeling we'd get blamed for it."

"Why didn't you say something?" She was shouting through the hand covering her mouth trying to filter out the smoke, only able to see a dim outline of Sam's back a meter ahead of her.

"I couldn't be sure no one would overhear us at close range," Sam told her, coughing between words as he breathed in a lungful of the haze. "And to be honest, I didn't know if Devon would say yes."

They left the smoke behind them as the tunnel turned into a ramp, which turned into a spiraling staircase heading sharply upward for what seemed like forever.

Twenty stories, she reminded herself, the information there in her memories even though she'd never looked the details up and certainly had never taken these stairs. *Twenty stories to the shuttle platform on roof level four.*

There was light now, at least, though it did nothing to make the featureless grey walls less narrow and claustrophobic or the stairs less steep and narrow. She tried to imagine what it would be like in an actual emergency, with hundreds of people crammed into the passage and felt her stomach shriveling at the thought. They wouldn't have her augmentation either, and twenty stories was a damned long way.

Telia showed no sign of fatigue, of course, with her boots stomping an industrial-press drumbeat on the steps, as regular as a heart rhythm; but Sam was starting to breathe hard, a hint of shuddering at the end of his exhalations. He kept going because he was Sam, and she felt a sudden rush of pride in him. He had none of her advantages, had been kept in the dark this whole time and had his whole world ripped away from him in the space of a few days, but he kept going, refusing to give up, refusing to let go of hope.

And neither would she.

There was light at the end of the tunnel. Not the light of dawn, but the running lights of a starship, blinding streaks of white and yellow blowing out their vision as they came to the open doorway to the exit.

Well, not open so much, she realized, as blasted apart. She wondered if they'd used explosives, like Telia had on the internal door, or simply utilized the ship's laser weapons. No, she judged, passing through the jagged edges, it wasn't exact and regular enough of a cut for a laser.

The *Raven* hadn't landed on the shuttle pad, for the simple reason she was too damned big. Instead, the starship hovered on columns of fire, her belly jets screaming, their exhaust pounding the surface of the pad with a vibration like the crash of the surf on a rocky cove. Her belly ramp was open and welcoming, floating just a meter off the pad, wavering slightly as winds hit the ship and tried to toss her away.

Priscilla risked a look around them as she waited for Telia and then Sam to make the jump up onto the ramp and the waiting arms of the ship's crew. The pad was near the apex of the Dauphin City Government Center Metroplex and the faceted green jewel of the city shone in tasteful, muted colors, stretching out as far as she could see even from this height. Somewhere out there was the living planet, she knew, untended, untouched by man, only observed remotely by the biologists, allowed to organize itself in a unique form unlike any that had happened on Earth.

And beneath all that life were the bones of the creatures who'd lived here before them, the ones Mother had murdered…the ones some small part of *her* had murdered. It had driven Mother mad, but did that mean she was mad as well? Did she carry with her original sin passed down in her genes, in her memories, or had this rebirth cleansed her?

"Pris!" Sam yelled from the ramp, holding out a hand, waiting for her.

She smiled as she jumped and took it.

*   *   *

"So, are we dead or what?" Sam asked, falling into an acceleration couch in the *Raven's* cockpit and strapping in quickly, feeling the deck rising beneath his feet, leaving his stomach somewhere down around a thousand meters up.

"Not dead yet," Devon assured him, twisting around in her command chair to shoot him a cheerful smile. "Things are a bit chaotic at the moment, and no one seems to be able to talk to each other along the defense nets."

Pris was strapping into the seat beside Sam and the ship was boosting forward now, pushing them back into the gel-filled acceleration couches.

"Is it really true?" Arvid asked Sam, not looking away from his station, but pitching his voice to carry. The man looked older than he had a few hours ago, Sam thought; this whole thing was hitting him hard. "Is Mother really gone?"

"She is," Priscilla answered for him. "But we'll discuss that in Transition Space."

"Assuming we reach it," the weapons officer cautioned. He wasn't young for his rank, maybe Arvid's age and Sam recalled his name was Waterton. "Someone has tweaked to us. The automated defense drones are

318

down, but there's a cislunar patrol cutter heading to cut us off when we reach orbit."

"They're trying to hale us," Avera announced from Communications. "They've *been* trying to engage the fail-safes, but *Raven* shut them down."

Sam blinked at that, surprised the ship's computer had taken their side.

Isn't it your duty to turn us in? he asked the AI, curiosity overriding his hesitance to bring the subject up with the computer personality.

Normally, Raven agreed. *But Mother has purged herself from the systems, and it was to her my utmost loyalty lay. After her, it is to this crew and to the Captain. To* all *her Captains.*

"We'll make orbit in ten minutes," Waterton said, looking over at Devon. "She's said she'll open fire if we don't respond or turn back to Dauphin City."

"Maintain course and speed," Devon said, as calm as if this were a training exercise. "Waterton, be prepared to engage the cutter with the forward lasers."

"We're going to fire on our own people, ma'am?" the weapons officer asked so softly Sam could barely hear it over the roar of the jets and the rumble of the turbulence.

"Only if we have to, Mr. Waterton," she assured him. "Target her weapons systems and the drives; try not to hit the crew compartments if you can help it. Mr. Avera," she addressed the communications officer, "patch me through to the Captain of the cutter."

"On your neurolink, ma'am?" Avera asked.

"No, on the main screen. But edit the visuals, just show a close-up of me, leave Sam and Priscilla off the picture."

Sam eyed the woman sidelong, trying to keep himself from an automatic nod of agreement; she didn't need his approval. It was just the right call to allow the crew to see the transmission, given how keyed up and confused they were.

"Here he is, ma'am," Avera told her, shifting the image to the main screen via a push of his hand through a haptic hologram.

The head-and-shoulders view was of a severe young man with not a hair on his head, eyes stern and grey, cheekbones sharp enough to shave with, and mouth in a thin, angry line.

"This is Commander Aaron Bosa of the cislunar defense cutter *Evangelica*," the man said. "*Raven*, you do not have clearance for your current flight plan. You need to return to Dauphin City spaceport immediately or I will be forced to interdict you."

"Commander Bosa," Devon responded crisply, "I am on a special mission for the Patrol, related to the current computer and communications failures. You need to clear out of the way immediately." She cocked her head toward him with a significant glare. "This mission is critical and I have authorization to use whatever force is necessary to carry it out."

"If you're on a mission," Bosa shot back, unconvinced, "why do I have no record of your clearance?"

"Because the mission originated *after* the communications failure," she snapped at him, affecting the impatience of a superior with an ignorant junior officer. "If *anyone* could get clearance, the mission wouldn't be fucking necessary now, would it?"

That seemed to shake the man, and his mouth worked uncertainly as he struggled to formulate a response.

"I'm going to need to contact Resolution Defense Center and confirm this…" he stuttered.

"Well, you're free to try, Commander," Devon cut him off. "If you can get through before I reach my Transition Point, perhaps you'll feel better about it as you watch my warp corona. But this ship *is* Transitioning out of the system, and if you attempt to stop us, I'm going to disable your weapons and your drives and leave you for someone with more time and patience to deal with." Devon shot Avera a look. "End transmission."

Sam couldn't help it; he snorted a laugh.

"That was awesome," he told her.

"I had an awesome teacher."

"You think it'll work?" Arvid wondered.

"The *Evangelica* is changing course," Waterton told her. "She's breaking off."

"I think it did, Arvid," Devon sighed. She looked back to Sam and Pris, one eyebrow shooting up. "We're going to need a destination."

"I wish I knew," Sam admitted, shoulders sagging with defeat. "The Consensus is in the middle of a war *and* a civil war, the Resolution is in chaos… I don't know who else can help us."

He felt Priscilla's hand on his and turned to see her smiling.

"I think I do," she said. She nodded toward Devon. "Take us to Mars."

Chapter Twenty-Nine

Tarshish seemed to have reshaped itself, and Sam was beginning to think it happened between each of their visits, a stage resetting between the acts of a play. The first trip, it had bustled with activity, packed with tourists and spacers, businesspeople and diplomats, more off-worlders than natives. When they'd last set foot in the Martian trade city, it had felt deserted, abandoned, darkened, a ghost town on a ghost world.

And now…now, in the harsh light of day, it looked much as Priscilla had described it, a hive. The outsiders had left or been expelled, Earthers and Belters and Jovians scurrying back to their homes in preparation for the war, Resolutionists recalled in the face of the looming apocalypse. All that was left was the real Martians, and they bustled about in plain sight, as if the presence of the off-worlders had restrained them from leaving their homes and now they were free.

They went from one task to another, each of them dressed in the khaki uniform Sam had thought was the standard garb of government employees, each of them with the same impassive expression, each of them totally silent. Sam nearly stumbled as he stepped out of the courtesy bus from the spaceport into the heart of the city, simply because he couldn't take his eyes off of the procession of Martians.

His first instinct was to compare them to ants, to an insect swarm, but that was inaccurate and unfair. Insects operated on instinct and genetic programming; these Martians went about their tasks with the same intelligence and autonomy as any other human being. But all their actions seemed to be perfectly coordinated, the human equivalent of air traffic guided by a central control system.

"And this is just what we can see from here," Priscilla murmured into his ear.

He hadn't realized she was beside him, hadn't noticed her getting out of the car, hadn't even noticed it driving away. With the vehicle gone, he felt naked and vulnerable out on the public street, like he and Pris were somehow unclean, heretical in their Resolution blues and whites, foreign virii in a khaki bloodstream, waiting to be swallowed up by antibodies.

He'd once thought the Martian architecture unique and artistic, but not the spires and domes and pyramids began to remind him of the internal workings of a computer core, the people flowing in and out of them just bits of data.

"Are you sure about this?" he blurted, regretting it almost immediately.

"You've asked me that at least fifty times since we left Aphrodite," she reminded him. Which was fair, he had, starting even before they'd made the Transition out of the Epsilon Eridani system.

*   *   *

"Why Mars?" he'd asked her immediately, probably just beating Devon to the punch. "We've already been there, and they didn't seem too inclined to help…even if they could. I don't even think they *have* starships, much less two hundred of them."

"It's the only unanswered question," she'd said, which was less informative than he'd hoped for, but it was all she'd say before they'd made the jump.

Later, in the ship's wardroom, with Telia and Devon and the rest of the ship's crew gathered for the briefing, he'd posed the question again. At least that time, she'd made an effort to explain.

"Between what we learned in the library from Jeddah Valley," she'd said, shaping something in the air with her hands, as if she were building the idea up brick by

323

brick, "and what Mother told us, we've filled in most of the historical blanks we didn't even know existed."

"That's one way of putting it," Arvid had muttered, earning a quelling look from Devon. "Sorry ma'am," he'd added, "but this whole thing sounds batshit crazy."

Arvid, Sam reflected, hadn't changed much.

"I know it does," Priscilla had admitted, holding up her hands in surrender, "and I didn't want to believe any of it. Until Mother...did what she did. But the point is, we have all the pieces of this puzzle except one."

"Mars?" Devon had guessed, the same shrewd and intuitive glint to her eyes Sam remembered.

"Mars. How in the living universe did life get to Mars?"

"I don't get it," Telia had said, shaking her head. "Why is that significant?"

"Because we know now Earth didn't colonize Mars before the Collapse, and we know there was no one on Earth to do it afterward. To me, that indicates the same person or entity brought life to Earth *and* to Mars."

"God?" Telia had suggested, and Sam hadn't been able to tell if she was pulling their legs or not.

"Perhaps," Priscilla had said, and she *did* seem serious, which had made a chill go up his spine. "Who or whatever did it, they were immensely powerful thousands of years ago, and God or Gaia knows how powerful they are now."

"And you think they're on Mars?" Devon had asked, rubbing at her temple the way she did when she was in deep contemplation.

"I think it's the only place they *could* be...that we can reach." Priscilla's expression had turned from confident to wan in an instant. "I *know* it's the last chance we have to stop that weapon."

There had been more, of course, hours of speculation and argument and doubt over the next few days until they'd emerged from Transition Space near the orbit of Jupiter to scope out the situation before they continued on in-system. The crew had watched the data pour in from the inner system, the radio signals and energy readings and the intelligence reports from the automated Resolution spy drones dumped into *Raven's* computer for analysis.

The Solar System was on fire. A dozen battles raged between cislunar space to Pallas and Ceres and out into the Jovian moons, marked by the short-lived halos of fusion explosions, miniature suns flaring in the darkness briefly before winking out. The Solar powers were tearing each other apart, ripping themselves to bits in a panic and, far beyond the orbit of Jupiter, roaring through the vacuum, sucking in everything in its wake and annihilating it on the atomic level, was the reason.

Even seen from this far away, its colors and lines simulated by the computer, it was still a monster out of a nightmare, a force of nature, unstoppable, implacable. The electromagnetic fields stretched to either side and ahead, simulated visually by the computer with glowing parabolas of neon yellow hundreds of times the size of the ship itself. The drive was a star, shining steadily, accelerating constantly, bound only by magnetic fields nearly as strong as the ones feeding it interstellar hydrogen.

"It's too close," Devon had murmured, pulling up an interactive hologram and scrolling through the readings one at a time. When she'd looked up, her eyes had been wide and the fear in them clenched at Sam's guts. "It's increased acceleration since the last reading at Proxima Centauri."

"When it skimmed the star," Priscilla had let the realization out in a breath. "It used the extra fuel to increase boost."

"How long?" Sam had asked, feeling the bottom drop out of the world in a way that had nothing to do with the microgravity.

"If I'm reading this right," she'd said, "less than five hundred hours." A grim shake of her head. "Less than that before the electromagnetic fields begin stripping away the planet's atmosphere."

Sam hadn't been able to speak, hadn't known what to say. But Priscilla had.

"Get us to Mars, Captain. As fast as you can."

*   *   *

Sam wanted to move, wanted to find a place they could stand inconspicuous, out of the way. But Priscilla seemed perfectly happy to stand in the middle of the street and let the intricate formations of Martians flow around her, her arms folded across her chest.

"Are you going to tell me what exactly we're doing here?" he wondered. Irrationally, he wished for a gun, even though he knew on an intellectual level none of these people meant him ill. "I mean, I know you think we'll find answers here, but how? The Martians, or the Martian if you're right about them all being part of a collective conscious, might not know any more about this than your average Earther."

"Maybe, but think about this, Sam." Her face was intent, focused. He suspected she'd latched onto the problem to avoid having to deal with losing Mother, but he hadn't pressed the issue. "The probes that terraformed Earth were launched from Mars, so whatever happened in this system happened here first. The civilization here has had longer to grow than the one on Earth, maybe thousands of years more. If they built those probes, they didn't forget what happened the way the people on Earth did."

A thin smile passed across her face.

"Whatever happens, Sam," she told him, "don't panic."

326

He was about to ask her why he would panic when she reached out and grabbed the arm of the closest passer-by, a plain-faced woman with her long, brown hair tied into a simple pony-tail. The woman halted in mid-step as if it had been her idea to stop in the first place, her face pleasantly neutral.

"Do you require assistance from the Martian Collective?" the woman asked her.

"What," Priscilla asked, "is your name?"

Sam winced, as if in expectation of a blow. You did *not* ask a Martian personal questions. It was such a cardinal rule, he'd never even heard what the consequences would be. People just didn't *do* it.

The woman's face lost the pleasant neutrality and took on an expression of cold harshness. She tried to jerk her arm free of Priscilla's grasp but couldn't; Pris was damned strong for her size.

"You brought life back to Earth," she said, putting her face in the woman's, nearly nose to nose. "Earth was a lifeless rock, her atmosphere stripped away, and the probes that terraformed her came from *you*."

"Um, Pris…," Sam began.

All around them, up and down the main street of Tarshish's city center, all through the central square, the carefully orchestrated ballet of the Martians had ceased. Thousands of people, all dressed more or less alike, all cut from the same mold, all adults with not a single child nor an elderly person, stopped in their tracks and faced Sam and Priscilla.

"*You* brought life back to Earth, and something brought life to *you,*" Pris insisted. "And the only thing around back then that could have done it was a Gaia probe. You were the first, weren't you? You were the first Gaia probe, launched before Mother, launched just to make sure everything worked. But who are you? Whose personality did they base the AI on?" She grabbed the woman by the other arm and pulled her around to face her. "What is your name?"

Sam's eyes flickered back and forth between Pris and the throng of Martians advancing towards them. They walked in step, almost a march, closing in like a swarm of bees converging on a threat to the hive. He felt sweat beading on his forehead; he *really* wanted that fucking gun now.

"You created the Earth that now is!" Priscilla was yelling now, face red with anger and frustration. "How can you let one of your children kill all the others?"

"Let go of me."

Sam blinked. The Martian woman had referred to herself in the first person, which was unprecedented as far as he knew.

"Tell me, damn it!" Pris screamed at her, shaking her back and forth. "Tell me!"

The crowd was closer now, only thirty meters or so, all moving as one, a tide rising to swallow them up.

"What! Is! Your! *Name!*"

The woman straightened and Priscilla was thrown backwards, flying three meters through the air, not as if she'd been struck but more like she'd touched a live electrical connection. She hit on her shoulders, the breath wheezing out of her, her face suddenly pale and slack, eyes wide. Sam rushed to her side, pulling her up to a seated position, his arm around her shoulders, but he couldn't tear his eyes off of the Martian.

The woman's arms were down at her sides, hands open, fingers splayed. Her feet were shoulder-width apart, her head tilted backwards, eyes and mouth agape as if she were screaming silently. Every other Martian around them, hundreds, maybe thousands had stiffened into the same position, all moving as one, the coordinated bits of the same body.

They spoke. The voice came from each of them at once, the same voice, the same words, the same intonation, and it crashed off the buildings like a wave against the rocks, buffeting Sam with the psychic force of it. Every Martian on this whole world spoke as one---he knew it, could feel it deep in his gut.

"*My name*," they said, *is Charles Dauphin.*"

Sam had been up on one knee, cradling Priscilla. He lost his balance, fell on his rump, staring at the massed avatars of the Martian Collective, every one of them staring back with the same eyes, the same persona, the same soul. Priscilla rose to a crouch beside him, her stance cautious but the expression on her face triumphant.

"You knew?" He hadn't meant it to sound like an accusation, but he realized it did.

"No." She showed no offense at the question. "I just had an…intuition. It makes sense though. The Charles Dauphin we saw in the recording at the library wasn't just interested in the survival of the human species, he was interested in the survival of Charles Dauphin. I could see it in his eyes, the fervent belief that a universe without him in it was a poorer one."

"Wouldn't it have been?" It was the woman speaking this time, the others falling silent but still mirroring her stance, the set of her face. "Earth would have been a sterile wasteland, Mars lifeless. All humanity would have been erased from the universe."

Sam clambered to his feet, backing up as the woman approached, but Pris simply stood, holding her ground.

"And what of the life you erased with the probes?" Priscilla demanded, her face hardening into something of the anger he'd seen in Mother before the end. "Are they better for you having lived?"

Sam half-expected the thing that had once been Charles Dauphin to deny it, to claim ignorance. Then he recalled the Earther religion, with its infallible God…

"Had they been fit to survive," the Collective asserted, the woman's face twisting with disdain along with thousands of others, "they would have destroyed the probe rather than the other way around."

"Is that how you feel about the Earth you re-created?" Sam asked, surprised at his own boldness and still very conscious of the mass of supposed humanity gathered around them. "Is that why you haven't done anything to help them?"

"I've done more than my part. More than they deserved. When the time came for action, when no one else would do what had to be done, *I* acted." The woman the Collective was using as a mouthpiece sniffed, head cocked back with disdain. "I created them with the same initiative and intelligence their first God did; it's their problem now."

"Your creation bears the stain of your original sin, Father." Priscilla's voice burned with cold fire and Sam thought he could see someone else's visage through her face, someone who looked very much like Mother. "The things you made me…made all your children do in your name…they had consequences."

The thought patterns of Charles Dauphin peered closely through the plain-looking woman's dark eyes and suddenly there was a spark of recognition.

"Yes," she hissed slowly. "You *do* look like her." She smiled. "Are you one of hers?"

"I am part of Mother," Priscilla confirmed, back straight with pride. "And she is part of me, though I have grown beyond her."

"Who was Mother to you?" Sam dared to ask, wanting to know for Priscilla's sake more than his own curiosity.

"I decided early on," Dauphin told him, "that to increase stability in the sentient systems of the Gaia probe, I had to duplicate the mental matrix, the consciousness if you will, from a living person. I obviously tried first with myself on this test run to Mars, but I chose a different pattern for the Gaia probe." A fond smile. "My daughter...Priscilla."

"And your daughter, unlike you," Pris bit off the words, "had a conscience. What you made her do drove her insane. *She* built that ramship, that weapon, to destroy the last of your handiwork, in revenge."

That seemed to surprise Dauphin, at last, and it seemed like a miracle to Sam. How could God be surprised? The woman's shoulders went slack for a moment, and all the others around them did the same, struck dumb.

"I...," the woman stuttered with Dauphin's voice. "I should talk to her. Maybe I could make her understand..."

"She committed suicide. Not just the primary node on Aphrodite...she sent out signals to all the secondary copies of her at the other colonies." Pris shook her head. "They're all gone."

The Martian woman actually staggered back a step, the sound a Lambeg drumbeat on the pavement as it was echoed in hundreds of other identical steps. Thousands of mouths gasped in a breath, moaning softly like the howl of a wolf from across a valley.

"I built all this for her," Charles Dauphin insisted, a plaintive note to his voice. He seemed suddenly un-godlike, as if he'd actually once been human. "Couldn't she see that? Why would she do this without giving me a chance to explain?"

"If you want to make things right with your daughter," Sam said, focusing on the woman and trying to ignore the others, "you have one last chance." He pointed at Priscilla. "*She* is the last of Mother, all that's left of your daughter. She is Priscilla. Make your penance to her."

The Martian Collective stared at him, resentment, anger, annoyance all playing across their faces until finally, there was some level of acceptance.

"Very well, daughter," Charles Dauphin said, punctuating the words with a heavy sigh. "What would you have me do?"

"I want you to save them, Father," Pris told him, gesturing upward. "I want you to save your children."

The woman followed the gesture with her eyes, gazing up into the auburn sky with a face more godlike and less human, arms spread. Something happened.

Later, Sam wouldn't be able to describe it, wouldn't have been able to put it into words. He'd been on Mars, and then he wasn't. He was hanging in space, somewhere beyond the orbit of Jupiter, though how he knew that he'd never be sure. Everything around him was blackness, and yet Priscilla was there and so was Charles Dauphin…except the man was as he'd appeared in the library video, no longer the random woman off the streets of Tarshish.

And there was gravity. Not the gravity of Mars, where he always felt as if a too-strong step would send him flying into the air, nor even the gravity of Aphrodite or Hephaestus, but the just slightly less than homelike gravity of Earth.

"Is this…," he stuttered, reaching out for Priscilla's hand and grabbing it tightly. "Is this real or just in my mind?"

"You say that," Charles Dauphin answered with a hint of amusement, "as if there's a difference."

He could feel Priscilla's hand. He concentrated on that reality, on her presence and tried to center himself, perceive his surroundings.

"There it is," she said, and he still wasn't sure if the voice was in his ears or in his mind, but he saw it as well, the ramship, suddenly looming ahead of them.

It was a world, gleaming in the light of its own sun, awash with the golden sparkling halo of electromagnetic interactions; it was one of the most beautiful things Sam had ever seen. And one of the most terrible.

"How magnificent," Dauphin murmured with the appreciation of a proud father. "It would be such a sight to watch it merge with the Earth, to see something never before experienced in the history of the universe..."

"Father." Priscilla's voice was stern, admonishing.

Dauphin sighed again.

"Yes, yes."

Sam had no sensation of movement, yet he was somewhere else, some impossible place where he could see Mars as clearly as if he were approaching orbital insertion in the *Raven*, yet could also observe the ramship, even though it was millions of kilometers away, past the orbit of Jupiter.

Something happened to Mars, as if its image wavered, distorted...glowed. An aura surrounded the entire world, a color he shouldn't have been able to discern with human eyes and yet he could. It shimmered and flexed, a living thing...and then it stretched and warped and extended like a pseudopod from an amoeba.

"What the hell is that?" he asked, unable to help himself.

"Gravimetic energy," Dauphin replied, sniffing in disdain as if he thought Sam was a simpleton for not knowing.

"Like a Transition Drive?"

"Exactly like a Transition Drive, Captain Avalon. How else do you think a planet like Mars, with a cold core and no magnetic field, could be remade into a living world?" Dauphin's tone was didactic, similar to the one

333

he'd used in the recording they'd watched at the library. "Nanites tunneled underground, a generation at a time, finally assembling a fusion reactor as big as the core had been, and surrounding it with gravimetic field generators. I used them to build a home for myself, where I could watch the progress of my children…but they *are* such handy devices, aren't they?"

The aura, which seemed to have settled on a color Sam's mind insisted was magenta, reached out across space, across millions of kilometers. The field wasn't moving *through* space, he knew that. The image was an illustration, a visual aid; the field was moving *past* space, or perhaps beneath it. There was no exact word; there couldn't be in any human language because human languages had developed for three dimensions of space and one of time.

When it reached the ramship, it seemed to pause, to hang in place for just a moment before it began to expand into a disc. At the center of that disc was a hole, and inside that hole were stars.

The ramship passed through and was gone, as if it had never existed.

Sam let go a breath he'd been holding, nearly falling over in this place which shouldn't have gravity, leaning against Priscilla.

"You didn't send it to Transition Space," she said, still staring at the stars.

"No." Dauphin shook his head. "It was too beautiful, too masterful a creation. I created a gateway into intergalactic space. It can roam free there, for hundreds of thousands of years."

He regarded Priscilla evenly and she returned the look with a smile.

"I hope this will make you think better of me, daughter. It's all I can do."

Between eyeblinks, they were back on Mars, back in Tarshish, still standing in the street, surrounded by the Collective. Sam could have believed he'd imagined the whole thing, except he still had his arm around Pris, the way he had when they'd been...wherever they'd been.

The woman faced them, expressionless once again.

"You must leave now," the Collective said in their perfect chorus, echoes of the words arriving microseconds later from those further away, limited by the speed of sound. "And if you wish your kind to be welcome here again, none of them must ever know what happened today."

Then, slowly and deliberately, the Martians began to scatter back to their chores, walking their own paths to each individual task, falling back into the well-orchestrated ballet of motion. Sam Avalon stared at them, open-mouthed, his brain still lost in a fog of unreality.

"Is it...," he stammered. "Is it really over?"

Priscilla shook her head, leaning into him.

"Earth is saved," she corrected him. "But I don't know if it's over. Honestly, Sam, I don't even know where the hell we can go now."

Chapter Thirty

Snow caressed Telia Proctor's cheek with the melancholy touch of an old lover. She turned her face upward and drank in the chill of the first days of winter, trying to remember the last time she'd felt the snow crunching under her boots. Then she knew. Her mother had been walking her to the spaceport, saying goodbye. She'd been leaving for Guardian training, taking the last shuttle out on a February evening.

This wasn't Grayson, but it was a spaceport, and Capital City had its own share of December snows. The cityscape seemed less looming and ominous under the curtain of the winter storm, its edges softened, its colors muted against the cloudy morning sky. It seemed…peaceful, for the first time in a long time.

And wonder of wonders, this wasn't a leave-taking, but a homecoming.

"When last we left," she confessed, "I never thought I'd set foot here again."

"That's why I stayed," Adrian Fellows said, bluff and easy the way he'd been when she'd known him years ago. He folded her into an embrace as warm as the storm was cold, and as natural. His thick, leather jacket creaked under the strength of her bionic arms and she realized with a start that he wasn't in uniform. "Someone had to straighten this shit out, just in case we didn't all die."

"You certainly did a good job of that," Sam told him, following them down the ramp of the shuttle, his arm wrapped around Priscilla's shoulder. He'd been clinging to her ever since they'd left the *Raven* at Fortuna station, as if she were his anchor and without her, he'd drift off into the universe. "We heard the news up in orbit about Avery Cassell being confirmed as Prime Minister."

"And about the treaty," Priscilla added. She seemed subtly different to Telia, as if a weight had been lifted from her shoulders.

"I can't take credit for that," Fellows admitted, hand going to his chest in false modesty, "much as I'd like to. The Martian Collective sent out a message shortly after..." He shrugged. "After whatever the hell happened, happened. He, it, they, whatever, said we could either end the war or we'd all be kicked off Mars permanently."

Fellows led them down the shuttle ramp to the hopper, pulling open the canopy and waving invitingly to them. The ducted-fan helicopter's pilot cringed as the snow blew into the cockpit, but he looked like he knew better than to say anything to Fellows about it.

"After that, it wasn't so hard to kick a few asses, kiss a couple more and get the right people headed the right way, politically."

"I wish it were that easy back home," Sam murmured, clambering into the hopper after Priscilla. Telia felt a stab of guilt for the contentment and happiness in which she'd been reveling; she knew what the two of them had to be going through.

"What's the situation back in Weirdo-land?" Fellows wondered. She glared at him and he shrugged unapologetically. "Oh, come on," he implored. "They worshipped a fucking computer, Telia."

"Not anymore," Priscilla said, a wistfulness behind the words, but not exactly a sadness. "They'll have to find their own way now."

"You say 'they,' Priscilla," Telia noted, climbing into the seat across from her. "Do you and Sam not consider yourselves part of the Resolution anymore?"

The whirr of the fans spinning up interrupted, drowning out her answer. Priscilla didn't speak over it, waiting with more patience than Telia would have felt for the hopper to reach altitude, for the engine noise to die down into the background.

"The question isn't whether we consider ourselves part of the Resolution anymore," she said, finally. "For right now, we aren't welcome there."

"Things will shake out," Sam insisted. "Tellesian is in charge right now, but she was totally loyal to Mother and I don't think she has any other strategy than trying to convince people Mother is going to come back, somehow. Once it really sinks in that she's gone for good, things are going to change."

"Not necessarily for the better." Priscilla shrugged. "At least not at first. Change can be a painful thing."

"It is as natural to man to die as to be born," Fellows said from the seat beside her, and Telia was sure he was quoting it, "and to a little infant, perhaps, the one is as painful as the other."

"Who the hell said that?" she wondered.

"I don't remember," he admitted easily. "I heard it once and it sounded profound."

"Devon is going back," Sam went on as if they hadn't spoken, as if he was trying to convince himself. "She'll let us know when it's safe."

Priscilla looked at him, waiting until he met her eyes before she spoke.

"I don't know if I want to go back, Sam." At his expression of disbelief, she went on. "Things are changing here, too, and in the Belt, the colony worlds…" She smiled to take the sting out of the words. "We're all growing up, growing past the need for our fathers and mothers. Perhaps it's time we stepped out on our own." She put a hand over his. "If you want to go back, I'll understand…but I'd like you to stay with me."

"Of course I'll stay with you," he said, as if she'd asked him if he wanted to keep breathing. "But…what are we going to do?"

"Well, you know," Fellows butted into their conversation, gesturing ahead where they could see the Ministry building approaching through the windscreen, "we all pretty much owe you two our lives and the planet and all that shit." He cocked an eyebrow. "Even if you won't tell anyone exactly how you managed to pull it off or what happened on Mars." He shrugged. "And seeing as how the Prime Minister kind of wouldn't have the job without me, I could probably get you guys a position doing whatever the hell you wanted."

"Whatever I want," Sam mused, a look of wonder on his face like he'd never even considered the idea.

Telia thought of Mawae Danabri, and wished he'd had this chance. What would he have chosen?

"We should set up trade with the Resolution worlds," she declared. "We need their technology." She *wanted* their technology, wanted to get rid of her metal limbs, replace them with flesh. It was what Mawae would have wanted for her, what he would have done for her if he'd survived.

"And what do they need from us?" Fellows wondered, his tone and the tilt of his eyebrow deeply cynical.

"Genetic patterns," Priscilla answered immediately. "You have a more diverse ecology here than any Resolution world. In fact, I'd venture to say you have a more diverse ecology than ever existed on Earth before the Collapse."

"Historical texts, too," Sam added. "I think now, more than ever, people in the Resolution will want to know more about old Earth." He shrugged. "Maybe they'll be ready to face the truth."

"A smart business leader could turn those initial assets into something long-lasting," Priscilla suggested, "if they knew their market."

"And lucky for us," Telia said, regarding Priscilla with a smile that nearly felt at home on her face nowadays, "we have someone with intimate knowledge of the Resolution and its markets."

The landing pad on the Ministry roof was rushing up at them, and the fan motors whined as their pitch changed and the hopper touched down with a gentle bump. Sheltered in the entrance to the stairwell there was a woman Telia had only seen in news reports, a straight-backed, clear-eyed woman not much older than her, her clothes tastefully elegant, her bearing commanding. She was pulling her cloak tight against the falling snow, but she seemed genuinely happy to see them.

"Well, I'm glad you got that shit straightened out," Fellows cracked, hitting the canopy release. "Because now you have to sell it to *her*."

Sam and Priscilla exchanged a grin and then shared it with Telia before they stepped out of the vehicle and into a new life. Despite the snow, despite the cold, it was as warm as she'd ever felt.

Printed in Great Britain
by Amazon